"Let Me Out!"

*A*corna was roused from a restless sleep by a hissing noise. She lay prone on the comfortless slab, her face turned to the metal ceiling . . . and the now open vent. A thin, mournful face was framed within the vent. A grubby finger was placed across the lips of a tear-stained and very dirty face.

The child slowly let a rope down through the opening. Acorna stood on the slab to be closer to the vent. There seemed to be just enough rope to reach her outstretched hands.

Read All the ACORNA Books

Acorna
by Anne McCaffrey and Margaret Ball

Acorna's Quest
by Anne McCaffrey and Margaret Ball

Acorna's People
by Anne McCaffrey and Elizabeth Scarborough

Acorna's World
by Anne McCaffrey and Elizabeth Scarborough

ACORNA'S
Quest

ANNE McCAFFREY
and MARGARET BALL

An Imprint of HarperCollins Publishers

This is a work of fiction. Names, characters, places, and incidents are products of the author's imagination or are used fictitiously and are not to be construed as real. Any resemblance to actual events, locales, organizations, or persons, living or dead, is entirely coincidental.

EOS
An Imprint of HarperCollins*Publishers*
10 East 53rd Street
New York, New York 10022-5299

First Eos paperback printing: September 2000
First HarperPrism paperback printing: July 1999
First HarperPrism hardcover printing: July 1998

Eos Trademark Reg. U.S. Pat. Off. and in Other Countries, Marca Registrada, Hecho en U.S.A.
HarperCollins® is a trademark of HarperCollins Publishers Inc.

Printed in the U.S.A.

OPM 10 9

Preface

A short recounting of events that took place prior to the opening of this book, events that are fully detailed in the novel **Acorna,** *also by Anne McCaffrey and Margaret Ball*

The asteroid miners Calum Baird, Declan "Gill" Giloglie, and Rafik Nadezda were at the beginning of one of their long collecting journeys when they discovered, floating in space near the asteroid where they were working, a life-support escape pod of unknown origin and its single, sleeping occupant. The occupant was clearly humanoid yet not quite human; this was not as much of a problem for the miners as the fact that they had suddenly been saddled with the care of an infant— and a female one at that! Yet, having no desire to stop working a profitable asteroid belt to bring the child back to their base, they had no choice but to keep and care for her as best they could. In a few days, they loved her as they would a child of their own. Then the child's unusual qualities became obvious—she could purify water and air, she learned with astonishing speed, and she matured even faster. Within the single year of their voyage she grew as tall and mature as an adolescent human girl.

When they did finally have a large and valuable enough load to return to their base, they found that MME had been taken over by a larger company, Amalgamated Mining. This change in ownership, as well as Amalgamated's desire to assume all control over the waif whom they had named Acorna, proved unacceptable to the three miners. When they and their "ward" fled, officials at Amalgamated pursued them with claims to ownership of the ship, which was the miners' only means of livelihood— untrue claims which could nevertheless keep Gill, Rafik, and Calum tied up in Federation courts while their resources were drained by legal expenses. In desperation the miners turned to Rafik's remarkable Uncle Hafiz, the wealthy and more than slightly shady owner of an interstellar financial empire.

Hafiz arranged to swap the identifying beacon of their ship for one belonging to a wrecked vessel with Kezdet registration. Although the miners were uneasy about adopting the registration of a planetary system with which they had had some difficulty in the past—a small matter of disputed mining claims—they had no option but to accept the offer and pay part of the price Hafiz demanded—a substantial percentage of their profits from the last mining journey. The rest of his price, though, was unacceptable to them. A dedicated collector of rarities and one-of-a-kind treasures, Hafiz was fascinated by Acorna's short horn and delighted by her precocious ability to understand the numbers he loved most— gambling odds. He demanded that the miners leave Acorna with him and clearly planned to keep them prisoner until they complied. Rafik outwitted his uncle in a series of clever maneuvers which freed them but left them on the run from even more enemies than they had had before: not only the minions of Amalgamated Mining, but also the Kezdet magnates who had caused the wreck of the ship whose identity they had "borrowed." In addition, they had a third enemy they did not even know about. Hafiz Harakamian was so impressed by the way in which Rafik had outwitted him that he decided this nephew was quite clever and crooked enough to be a worthy heir to the Harakamian financial empire — in contrast to his worthless, bungling son, Tapha. Hearing about his father's plans to disinherit him in favor of Rafik, Tapha decided that the only way to keep his inheritance was to find his cousin and kill him.

After a precarious time spent moving from system to system, trying to sell off their payload without being caught by any of their numerous pursuers, the miners were finally captured by Pal Kendoro, a young man working for Delszaki Li. Li had been a friend of the real owner of the ship whose identity they had borrowed, and when his agents discovered the ship's beacon again in use they assumed the miners had killed the owner and hijacked the ship.

Although based on Kezdet, Delszaki Li was no friend of the Kezdet government and their quasi-military police, the so-called Guardians of the Peace. In fact, he had quietly funded an organization which worked to subvert the ruling class of Kezdet. The wealth of Kezdet's few was based on the sufferings of the many; its low-tech mines and factories were served by unwanted children brought from nearby systems and kept in bondage by a semilegal system which treated them as debtors who must work off their debts. The factory owners saw to it that the children's nominal wages were so low and the charges against them for food and shelter so high that they never "worked off" any debt, but remained in perpetual bondage. Few survived to adulthood, and those who did were so debilitated by years of poor food and crippling work that they had no energy to challenge the system that had enslaved them.

Heir to a financial empire that rivaled that of Hafiz Harakamian, Delszaki Li had first freed his own interests of any connection with the Kezdet child-labor system, then had begun working secretly to help the enslaved children in any way he could. Although physically disabled by a wasting neurological disease which had almost totally paralyzed him, he was still brilliant and wealthy and was able to recruit others to his cause—among them Pal Kendoro and his two sisters, Mercy and Judit. The Kendoro siblings had been among the orphans brought to Kezdet for slave labor, but Judit had escaped by winning one of the scholarships established by Delszaki Li to encourage education among the bonded children, and by hard work she had soon earned enough to buy her young brother and sister free. Now grown, all three were determined to take whatever risks were necessary to free the children who remained in bondage.

Their attempts to effect peaceful change by educating the enslaved children and helping them to demand better conditions were continually frustrated by the wealthy class that controlled Kezdet's government, and by the time he encountered Acorna, Delszaki Li was on the verge of despair. It seemed as though nothing short of a revolution would free the children—and it would take a miracle to overthrow the solidly entrenched government of Kezdet.

In Acorna, Delszaki Li thought that he recognized that miracle. Half-Chinese, he saw in her a *kilin*—the legendary unicorn of China, whose appearance is an omen of great and beneficent change. The fact that she came accompanied by three asteroid miners only increased his belief that she was sent by the heavens to bring good fortune to his enterprise, for it happened that he was in particular need of such expertise as they might supply. Before he met Acorna, Mr. Li had subtly acquired the mineral and mining rights to Kezdet's three moons—Maganos, Saganos, and Tianos—seeing in them a possible place for the children he wished to rescue from Kezdet's factories and mines. None of the planetary mining companies wanted to bother with the problems of building moon bases when it was so cheap to use child labor on . . . or rather below . . . the surface of the planet. But Li's plan was ambitious as well as altruistic. He meant to use his great fortune to create mining bases on the three moons, where the children he freed could work part-time and be schooled parttime. With love and care and decent nourishment, upon reaching adulthood they should be ready to take over the mining bases and make them truly selfsufficient. But until he met the three asteroid miners and their "ward," the mysterious unicorn girl,

Acorna, Mr. Li's plans had moved so slowly that he
despaired of their coming to fruition in his lifetime.
There were too many problems for one man to overcome: the entrenched opposition of the wealthy families of Kezdet, the bureaucratic obstacles which the
Kezdet government threw in his path, and, most of
all, the fears of the children who had been taught
from arrival on Kezdet to flee strangers—even
benevolent ones. When the factory owners would
not admit to employing children, and the children
themselves had been trained to hide, how could they
be found and freed?

Once it was clear that Calum, Gill, and Rafik
had not caused harm to his friend, but had merely
exchanged identities with the wrecked and derelict
spacecraft in an effort to evade their own pursuers,
Li recruited them as his allies and offered to adopt
Acorna as his own ward. Recognizing that the child
they had raised was now maturing to the point
where she needed a permanent home and an education in the ways of "normal"—i.e., planetside—civilization, the miners agreed to help Mr. Li with his
project. But when Acorna learned of the plight of
Kezdet's enslaved children, she precipitated a crisis
that affected all of Delszaki Li's slow and careful
plans. Unable to wait and do nothing where she saw
obvious cases of need, she became entangled in any
number of projects that aroused the wrathful attention of Kezdet's ruling class—rescuing one child
from a brothel, another from begging on the streets,
giving shoes to the barefoot slaves of a glass factory
and using her horn to heal their wounds. The furor
aroused by her actions forced the Child Liberation

League to forgo their years of patience and incremental improvements in favor of a bold stroke for freedom.

While the miners worked desperately to get the first of the planned moon bases in condition to receive children, and Delszaki Li fought Kezdet's bureaucracy to get permission to open the base, Acorna solved the problem of finding and freeing the children. They might have been taught to flee strangers, but the mystical rumors which identified Acorna with the protective saints and goddesses of the children's manifold belief systems ensured that she alone, of all the beings on Kezdet, was accepted by all of them. Believing that the silver-haired girl with the horn on her forehead was an earthly manifestation of Lukia of the Lights, or Epona, or Sita Ram, at her call they came willingly from mines and factories and followed her without fear. With the help of Calum, Rafik, and Gill to implement plans for a working mining base on Maganos Moon, and the sometimes overenthusiastic help of Acorna to reach out to the neglected children of Kezdet, Delszaki Li had the immense gratification of seeing his plan become a reality. He also saw that he had made many implacable enemies among those formerly wealthy who were now, as a result of his machinations, merely well-to-do. But it did not appear that this fact disturbed him particularly.

By the time that Maganos Moon Base became a reality, the miners' lives as well as Delszaki Li's had been changed—as much by Pal Kendoro's two sisters, Judit and Mercy, as by the implementation of the moon-base plan. Gill and Judit Kendoro had agreed to act as foster parents to the children brought to Maganos. Rafik's cousin Tapha had died in an attempt to assassinate him, and Rafik felt it was his responsibility to work with his uncle Hafiz and learn the ins and outs of the Harakamian family businesses that he was now slated to inherit. As for Calum, he was as taken with the shy, quiet Mercy as Gill was with her more outgoing sister, but he felt that with the defection of his comrades it was even more his responsibility to help Acorna in the search for her home, especially as it was his mathematical analysis of the partial results given them by Dr. Zip that had narrowed down the possible location of her home planet to a searchable sector of space.

Even Acorna was not romantically untouched; Pal Kendoro had fallen in love with her, and she was, like any young girl, flattered though distressed by his devotion . . . but unlike most young girls, she had to wonder whether their two species were even compatible! In any case she felt that she could not commit herself and her life to this young human while she still did not know where, or even if, others like her might exist.

Where did she truly belong? And how much time did she have to find a suitable mate? In the three years that had elapsed since the establishment of Maganos Moon Base, she had matured from an adolescent into what appeared to be a fully adult female of her kind. Knowing nothing of her origins, she had no way to guess whether her body would stabilize or whether she would age and die as rapidly as she had matured.

Although the search for her home world was of

prime importance to Acorna and almost as much to Calum, Acorna's other friends and guardians were reluctant to see them start out on such a long and potentially perilous journey. They had become used to protecting Acorna—not only from the enemies she and Delszaki Li had made on Kezdet, but from the genuinely ill who wanted access to her healing powers and the charlatans who thought to grow wealthy by exploiting her unusual capabilities.

To protect her from wearing herself out in an attempt to heal everyone who might approach her, they had grown into the habit of shielding her from the world, screening her mail, and otherwise treating her as someone to be sheltered and hidden. Sometimes it seemed that it would take another revolution to free Acorna from her well-meaning friends, and as *Acorna's Quest* begins, just such a revolution is about to take place. . . .

ACORNA'S
Quest

One

*A*corna's office in the Dehoney facility on Maganos Moon Base was far too full for her comfort, and the meeting had been going on so long that she was developing an alluring fantasy about escaping the comfort of the base for the freedom of a good planetside gallop—any planet, anywhere, just so it offered her clean firm earth to run on and a horizon very far away. The need for earth and sky and open space was becoming almost an obsession for her as the meeting dragged on—just as dreaming up all these new ways to stop her and Calum from starting on their mission to find her species' home world had become an obsession for Pal.

She tried to compose herself, remembering that it was probably even worse for Calum. He considered finding her home world his first duty to her, even before his love for Mercy. The sooner Acorna could release Calum from that self-imposed quest, the sooner he and Mercy could marry. Acorna understood why some of her friends were reluctant to see the *Acadecki* depart. Gill and Judit were happily settled now, overseeing the care and education of the bondchildren still arriving to study and work at Maganos; and Rafik was presumably satisfied with his new career as assistant and heir apparent to his uncle Hafiz, the head of House Harakamian. But couldn't they see that Calum needed to complete his quest for her home planet—and that she needed to find her own people before she could be content anywhere?

Pal continued inexorably to read on from the notepad in his hand. "Supplies and munitions are still not completed. But right now"—and he looked directly at Acorna and then Calum, shaking his head sadly—"the worst problem is that of reinstalling and testing the *Acadecki*'s defense system. My people estimate it will take at least four weeks to be certain that the new defenses are accurately installed this time."

"Wait a bleeding minute!" Calum jumped to his feet. He and Acorna exchanged a glance that told her he felt sure this was yet another one of the many phony little delaying tactics thought up by Pal in collaboration with his sister Judit and Gill. Possibly even Delszaki Li had had a hand in this one; although the *Acadecki* had been supplied by Hafiz Harakamian, Mr. Li had offered to finance its refitting to make it the perfect vessel for this long-distance quest. Had that generous offer really been a sneaky way of seeing that Delszaki Li retained control over the ship and could drag out the refitting until they gave up the search?

Calum shot a second, almost accusing glance at

Mr. Li, who was floating quietly in the chair which allowed him such mobility as his increasing paralysis permitted. Some people had made the mistake — sometimes a fatal mistake — of underestimating Delszaki Li because of his great age and the debilitating neurological disease which had all but paralyzed him. Not Calum! He was all too aware of the clear, penetrating mind encased in that ancient body. Delszaki Li was a force to be reckoned with — benevolent, powerful, astute, and, Calum thought wryly, about as straightforward as a spiral staircase in an Escher print.

Calum knew that Mr. Li found it hard — deep in the heart which Acorna's beauty, charm, bravery, and intelligence had thawed — to let her start out upon her search. He did make every appearance of helping to secure her ambition of finding her folk; but he was easily tempted into thinking up new ways to delay her actual departure. And Pal Kendoro, his personal assistant, was not limited by even the pretense of wanting to help Acorna on her quest! He considered himself in love with Acorna, could not or would not see why she couldn't settle down happily with him while remaining in ignorance about her own race, and absolutely did not want her going off alone for months, possibly years, with Calum. Neither of Pal's sisters could convince him that Calum Baird had absolutely no interest in Acorna, apart from completing his self-imposed task of finding her species.

Cal might seem totally immersed in technologies, improvements, designs, star systems and analyses thereof, but he wasn't oblivious to Pal's obvious jealousy, and he did his best to defuse situations which fed that unreasonable attitude. Sometimes he wondered if it wouldn't be better to openly declare his love for Pal's youngest sister Mercy and his desire to marry her as soon as he had completed this mission—though that would not be fair to Mercy; she should not be tied down while he went away on a quest of unknown duration. But right now, all Calum's good intentions of calm, rational behavior had gone out the nearest air vent as, once again, Pal seemed to be sabotaging the start of their voyage.

"If you think," Calum went on, his anger apparent in his acid tone of voice, "that a lousy defense system is going to stall us another few months, you're crazy. Crazy!" And he scissored his hands to emphasize his denial.

"Why we should require a defense system," Acorna jumped in to support him, "so far beyond what was originally designed for that class of ship, I do not know."

"Is not sensible to send you so far without every possible consideration taken for your safe return," Mr. Li said.

"We have communications devices that can reach a habitable system soon enough to summon help if the long-range missiles, the mines, the warheads, and the laser cannon do not dissuade a pirate," Calum went on. He was seething with resentment.

"First"—and Acorna held up one of her blunt, two-jointed digits—"what could a ship the size of our scout possibly have that anyone would want?"

"You," Pal said in an unequivocal tone.

"Second," Acorna said, ignoring that, "the built-in weaponry already installed allows us to defend ourselves against ships with three times our capability. . . ."

"Not to mention our built-in speed," Calum interjected. "Why, that drive could outstrip the fastest drone ever manufactured. And that's saying something." He gave an extra nod in emphasis.

"Third, Uncle Hafiz has supplied us," Acorna continued, "with so many identities and drive-variation signatures that anyone looking for us from one port of call would never recognize our ship in the next one. And he has already taken long enough to supply such multitudinous identities!"

"You, Acorna, are valuable for so many reasons and to so many people," Pal said, his tone almost as angry as Calum's had been, "that of course House Harakamian desired to support you with alternate documentation and drive-emission camouflages."

"Nineteen of them? Requiring six months to develop? To be any safer, I would have to be dead already!" Acorna said, unusually sarcastic for her characteristically gentle self.

"You can stay here, safely, and let Calum find your folk," Pal said, desperation creeping into his tone.

Acorna straightened her narrow shoulders, tossing the magnificent mane of silvery hair behind her. "These are my people we are trying to find. How will they know that Cal is on a genuine search unless I am with him to represent myself? We know so little about my circumstances." She shook her head sadly. Her brilliant silvery eyes filmed over, ever so slightly, with the melancholy that was deepening within her daily, almost drowning her with an urgent need to be resolved. Sometimes, at night, she was nearly overwhelmed by the intensity of her need to find her own kind.

"Why was my life pod evacuated from the ship in the first place? Who did it? Enemy or friend? Why was it done? To save me or to destroy me without trace? Why have no vestiges of my kind been discovered with all the explorations that are being undertaken in every direction of this galaxy?"

"That's another point," Gill said, speaking for the first time and squeezing Judit's hand in his big one. "You may not even come from this galaxy. The search could take decades."

"Decades it could be," Delszaki Li said, sadly nodding.

"Oh, Mr. Li." Acorna leapt from the chair she was seated in and lowered his float so she could take his almost useless right hand in hers and stroke it lovingly. "I will not tarry a moment longer than necessary to hurry back to Kezdet and you. You will receive a message the moment we have found my home world."

"I know this, Acorna," Mr. Li said in a gentle, understanding voice. He nodded as if he were patting her hand, an action he could no longer perform.

Acorna bent her head, touching his hand with her horn, wishing she had the power to eradicate completely the wasting disease which slowly consumed him. She could, and did, ease his discomfort. But she need not stay for that; there were medicines which did as much as she could to alleviate his pain. And she was more and more "urged" to begin the search. Before it was too late? The phrase sprang into her mind. Startled, she looked up at Mr. Li's black eyes, wondering if he had a vestige of telepathy. But she saw nothing other than his real love and concern for her.

"Acorna, my love," thundered Declan Giloglie, "you're not going without the best defenses we can fit you out with, and that's me final word on the subject!"

Calum heaved a dramatic sigh. "I see there's no changing your minds."

Acorna glanced at Calum, aghast at this apparent collapse of resistance. The side of his face that was turned toward her, away from the rest of the group, flickered in what might have been a brief wink.

"I suppose you are right," she said, bowing gracefully toward Mr. Li. "Please forgive me for causing you anxiety. It was indeed extremely selfish of me to wish to find my own people before I die of advanced old age." She could not restrain that comment, even though she recognized as she made it that her words might destroy Calum's pretense at acquiescence . . . if it was indeed pretense?

"Women!" Calum said in a disgusted tone. "All sentiment, no logic. But I do see the force of your arguments, and I'll explain it all to our pretty one here until she understands."

"Oh, no, you won't," Pal said. "That's my job."

"Convince me later, Pal," Acorna said sweetly. "Right now—since we are all agreed on the necessity for installing the revised defense systems—I wish to go over some matters of the ship's living space with Calum. I am afraid we may need to completely remodel a portion of the interior."

"By all means," said Delszaki Li, beaming in a way that reinforced Acorna's belief that this talk of the new defense system was just another faradiddle designed to delay her departure yet again.

"Make whatever changes you wish. My architect will accommodate." Li bowed to Acorna.

Once they were alone on the *Acadecki*, Calum looked at Acorna.

"You didn't really want to redesign the living space again, I trust?"

"You don't really want to wait six more weeks, which will probably turn into six months if Mr. Li and Pal can arrange it, before we take off, do you?"

"No!" they both said in chorus.

"We're well enough supplied for the initial voyage right now," Calum said thoughtfully.

"If something happened to distract the others for just a little while . . ." Acorna murmured.

On their return to the base, it seemed that distraction might just be at hand. Pal and Gill were fuming out loud at one of the com techs, who had innocently sent the requested acknowledgment for delivery of a message to Acorna.

"What is the problem with this?" Acorna asked. "It seems perfectly standard behavior to me."

Gill gave her a disgusted glance. "For people who aren't celebrities, maybe. For you—the acknowledgment tells whoever-this-is that they have found your Lattice node. Now you'll be inundated with junk mail and worse. Damn it, people send these test messages out like confetti, hitting every node where they think they might find their target, and I thought we had trained all the com techs never to acknowledge anonymous messages!"

Acorna put her hand on the tech's shoulder. He was young enough to have been trained at Maganos in the past two years, thin enough to have come from one of Kezdet's factories before that, and he was shaking under her hand. She sent soothing, calming impulses to the boy until she could feel that he was steadier.

"If you upset the people who work here for no reason at all, Gill," she said, "how can you expect them to remember your wishes? Do not worry," she said to the tech, "it is a small matter, soon forgotten."

"That's what you think!" said Pal darkly.

Acorna shrugged. "I've never had an anonymous message before, so there is no reason to suppose this one is the beginning of a flood."

"Never—had—" Gill plunged both hands into his curly red beard and tugged as if he were trying to root it out. "Why, we must have bounced half a hundred of these confetti jobs back in the last week alone!" He glared at the younger man. "Didn't you tell her, Pal?"

"I didn't think," Pal said unhappily, "it would be a good idea to mention that we were screening her mail. . . ."

"You were WHAT?" Acorna demanded in outraged tones. "Gill, whatever gave you the colossal gall to intercept my personal messages? And Pal, did you think that because I hadn't absolutely rejected your declarations, you owned me and my communications?"

"See here, Acorna acushla," put in Gill, "you can't be talking to me that way, me that bathed you when you were a baby and that's not so very long ago neither!"

In a few short, scathing sentences Acorna demonstrated that she could and would talk to Gill that way and worse. By the time she stalked away, Gill's face was as red as his beard, and Pal later swore that he had seen small puffs of steam coming out of the miner's ears.

"I knew it wasn't a good idea to tell her," Pal said.

Gill glared at him. "You could have explained why we had to do it!"

"Did you hear her give me a chance to get a word in edgewise?" he replied. "Besides, you could have explained, too, and I didn't hear you saying anything!"

Gill's deep laugh rumbled through the com center, and he wiped his sweating forehead. "You've a point there, young Pal. Tell you what, let's get a printout of all the messages we've deleted in the past ten days or so. That'll explain it to her without us having to get that word in past the young lady's offended fury."

"Where'll we send it? The mood she's in—"

"No matter what kind of a mood she's in," Gill said, "you can't stalk off very far on a lunar mining base. And you should be able to guess as well as I where she'll go to let off steam. Why don't you give your sister a call, let her know what to expect?"

He leaned over the desk and began explaining to the com tech exactly what arcane procedures he'd have to follow in order to retrieve the massive amounts of "junk mail" that he and Pal had deleted from Acorna's files before she ever saw them.

"They treat me like an infant," Acorna declared, stalking around the circular floor of the main dome in the living space Judit Kendoro shared with Gill. "I am not to search for my own people . . . I am not to read my own mail . . . I will not have it!" Her head came up, her nostrils flared, and the silvery mane that cascaded down her back quivered with the force of her indignation.

"Of course you will not," Judit agreed, taking Acorna by the hand and leading her to a comfortable couch designed with her equine proportions in mind, "but perhaps you will have a cooling drink before you quite explode with indignation? Iced kava, perhaps, or madigadi juice?"

"If you are trying to make me forget about it," Acorna said, seating herself, "I should tell you that it will not work! I am no longer to be treated as an ignorant child!"

"Of course you are not," said Judit Kendoro understandingly. "You have grown up quite amazingly in the last two years. You never lose yourself galloping in the park anymore, or get into fights with street vendors, or . . ."

Laughing, Acorna stopped her. "Enough, please!

I do not deny that I did some very foolish things when I first came to live with Mr. Li—but remember that nearly two years aboard a mining ship is not much preparation for social life on a planet! And I was much younger then."

"That's true," said Judit, "and Gill and Pal now realize that they were wrong to screen your mail for you."

Acorna looked at her suspiciously. "Then why did they not say so? And how do you know?"

"Did you give them a chance to apologize?" Judit asked. "Or did you just stalk off in high dudgeon, O mature and sober woman of the world? Pal guessed where you would go and called to tell me that he and Gill would be sending your intercepted mail from the last ten days over as soon as it could be retrieved and printed—and here it is now," she said as the delivery bell chimed to signal arrival of a parcel.

And chimed.

And chimed.

And chimed . . .

"Two dozen boxes!" Acorna exclaimed when the last of the boxes of printouts had been dumped on Judit's floor. "Impossible! I do not know two dozen people apart from the children, and most of those people I know are right here on Maganos and would have no need to send me any mail. Gill is making a joke."

"Well, this one seems to be addressed to you," Judit said, picking a flimsy at random from one of the boxes. "Don't you want to read it?"

"Let Karina, Psychic Healer, make your fortune?" Acorna read aloud. "What is this about? I do not know any Karina, and if I did, why would I wish to join in partnership with her to sell my healing abilities at so much for each millisecond of time expended? It sounds like a most immoral notion to me!"

"It may not be the most immoral notion you come across today," Judit said softly. "Read some more."

By the time Acorna had worked her way through half a box full of requests for money, suggestions for a line of gilt plastiflex visors called "Acornas," offers of partnership, and demands that she submit herself to some research institute or other for immediate examination, she began to understand why Gill and Pal had been so protective.

Judit, for her part, silently blessed the men for leaving all the heartrending pleas for help and healing at the bottom of the heaviest box, where with any luck Acorna would never see them. She would never be able to resist those cries for help . . . yet to heal even one percent of those who needed her would so sap her energy that she would be unable to do anything else. *We must find a better solution for her,* thought Judit. *We cannot go on hiding her from the world—the world is catching up with her, and it will destroy her.*

But, of course, Judit realized, with a catch in her breath and a queer ache in her heart, the solution was there—had been there all along. If they hadn't been interfering with Acorna's desire to go and find her people, she would long since have left Maganos Moon Base to explore distant regions where even junk mail had not yet penetrated. And now that one of these messages had been acknowledged, whoever had sent it was sure to be on his or her way to Maganos . . . to be followed by newscasters, charlatans, and the terminally ill. The fiction that Acorna's healing abilities had faded as she matured would be exploded the first time Acorna's soft heart was touched and she touched her horn to an ill or injured person.

The only solution, after all, was for Acorna to leave Maganos before she was tracked down here. And even if she never came back . . . she would come back. Judit blinked away incipient tears and set about the task of persuading the lost youngling of an alien species, whom she had come to love like a younger sister, to leave immediately.

It was not, after all, much of a task. So, feeling as if she was doing something heinous, she contacted Pal's missile-defense supplier and told him that Mr. Li wished that the installation would take longer.

Mendaciously, she also told Pal that she had received a call to that effect: there was some difficulty in supply. She told Calum, who exploded, and Acorna, who gratified her by assuming the most rebellious expression ever seen on that lovely, tranquil face. Judit decided that frustration would have the desired result.

It did. Calum and Acorna made discreet plans, stowed the few items they wished to take with them on this history-making voyage, and took off without waiting for permission. The *Acadecki* had been "ready" for all practical purposes for weeks. The hydroponics tanks had even been replanted since the original plants had gotten out of control in size or disuse, and some of Acorna's favorites had gone to seed. The alfalfa had had to be harvested three times already and was back to lawn height.

Since the *Acadecki* had long been in one of the Dehoney takeoff bays, it had been no trouble at all to board her. Nor had the Tower seen anything odd in a request for her launch, since the *Acadecki* was constantly being taken out for trial runs on this, that, or the other new ramification to its engines, com units, whatever. Calum and Acorna were up, up, and away and into the star-studded sky while those nearest and dearest to them slept.

Calum had spent the entire first few hours whistling happily or chortling at having escaped so deviously. It eased Acorna's nagging conscience that he evidently suffered from no guilt about their precipitous departure. She herself still felt pangs of grief and guilt about sneaking away without a proper farewell to Gill and Pal and Mr. Li—not to mention Rafik, who had been away, as usual, on business for his uncle Hafiz. But she could not have said good-bye without warning them . . . and it had seemed essential to take advantage of Judit's offer to keep all three men busy and out of communication until the *Acadecki* was well clear of Maganos.

"Are you sure even Rafik won't be able to deduce our course, Calum?" Acorna had asked when they were outside the heliopause of the Kezdetian primary.

"Not even Rafik, Acorna. He may be subtle in dealing with people, but I'm the engineer and navigator," Calum said proudly.

"But they all know our destination: the Coma Berenices quadrant."

"Ah,"—Calum's smile was devious as he held up one finger—"there are nine and sixty ways of getting there, and we're taking almost, but not quite, the most illogical. I don't trust Rafik not to think of the most illogical, so I plotted in the course he is least likely to suspect. Therefore, there is no logical or illogical way for him to figure out what way we did go. See—here's the space we're navigating in." He put his hands in a position to encircle a globe, then drew out the left side. "Milky Way," he explained, "then we are going down . . ." He let his right hand describe a direct downward line. "That is NOT the shortest distance to where we want to be." And his right hand made his planned deviation. "Except that, actually and spatially, it will be. But I don't have to make a course correction for a few days."

"Well, in that case . . ." Acorna allowed herself to be reassured, at least that they could not be followed and talked out of their project by Rafik's eloquence. "I am surprised, now that we've been gone nine hours, that they haven't discovered we've gone."

The com unit bleeped.

"You spoke too soon," Calum said.

"Urgent you return to Dehoney immediately. Acc—"

Calum's hand disconnected the com unit. "Well, I'm surprised it took them so long.

"'Acc?'" Acorna asked, blinking a little anxiously. "Maybe we should at least listen to the message? It sounded like Provola."

"So? They all know we respect Provola and might listen to her, where we've given UP listening to them!" His tone was caustic.

"But she's never been an alarmist," Acorna responded, weighed down once again with guilt about their stealthy action.

Calum shrugged. Provola Quero was now in charge of the Saganos operation; she couldn't have anything that urgent to say to them; she was probably just relaying the expectable protests from Acorna's other "guardians."

"We can't swerve from this departure, Acorna, love, or they'll just find another way of stopping us."

It was not until the third day out that their euphoria at escaping so neatly received a slight check. Acorna had by then used up the greens and vegetables that she had brought on board. She also needed to replenish Calum's supplies from the storage area. She came rushing back into the main cabin.

"It's not there anymore," she cried, her silvery eyes wide with distress. "What could have happened to it?"

Calum rose from the pilot's chair and took her by her slender arms, which were far stronger than they looked.

"Easy, girl, what's not where?"

"My escape pod."

"What? But it was there when I inspected the ship five days ago."

She followed him as he ran to where he knew, damned well certain he knew, that the escape pod in which they had found her five years ago had been carefully netted in. The net was still there, but the escape pod was not.

"Blast Pal and his retrofitting nonsense. It was there." He picked up a piece of the netting as if by shaking it he could restore the missing escape pod. "They must have removed it for safety before they started their damned defense installations. The tubes would have had to be settled against the inner hull. Damn!" And he forcefully threw the netting down again.

"Oh, well, it is not all that essential," she said, now taking the role of comforter. "After all, there is no counterfeiting me," she said, giggling as she swept her hand down her obviously alien length.

"Yes, but the glyphs . . . they might establish your lineage or rank or something."

"We have holos of them in the files. For that matter, I can draw them quite well, you know."

"Yes, petal, I know you can." Calum absently patted her arm. But he, too, was shaken by the disappearance of the pod—not crucial in itself, but what else might they have overlooked in their eagerness to get away?

The second shock to their seemingly smooth escape was the failure of the legume crops to sprout any pods as they should have done by this point in their growth, followed the next day by a decided yellowing in the stalks of alfalfa. Acorna spent a good deal of time on the agri channel and the microscope, trying to determine why that crop was failing.

"Somehow, the valve to the nutrient reservoir has been tampered with. Damn it."

Her mild cussword surprised Calum enough,

but the fact that she had not spotted the problem earlier was even more unnerving to him. Acorna was usually instantly aware of the slightest change in atmosphere or water.

"It's just fed the entire stock of trace elements into the water supply at once—zinc sulfate, copper sulfate . . . no wonder the chard looks so sick!" Acorna sighed deeply.

"Something the matter with your famous nose?" Calum asked, since Acorna could often just smell an imbalance.

"The ship has many new smells, most of them chemical. I guess I thought it was just normal." She paused, thinking. "Maybe we should listen to Provola's entire message. 'Acc' . . . where you shut her off, could have been the beginning of 'accident' as well as the start of my name."

"So we will now dutifully listen." Calum keyed in the interrupted message.

Urgent you return to Dehoney immediately. Accident risk warning! Supervisor's report lists a broken valve in the hydroponics' unit, which was to have been repaired first thing this morning. Only you left before they could repair it. There was a hint of humor in that final sentence, and Acorna winced. *Advise immediate return to effect such minor repairs which could totally damage entire hydroponics and grazings if not made. It won't take long.*

The plea was unmistakable even in Provola's unmistakably prosaic tone.

"Now, now, petal," Calum reassured her. "At least it was a mistake."

"Like unloading my pod?" Acorna asked, then thinned her lips over her front teeth.

"How bad is it?" Calum asked anxiously.

"Well, the chard could be toxic. The old, tough spinach leaves"—Acorna wrinkled her nose—"should be okay since they were fully grown when we left, and one vat of timothy was well grown before the trace-element dump, but the rest I'm not sure about. I'll have to purify the rest of the 'ponics . . . and the alfalfa will have to go; if it's picked up even a small percentage of that zinc, I'll come out in spots."

"Now just a moment," Cal said soothingly, and twirled his chair around to the astrogation-control panel. A flash of knowing fingers across the touch pads, and he beamed. "We're not that far, spatially speaking, from Rushima. We can stop there . . . two, three days. Basic agri world, colonized by the Shenjemi Federation. It'll have everything we could possibly need."

"Well, I suppose I can exist on what's available," Acorna said with a sigh. She swallowed hard and scratched a bit, thinking about how near she'd been to chewing her way through her original notion of lunch—a long swath down the alfalfa bed.

Two

*T*he unused 'ponics tank was cold and hard. The lightweight protective mat that covered it and hid Markel also blocked the warmth of the sunlamps that fed the plants in the working tanks with a steady diet of golden, artificially balanced light. He had padded his sleeping place as best he could with fragments of worn-out mats, but it was still so cold that he was unable to take advantage of the space he'd exulted in when he found this hideout. He slept, when he slept at all, curled around himself like a sprout coiled within its pod, trying to hold on to the warmth of his own body. It was so dark and cold under the mats . . . almost as cold as the empty space that surrounded the *Haven*. . . . He was not, he told himself firmly, going to think about that. He curled up, arms wrapped around his knees, and drifted off into an uneasy doze. The hard white surface of the tank was soft, he was floating, spinning, and the stars floated around his head. . . . No, they didn't. If you were spaced without protective suiting, your eyes and everything else exploded, and you couldn't see anything!

Markel jerked awake, shivering. He wasn't going to think about his father, Illart, floating forever in absolute cold and darkness, empty eyes gazing unseeingly on the stars that he had loved. He wasn't going to think about anything except the immediate practical problems of surviving another day on the *Haven* without getting caught.

Huddled in another cramped position, he worried at the problem with his conscious mind. A person could get warm enough in the heating vents that led to the food center. He would try that in a little while, but he didn't dare now; he was so tired, he might fall asleep in the vent and be scalded to death when the steam blasted through to clean and sterilize it. He would have to wait, and if he timed it right, he might be able to nip out of the vents and steal some scraps of food from the recycling bins. His body needed protein to supplement the fresh greens he stole from the working 'ponics tanks in tiny nips and pinches.

And he needed to steal a blanket from somewhere. Due to recent events, there should be enough to spare now . . . enough blankets and warm clothes for anybody. He wondered if one of Nueva's lieutenants had moved into his family's old quarters, or if he dared try and make it back there to get some of his clothes. . . . No, not his clothes, that might make them suspicious. Illart's. They knew his father was dead—everybody knew, had seen. . . .

Markel struggled soundlessly against the dream of space, the cold and the brightness of distant suns and the pressure of his own blood exploding outward; he snapped out of the nightmare once more and felt his heart thumping in his chest. It had all happened so fast, almost as quickly as the dreams that trapped him whenever he tried to sleep.

Only three, no, five shifts ago he had been safe in his own quarters, and the only thing that worried him about the quarrel between Illart and Sengrat was that Ximena would take her father's side. *She'll never look at me now,* he had thought—as though she had ever noticed him before! But he'd been a child then. Five shifts ago. Or was it six? It seemed terribly important to remember.

Somebody had to remember. Somebody had to tell the truth, counteract the lies they meant to spread about . . . about the ones who could not speak for themselves anymore. The ones who would never be warm again.

The quarters Markel had shared with his father were spacious by *Haven* standards, as befitted Illart's rank as one of the three Speakers of the Council. Naturally there were separate sleep bunks for the two of them, with their own carefully engineered storage areas for personal belongings; any citizen among the Starfarers was entitled to that much space, and any working citizen, or parent raising small children, was also allotted a private sitting space and a desk console.

But nobody else Markel knew, even Third Speaker Andrezhuria, had a space so large that all three Speakers could sit down at one time without even feeling crowded. Where else, except in a public hall, could a person enjoy such luxury? Markel could never understand his father's wry comments about how his rank in Council as First Speaker bought him almost enough room to swing a cat. But then, Markel's only knowledge of cats came from the vids he called up on his personal console, and he never had figured out why anybody would want to swing one.

The Old-timer generation was full of quaint sayings like that, like their insistence on calling a period of two and a half shifts a "day." Ximena said it was better just to humor the old folks and not to demand explanations for all their quaint old folk sayings.

Anyway, it wasn't the presence of the other two Speakers that had made the sitting area so crowded that Markel had retreated to his sleep tube with his personal console; it was Sengrat. Really, Markel thought, it was Sengrat's overinflated ego that seemed to fill up all the space and use up all the oxygen. The man had a voice like a file going through sheet metal; once you started letting it get to you, it could saw through earplugs and ruin your enjoyment of a good classic music vid. Markel blinked twice to stop the vid. No sense in letting his pleasure in the ancient music be ruined by irritation at Sengrat. He would just wait until the visitors left.

Sengrat was always going on about something; it seemed he never agreed with any of the Council decisions. And Illart said he wouldn't speak up during open Council; he just sat there and simmered and waited to buttonhole one of the Speakers in private, later, and tell them how wrong they were. Right now he was disputing the decision to leave their present orbit as soon as the nav officer on duty identified a good pattern for quadrant departure.

"We've done what we came to Khang Kieaan for, Sengrat," Andrezhuria said wearily. "We've presented our case, we have the promise of their support in the next Federation meeting. . . ."

Sengrat snorted. "'Presented our case,'" he mimicked Andrezhuria's precise, cold tones. "'Zhuria, wake up and smell the kava! We've been presenting our case for ten years now. All the moral support in the world won't make Amalgamated Mining cede Esperantza back to us—and if they did, they couldn't repair the damage they've already done to the planet. It's time to move on, make a new life for ourselves."

"Are you saying we should have accepted Amalgamated's joke of a resettlement offer?" Gerezan, Second Speaker, inquired. "A bit late to be arguing that, don't you think?"

Markel could tell without looking that Sengrat would have flushed a deep purple. His anger came out in the plummy resonance of his next words. "Don't twist my words, Second! I'm not the one who's living in the past—you three, and the Council members who follow you around like dullbots, are the ones who do that. You're still talking as if we could get Esperantza back and settle to dirt farming. I don't want to do that. I'm not even interested in that. Our 'case' against Amalgamated was settled in Federation court—"

"Unfairly," Andrezhuria cut in. "If we can get evidence of the bribes Amalgamated paid out and the records they had doctored, we'll have grounds to reopen it. And we will get it; the kids in my data study group are sharper than any dirtside hackers, and they're getting through Amalgamated's data firewalls one at a time. Until then, our mission is to keep the story of Esperantza alive. Not to let anybody forget what an injustice was done, not to let Amalgamated get away with it!"

"You're dead wrong, my dear 'Zhuria," Sengrat drawled. "Our mission is to survive. Anything else comes second. And in the interests of survival, as Chief Maintenance Officer, it is my duty to point out that the *Haven* is long overdue for retrofit and replacement."

"Well, I hardly think we should request permission to dock on Khang Kieaan for maintenance work," Illart said, chuckling. "Even if we could afford it, some of the folks down there may just not feel too friendly toward us after the way we took over their planetary communications system to state our case. Sure, we got a lot of popular sympathy, but I bet the government's going to be nervouser and nervouser the longer we hang around here. All three governments," he corrected himself after a moment's mental review of Khang Kieaan's troubled political situation.

"We don't need to request anything of Khang Kieaan," Sengrat snapped. "We had their communications system under total control. That should have paid for all the maintenance we need."

"Exactly how do you figure that?" Gerezan asked. "They weren't going to pay us to run their planetary communications when they had a perfectly good working system of their own."

"But they didn't, 'Zan," Sengrat purred. The rasping tone was gone from his voice now, and Markel pulled the vid plugs out of his ears to hear better. When Sengrat's voice softened, he was happy; when Sengrat was happy, there was trouble coming.

Sengrat'd sounded just that way, smooth and velvety and jovial, when he told Markel that Ximena was too old for him, and he didn't want any good-for-nothing teenage kids hanging around his daughter.

"They didn't have a working system of their own," Sengrat went on, "not while we'd intercepted all communications to make our own 'cast. With a little diplomacy, we could have gotten a contract from the Night Sky Lightning party granting them exclusive use of planetside communications . . . through us."

"You're talking about making them pay us to stop disrupting communications? We're not racketeers," Illart said sharply.

"And just what do you think the Sun Behind Clouds and the Spring Rains parties would have done about that deal?" Gerezan demanded.

"Nothing," Sengrat said simply. "I checked. Night Sky Lightning is the only group with the technology to attack us in orbit; the other two parties are exhausted from three generations of constant fighting. The NSL is the clear technological leader; with a little help from us, they could control Khang Kieaan now. We'd be doing a public service, really. End the fighting now, instead of two or three generations down the line. And ensure *Haven*'s survival." He sounded as though he was beaming, turning his face this way and that so that all three Speakers could get the benefit of his confident looks.

"We don't interfere in other planets' internal affairs," Illart said. "In case you've forgotten, that is part of the original charter agreed upon when we decided to refuse Amalgamated's resettlement offer and live on our colony ship until we got justice. We offer to all other peoples the respect and noninterference we desired for ourselves. That is the way of the Starfarers."

"Your way, you mean," snapped Sengrat.

"The Council's way," Illart corrected him. "You wish to discuss changes in the charter, Sengrat? If so, you should have convened a full Council meeting instead of buttonholing the three of us privately. Nothing less can change the original charter."

"Nothing is less likely to change it," Sengrat riposted. "I already know it's no use going through the Council; they'll do whatever you three want. And you're living in the past. I should warn you that not all the original Starfarers see things your way. And the political refugees we've taken in from other places—why should they care about a dead planet they've never seen? People like Nueva Fallona aren't interested in being permanent refugees crowded into a ship that's turning into a slum, Illart."

"If we hadn't taken in Nueva and the other refugees from Palomella, the ship wouldn't be so crowded," Andrezhuria pointed out. "If it weren't for our charter and our commitment to aid other victims of political injustice, she wouldn't be here. Perhaps she should bear that in mind before agitating to change the charter."

"She said you'd do that." The metallic rasp was back in Sengrat's voice. "That's why I was chosen to present the opposition point of view to you. The Palomellese and other newcomers are underrepresented in Council—"

"That will change with time," Gerezan put in quietly. "They have the same voting rights as any other Starfarers."

"Some of us," Sengrat said, "don't think we should wait any longer. Some people don't see any point in trying to work through the Council; whoever's elected, it's you three Speakers who run it, and Nueva was right—your minds are stuck in the past. I'm looking toward a future in which the Starfarers are truly free, not begging for favors from the Federation, but expanding in space and answerable to no planetary bureaucrats. If you're wise, you three, you'll join me. It's past time for some real changes around here."

"Always so pleasant chatting with you and hearing your views, Sengrat," Illart said. "Are you sure you can't stay for kava? It's a new strain, compliments of the genetic researchers from Sun Behind Clouds. They think we might actually be able to get enough yields from this strain to justify raising our own kava onboard. Of course they don't understand dark-roasting, so I'm afraid it's not as strong as you like it, but there's a nutty flavor reminiscent of hazelnuts that I personally find quite enticing."

Sengrat's rejoinder about frivolities and frippery was drowned out by the crackle of the shipboard com system. Sengrat wasn't all wrong, Markel reflected as he stretched out in his tube and reached for the earplugs. Like far too many systems on the *Haven*, the com speakers desperately needed upgrading and refurbishment. The Starfarers might have the scientific and technical know-how to take over entire planetary systems and hack into intergalactic corporate data bases, but their own equipment was held together by duct tape and prayers. The speaker in Illart's quarters was so bad that whole words and phrases were drowned out by static. All Markel could make out was, "Kava shipment . . . message. . . . Xong . . . join . . ."

Oh, great, he thought. *Another political refugee, sneaking a cry for help out in the kava beans. Just what they needed, one more person on the overcrowded* Haven. *Or maybe fourteen or fifteen more people,* he reflected gloomily. These Kieaanese ran to large families.

He had just inserted one earplug when his father's yell of excitement all but pierced the other ear. "Xong who?"

"Not Hoo," the voice on the speaker crackled, "Hoa. Ngaen Xong Hoa."

Gerezan and Andrezhuria burst into excited babbling until Illart hushed them. Whoever this Ngaen Xong Hoa might be, they seemed to think he would be worth his space on the *Haven*. Markel put the vid system aside again and wriggled out of his tube. Might as well find out what all the fuss was about. He would take his vid off into one of the service tunnels later and enjoy it in peace and quiet. The desire for privacy had long ago inspired Markel to explore all the nooks and crannies of the *Haven* where a slender boy could fit unobserved. He knew every supposedly unusable space where outmoded equipment had been yanked out and sold for scrap, as well as the whole system of the narrow air vents and the crawl spaces designed for access to the ship's electrical system.

The three Speakers were grinning and hugging one another when Markel entered the sitting area.

"Such a pity Sengrat didn't stay a little longer," Andrezhuria said happily. "Then he could have heard the news ahead of everybody else!" She looked almost as young as Ximena, flushed with excitement, curly tendrils of her blond hair escaping from their severe braids to frame her face in light.

"Just as well," said Gerezan. "Why give him extra time to think about some way to put Ngaen Xong Hoa's research to unethical uses?"

"Oh, come off it, Gerezan. Even Sengrat couldn't think of a way to misuse a weather-prediction system!"

Illart cleared his throat. "I'm not so sure about that." He tapped the data screen set into the wall behind Gerezan. "Here's the complete text of his message."

Although still slender enough to fit into the air vents, Markel was already a good head taller than Andrezhuria. He had no trouble seeing the screen over her head. Ngaen Xong Hoa—and Markel still didn't know who he was—requested political asylum on the *Haven* because he feared that one of the three governments of Khang Kieaan would misuse the results of his latest research.

"Oh, he's just saying that to make sure we'll have him," Andrezhuria said blithely. "And of course we will. If he's finished the model he was discussing at the Chaos and Control Seminar, we should be able to sell it to agri planets for enough to take care of all the *Haven*'s maintenance problems forever!"

"Not sell," Gerezan said. "Rent. We keep control of the model."

"Are we counting our chickens before they're hatched?" Illart inquired dryly. "We don't even know he's still working on the same thing. He may have given up on the chaos-theory problem and turned to some other line of research entirely."

In the brief silence that greeted this suggestion, Markel finally got a word in edgewise. "Who is this Ngaen Xong Hoa, anyway?"

Illart reached out to put an arm round his son's shoulders. "It's kind of hard to explain if you don't remember living planetside," he said, "but . . . I guess you'd call him a weatherman."

"And that's all he would say about it," Markel complained later to Johnny Greene. Even if Johnny was of the same generation as his father, he wasn't as stodgy as the original settlers. He'd only joined the *Haven* a few years earlier, after a near-calamitous escape from MME when Amalgamated had taken over the large mining company and caused huge redundancies among the specialists. In some ways Markel found Johnny could bridge the gap between his father's generation, who could remember digging and growing things in dirt, and the young people of his own generation, who had been raised in space. "What's a weatherman, anyway? I looked it up on the ship's net, and all I could find was some junk about solar winds. I don't see how that's going to make us rich!"

"Oh, that's space weather," Johnny Greene said. "Ngaen Xong Hoa's work is on planetary weather systems, and he's the prime researcher in the field. Although last I heard, even he hadn't solved the chaos aspects."

"Who cares about planetary weather?" Markel demanded. If dirtsiders didn't like being rained on, why didn't they live in space like all sensible folk?

"Markel," Johnny said sharply, "stop pouting and use your brains! I know you've got some, heard 'em rattling round in there just the other day. Turn on a couple of processing bits, will you? Okay, so space colony ships like *Haven* don't care about dirtside weather, neither do lunar colonies or high-tech cities in domes. But there are still plenty of people out there who live by growing food or raising animals on planetary surfaces, who have to guess right about the upcoming weather if they and their children are going to eat next year. Ninety percent of Khang Khieaan's habitable surface is good agricultural land; naturally they care about knowing whether it's going to rain enough to raise their crops . . . or enough to drown them."

"Sounds like a simple enough question to me," said Markel. "Just model the atmosphere and the ground surface and plug in your numbers. Nothing like as complicated as plotting a course through four-space to shortcut from one quadrant to another without meeting a neutron star."

"You think so, do you?" said Johnny. "Well, here. I'll give you references to the latest weather-modeling theories, and you can download a complete data set on Khang Kieaan's current weather. We'll likely be here another two–three shifts to collect Hoa, so you'll have plenty of time to predict . . . oh, the rainfall over the Green Sea, and the expected high temperature in the central plains area, that'll do for starters. Just take a look at the models, decide which one works best, and . . . what was it you said? . . . plug in the numbers. Then we'll see how close you came."

Markel hadn't come to Johnny for extra home-work, but he'd learned that if he did what Johnny Greene suggested, it usually worked out to his ben-efit in the long run. Besides which, once Johnny had given him a learning assignment like that he wouldn't talk to Markel at all, not even to tell tales of mining adventure among the asteroids, until Markel could show that he'd done the work. So he copied the references over to his private storage files, set the system to download Khang Kieaan's current weather data, and skimmed papers on weather modeling while he waited for the data to come in.

He was waiting when Johnny came off duty two shifts later. "This stuff is crazy," he com-plained. "Look, I programmed three different models—well, okay, I didn't have to do them from scratch, most of the code was in files attached to the papers—and fed in the same numbers, and look at the results! This one says the Green Sea is going to get two inches of rain between dawn and noon tomorrow, this one says thirty percent chance of typhoons and doesn't tell me anything about rain, and this one"—he waved the printout for emphasis—"this one only says, 'If a butterfly flutters its wings in the rain forest, what is the probability of snow in Alaska?'"

Johnny laughed. "Okay. Welcome to chaos theory. That last one is telling you it doesn't have enough data."

"I gave it the same data set the others had."

"It's more persnickety. The other two models are designed to give you their best guesses regardless of how close on they are—sort of the way traditional weathermen operate. This third one"—Johnny tapped the printout—"won't give a prediction that can't be relied upon. And it just happens that planetary weather is what we call a chaotic system—meaning that its adjacent solutions diverge exponentially in time. Such a system is very sensitive to the initial conditions, which means that a very slight change in the starting point—like the fluttering of a butterfly's wing—can lead to enormously different outcomes."

"Then this last model is a joke," Markel muttered.

"Nope. It's making a point: that none of the existing models is accurate. Did you look at the author's name?"

"Ngaen Xong Hoa. That's the guy who's supposed to be delivered with the last load of supplies from dirtside," Markel said before realizing that he probably wasn't supposed to have read the memo detailing exactly how the *Haven* planned to collect their scientist . . . even if there was nothing particularly new about the plan. "So?" Markel went on hastily to distract Johnny from the fact he'd been hacking into Council memoranda again. "They're all excited about getting somebody who tells you Zen proverbs about the sound of one butterfly wing clapping?"

"I think," Johnny said cheerfully, "they're excited about the chance that he's solved the problem by now. And even if he hasn't . . . take another look at that model. I bet you incorporated the code without reading it thoroughly. Want to bring it up on the screen in my quarters, take a second look?"

A few minutes later Markel was following lines of code as they scrawled across Johnny's screen in the highly abbreviated format of upper-level languages. "I don't see the point in untangling this code," he grumbled under his breath, "it's just what he says in the paper. Put the data into canonical form, apply a series of nonlinear equations, and . . . oh."

"Now you see it?"

Markel nodded. "If you don't stop with the initial data set, but keep entering small changes as they're monitored . . . but then you have too many variables. In fact, you could have an infinite series of variables. So you can't define your nonlinear system until you know how many variables you're dealing with, but you can't tell how many variables you need until you've defined your nonlinear system, but . . . my head hurts," he groaned. "But, okay, okay, I see what you mean. If you follow this path through the program, you don't get a Zen proverb, anyway."

"Good. What do you get?"

"Probably a system crash," Markel said absently, studying the complex system of data structures and temporary processors that would have to be created, and then, "Johnny! You told me to implement a model that would've brought the *Haven*'s computer system down?"

"Actually," Johnny confessed, "I didn't think you'd get that far. I thought you'd get bored by the time you'd implemented even one model, and then you'd bring the results back, and then we could have looked at the discrepancies between the prediction and what was actually happening dirtside, and that would be enough to convince you it wasn't so simple."

"And then," Markel said, "you'd have implied that I screwed up by not following through all three models in rigorous detail, and I'd have been embarrassed and quit bugging you about this stuff. John Greene," he said slowly, "you are one twisty, devious s.o.b."

Johnny beamed. "Thank you, son. Does my heart good to have somebody recognize my true talents. And by the way . . . that last model wouldn't have brought the whole system down. We do have fail-safes against infinitely expanding neural networks. Can't ever tell what some kid might code in to run his sim games, you know," he chuckled, referring to the time Markel had used up sixty percent of the system's resources to simulate a series of space battles in real time for one of his war games.

Markel flushed. "That was a long time ago," he muttered. "I was just a kid then . . . fifteen. . . ."

"Last year," Johnny grinned. "Sixteen is, of course, ever so much older and wiser than fifteen."

There was a tap on the door.

"Johnny?" called a soft voice that sent Markel's heart rate into fifth gear.

Ximena Sengrat opened the door a crack. "I am sorry to disturb you," she said, "but the com unit to your quarters is malfunctioning again."

Johnny snapped his fingers. "Damn wiring!" he said. "I really gotta get in there with some duct tape."

As Markel, Ximena, and everybody else knew, Johnny had the highly unauthorized habit of disabling the com system in his personal quarters whenever he got tired of the continuous flow of scratchy, squeaky announcements from Central; so they gave this "explanation" all the attention it deserved.

"My father thought you would wish to know," Ximena went on, "that Dr. Hoa is now on board, and he has brought with him the code for his new weather-modeling system. The Council feels it might be tactless to try to sell the results to Khang Kieaan." She smiled and brushed her dark hair back, revealing more of the perfect oval of her face. One curling lock clung to her neck; Markel could have leaned forward and moved it with one finger. Instead he hunched over the data console and piled his printouts on his lap. "It has been suggested we should visit Rushima instead. As a primarily agricultural colony, they should be in desperate need of our services, and certainly the Shenjemi Federation can afford to pay for them."

If he didn't know Ximena was only four years older than he was, Markel thought, he would've taken her for a Council member herself instead of just somebody's kid running an errand. She sounded as if she'd been in on the discussions. Sengrat was probably right . . . she was too old for him. She'd never look at a sixteen-year-old kid.

"They want all our best mathematicians and computechs to familiarize themselves with Dr. Hoa's model en route," Ximena went on. "So I'm afraid you two will have to give up your sim game, or whatever you were playing at."

Markel wanted to protest that he had not been playing sim games, he was way too old for that kid stuff, but realized saying so would only make him sound younger.

"You're supposed to study the math, Johnny," Ximena said, "and Markel, you're assigned to the team to analyze the code."

"Me?" Markel's voice broke on the word in a humiliating croak, the sort of thing that hadn't happened to him since he was thirteen . . . except around Ximena.

"But of course," Ximena said, dark eyes wide as if she couldn't imagine why he was surprised. "We couldn't do without you on this, Markel Illart. Everybody knows you're the fastest computech on the ship."

A part of Markel's mind noticed the way

Ximena said "we," as if she identified herself with the Council, but most of his mind was floating off into hyperspace. She knew who he was—not just his name, but what he was good at—and she respected it!

"Even if you are the youngest," Ximena added, and Markel came back into ordinary flat three-space with a dull thud.

For the three shifts it took them to reach Rushima and attain a stable orbit, Markel was lost in the efficient beauty of Dr. Ngaen Xong Hoa's approach to modeling atmospheric processes in terms of their electronic-potential differences. The paper which had been issued to him, modestly entitled, "On Certain Aspects of Chaotic Systems and Operations Theory," outlined a global-weather model that was both more general and much more elegant than the one Johnny Greene had had Markel working from. And yet . . . ?

Markel frowned at the screen. Once you cut through the code to the underlying structure and mathematics of the model, this seemed essentially the same as the one in the earlier paper. True, Hoa had replaced his flip comment about the butterfly with weather predictions graded by reliability, but it was still true that until you got into the infinite loop of adding variables and revising the nonlinear-equations system, there were no predictions Hoa graded as reliable enough by his standards. He still had not solved the problem of the unpredictably large results owing to small variations that, according to Johnny, plagued all attempts to model complex chaotic systems.

Markel had just reached that point in his reasoning when Illart announced that it was time for their
sleep shift. Under the circumstances, the only thing
he could possibly do was wait until his father started
snoring and then sneak a portable console into his
sleep tube to try out the new model for himself.
Despite Johnny Greene's certainty that the built-in
checks in the system would prevent his inadvertently
crashing the ship's computers, he decided that it
would not be prudent to test the new model directly.
Besides, it would take half the shift to download the
amount of weather data he'd need. Instead, he wrote
a quick and dirty driver program that would simulate
the running and systems requirements of both Dr.
Hoa's models, given unlimited data.

The results were almost identical. The new version could handle more nonlinear equations than
the old one before it crashed, but it still didn't get
anywhere near the predictions stage of the program. Markel switched off the portable console
and lay with his arms behind his head, thinking. If
Dr. Hoa's work was this far from completion, why
had he found it necessary to flee Khang Kieaan?

Next shift, the *Haven* was settling into orbit
around Rushima, and Illart was too busy preparing to negotiate for the Council with Rushima to
answer Markel's questions. Markel wound up, as
usual, perched on Johnny Greene's cluttered
worktable in the CaN, or Computation and Navigation.

"Hoa hasn't actually been working much on the
prediction model since that paper you first saw,"
Johnny said, supporting Markel's deductions of

the shift before. "He's a meteorologist by trade, not a mathematician, and he says what that model needs is some new mathematical insights—and he sure hasn't got them."

"Then why did he really want to leave Khang Kieaan? The original work has been out for over a year. Isn't it a little late for him to worry about somebody misusing his research? Besides," Markel added, as snidely as befitted somebody who'd been up for most of his sleep shift comparing a cleverly disguised "new model" with its virtually identical predecessor, "you can't even use this one, let alone misuse it."

"Oh, don't underrate Hoa's work," Johnny said, "it's the best weather-prediction model going, and even if it's not long-range or perfect, it ought to be a considerable improvement on whatever the Rushimese are currently using."

"I still don't get why he had to be smuggled out in a sack of kava beans."

Johnny sighed and touched his console with one finger to halt the program he was running. "And you're not going to stop asking why until you get some answers, are you? Pestilential brat," he added, but his voice was warm. "What you need is a walk in the Garden. Get some exercise. You've been staring at your data console all night again, haven't you? You'll addle your brains that way."

"I'm not—" Markel began. Johnny hushed him with a hand signal that dated back to the time of his first arrival on the *Haven*, when he'd spent hours playing Miners and Martians with a lonely kid whose father was wrapped up in Council business and in grieving for a mother Markel could barely remember. That waggle of the fingers, Markel remembered, meant, "Hush, we are observed." And the slight crook in the thumb meant "Follow me silently."

The "Garden" was actually the part of the *Haven*'s hydroponics unit that was open to general view: a network of narrow trails on the spongy damp flooring of the unit, past flowers and fruits and greens that had been carefully trained to drape over the edges of their ugly tubs. Markel had never seen the point of it, but the Starfarers of his father's generation, who had actually wanted— wanted! he thought in amazement—to become dirt farmers, who remembered living dirtside in the inefficient alternation of light and darkness that didn't fit human biorhythms, insisted they needed this gardenlike section to remind them of their past lives.

Today, though, there were no visitors other than Johnny and him. Probably everybody was too busy preparing for the Rushima negotiations, or too anxious to hear the results, to take time for smelling the flowers.

"You're not cleared for this information," Johnny began abruptly once he had ascertained that there were no other visitors to the Garden. "I'm only telling you because I know how hard it is to stop you when you've got your teeth in a problem, so I know you'll be worse trouble and probably uncover more stuff if I don't give you a little now. But I'd hate to have to explain to the Council that I couldn't head off a sixteen-year-old's ''satiable curiosity,' so just keep it to yourself, will you, Elephant's Child?"

The nickname came from an old story Johnny had once told Markel, about a baby elephant who got into terrible trouble and had its nose pulled until it became a trunk, all because it refused to stop asking annoying questions.

"You haven't actually told me anything yet," Markel pointed out, "except that there's something to tell. Now that I know that, of course I'm going to be curious." He grinned at Johnny.

"All right. I told you Hoa hasn't been working on the weather-prediction model for over a year, and that's true. This paper we've been given to read is just a rehash and slight improvement of his earlier stuff, put out to convince the heads of his research lab on Khang Kieaan that his more recent work has not been productive and that he is going back to the prediction model. The fact is that his experiments have been quite successful. Terribly successful," Johnny added in somber tones. "He didn't want them to fall into the hands of any of the three Khang Kieaan parties for fear that whichever party had it would use his work to destroy the other governments, and probably destroy the planet in the process. And there were too many people involved in the work to keep it secret indefinitely; even though he was the only one who knew all the parts of the project and could put it together, he was afraid some lab assistant or graduate student would let out enough to get the head of the lab interested. He had already converted his notes to a single datacube and erased all his working files, and he was prepared to blow up the datacube and himself if they came for him before he found a way off-planet. You can imagine that he was very glad to learn of the *Haven*'s visit."

"Okay, okay." Markel was practically dancing with impatience. "But what is this 'terribly successful' work, and when do I get to see it?"

"You're not having these papers," Johnny told him. "Nobody but Council heads and a few selected experts have been invited to study them."

"Like who?"

"Well . . . yours truly, for one, which is how come I know enough to know that you shouldn't be asking questions right now, Sengrat, because if we can find a useful application for the work, he'll be in charge of building the equipment needed. I don't know who else. Not many."

Markel could tell when he was beaten. "You could at least tell me what it's about."

"I could at least get my head ripped off by your father for breaching security to the extent I already have," Johnny muttered. "Look, kid. If I tell you the general area Hoa's been working on, do I have your word of honor that you'll stop asking questions, and you won't hack into the ship's system to get any more information on it, until it's released for public consumption? He's taking a big step here. He doesn't trust his own people to use this work wisely, but he does trust the Starfarers. Do you have any idea what that says about the reputation men like your father have built up in a decade of fighting for justice? And do you see what a betrayal of Hoa's trust it would be if we let word of the results spread as soon as we knew what he'd been working on?"

Dry-mouthed, Markel nodded. "Okay," he said. "You have my word I won't ask any more." The next thing cost him an effort to say, but he managed it anyway. "You don't even have to tell me what it's about, if you don't want to. Besides," he couldn't resist adding, "I bet I can guess."

"Anything but that," Johnny exclaimed in mock horror. "Better you should know than we should be subjected to the guesses you'll dream up. . . . He's moved from studying weather prediction to studying weather manipulation. Everybody knows that if you zap a planet's ionosphere with enough energy you can disrupt communications and cause unusual weather patterns; well, Hoa's been refining on that, getting more accuracy, working with a series of targeted laser beams and precise timing sequences. From what I've seen of the preliminary results, it wouldn't be an exaggeration to say that he can call down lightning out of the heavens."

True to his word, Markel did no more investigating of Dr. Hoa's recent research. Instead, he put in a casual quarter of an hour answering the questions the electronic math tutor had allocated for that week, then decided to revert to last year's childish pursuits and play a few rounds of SimArmageddon. But the console beeped a warning at him instead of bringing up the sim game, and neon green capital letters flashed a message on the screen.

YOUR ACCESS TO GAMES HAS BEEN RESTRICTED UNTIL YOU WRITE THAT TERM PAPER FOR THE LANGUAGE AND COMPOSITION TUTOR. LOVE, ILLART.

Markel hated actually composing papers—language was so clumsy compared to the pure, sparse beauty and rigorous meanings of mathematics and computer languages. He felt sure that he could easily enough hack his way around whatever restrictions Illart had imposed. No First-Gen Starfarer could know his way around the *Haven*'s computers the way the children of the Starfarers did. But Illart would probably consider that dishonorable.

With a sigh Markel settled down to think over the assignment. *Research and write the biography of an adult with whom you are personally acquainted. Verify all statements with documentation and interviews. Where there is a conflict between documentation and the personal account, resolve the conflict without either falsifying the documented facts or offending the interviewee.* Oh, great. Not only was he going to have to write complete sentences and paragraphs and do footnotes, he was going to have to practice Tact and Diplomacy 101.

Well, let's see. Doing Ximena would give him an excuse to "interview" her . . . but he felt sure the tutor would not count a Starfarer of his generation as an "adult," even if she was four years older than him and inclined to identify herself with the older generation. Johnny Greene wouldn't take offense at anything Markel wrote, but he was a slippery customer; Markel had already discovered that Johnny was vague about certain episodes in his past and that a lot of his life had somehow slipped through the bureaucratic meshes of the galactic Lattice.

Everybody else would be doing some First-Gen Starfarers; Markel cringed at the thought of hearing all those histories of the Theft of Esperantza from various points of view. He would have to do something different . . . there was that woman Sengrat had mentioned, Nueva Fallona of Palomella. She must be quite old, at least thirty, but Markel wouldn't mind interviewing her one bit. He thought about glimpses of a curtain of straight, iridescent, reddish bronze hair, a firm chin, eyes that always seemed to be looking into some distance only she could see. And she was intriguing, with that slight limp and the elegant cane she used, made of a reddish bronze to match her hair, turning her disability into an affectation. Probably she'd been tortured by the Palomellese government and was too proud to talk about her past sufferings. Yes, she'd definitely be an interesting subject. Besides, Markel would bet nobody else in his age class would think of doing a Palomellese; it wouldn't have occurred to them that they could access Palomella's data bases via the Lattice. True, there'd be just a little hacking involved . . . but it was research for an assigned paper, Markel told himself virtuously.

And the *Haven*'s computer-tutor seemed to agree, or else Illart hadn't thought of restricting Markel's access to anything other than games, for it let him access a gateway to the Lattice with no trouble at all. He didn't really have to start working until he reached Palomella's first level of security. When Illart returned upset from a two-shift-long Council meeting, Markel's mood was somber enough to match his.

"How did it go?" Markel asked from the tube, where he'd been lounging and watching old music vids. "You missed our mess time. Want me to go to the kitchens and get a bowl of hotchpotch for you?"

"No, thanks," Illart said. "They sent in food between shifts, so we wouldn't have to break for mess."

"How come?" Markel thought he knew the answer, but he wanted the satisfaction of hearing it from his father. "You always said it was a good idea to break up long meetings, give everybody a chance to simmer down."

Illart rubbed the back of his neck with one hand, and Markel knew from the gesture that his father was suffering one of the agonizing tension headaches that had plagued him ever since he took over from Andrezhuria as First Speaker. Perhaps it was time he handed over to Gerezan. Markel slipped out of his tube and squatted behind Illart to rub the tense cords of muscle in his neck.

Illart sighed with relief. "That's better. You've your mother's touch. When I came in hot and sweaty and aching from the fields, Aiora used to rub the ache out of my muscles as lightly as a butterfly's wing."

Markel could almost remember the scene—or was it just that Illart had reminisced about it so many times? All that Markel could truly remember of their life on Esperantza was the communal crèche where Illart had left him for the long hours of daylight after his mother died. He couldn't even remember what his father had been like in those days; he was usually asleep by the time Illart came in from the fields to collect him. He'd been looking forward to turning five, when he would be old enough to follow Illart into the fields and collect stones, or help with some other farming task, instead of staying in the crèche with the babies. Life on the *Haven* had been a joyous adventure of freedom and exploration compared to that, an unexpected boon from the heavens. . . .

Markel abruptly switched his thoughts back to the present, as he always did when his reminiscences reached that point. It seemed disloyal to Illart and the others who had given more than ten years of their lives seeking justice, to admit that he for one didn't really want to go back to Esperantza or any other dirtside life. Crowded and dilapidated the *Haven* might be, but it was far more home to Markel than any vague memories of dirtside life.

And he mustn't let Illart guess that, ever. It would hurt him too much.

"So tell me about the meeting," he said instead. "How come you didn't break for mess, and didn't 'cast any of the discussion?" Usually, although not always, the Council meetings were broadcast on a separate channel for any interested citizen to view through the data console.

"We were discussing . . . classified matters," Illart said.

"Why would the negotiations with Rushima be classified?" Markel asked in his most innocent voice. "After all, everybody knows that's what we're here for."

"They're not going well," Illart said.

"I'm not surprised. After I looked at Dr. Hoa's

weather-prediction model, I can see why they
might not want to pay for it. It's not that much of
an improvement on current systems."

"Yes, but they don't know that yet," Illart said.
"They haven't seen the code . . . they just said no
thank you, they've had three years of bad harvests
planetwide and they owe so many back taxes to the
Shenjemi Federation that they can't even imagine
throwing away their credits on high-tech frills. The
wording," he added dryly, "is Rushimese, not
ours."

"So it took two full shifts for them to turn us
down?"

"Oh, no. That happened about ten minutes after
we opened negotiations. The rest of the meeting,"
Illart said wearily, "concerned what we do next."

"Try somewhere else?" Markel hazarded.

"That seems to me our only option. But Nueva
Fallona had another idea. You see, Hoa brought
with him the results of some other research he's
been doing recently . . . I can't tell you exactly
what, you're not cleared, but it has to do with actually modifying weather patterns rather than just
predicting them. Nueva and some of the other
Council members thought we might be able to use
that research to convince the Rushimese that they
needed our services." Illart sighed again. "If Hoa's
work were accurate enough for us to guarantee a
season's worth of good growing weather, and if we
could afford to wait around during that growing
season, it might not be such a bad idea. But he
doesn't have that kind of control yet, as Nueva
ought to know; she's seen the abstracts Johnny

Greene put together for all the Council members. I pointed out that we couldn't predict what would happen if we started discharging pulsed energy into Rushima's ionosphere—we could cause terrible catastrophes on the surface—and do you know what that woman said?" Illart's voice rose in indignation. "That it didn't matter what happened; if we could make their weather interesting enough, they'd be very happy to pay for our services. As if we'd stoop to running a 'protection' racket—pay us or we'll destroy your climate! None of the original Starfarers would stoop to such a thing. Naturally, Andrezhuria and I quashed that idea. But it took forever. Some of the Council actually couldn't see that Nueva was proposing to threaten Rushima until I spelled it out for them in plain language, over and over. The funny thing is," Illart said, yawning hugely, "Nueva herself didn't seem to be that unhappy when I made it clear that we'd never consider such an unethical procedure. The other Palomellese on the Council were griping and muttering, but Nueva actually seemed pleased that I wouldn't even consider her proposal."

In view of what Markel had learned about Nueva during his afternoon of hacking into Palomella's secure data bases, this surprised him even more than it did Illart; but his father fell asleep before he had a chance to tell him what the Palomellese aboard ship had been tactfully not mentioning.

Later he thought that he might never forgive himself for that omission.

A dream of flashing lights, laser pulses calling lightning from the clouds, cities going up in silent waves of flame, resolved into the steady three-pulsed flash of the cabin lights that signaled an emergency alert. Markel half fell out of his sleep tube, rubbing his eyes, and turned to Illart for an explanation of this emergency.

Only Illart wasn't there. He must already have gone to deal with the problem . . . but what sort of emergency could call the First Speaker out in the middle of his sleep shift? For engineering problems, Sengrat would have been called; for computer systems, Johnny Greene or one of the other hotshots who carried the CaN. Much as Markel respected his father, he knew that Illart's high position on the *Haven* was due not to technical expertise but to his reputation for probity and plain speaking. Illart wasn't even that much of a diplomat; when they needed somebody to weasel-word around some system's regulations, Gerezan was the Speaker they called upon to phrase the careful sentences.

Well, it was dumb to stand there trying to guess what had happened instead of using the ship's information channels. Markel turned toward the main data console built into the wall of the sitting area, but before he touched it, the screen came to life of its own, casting an eerie pale glow over the darkened chamber. "FREE CITIZENS OF THE *HAVEN*!" blared the speakers. For once, the sounds came through clear as a bell, with no ominous cracklings in the background. "Please assemble before your screens for an important announcement!" The emergency lights flashed three more times, a siren went off, and the lights

pulsed again before the gray background of the
screen dissolved to show . . . not the Council cham-
bers, as Markel had expected, but one of the cargo
bays where technical equipment and supplies were
stowed. Confused-looking people, disheveled from
sleep, stood to one side of the bay; among them
Markel saw his father and Andrezhuria, the Second Speaker. On the other side of the bay stood
those who must have been on shift when the emergency, whatever it was, had occurred; their faces
were bright and alert, and they were wearing
crisply pressed black fatigues. The majority of
them seemed to be Palomellese, although Markel
recognized Gerezan, Third Speaker, and Sengrat
standing with them. With mounting disbelief
Markel saw that two of the Palomellese had drawn
phasers and were aiming them at the other side of
the bay. He had no time to see more before Nueva
Fallona's sharply chiseled features filled the
screen.

"Free citizens of the *Haven*," she began crisply,
"you have been betrayed, not once, but over and
over again through the years, by those who pretended to care for your welfare above their own.
This ship, our only home, is in grave disrepair, and
the *Haven* has no funds for refitting and repair. Yet
the Speakers of Council who are supposed to
guard your fate have paid no attention to your desperate situation; they care more about acting the
part of noble and disinterested statesmen than they
do about protecting those who depend on them!
Furthermore, though they pretend to have a system of democratic elections, the fact is that the

power of Council is controlled by the three Speakers, and they have not changed since the first charter of the Starfarers."

Markel frowned. That was true, now he came to think of it. Andrezhuria, Gerezan, and his father had shifted the burden of being First Speaker from one to another over the years, but he could not remember any other Speakers ever being elected. In fact, nobody ever ran for the office; it was the lesser Council posts that were disputed in the lengthy political debates the older people loved so well. But Nueva didn't understand. Who'd want to be a Speaker? It was a heavy responsibility, one that had lined Illart's face before his time, one that had broken up Andrezhuria's marriage to Ezkerra when he complained that she cared more about the Starfarers en masse than about her husband.

"As a loyal Starfarer, I can no longer stand aside and see this travesty of a government go on until our tanks are empty of water and our atmosphere is poisoned by failing recyclers," Nueva went on. An abstract part of Markel's mind was impressed by the way she harped on the issues that would immediately excite any space-faring group, while the rest of him was beginning to panic. Something terrible was going to happen. He knew about Nueva and the rest of the Palomellese now; he had to tell Illart immediately, before whatever this was went any further.

The cabin door would not move under his hand. He tugged at the latch to no avail; it wasn't stuck, it was electronically locked. Probably by a command from Central Systems.

"At the eleventh hour we have found a way to salvage ourselves through the work of a new Starfarer, Dr. Ngaen Xong Hoa," Nueva said from the screen. "Proper application of his research can give us the power to control the weather and communications of any planet we visit. Rushima and many others will pay well for the use of this technology, but the fainthearts who control the Council will not permit it. They would rather see you suffocate in a dying ship than take the risk of using new technology!"

Illart started forward. "No!" he shouted. "That's a lie, Nueva, and you know it! Tell them what Hoa's system will actually do to a planet! Tell them that you don't know the effects of using it, that nobody can predict—"

A Palomellese swung his phaser up into Illart's face. "No interrup' La Fallona!"

Markel held his breath until Illart subsided. For a moment he'd thought he was about to see his father murdered before his eyes.

"We, the loyal Starfarers, have been forced to take over from the Council in this emergency," said Nueva. "Those who are with us stand here. Those who are not with us may now leave the *Haven*."

Markel exhaled a long sigh of relief. The Palomellese might be criminals, but they weren't homicidal maniacs. They meant to exile the Speakers to Rushima. It was a crazy plan, but it wouldn't—it couldn't—last long. The Starfarers would never stand for this . . . would they? For the first time he felt uneasy about the sight of Gerezan and Sengrat, fully dressed and alert, standing comfortably among all these armed Palomellese.

Andrezhuria spoke into the silence left by Nueva's last words. "I will happily take a lifeboat to any system you name," she announced, "rather than lend my countenance to your extortion schemes. But we'll be back when the Starfarers realize what you're up to!"

Nueva's smile did not reach her eyes. "Back? Oh, no, I don't think so," she said softly. "Whatever gave you the idea we meant to waste precious resources like lifeboats and oxygen tanks on the fools who have already wasted so much of the *Haven's* substance? If you won't earn the air you breathe, then you can find your own—out there." She gestured with her phaser toward the door to air locks at the end of the cargo bay.

"Now, just a minute, Nueva," Gerezan protested uneasily. "I never meant—"

"No? Then you, too, are a fool," Nueva said. "Perhaps in sentimental vids people leave their enemies alive, to recover and strike at them again. On Palomella we learned better." She nodded at one of the other armed Palomellese. "Esposito, the prisoners here are those who cannot be rehabilitated. You may escort them to the air locks." She turned back to the screen. "Citizens, you have been confined to quarters for your own security during this changeover. As soon as the prisoners have been disposed of, members of the new Council will come among you to release you from your quarters and take your oaths of loyalty."

Markel stood like an idiot, staring at the screen

as he saw the men and women in their sleeping clothes shuffle forward under the phasers of the Palomellese guards. He recognized nearly all the faces in the group: Council members, First-Generation Starfarers from Esperantza, the sort of people who would have agreed with Illart that it was unthinkable to use Hoa's weather control as a weapon against peaceful planets. How much of this had been planned? An extended Council meeting, to make sure that all the dissenting members would be sleeping on the next shift; easy then to surprise the CaN and Engineering departments, and to round up unsuspecting, sleeping people for . . .

"NO!" Markel hammered at the door, weeping tears of rage and fury. On the screen, the image of his father said, "Esposito, quit waving that thing around, somebody's going to get hurt. If you're going to run this ship, you'd better learn to think ahead."

Illart sounded so calm that Markel thought for a minute he had secret control of the situation, that in a moment he would snap his fingers and the Palomellese would discover themselves outmanned by a large force of armed Starfarers.

But instead, Illart strolled toward the air lock as casually as if he were going for a walk in the Garden. "Aiora, my love," he said to the slowly opening door, "it has been too long." He looked directly toward the screen for just a moment. "And we leave those behind who will remember and avenge this treachery."

That was his farewell to Markel. Later Markel realized that Illart had not mentioned his name because he did not wish to remind Nueva Fallona that he left a son who would never forgive his execution. At the time he only watched, eyes blinded by tears, as his father passed beyond the inner doors of the air lock and out of his life forever.

Behind Illart, Andrezhuria shook off the Palomellese who had a hand on her arm. "I go with the First Speaker," she said coldly. Her eyes glanced at the group of Palomellese. "Gerezan, your honor goes with us. Will you not accompany it?"

"I did try to get you to see reason, 'Zhuria," Gerezan mumbled.

Andrezhuria lifted her chin and tossed the tumble of blond ringlets back over her shoulders. Without another word she stepped forward through the inner doors of the air lock, hand in hand with her former husband Ezkerra. The other prisoners followed her, one by one, some protesting, others accepting their fate in benumbed silence.

When the inner doors closed behind them, Markel went temporarily mad, beating on the unyielding door and twisting at the walls until his hands were raw and bruised. This could not be happening — it was some sort of nightmare!

"No nightmare," said a raw voice he hardly recognized as his own. "You knew what Nueva Fallona was. You knew, and you did not tell Illart." He had a debt to pay for that failure, a task Illart had laid on him in those last words: to remember and avenge.

And he could accomplish nothing by crying like

a baby or wrestling with the doors as if they could hear his desperation. Markel put his grief aside, and with it the last of his childhood, because he did not have very long to decide what to do before the new guards came for him. They must know that he would never swear loyalty to the regime that had killed his father. Even if they were blind enough to believe in any oath he took, wouldn't the words choke him?

There was only one alternative: he must not be there when they came. It was a good thing he knew the secret insides of the *Haven* so well. In the icy calm that he had imposed on himself, Markel mentally went over at least three separate ways to exit the cabin without using the locked doors, any one of which would leave no trace. But just to confuse the issue, he would hack into the central computer and see what trouble he could make before leaving. No telling when he'd next get a chance at a data console.

Three

Laboue, Unified Federation Date 334.05.12

*H*ouse Harakamian received an emergency call from the *soi-disant* senior members of the secluded and elusive planet of Laboue, where Hafiz Harakamian made his home when he was not scouring the galaxy in search of rarities for his collection and profits for his businesses.

"Surprised by your call? Why, no, my dear Qulabriel," Hafiz said urbanely. "I assume you wish to enlist my help in communicating with the strange ship that has been in orbit about our world for the past six hours."

An irritated crackle came from the speaker, ending on a note of inquiry.

"But of course I am aware of it. House Harakamian's defenses are, as I am sure you are aware, planetwide; and information, my dear Qulabriel, is the first requisite for proper self-defense."

But Hafiz had not been aware of the reason why Qulabriel was enlisting his aid. When he learned of it, his eyebrows rose in surprise — not so much at the news that beings similar to the horned girl Hafiz had once sheltered were apparent in vids transmitted from the strange ship, as at the discovery that Qulabriel knew all about his unicorn visitor of four years previously. Something was very wrong with the Harakamian security arrangements, to allow Qulabriel access to such information!

But concerns about his private security system vanished when the broadcasts coming from the ship were transmitted forward to the Harakamian house screens.

What it was broadcasting was not a known language but files of the most awful atrocities he'd ever seen committed, inflicted by vicious-looking members of an alien race on what Hafiz instantly identified as members of Acorna's species. Some, and these must be the males writhing within their torture structures, had larger horns, were obviously taller than Acorna, but helpless. Then the awful visions altered to a spatial map, showing the planet Laboue where House Harakamian was sited. Clearly displayed were the bridge of a ship occupied by members of Acorna's species, and then a second view of the galactic area in which this solar system was located as well as a five-ship vanguard of what had to be the vicious torturers aiming straight at this retreat. Then images of the unicorn people, this time standing upright and free, appeared, their arms outspread in what appeared to be a gesture of greeting—or a cry for help.

"So?" asked Misra Affrendi, a trusted family

retainer who had recently celebrated his 110th year of life, "what do we do?"

Misra didn't sound desperate, but there was an edge to his voice.

"Is there a channel from our satellite open to the horned ones' ship?"

"Of course, and everyone with any linguistic ability is trying to analyze their language."

Hafiz grimaced. He did have a cube of Acorna opening the Maganos Mining, but he didn't have Rafik, who might or might not remember the few words Acorna had initially used before she had sopped up Basic Universal Interlingua like a sponge. And, as far as Hafiz knew, the escape pod was at Maganos Moon Base, too, and he'd no cube of THAT to display.

Qulabriel had wondered if the vids were some form of threat, but to Hafiz it was obvious that the horned folk felt some warning was required to another sapient race standing in the path of such a viciously predatory race as those videoed. Hafiz shuddered at the thought of Acorna's lovely slender body encased in any of the instruments of torture displayed. And then at the thought of his own in a similar condition.

"What else is being done?" Hafiz huffed. "As the Third Prophet said, 'Before thine own life and thine own honor, redeem and protect the house from whence thou camest.' First we must protect House Harakamian—then we can analyze this message at length and attempt to establish communication."

"That has already been taken care of. We've

activated the Shield, of course," Misra said, his elderly voice croaking with impatience.

"Have we warned all our shipping and affiliates?"

"Those in immediate peril, yes."

"But once the Shield goes up, no one can get in or out."

"Exactly," Misra said with great satisfaction.

"I must contact my heir immediately. . . ."

"You have six minutes before the Shield goes up."

For the first time in his life, Hafiz wondered if the Shield, which had cost so much and had been kept so secret, would prove sufficient to the need. As soon as he sent a message to Rafik, he would initiate his own special invasion procedures. They would have been sufficient against any known hazard, but he didn't like the look of these new predators. Especially if the little Horn ship had felt obliged to warn any other sapient species it encountered.

Why could he not remember the few words that Acorna had said to him in her own language?

"Ah!" Now they came floating back to him. "Avvi," she had cried in her sleep once. "Avvi, Lalli . . ."

"Misra, I must speak to these Horned Ones!"

"Why? Have you suddenly a method of learning their language unknown to us?"

"For once, Methusalitic relic of a thousand of an era no longer even understood, stop asking questions! PATCH ME THROUGH!"

If the beauty of the four obviously mature specimens of Acorna's species startled Hafiz, they were dumbfounded to hear him use the two words of their language that he knew.

"Aavi," one of them repeated, giving the word a slightly different emphasis that made her sound exactly like Acorna. "Laali?" Then, blast it, she started chattering their gibberish at high speed.

"What is she saying, what is she saying?" demanded Misra.

"I have no idea," said Hafiz, although in fact he was pretty sure she was saying the Horned Ones' equivalent of "Praise to Allah, at last someone who speaks a civilized language!"

That attempt at communication had backfired, but at least he had a vid of Acorna to show, taken secretly two years ago when she had visited him, and kept by Hafiz for his private enjoyment. When he displayed the pictures of young Acorna romping on the grass and dancing to her own music on the Singing Stones of Skarness, he saw the amazement of the envoys increase. They fell silent, but their moving eyes and animated gestures indicated that a lively discussion was going on. Why could he not hear it? Oh, well, what difference would it make if he could? He wouldn't have understood what they were saying anyway.

When he also produced the graphic of the inscription on her escape pod, they became so agitated that he wondered if he had turned the information about Acorna over to the wrong sort of Horned Ones.

Hafiz had never been good with charades as a method of communication, but he had the sense to record the movements: the blunt two-jointed hands mimicked a small member of their species, then outspread and uplifted arms and a universally understood expression of query.

In response he nodded, smiled, and gestured to the latest height of Acorna to indicate her maturity.

Then they obviously were trying to extract from him her current location, showing him star maps and pointing urgently at them. They spoke all the time in their own liquid language, slightly nasal, as Acorna's Basic was, but he was totally out of his depth. He'd always left navigation to his highly trained space crew and wished desperately that he had Rafik to hand just then.

A chance look at the timepiece showed him he had little time to fool with gestures and expressions. He compressed their interview into a message cube, slotted it in with the *Uhuru*'s code, and sent it off. No sooner had he done that than a great shadow seemed to float through the window and over his house. The Shield had been put in place.

Lost was any contact with the courier ship, and he could not be certain that the message had made it through that device and on to Rafik.

"Well," Misra's acid voice now violated his ears, "did you find out anything?"

"If I did, that damned Shield, ten thousand djinnis fly away with it and drop it into the hell of molten rock, may have prevented it getting through to where this information will be most valuable. Rafik HAS to have that information."

"They call themselves Linyaari," Misra said with that odiously superior tone he so often adopted.

"We know their planet of origin, but it has been totally destroyed by these invaders whom they call the Khleevi. They have reestablished a home world only to be forced to run again from these . . . these things. They thought to warn us, and they have other couriers doing the same task in the hope of finding some group strong enough, or militaristically advanced enough, to overcome the threat the Khleevi so obviously are. Let me remind you that all communications would now cease even if the Shield were not in place, in case these . . . predators . . . have equipment able to detect even planetary-based signals."

"That," Hafiz said, "could prove as expensive as not having the Shield at all." No communications meant no trade, and how long could Rafik carry all the burdens of House Harakamian's multitudinous business schemes by himself? Not only that, but he would be absolutely unable to complete some agreements without Hafiz's personal authorization, and there were others he had not been told of. . . . Well, the boy had already proved his worth as heir to House Harakamian; he wouldn't be a worthy heir if he didn't have, somewhere, a source of information about ALL the House's business plans, as well as a code key that would allow him to forge his uncle's authorization. In that sense at least, one could always trust one's family. . . . But to do exactly what? Rafik couldn't protect Acorna and manage Hafiz's business simultaneously. Hafiz paced his study and could not decide which choice would cause him most distress.

***

Rafik was somewhat surprised to receive a message from his uncle, who should know that the *Uhuru* was already orbiting Laboue and that Rafik would be reporting in person shortly. The message had obviously suffered some damage in transit, and the only word that came through unmutilated was "Acorna's . . ."

Rafik fired off a request for a repetition of the message while he waited for confirmation of his first message, requesting permission to land.

The com board gave a warning beep; Rafik glanced over to see that his second message had been returned as undeliverable. There was still no response to the first one . . . and a new series of beeps alerted him to the possibility that there would be none. Laboue's main communications satellite had stopped transmitting. "Check alternates, display visuals, trace," Rafik snapped, and the visual-display screen came up showing a sphere of cloudy gray, to all appearances completely enclosing the green planet where he had just been preparing to land. The test of alternate communications routes returned a null; apparently none of the backup satellites was transmitting or receiving messages either. The red tracer line that showed the futile progress of his communications burst from one possible node to another also showed a strange ship, one whose beacon signal, if any, was unknown to the *Uhuru*'s computer . . . and Rafik would have sworn that his uncle Hafiz had access to every ship-recognition code, registered or unregistered, in known space.

What sort of threat had that little ship posed, to

make Hafiz take the unprecedented step of shutting Laboue off from the rest of the universe with the Shield? Should he stay and try to help from here? After a moment's agonizing debate, Rafik decided against it. He had every confidence in Uncle Hafiz's ability to take care of himself. Besides, if this confidence should prove to be misplaced for once, Hafiz would surely not be pleased to see his heir run into the same noose that had captured him. And that garbled message had said something about Acorna . . . perhaps to warn of some danger threatening her? Clearly his duty was to return to Maganos Moon Base at once, to check up on Acorna, and once there perhaps to enlist Delszaki Li's aid in finding out what disaster had cut off his uncle's communications.

On board the *Balaküre*, joy and confusion almost overwhelmed the Linyaari envoys at this evidence that one had survived who had long been considered dead to them. They were not, however, so overset that Melireenya, the communications specialist, failed to copy and trace the single message that emerged before a shield impenetrable even to their sophisticated equipment blanked out transmissions from the planet below.

Among themselves they did not bother to speak aloud; after so many months of travel, the small crew were all perfectly attuned to one another's thought-patterns, so that the rudimentary short-distance telepathic communication of their kind was even less effort than speaking.

(That pod was marked with the names of Feriila and Vaanye.) That was Neeva, Feriila's sister, one of the two senior members of the envoy team. The hope that some member of her family might have survived had overpowered her emotions; her golden eyes were narrowed to vertical slits, and the gilt tendrils of her mane quivered in the still air of the ship.

(But we know they destroyed their ship rather than be captured by the Khleevi. How could one of the survival pods have come so far, to be in the possession of these barbarians?) Thariinye, young and beautiful and arrogantly male, prided himself on his unemotional analytical reasoning.

The thought-streams of the whole crew blended, coalescing and separating like partial conversations at a very crowded party.

(We don't know they are barbarians. They may be perfectly civilized people.) The thought-shape that accompanied this concept was of a group of hornless unicorns with flimsy, soft hands and feet. If Khaari had been speaking, the words that went with this thought-shape would have been "people like us."

(Then why won't they treat with us? Anyway, they look like carnivores to me. Did you see those pointy side teeth?)

(We still don't know all the properties of the device Vaanye used to destroy the ship; his research notes went with him. But we can postulate it was developed as an offshoot of his research into space topology and transportation.)

(Who cares about the research! I want to find Feriila's child!)

(Neeva, calm yourself. That they have a vid does

not prove that they have the child, only that there has been some previous contact with our kind. The vid was of a young girl; it's been three ghaanyi since the explosion; if Feriila's youngling had lived, she would be fully grown by now.)

(My point about the research was, Vaanye said the new weapon worked by folding space to make two distant points contiguous, but there were still a few minor problems to be solved.)

(So?)

(So maybe what he meant by "a few minor problems" was that objects close to the fold might be unpredictably transported to an unknown distant point. Physicists think like that, you know. And when he used his experimental weapon to blow up his ship and the Khleevi attackers, maybe as a side effect, the youngling's escape pod was transported into this sector.)

(A lot of "maybes" there.)

(Okay, you explain how they got hold of a pod from a ship that was supposed to have been destroyed down to the molecular level three ghaanyi ago.)

(I'm sure she survived. I'm sure of it. The barbarian was holding his hand up to show us how much she'd grown. And that word he kept saying— "Acorna"—that must be what they called her.)

("Acorna"? That word was in the transmission that was sent just before the Shield closed down. It was the only signal I picked up clearly. But it was enough to send that neighboring ship out of orbit.)

(Can we follow it?)

(Of course we can, if Melireenya will give me

details of the ship's signal. I didn't get this for nothing.) Khaari tapped the crescent-shaped silver medal that proclaimed her a senior tutor in the Navigators' Guild.

(Might as well do so, then. It certainly doesn't look as if we're going to get any more out of this lot of barbarians. Why did you have to scare them with those vids of Khleevi tortures, Melireenya?)

(Me? I like that! It was your idea to start with vids instead of first collecting enough samples of the language to run the LAANYE, Thariinye!)

(Well, they're scared now, no matter whose idea it was,) Neeva interposed pacifically. (We'd better cloak the ship; if this one notices us following, he might think we have hostile intentions toward him.)

(Why don't we just capture him for our language sample?)

(Thariinye. I. Want. To. See. Where. He. Goes. All right?)

Thariinye's handsome young face flushed dark, and his silvery pupils narrowed to slits at Neeva's scolding tone, but he realized the justice in it. His attempt at first contact with the barbarians had failed miserably. In the democratic fashion of the Linyaari, it was now Neeva's turn to take the lead, and he was obliged to support whatever decisions she made in her own attempt to initiate contact—even if those decisions did seem to him, as now, to be excessively guided by personal concerns.

To be even more than fair, Thariinye reminded himself that a possible missing one of the Linyaari should be of the greatest importance to them all. It was just coincidence that this particular one, if she lived, might turn out to be Neeva's sister-child.

All the same, he felt embarrassed both at his failure and at this public reprimand, and was eager to distinguish himself before the older envoys; a desire which was to cause far more trouble than this brief squabble on board the ship.

Cloaked and shielded, the *Balaküre* followed Rafik's *Uhuru* at a discreet distance, a momentary darkness in space that hovered always in the other ship's blind spot. For fear of alerting their quarry, the Linyaari shut down transmissions with their home base, difficult in any case at this great distance from the civilized world; but within the ship, they discussed their next step endlessly until everybody's thought-patterns converged by minute increments onto the same plan. They had been mistaken to try and skip the language-acquisition phase of initiating contact with a new people; this would, therefore, have to be their first priority after they discovered the other ship's destination.

For many generations the Linyaari had relied more and more upon their late-evolving telepathic abilities and less and less upon spoken language, except as a way of communicating with younglings whose brains were not yet mature enough for thought-speech. Only when they first came into contact with other races did they discover the problem presented by their total inability to make thought-contact with Others who showed signs of being as "linyarii," in their own way, as the Linyaari themselves. With highly advanced technology but no experience in learning second languages, they had taken the obvious step of devising a learning device that, given a sample of an alien language, could be used in a few overnight sleep-training sessions to connect the forms of that language with the thought-forms of basic Linyaari communication. The device did have the one minor drawback—that it was necessary to establish some rudimentary dialogue with one of the aliens first, as a basis for further learning; and they had learned through experience that it could be extremely difficult to get cooperation before proper communication was established. The nesters of Khorma V had been sedentary creatures, the adults bonded to their nests by a complex set of chemical interactions. That first translation task had been easy enough; the Linyaari envoys needed only to camp beside a large nest and wait until the inhabitants grew curious enough to begin interaction. But the scurrying little dharmakoi of Galleni had been shy, easily frightened little creatures with a unique ability to disappear into shadows. The Linyaari had slowly established trust over a long period of cautious contacts, until the dharmakoi learned that not all Others were predators and came trustingly to converse with the large horned ones . . . a lesson the Linyaari now regretted teaching them, since the dharmakoi had greeted the first Khleevi with the same trust and hence were now extinct.

Memories of the time it had taken to gain the trust of the dharmakoi had inspired Thariinye's suggestion that they initiate contact with vids from Khleevi torture ships, showing these barbarians what a mutual enemy they and the Linyaari had. At the time it had seemed like an excellent idea. Now they had returned to their basic contact methods, with a slight difference that was argued out while they followed the other ship.

(We don't have time to spend months taming a barbarian. Besides, they are many, and we are only four—in this sector. What if they decide we're dangerous and try to kill us? We have to establish communications right away,) Thariinye argued.

(I'm not even going to mention where I've heard that idea before, or what just happened when we tried it.) Neeva's thought-images were accompanied by an emotion, or rather, by the haughty repression of all emotion; they seemed to float in a cold empty space.

(It wasn't a total failure,) Melireenya pointed out. (We did learn that your sister-child may be alive and in this sector, Neeva.)

(I'm just saying that next time I'd like to have a little more meaningful dialogue and a little less hand waving, all right? It's clear we can't do anything until we have their language.)

(I didn't say we don't need the language, I said we don't have time to sit outside their burrows and win their trust little by little, like the Second Envoys did with the dharmakoi.)

(So what do you suggest, Thariinye-always-in-a-hurry?)

(Isn't it obvious? We'll have to catch one. The one we're following is handy.)

(That's unethical! We can't deprive a sapient being of liberty without its understanding and consent!)

(So we'll calm it down until it consents.)

(Wait a minute, Neeva. Thariinye has a valid point. It could take a long time to win these barbarians' trust . . . and they seem to have formidable weapons systems. If they are more khlevii than linyarii [more like vermin than like us, the People] then they might well exterminate us before we can even begin negotiations.)

(If they are so khlevii that they kill strangers who come to them peacefully, there's no point in negotiating. Those are not the kind of allies we need.)

(Agreed, Neeva, but if you don't terribly mind, I would prefer not to die finding this out!) Khaari thought with a wry twist of her mind that set all four Linyaari laughing in agreement.

(Perhaps if we could win the barbarian's consent after we have captured and tamed it . . . ?) Melireenya suggested.

(Bending our laws instead of breaking them, Melireenya?)

(Any good system must be flexible,) Melireenya stood up for herself.

(Hmm. Well . . .)

(We might want to use the barbarian as an envoy, too, rather than speaking with them directly. Just at first, while we're finding out what happened to your sister-child. It might be better—if they think it's one of their own people inquiring, then they won't get scared and hide her.)

(You're assuming a lot of cooperation from this captive barbarian whom we don't even have yet.)

(If this people are at all linyarii, then surely every one of them will be happy to reunite a youngling with her family.)

(And if they aren't?)

(Then it's best we find that out first—even if it does mean bending the Linyaari code of ethics slightly. After all, our forebears who devised the code governing first contacts never envisioned encountering something like the Khleevi.)

(I should hope not! Who could imagine anything like that?)

(But now that we know such beings exist, it is only rational to amend our code accordingly. Ethical interspecies contact should not require that we put ourselves into avoidable danger.)

(Ah, but which is more important—our danger, or the fear and anguish we shall inflict on this hypothetical captive barbarian who will have no idea what is going on?)

(We can dampen the fear and anguish.)

(Even if it were ethical to mess with its mind, we don't know the effects we might have on its memory. This one may know something about our little lost one; we daren't use it for a teaching tool.)

Eventually a compromise was reached. They would not attempt long-distance contact at first, but neither would they kidnap any members of this species. Nor would they approach whatever sentient beings were on the ship they were following, for fear that the necessary clouding of their minds would also cloud their memories of the desired information. Rather, they would ascertain the ship's destination, then intercept and board some other ship headed for the same destination, relying on signs and whatever telepathic abilities this species might have to make it clear that they came in peace and meant to harm no one. If one of the barbarians on the ship would come with them willingly, they would use it for a language sample and maybe later employ its services as an envoy. If not, they would let the ship go on its way and try to think of some other stratagem. In either case, since they would be physically present on the vessel, they would have the power to heal any fear experienced by the barbarians during this brief captivity, as well as to blur their memories of the experience so that they would be hesitant to speak of it to others.

(What if we find we cannot heal this species?) Neeva fretted. (And even if we can, isn't it just as unethical to fool with their memories as it is to take one of them captive?)

(Bend, not break, Neeva,) Khaari said firmly.

The shuttle for Maganos was delayed on the launching pad, giving Karina ample time to suffer from the tasteless décor of deep red and orange that clashed horribly with her personal colors of lavender and creamy white. And the shuttle was fully booked, every seat filled, and in some cases overfilled; the old woman next to her filled up her own space and overflowed into Karina's. And somebody quite nearby had been eating Thai food: the whiff of garlic and cilantro quite overpowered the usual shuttle smell of carpet cleaner and recycled air. Karina whiled away the long wait for takeoff by explaining to the old woman next to her, who was going up to try to identify a long-lost great-nephew or something of the sort, how extremely trying she found experiences like this, with the crowd of humanity pressing so close against her.

"I know just what you mean, dearie," the old bat said comfortably. She shifted position and propped her legs up on Karina's carryall. "They don't make these shuttle seats near big enough for full-figured women like us, do they?"

Karina glanced at the old broad's shapeless bulk, bulging out of a shiny stretch dress two sizes too small and thirty years too young for her, then smoothed a reassuring hand down the flowing curves of lavender silk that she herself wore. Surely there could be no comparison . . . could there?

"Oh, it's not physical crowding that troubles me," she said with a little laugh that someone, a long time ago, had mistakenly likened to the gay tinkle of water falling onto smooth stones. Karina had been tinkling gaily ever since. "It is the presence of so many souls, each with its own weight of misery and secret fears and bodily pains. I am a Sensitive, you see: I can feel these things." She pressed a hand to her heart.

"Me too," her seatmate agreed amiably. "I feel it most particular after I eat fried foods. Looks like that's where it's getting you now. A burning pain, like, right under the breastbone?"

"Not in the slightest," Karina snapped. "Besides, I never eat animal fats or take alcohol."

"Can't be too careful when you get to our age, can you?" The old woman chuckled comfortably and reached into a capacious silver-mounted traveling bag. It looked as if she were bringing out her portable photo album . . . and it was huge.

Karina decided it would be hopeless to try and explain to the old bat that the pain she referred to was one of empathy, sharing the sorrows of humanity and knowing that her own poor talents would never suffice to heal the griefs of all those she encountered. In sheer self-preservation she was obliged to limit her healing work to those with whom she felt a certain spiritual oneness. At first she'd thought her seatmate might turn out to be one of those—the gaudy display of rainbow-flashing rings and bracelets on her fat white wrists and fingers suggested someone who could pay adequately for healing whatever pained her. Now Karina began to think it would be wiser to pass the rest of the flight in contemplative silence.

She announced that it was time for her personal meditation, leaned back, and closed her eyes, trying to ignore both the plump thigh pressing against hers and her seatmate's agreement that a little nap after lunch was a good thing at their age. Irritation would interfere with the alpha waves, and she wanted to arrive on Maganos projecting a serene calmness that would reassure this Acorna. Poor child, she had had no guidance in how to handle her psychic powers; no wonder she had fled to a remote lunar base! Indeed, a time of withdrawal from the world might have been most healing for her. But now it was time for her to come back to the world; Acorna herself must have sensed it, which was why she had acknowledged Karina's fifty-seventh message. Now she would take the unicorn girl under her wing, teach her how to use her powers for the good of all without exhausting herself and, above all, without simply giving it away as she'd done during her weeks on Kezdet two years ago. The very thought made Karina feel slightly ill. Never mind; once she and Acorna were partners the girl would learn better.

Karina fingered her pendant of opalescent moonstone set in silver and visualized a pink light of love all around herself, reaching out to envelop Acorna in its roseate glow. She felt an answering pulse, alien and surprisingly strong, and definitely welcoming. Wonderful! The shuttle couldn't be more than halfway to Maganos, and already she could feel Acorna's presence . . . it had to be the unicorn girl, didn't it? Karina willed herself to sink deeper into trance. It was awfully hard to concentrate with that silly speaker squawking at them about minor course corrections and telling her not to panic. Of course she wasn't going to panic . . . strange! The seat felt as if it were dropping away from her. She must be achieving a really good trance, almost levitational. And there was definitely a sense of an alien presence, very close now and quite different from the babbling, grumbling minds all around her.

A firm tap on her shoulder and a warm, mint-flavored gust of breath broke the trance.

"Have one of these, dearie," her seatmate said, holding out a mint that had suffered from being clutched too long in a hot, sweaty palm. "Wonderful for the motion sickness, they say."

Before Karina could explain that she never permitted her mind to experience such illusions as motion sickness, the shuttle gave a sickening swoop and a sideways lurch that took her breath away, then steadied. Someone across the aisle made retching sounds. Karina had to close her eyes and remind herself firmly that she was thinking of Higher Things and that motion sickness was a false messenger. Someone farther up the cabin gave a faint shriek that was echoed from various seats around the body of the shuttle. Karina concentrated fiercely on her mental image of Acorna, tall and silver-maned and welcoming her partner-to-be, before she allowed herself to open her eyes and see what the screaming was about.

Which was why she, alone of all the shuttle passengers, was neither frightened nor amazed to see a tall, silver-maned being with a golden horn stepping lightly through a door that should have been closed and double-locked until the shuttle entered the artificial atmosphere of Maganos. Outside the open door could be seen a stable, sourceless, golden glow where there should have been empty space, blackness, and immediate death for all the shuttle passengers.

"Don't scream, you idiot, it's only Lady Lukia!" one of the passengers admonished another, using one of the names by which Acorna had been known during her brief stay on Kezdet.

"She's comin' to take me, and I don't want to be took!" cried the girl who'd first screamed, burying her head in her trembling arms.

The unicorn-person said something in a liquid, slightly nasal language, and touched the girl's head. She looked up, trembling, and met those golden eyes. Immediately her body relaxed, and she sat back in her seat, limp and smiling slightly.

Whatever had been done to the girl appeared to be contagious, for within seconds, the people sitting on either side of her were similarly relaxed and vacant-eyed.

The old lady beside Karina was clutching the arms of her seat, white-knuckled, and saying prayers under her breath. Karina realized that the other shuttle passengers had no idea what was really going on.

"Excuse me," she said tightly, pushing herself out of the seat and starting for the aisle. "Excuse me, please, thank you, if you could move your knees a little, sir, thank you. Sorry about that, there's nothing to worry about, it's me they've come for. . . ."

Finally, disheveled and breathless, she reached the aisle amid disgruntled murmurs about people who didn't have the consideration to go before they got seated and people who ought to pay for two shuttle seats if they were going to take up all that space.

Idiots, Karina thought. *We've been lifted into Another Dimension and Acorna has come personally for me, and all they can think of is their paltry human bodies. Throwing up, screaming, and kvetching about having their toes stepped on—what must she think of us? It's up to me to show that some of us are Above All That.*

Smiling resolutely, and ignoring the tiny part of her that squeaked that it, personally, was worried about its paltry human body and didn't want to go away with aliens no matter how benevolent, Karina walked down the aisle and held out one hand gracefully to the unicorn-person.

"It's all right," she said. "I know you've come for me. Don't worry about these others; they're not used to psychic manifestations on this plane of being."

Acorna—for surely it must be she: there was no other like her—tilted a long, shapely face and said something like, "Lllrivhanyithalli?"

"Charmed, I'm sure," Karina replied. Why hadn't anyone mentioned that Acorna didn't speak Basic Interlingua? Oh, well, they could communicate on a psychic level. She beamed and projected, as strongly as she could, the image of herself and Acorna together and surrounded by the rosy pink light of perfect love and accord. When Acorna still looked puzzled, she put one hand to her moonstone pendant and asked it to lend her its energies for the projection.

Acorna turned away from her!

(See, Neeva? This one wants to come with us! Can't you sense it?)

(It feels confused to me. If it can thought-talk at all, it's doing so very weakly. Are you sure about what it wants?)

(Thariinye, I'm not so sure either,) put in Melireenya. (From your thought-images, it seems to be baring its teeth. In carnivores, isn't that usually a threat?)

(Not in these carnivores.) Thariinye had watched randomly captured vids from intercepted satellite transmissions while they had followed the other ship across space to the lunar base where it had landed. (They bare their teeth to indicate sociability and greeting.)

(Oh, all right, if you say so. Anyway, I suppose we can reassure it later.)

Karina let out a sigh of relief as Acorna turned those large golden eyes back upon her and extended a . . . hand? Whatever—the digits were thick and clumsy compared to human fingers, but soft like a hand. Karina grasped the offered hand and felt a twinge of unease. Was she picking up some trouble from Acorna's mind? Or was it the fact that Acorna's eyes were golden, not silver as in the stories? Or was it the fact that she seemed taller and more muscular than Karina had pictured her? Almost masculine in her aura. Perhaps it was the effect of the loose navy blue tunic she wore; it was so severe-looking, not the way you'd expect a young innocent girl to dress—unicorn or no. Well, perhaps Karina had been Sent to teach Acorna how to dress . . . among other things.

"Just a minute," she said firmly when Acorna beckoned her toward the open door. "I need to get my bag."

That occasioned another interlude of panting, wriggling, and apologizing as Karina fished her carryall out from among other passengers' feet. She emerged from the struggle flushed and anxious that Acorna would have become impatient, so she did not demur when Acorna gestured that she was to go first up the aisle and through the door. The golden glow outside the door blinded her, and she thought about Higher Powers and stepped into it with complete—well, nearly complete—Love and Trust anyway.

Only when the other ship appeared in the glowing light, when she saw even more unicorn-people excitedly awaiting her appearance, did Karina realize that she was just as badly off as the other passengers on the shuttle.

She didn't have a clue what was really going on.

Four

Rushima, Unified Federation Date 334.05.17

While the Starfarer vessel was orbiting Rushima, it was not at the moment in a position to see the arrival of the *Acadecki*. Nor did Calum bother to check on any orbiting spacecraft since the Galacticapedia résumé on Rushima indicated the planet was in the early stages of its agricultural development and had only a message beacon. As he and Acorna saw no need to leave a message that would undoubtedly not be retrieved until whenever the colony remembered to look for messages, they thought they would simply identify a decent-sized settlement and land there. Rushima, being new with only one generation born on-planet, would not be startled or surprised by a single ship arriving. They could pay for anything they needed by transferring credits from the Li Mining Company to whatever credit institution the Rushimese nominated.

But as the *Acadecki* made its approach, Acorna frowned.

"This is the sickest-looking agricultural planet I

have ever seen. Whatever can they be growing? It looks all brown, and yet this is the summer for this hemisphere. Something should look green. Even the forests look sick."

"You're right. Maybe we should try the northern hemisphere. This planet, it says right here"—Calum pointed to the entry from Galactic which was displayed on another screen—"has little axial tilt, so it stays more or less the same temperate climate year-round. Hmm."

As they got closer, into the atmosphere, they spotted larger lake areas than were apparent in the official entry orbital scans.

"What could have happened?" Acorna said. "Floods?"

"Sure looks like 'em," Calum had to agree. "But planetwide? That just doesn't figure into"—he tapped out some directions to the screen showing the Galactic—"the sort of weather they're supposed to have."

Then they overflew a vast wasteland with withered trees which had given up the struggle to survive without the rain they required. "If they don't do something quickly, erosion will ruin this land forever," Acorna said, for she had studied ecology along with many other subjects during her years aboard the mining ship. They continued on, over a low range of mountains, covered with sun-seared vegetation.

"Noah, you been at it again?" Calum said facetiously, to cover his shock at the devastation: one area of land drowning next to one that had been sun-baked to extinction.

"There's a sizable settlement over there, to the right, Calum. And what looks like an airfield."

As they closed the distance, Calum snorted. "A very wet airfield, but safe enough for us to land on. The settlement's not far away.

"Not far for aquatic animals," he amended later, when they opened the outer hatch and surveyed the lake which was the field: a rather muddy lake since their landing had stirred up the drowned soil.

"Phew!" Calum said, turning his head away from the smell that now rose to their nostrils. Acorna's nose twitched, but her main concern was food, not water.

"What's happened?" she asked. "Think the soaking's reached the sewage-disposal units?"

He pinched his nostrils. "I'll just get me a set of plugs." He paused as he passed Acorna: there were no plugs for her wider nostrils. But then she wasn't as particular about smells, bad or good, as he was. She seemed to like them all—the more intense, the better.

"There's no one around, either," Acorna said, shielding her eyes to peer around and adjusting to the odor. "I don't understand this."

Her digestive juices gurgled in complaint. She hadn't seen a need to ration what remained edible on board and had really been looking forward to a decent graze on Rushima. As far as her far-seeing eyes could perceive, there wasn't that much to tempt her. But she needed to eat something.

"Trees, over there, Acorna," Calum said, pointing beyond and behind the ship toward a distant hillock. "Look! You go see if there's anything edible there. I'll"—he looked down at the water surrounding them—"wade over to the buildings and see what I can see. Maybe even ground transport . . . delete that: what we'd require is aquatic transport." He looked at the landing ramp. "Doesn't look all that deep." The ramp's edge was only centimeters into the flood.

Blithely he stepped off, into water up to his ankles. The next step had him in water up to his knees. And he grinned sheepishly back at Acorna.

"Must've been a rut or something," he said.

"Well, I can at least help us see where we're going," she said, and, kneeling on the ramp, bent over so that her horn touched the water. A few swirling motions and the silty, smelly floodplain cleared magically. She dropped her nose into the clear water and drank. "Hmm, rather nice without the effluvium. There were fertilizers dissolved in the water, too."

"Really? They must be in bad shape here. One-half the planet burned to a crisp and the rest of the real estate underwater. Something's peculiar. That's unnatural."

Acorna stepped off the ramp. "It feels cool around my hooves." She grinned with childlike pleasure. She rarely used footwear on the ship. "I shan't be long. Now that I can see where I'm going, it's all about fetlock height across to the hill."

With that, she started off, splashing through the water at a dead run, occasionally leaping a few strides, her delighted laughter trickling back to him.

Now that he could see through the water, Calum stepped over the minor ruts that had nearly sunk

him before Acorna purified things. The grooves in
the dirt had probably been made by vehicle wheels
on the soft ground of the landing area. Odd that
they wouldn't have paved this area over with something solid. Still, this was a new colony, and most
likely it didn't have time or money for refinements.

Time or money for much at all, he decided when
he saw the condition of the airfield buildings. They
had an uninhabited and disused look to them, with
dead vines clinging to the walls. The plants were little more than mushy stalks that hadn't yet fallen to
join the rest of the plant in the mud. The building
was on slightly higher ground, so the water had not
yet quite reached it . . . although it looked to have
been flooded quite recently, perhaps during whatever disaster dumped all this water on what was
supposed to have been growing here. A badly
warped and distorted sign over the door, half-
covered with mold, read,

LOADING CENTER WEST—
AUTHORIZED PERSONNEL ONLY.

When he touched the door panel, it was slimy.
Wiping his hand, he pressed harder for admittance,
and, creaking badly, the door gradually opened.
Obviously no one had been here for yonks. It must
have been in use once, for there were benches,
tables, openings in the sidewall which had led to a
ticket counter, and to a weighing office. The size of
the platform suggested heavy cargoes had been
shifted through here.

Only one door was locked, and that gave with

just a little push, as the damp-soaked locking apparatus fell from the softened wood. Calum had hit
pay dirt—he'd found the main office, to judge by all
the files. Someone had spent time and energy to pile
the plastic cabinets on footings to keep them above
water level.

The room had several communication devices,
good ones, but Calum had to wonder if they were
still serviceable under all the mold. He brushed as
much gunk as he could away and depressed the com
toggle. It clicked uselessly several times before he
decided that there was nothing powering it.

Frowning, he went back outside to see solar panels on the roof. Not much would rot or otherwise
damage the materials from which such panels were
usually manufactured, but they did have to have at
least four hours of sun to operate. Clouds were
already gathering to the west. Rather fast, he
thought, remembering they'd landed in clear skies
and hadn't even seen a weather front moving in on
their approach from the west. Odd that! And there
wasn't so much as a breeze to ruffle the flooded
field.

He caught sight of Acorna in her grazing posture
and was delighted that she, at least, had had some
luck. He hoped he'd have his share as well. There
had to be something wrong for the solar panels to
fail. Possibly the cable connecting the panels to the
reservoir had perished. Then he spotted the ladder
attached to the gable end of the roof, which would
give him access to the panels. He'd just check. Sure
enough, the cable connections had fallen away from
the rain-soft wood, and the cable itself lay half in a

puddle, the insulation rotting away from it. Well, he had plenty of cable that size back at the ship, so he climbed down and splashed to the *Acadecki*, got a belt of the tools he'd need, and waded back to the building.

It didn't take him long to splice the cable and, since he rather thought there'd been some sunlight, maybe he could just rouse someone on this planet on the com unit. He headed into the run-down building. Power he had, and he sent a brief message, asking to be met by someone in authority at the field so he could transact business in acquiring new seeds for a hydroponics tank system. Then he trudged back to the *Acadecki* to get himself a bit of lunch and await the arrival of anyone who'd heard the call.

That was why he didn't see Acorna waving frantically in his direction, or hear her distant voice trying to warn him of the flotilla of assorted water vessels heading in his direction, bristling with all sorts of makeshift weapons. The first he knew of danger was an unfriendly challenge from the leading boat: "Hold it right there, y'damned pirate!"

Whoops, Calum thought, suspecting that Kezdet's new improved interstellar reputation might not have spread as far as Rushima. For the first time he felt fervently grateful for the hasty departure that had precluded his suggesting that Mercy might accompany them on the journey—ostensibly to provide Acorna with feminine company, that would have been his excuse. His sweet, gentle Mercy had already been exposed to too many dangers in her time—as a spy for the Child Liberation League within the offices of the corrupt Kezdet police. She didn't need to deal with floods, famine, riots, and whatever else was now coming their way, clearly spoiling for a fight.

He girded himself quickly with an arms belt, snapped on the field that would keep them outside and him safely within the ship, and just made it to the hatch before the first of the paddled boats arrived with its cargo of many men and women. Most of them were carrying sharp-edged or heavy tools; all of them looked distinctly unfriendly. What had ticked them off so quickly? Were they that serious about that AUTHORIZED PERSONNEL ONLY sign on the derelict loading shed?

"Hold it there yourselves," he called, raising both arms to show that he was not holding a weapon. Those at his belt could be clearly seen, and he wanted to keep folks far enough away from the ramp so that he could grab a stunner if he needed to. "I'm Calum Baird of the *Acadecki*. We've had a 'ponics failure and need to buy plants and seeds from you."

"Plants and seeds, he wants," a bearded man cried, laughing almost hysterically. That was the general mood of those who poled or paddled their craft to surround the *Acadecki*. They kept repeating his words with variations of derision and angry frustration.

"This is Rushima, isn't it?" Calum asked, perplexed.

"What you bastards have left of Rushima, you mean," the spokesman said, and the muttered growls of his companions did nothing to reassure him as to the general hostile mood.

"We're from Maganos Moon Base at Kezdet on our way to Coma Berenices on a private mission," Calum went on, making his voice sound as reasonable as he could even though he was scared stiff. Why hadn't he listened to Pal about defense systems? Not that anything a spaceship carried would have been useful in his present circumstances.

"Pull the other one, it's got bells on," growled the spokesman.

"Hey, now, he could be telling the truth," a tenor voice suggested. A young man in a raft with ten-centimeter sides glided to the side of the *Acadecki*, and read out their current alpha-numeric identification code. "That's not a Starfarer ID. Could be from Kezdet."

"So could half the pirates in the galaxy," said the leader, who evidently was all too aware of Kezdet's lax registration laws, which attracted all sorts of illicit business, "and if those Starfarers are as far-flung as they keep telling us they are, could be one of theirs anyhow. But it's shortly going to be ours. . . ."

There was movement as some of the bigger men slipped into the water and started for the ramp.

"Hey, the water out here's clear," a woman said, astonishment and delight in her voice. She scooped up a handful, tasted it cautiously, and let out a whoop. "How'd you do this, mister?"

Immediately others were sampling the water. And then almost everyone, at the risk of tipping over their basically fragile craft, buried their faces to drink so thirstily that the sight transfixed Calum.

Water, water, everywhere nor any drop to drink —the

phrase popped in from some distant corner of his brain.

"I did it." Acorna stepped gracefully around the after section of the ship. She also held her hands up, not that she could have hidden anything in the short, skintight tunic she was wearing. "Purifying water is one of our skills."

Calum closed his eyes in what could have been prayerful exhortation. Acorna had learned a great deal about humans during her experiences with Kisla Manjari and Didi Badini's attempts to kill her, but she was still far too trusting. These people might have softened a little during their brief talk, but they had started out as a mob out for vengeance. And, if purifying water just happened to be a must for this section of a waterlogged planet, Acorna might find herself an unwilling resident of Rushima.

At least she had said "our," instead of "my" skills, so they might not be aware that she had the power to cleanse the water all by herself.

He eased himself slightly to the right side, where the controls were. If she could just get close enough to dive through the hatch, he could have the field off and on before anyone else could capture her. He gave her the slightest signal with the fingers of one hand, trying to convey the necessity of boarding the ship as quickly as possible. Even the few who were out of their boats wouldn't be able to move as quickly through the water as Acorna could.

"Can you tell us what has happened to your planet? For something most disastrous has," she said in her sweet and calming voice. Even Calum began to feel more serene, less anxious. He blinked. With water still dribbling down the corners of his mouth, the spokesman regarded her with considerably less animosity than he had accorded Calum.

"Them Starfarers"—he jerked a finger heavenward—"they're running a bloody bandulu bidness."

"Huh?"

"Protection racket," the young man who'd read the *Acadecki*'s registration translated. "They offered to give us weather-prediction services for a fee, and when we said we didn't need 'em as our climate is so even—"

"That baggy on the com—"

"Woman," the younger man interpreted. "Give a nasty snigger, she did, and said we might be getting some climate changes. We've had nothing but rain since then . . . drowned all our winter crops before we could harvest anything, and there's no point in trying to raise anything in this." He pointed to the floodland. "And if we tried rice, they'd fry us."

"WHO?" Calum and Acorna said with such incredulity and outrage that their chorus provided more evidence of their innocence than any eloquence.

"Starfarers," was the universal reply. "They've been making a mess of the weather."

"Starfarers? I thought they were just a political protest group," Calum said.

"They've been 'making it rain'?" Acorna was still dumbfounded and glanced at Calum, but she was also surreptitiously moving nearer the ramp.

"Can *you* manipulate weather like that?" she

asked Calum with such incredulity that it pro-
voked sour laughter from several sources.

"Not with any accuracy," Calum said, "and you
have to work off existing weather conditions."

The spokesman gave a hollow laugh. "Well,
then, they got 'em some kin' obeah beyond any you
know. They got half our fields soaked and t'other
half dried up like a desert, and it ain't gonna get
better till we pays up."

"That's extortion," Acorna said indignantly. She
had learned a good deal about extortion, black-
mail, and such terrorizing activities on Kezdet, but
those had been industrial or economic, not ecolog-
ical. There was humorless laughter from the
crowd, but Calum was relieved that the belliger-
ence apparent at their arrival seemed to have
eased.

"And how'd you fix the com unit?" the spokesman
said.

"A new length of cable was all it needed, and the
sun we had this morning."

"First sun we've seen in yonks." Then the man
gestured to the flooded land. "Not that it'll do much
good. We're promised"—and his expression was
sour—". . . another six inches of rain if we fail to
accept their 'protection.'"

"You say this has been going on since the Starfarers arrived?" Calum asked. "By the way, I'm Calum
Baird, Li Moon Mining Enterprises, and this lovely
lady is Acorna Delszaki-Harakamian."

"Know those names," the younger man said.
"You're connected with the House Harakamian?" he
asked Acorna, and didn't seem to realize that she had

edged closer to the side of the ship, nearer the ramp.

"Mr. Delszaki Li and the House Harakamian are my guardians," she said proudly. "If you know them, then you realize that we have nothing whatever to do with . . . this!"

"I'm Joshua Flouse, mayor of this." He gestured contemptuously at the lake. "Is that purifier device of yours on the market?"

"Why, yes, it is," Acorna said with a bright smile, taking one step closer to the ramp. "I'll just get you one, shall I?"

Calum's left hand depressed the field-generator switch, and he gave her a nod. With a nimble and unexpected leap, she was on the ramp and moving inside while Calum reinstated the protective field just in time to slow the startled Flouse, who had lunged forward after Acorna only to find his arms slowed as if swimming through cold molasses.

"That is," Calum said crisply, feeling more able to take a firm line now that Acorna was safe, "we'll trade our water-purification services for seeds—legumes and broad-leafed greens for choice. Oh, and zinc and copper sulfates to replace the trace elements our system accidentally dumped. We'd only need small quantities."

Flouse's expression showed his disappointment at Acorna's escape. But she was smiling at him so charmingly that he shook his head, abashed, and shrugged.

"Whaddawe got left?" he asked, turning to those in the boats around him.

"Just about everything we've been able to keep dry enough to plant if we ever get the chance," a woman said. "But right now I'd settle for clean water, Josh."

"We'll also undertake to inform the authorities of these Starfarers who are blackmailing you," Calum said. "Unauthorized interference with a developing planet is a serious offense."

"Tell them!" half a dozen voices chorused as even more fingers pointed skyward.

Joshua pointed to the group in one of the motorized boats. "Jason?" he called, and the man at the tiller answered with a loud "Yo!"

"You got the security code. Get us some chicka-chicka peas and greens seeds. And bring a few seedling chard and rhubarbs. And a canister of Solution B." He turned back to Calum and Acorna, showing his eagerness to complete the deal. "Anything else?"

"You wouldn't happen to have alfalfa seeds, would you?" Acorna asked wistfully.

"A sack of alfalfa it is, ma'am. Now, lemme see this purifier of yours?"

"I'll just get one," she said, and before Calum could ask her what the hell she had in mind, she was down the companionway, moving in the direction of the storage compartment.

When Calum turned back to the flotilla, he saw that some children were splashing about in clear water up to their knees, laughing as they whooshed water at each other.

"It's been lack of clean water that's been the worst part to bear," Flouse said, shaking his head. "Boiled water isn't the same, and we couldn't even bathe or wash clothes without the smell staying in.

Flooded out our sewage system by the third week, and we hadn't a chance of stopping it. Some folks"—Flouse jerked his head in a northerly direction—"have tried sending tankers just to get our water to keep crops going, but the convoys keep getting blown up by lightning. Midday, at that, and not a blink of warning. Just zap!"—he brought both hands together in a resounding slap that momentarily stopped the kids playing—"whole damned convoy's crisped."

"How do they expect you to pay them if they've ruined your economy?"

"They'll lift the weather controls if we agree to supply them with all their food and the other agricultural stuff we were producing to pay off our colonial debts."

Calum nodded, understanding the basic crunch of producing sufficient to feed themselves with an excess to export to acquit the indebtedness of the initial expense of colonial expansion.

"Only they're going to send . . . administrators to see that each town and county supplies the quotas they're setting."

From the dolorous expression on the faces of Flouse and the others, Calum quickly saw that the Rushimese would be left with barely enough to feed their own families.

"Any idea where they came from?"

"Dunno. They're mighty short on explanations."

They both could hear metallic whangs and bangs echoing down the companionway, and Calum had to pretend he knew exactly what Acorna was doing . . .

when he was dying of suspense and anxiety.

But while she was contrapting whatever she was making, he found out all he could extract from Flouse and the others. The return of the launch coincided with Acorna's reappearance at the hatch, carrying a length of ordinary three-centimeter pipe, with valves on each end which were obviously meant to be attached to an intake point of the main town water supply.

"Now, this purifier has interstellar patents from here to the last century," Acorna said, pointing to the center piece. "I wouldn't try to investigate, as the purifier is also delicate—useless once it has been unsealed. But I can guarantee that any water running through the purifier will come out one hundred percent pure."

The launch slowed beside the ramp and willing hands transferred the seeds, seedlings, and nutrient canister to Calum just as Acorna placed the "purifier" in Flouse's eager hands. That was when he noticed the small slice that she had taken from her horn. Was she going to be read a riot act when they were safely away from here!!! Calum did not forget to switch back on the field that separated them from the crowd. But they had what they needed, and so did the *Acadecki*.

"I promise you, we'll send out word of this to the authorities as soon as we're clear of planetary interference," Calum said. "Now, if you'll just step back, we'd best be off."

Acorna had disappeared the instant she had the 'ponics' replacements, so it was up to him to get them safely away.

Calum carefully lifted the *Acadecki* in low-energy mode before touching the thrusters lightly enough to move far enough away from the flooded land to start an ascent. He wasn't sure who he was maddest at: Acorna for using a piece of her own self to provide the purification for those poor farmers, or the frigging bastards holding an entire world to ransom with weather tricks. And where had they gotten such tricks FROM in the first place?

He was far too busy laying in a course to access the Galacticapedia, but he would as soon as he had a finger free. As far as he knew, there was no process that could deliver rain to one area of a planet, lightning on command to another, and relentless sun to bake a third. That was undoubtedly why he didn't check the screen until he felt the unmistakable yank of a tractor beam . . . a very powerful tractor beam . . . snatching the *Acadecki* right off her ascent and inexorably into the maw of a massive spaceship, no doubt owned and manned by the Starfarers.

Five

C alum tried desperately to send a Mayday to Maganos, but they'd been ahead of him all along, and his signal bounced harmlessly back.

Calum was damning himself left, right, and center before Acorna came running to the bridge.

"What are you doing, Calum? I nearly lost the can . . ." Her complaint trailed off as the lights from their captor nearly blinded her.

"The Starfarers?"

"Sorry about this, Acorna," he said, mortified. "Rafik and Gill would never have been so stupid as not to check the trajectory, much less the proximity screens."

"Well, I've a few choice words for such scummy piratical opportunists. . . ."

She was so angry her horn glowed, and Calum buried his head in his arms. He'd done it now. Truly he'd done it. How was he going to save Acorna from this? He only hoped the Starfarers had been so busy with their felonious extortion that no hint of a strange species with a horn had reached their com unit.

"Acorna," and his voice cracked in his anxiety, "could you pretend to be a pet?"

"A pet?"

"It's the only thing I can think of."

Acorna stood very still, her tall form dwarfing him in the pilot's chair. She gave a little sniff, her wide silvery eyes regarding him. "I don't think they'd buy that."

"Then let's play it as cool as possible."

"That makes sense."

"And this time you've never heard of Delszaki Li and House Harakamian. When I can think what they'd hold Hafiz up for, much less Mr. Li, my heart fails me."

"You've made a very good point."

The *Acadecki* shivered, if a metal ship can be said to do such a thing, as she was locked into place aboard their captor.

"While I can't be a pet, Calum, I can be a Didi," she said, and was off down the corridor, shouting over one shoulder, "You be the pet, this time, Calum. Just bright enough to speak when spoken to."

He reviewed that in his mind as he felt other things happening to the *Acadecki*, like the clang of metal against the main hatch. They were unlikely to be able to break through, but what if they decided to blow or shoot the hatch off? Better to surrender and maintain the ship intact. He quickly keyed in a code and turned off the system with the special switch he himself had installed. *Let 'em try to break that,* he thought with some satisfaction.

Then he switched on the exterior speakers. "Wait a damned minute, will ya?" He flipped off the security lock on the hatch. Anyone could open it now from outside. "I'm coming. I'm coming. Doan like no one messing up the ship. My Didi'll get back at me if'n you do."

He was at the hatch when the first of the Starfarers showed up, and he did not like the look on this surly bunch of muscle-bounds at all.

"Hey, boys, take it easy. The Didi's coming." He waved them on in as if he weren't the least bit impressed by their menacing appearance.

The leader backhanded him with such efficiency that he careened from side to side of the narrow passageway before falling in an embarrassing heap to the deck.

"Really!" came the sultry remonstrance from an Acorna Calum didn't recognize. He blinked, as much to clear the shock of that backhanded blow as to make sure his eyes still functioned. "Was that necessary? Poor Calum doesn't have many brains anyway, and the ones he's got don't need to be rattled. He'll do whatever you tell him anyway. He's been trained to."

The attention of the heavies was immediately focused on the vision in black. Calum vaguely remembered Judit, Mercy, and Acorna giggling over some of the outfits that had been concocted to either emphasize or hide her horn. This outfit was not only skintight, but the high collar disguised the long fall of Acorna's silvery mane. It was cleverly attached to the ravishing black hat which sat at a jaunty angle on Acorna's head. The peaked front completely hid the horn and almost covered her right eye.

"Let me introduce myself: Badini, the Didi of Kezdet's best . . ." she paused, her voice heavy with significance, ". . . establishment. You wouldn't happen to have any children you consider excess baggage, would you? They certainly didn't down there." She pointed a contemptuous gloved hand down, indicating Rushima, which they had so obviously just left. Acorna's gloves effectively disguised the differences in her hands, and her cloven hooves were hidden within the apparently stack-soled boots just visible under her long pantaloons.

"What's a Didi?"

A disembodied voice echoed outside. "Bring them aboard. I want to question them if they've been on Rushima," said a woman's voice.

"Anything you say," drawled Acorna's imitation Didi Badini in what Calum decided was an excellent imitation of the real bonk-shop owner's voice.

With an elegant swaying step, Acorna the "Didi" made her way past the first of the guards, deliberately brushing against him in such an enticing fashion that Calum hoped she wasn't overdoing her role.

"I suppose you'd better come, too," she said, deigning to notice Calum just before she went through the hatch. She put just the right inflection in her voice to suggest to anyone listening that Calum was of no importance whatever.

Of such little importance, in fact, that when he had been given the most cursory glance by the

hard-faced woman standing slightly ahead of two
obvious henchmen, he was immediately hauled
away, probably by the man who had backhanded
him. As his collar was tightly held by whoever
kept pushing him forward, he couldn't be sure.
But he was pushed down a few miles of antigrav
tubes to the bowels of the enormous spaceship
and shoved into a bare cell. It was equipped with
two slabs of some plastic, strapped up against
opposing walls, a sanitary appliance, and that was
all. Not even a water supply.

"*Nor any drop to drink,*" he murmured, then
reminded himself that this cell was likely bugged.
So he released the fastening on one slab and sat
down on it. And began to worry about Acorna.
Could she pull off her fancy-dress persona? And
what good would it do? These people were the
type who'd think nothing of spacing superfluous
bodies. He was suddenly not so happy to have
been cast in the role of "expendably unimportant."

"WHERE did you say you came from?" asked
one of the three facing her.

"Kezdet," Acorna promptly replied. "I'm looking for . . . replacements."

"Replacements for what?" the woman asked,
but the first man laughed.

"Dirtsiders need certain types of entertainment
I'm sure this woman provides, Nueva."

"Oh. And you had no luck on Rushima?" This
seemed to amuse the woman.

Acorna snorted contemptuously. "If it isn't

flooded out, it's desert or burned out. Not what I was told to expect," Acorna said indignantly. "No one would even come out to speak to us, no matter where we landed. Ruined one outfit in the wet, and another has sand just driven into the seams." She let her voice flatten with annoyance. "Wasted time and fuel. As I said, I'm Didi Badini. . . ." She cocked her head, as if she expected to be informed of her interrogator's name.

"Welcome to the *Haven*, Didi Badini. I am Captain Nueva of the Starfarers."

"You wouldn't happen to have a few excess . . . children, or females . . . or even that sort of male type . . . I could relieve you of?" Acorna said.

"We've . . . sort of . . . relieved ourselves of the excess."

That was when Acorna realized she and Calum were in big trouble. Maybe she should have remained Acorna Delszaki-Harakamian, and worth a sizable ransom.

"Really," she replied as if amused at such a mutual circumstance, "then, if you'll just return my . . . my little friend, we'll be on our way. I really do need to find a few replacements, you know. Tastes get jaded so quickly."

Nueva made a motion, and two of the guards behind her grabbed Acorna by the arms. She could have thrown them off easily enough, being far stronger than she looked, but unless she also had Calum, displaying any of her discreetly concealed abilities was futile and possibly dangerous to them both. As she was turned and taken off in the direction Calum had been hauled, she saw that the *Acadecki* was tightly held by deck clamps fore and aft.

"Let's see how quickly your tastes jade," Nueva said, with an unpleasant laugh.

Over her shoulder, Acorna saw Nueva signal a waiting group of men and women, carrying various kinds of testing equipment and tools, to board the ship.

Acorna didn't think that Calum would have forgotten to disable the *Acadecki* before he'd opened the hatch. Of course, a personality like Nueva—and she made Kisla Manjari seem angelic in comparison—would have ways of extracting the information she wanted.

Nor was she, as she had half hoped, flung into the same cell as her guardian. Five of the doors on the narrow aisle she was pushed to were blue with force-field lights. So another time consuming puzzle would keep her from being totally jaded. Insane, maybe, but not jaded. Did they fill the cells in order? Or had Calum been pushed into the first empty one . . . since this Nueva person had boasted of relieving herself of excess personnel?

After using the sanitary appliance, with a deft but concealing shift of her pantaloons, Acorna unfastened one of the two slabs and lay down on it. She also decided to keep in character. She didn't doubt for a moment that anything she said would be monitored. So why had they separated her from Calum? Two people in the same fix would certainly exchange information. Oh, dear, perhaps she had laid it on a bit thick that Calum was useless. At that moment she would have given anything to be comforted by her "uncle."

She was roused from a restless sleep by a hissing noise and, as she lay prone on the comfortless slab, her face was turned to the metal ceiling . . . and the open vent. A thin, mournful face was framed within the vent. A grubby thin finger was placed across the lips of a tear-stained and very dirty face. But Acorna was not in a mood to quibble; she welcomed any friendly contact right then.

The child slowly let a rope down through the opening. She stood on the slab, thinking to assist by being closer to the vent. But instead the kid made violent gestures for her to refasten the slab to the wall.

As if she'd never been there. Good thinking.

There seemed to be just enough rope to reach her outstretched hands.

If this is all he's got, we'll never reach Calum even with the slab down, she thought.

She heard a soft, interrogative "Mmm?" from above, as if her rescuer was afraid to say out loud, "Come on, what are you waiting for?" Somewhat dubiously, Acorna gave a tentative pull on the rope. The thin youngster who was her unexpected savior couldn't have enough muscle to pull her up, light as she was. But he had tied the rope to something reassuringly secure. Hand over hand, she pulled herself up, grasping his hand as she reached the frame and angled her shoulders to the diagonal of the vent. Despite that, she scraped her arms badly getting through.

There was only the light from the narrow vent to see with. It reflected off a tube wall that wasn't very big, so she had to sort of slither the rest of her body out of the cell. Her rescuer quietly replaced the vent grill, screwed the fasteners back in, and began to recoil his rope. Once more he put his finger to his lips, then began to wriggle along the tube, looking back once to indicate she was to follow.

Fortunately, Acorna's gown was made of a fabric much more durable than it looked, but the fashionable boots that hid her oddly shaped feet were very clumsy and might make enough noise to be heard. How she finally got them off she never knew because it involved contortions of her lithe body she'd never had to make before, even in her self-defense exercises. Lying on her back, she sort of inched her feet up to where she could grab the boots and untie the laces. She would have loved to abandon them right there, but it seemed unwise to leave this proof of her escape route. Turning back on her stomach, she managed to tie the boots around her waist to keep them from hitting the tube walls. "Good idea," her rescuer approved in a bare thread of a whisper. After that they made better, and much quieter, progress along the tube. She wondered once or twice if her blood pounded more loudly than her body slithered, but no alarm was sounded.

She did sneak a peek through the other vents, but Calum was not in any of the three cells she could see into. The apathy of the detainees did nothing to reassure her about his safety.

They came to an intersecting tube, and the boy swung his body expertly to the left and wriggled down it. How long she followed him in this snakelike fashion Acorna had no idea, but suddenly they were in a much wider place—wider by comparison, at least—and she could sit without hitting her head on the ceiling. She was breathless and dry-mouthed from all her exertion.

"It's safe enough here. We can talk now," her savior said, but his voice was only a faintly raised whisper, warning her that their "safety" was only relative.

"What about Calum?" she whispered back.

"Who?"

"My . . . pilot."

The boy shook his head. "Must have been held in another area. I didn't see anybody but you and some of our own people."

Acorna's heart sank at this information, but she tried to put a brave face on it. "We must search for him," she said. "But first, I should thank you for rescuing me. I am Acorna. . . ." She let her voice trail off as she could not decide how else to identify herself. Was it safe to tell this unknown rescuer of her connection with the houses of Harakamian and Li? It might be better to find out a little more about him first.

"I'm Markel Illart. My father . . ." He gulped. "They . . . the ones who caught you . . . they're not Starfarers, not really. They were refugees we were helping out, and then that Nueva had a coup and spaced practic'ly all of the First Gen. I couldn't do anything, they'd locked the cabins. I couldn't do anything," he repeated, his voice rising dangerously.

"No, of course you could not," Acorna said at

once, though she was not at all clear on the situation—except that her rescuer, having shed his self-confident air, was clearly only a boy, a lost youngling in need of comfort. Despite, or perhaps because of, her sympathetic reassurance, Markel suddenly crumpled into sobs, even though he tried very hard to suppress them.

Immediately Acorna transferred herself to his side of their refuge and pulled him into her arms. Despite the hat, which had somehow remained in place through all her recent gyrations, she could touch his head with her concealed horn, to help relieve his anguish. The hands that he held to his face to muffle his sobs were bruised and bloodied as well as filthy. She could, and did, heal them. If he was to be of any further assistance to her, he needed to be whole. She left the dirt, having no water anyhow to clean him up. That reminded her of her own thirst.

"I'm terribly sorry, my dear," she said, hoping that he could feel the sympathy and reassurance she longed to give him. "How long ago did this happen?"

"Days, weeks, months it could be. It . . . it isn't easy to keep track of time up here." His voice wobbled dangerously.

"No, it certainly wouldn't be," Acorna agreed at once, "and I can't tell you how grateful I am to you for rescuing me."

"I had to, if I could. I'll do anything I can to get back at them for my father." He pressed his lips together as if holding back another outburst of unmanly sobs. "And they're going to make you tell them how they can get control of that ship of yours. It's a beauty."

"How would you know that?"

Markel's eyes lit up, and for a moment he seemed to have put aside his grief and his too-adult mannerisms, to be a normal cocky teenager enjoying a chance to boast of his expertise. "Oh, I know every tube and conduit in this ship. I can go anywhere, and I can even listen in on their coms. They think they're so smart. Well, they're not all THAT smart. I even know where they came from. They got on board the *Haven* by pretending to be Palomellese political refugees, but what really happened was Palomella decided to dump its worst criminals and scammed us into taking them on. That Nueva was running an extortion racket on Palomella, and now she's trying the same thing on the *Haven*. If only I'd warned Dad before—" He broke off and swallowed hard.

Acorna realized he was fighting back a sob, but the gesture still made her thirsty. She tried to moisten her mouth by running her tongue over the tissue, but she really needed some water. She thought rather wistfully of all the water they had so casually left behind.

"You wouldn't possibly have access to some water, would you?"

"Ha! I have access to anything I want," Markel said. "For all the good it does . . ."

Acorna sensed that he needed bolstering up, needed to think more about what he could do and less about the past that he could not change.

"I'm very thirsty," she said wistfully. "And,

when I think of the floods there were down on Rushima. . . ."

He reached behind his back and pulled out a water bottle, complete with nipple, the kind used for free-fall supplies.

"Oh, that's wonderful!" Acorna said, and there was no need to feign pleasure for Markel's sake. She enjoyed a long, luxurious drink of the water; it tasted stale and metallic, and she would have liked to purify it before drinking, but she didn't want to insult the boy.

"Go ahead," Markel urged when she paused after that first restorative drink. You can have all of it," he added with a casual flick of his fingers. "I've got more whenever you need it. Are you hungry?"

"Why, I am. Don't tell me you can find food, too! Is there anything you don't know about this ship?" She exaggerated her admiring tone slightly and saw the praise work on Markel as the water had done on her, restoring the parched tissues of his soul. "Only . . ." she thought to warn him before he made promises he wouldn't be able to keep, ". . . I cannot eat meat; only grains and vegetables."

Markel looked slightly relieved at this statement. "That's as well because it's much easier to snitch plants than anything else, like cooked food. Finish your drink. We're not far from the 'ponics."

Acorna's stomach made a joyful noise she was certain would echo down the tubes, but Markel had already turned to lead her to food. She slipped the bottle into one of her boots—as long as she had to drag these things along, at least they could be useful as carriers. The laces were long . . . maybe if she could add them to Markel's rope, they'd be long enough to reach Calum.

Over the other reeks of the ship, Acorna smelled vegetation: lots and lots of different kinds of vegetation, and the slightly chemical smell that her sensitive nostrils could identify as 'ponic nutrients. She wondered wistfully if the seedling chard she had planted on the *Acadecki* would ever leaf for her.

"Be very quiet now," Markel said, once again more mouthing words than actually speaking, as he deftly inserted a tool and withdrew the fasteners of a much larger grill.

The smells were almost unbearably enticing to Acorna, but she waited on his signal to enter after he had done a preliminary prowl round on hands and knees. The scent of chard drew her like a magnet, and it was fortunate indeed that it was nearer to her than the root vegetables he was deftly, and cleverly, harvesting. She noticed that he was careful to take only the small ones that were likely to be culled anyway. He took carrots and turnips and potatoes and several other brightly colored things that she did not recognize. Hybrids, probably. She carefully augmented his selection with chard leaves, then some lettuces, and one head of cabbage, stuffing what she could into her other boot. She was glad she hadn't been wearing the boots for very long before using them as food and water carriers.

The surreptitious harvest didn't take long. Both Markel and Acorna had nimble hands and were agile on their hands and knees. They gathered up their booty and retreated to the tube, and Markel refastened the grill behind them. He beckoned for her to follow him some distance away from the 'ponics unit before he signaled her to stop and start eating. Which was perfectly understandable, for carrot chomping could be heard if one was listening for it. Even, perhaps, if one was not, because she was chewing as fast as she could. She took chard next, then experimented with the dark red thing he handed her, and that was good, too. Well, almost anything would have tasted good to her at that point.

After those sorely needed restorative mouthfuls Acorna thought again of Calum. He, too, would be hungry and thirsty. If only she knew where he was being held!

She tapped Markel's shoulder as he was chewing away at a raw potato and indicated she wanted to speak. He nodded but cautioned her with a finger across his lips to speak quietly.

"My friend will have no food or water. If only you could figure out where he is being kept, could we get to him with something to eat and drink?"

Markel considered and finally gave a sharp nod. "He'll be in the secure area," he whispered, "where they keep the important prisoners."

Acorna's heart sank. "I tried to make them believe he knew nothing."

"Didn't work," Markel told her, "or they'd've tossed him in the holding cells like they did you.

It'll be a lot harder to sneak into the secure cells—but you're right, we gotta try. Even if we can't break him out—and I ain't promising, those cells are a lot tougher—we can prob'ly slip him a water bottle and some greens. He'll need it, too! Sometimes they 'forget' to feed the folks in detention. I hate it," he whispered. "I keep thinking, what if somebody dies, and I could have saved him . . . but some of the ones they throw in the cells are Palomellese. If they found out I was free, they might sell me out to gain favor with Nueva."

Acorna's heart ached at the decisions that had been forced on the boy, decisions that would have been heartbreaking for a mature adult. "Well, I can assure you that neither Calum nor I will sell you out—no matter what happens!"

Six

nce she got over her shock at being surrounded by four unicorn-people instead
of facing just one, Karina realized that
she might really be onto something here. The
entire rest of the populated galaxy thought that
Acorna was the only one of her kind. But here
were four more of the unicorn-people—and she
was the one who had been Chosen to act as their
guide and interpreter! Once it had been established, with a great deal of pointing and head tossing and shrugging and mane twitching, that none
of the four around her was Acorna, Karina was
able to guess that they were looking for Acorna. It
was strange, the way their meaning seemed to
come into her mind if she just let them say their
strange nasal words and didn't try to understand.
The trick seemed to be not to think about it, to
convince the busy part of your head that you were
actually thinking about something else and just
sort of accidentally overhearing their conversation.

In the first minutes on the unicorn-people's spacecraft, Karina found that trick quite easy to pull off. Everything was so different, so . . . magical? Or just alien? She couldn't decide. The soft, flowing draperies they wore, the glowing translucent horns on their foreheads, the couches where they reclined so gracefully, even the gentle radiance that lit the interior of the spacecraft all spoke to her of a Higher World guided by thought and love, the Upper Realm she had so long been seeking to contact. But when one of them went through a slitted opening into another part of the spacecraft, she saw a board covered with twinkling dials and long projecting levers that had not been made for any human fingers to manipulate. That made her nervous, so she decided not to think about it but to concentrate on boosting her psychic awareness so that she could communicate better on a pure and spiritual level.

But every time she achieved the kind of calm that was supposed to bring connection with one's spirit totem and access to higher levels, she lost that sense of almost understanding what the unicorn-people were saying. It was most irritating and not at all what she would have expected.

(Do you have enough data from its thought-images to use the LAANYE yet, Melireenya?)

(Not quite, though I have learned that it is a she-creature.)

(Had to be, with those engorged mammaries. Don't they hurt?)

(Well, those could be the result of some kind of

illness. They certainly don't look natural, do they? But her images are distinctly feminine . . . what I can read of them. You've noticed how weak her transmissions are? And every time I think we're communicating, something breaks it off and all I get is this image of a long, pointy crystal—see?)

(Maybe she's trying to tell us that they use something like that to amplify their naturally weak thoughts.)

(Good idea! I hadn't thought of that. Shall we make one?)

(Might as well try it. If we have to build the data for the LAANYE by pointing our horns at things and listening to her grunt their names, it'll take forever.)

Something heavy and sharp-edged dropped into her lap and interrupted Karina's meditations and earnest efforts to establish communion on the spiritual plane.

"Hey!" she exclaimed, opening her eyes. "Be careful what you're tossing around, will you— Ohhh. . . ." Her indignant comment died away into a long gasp of awe and wonder as she lifted the ten-inch, doubly terminated quartz crystal. "Now where did you get that, I wonder?"

(Well, that came through loud and clear. She doesn't like us dropping rocks in her lap.)

(She likes the rock, though. Look how she's holding it!)

(Great, we can generate as many of those as we need from the spare-parts assembler. Maybe we can use them as trade items. Go on, now, get some more complete utterances from her. The LAANYE needs syntactic data as well as semantics, you know!)

(Barbarian! Can you say . . . shit, I've lost her again.)

Holding the quartz crystal, Karina was deep in meditation, imagining the flow of energies that moved in a stream of golden light through the crystal, into her hands, through her body, and out to embrace the Guides around her. She imagined so effectively that she was completely unaware of the thought-images directed at her by Melireenya.

(We got a burst of transmission when we gave her that crystal. Maybe she wants another one.)

(Maybe we should just drop something heavy on her foot and see what she says.)

(Thariinye, when are you going to grow up?)

After a bit of tinkering, the spare-parts assembler was able to produce not only quartz crystals but also a number of other crystalline mineral specimens. They started with the varieties of quartz, showering Karina (gently) with rose quartz, amethyst, and citrine; then, for variety, Thariinye adjusted the assembler to produce other silicates such as tourmaline and iolite, orthoclase and microcline. He was particularly proud of a large, tabular orthoclase with a bluish white sheen in two directions. Their biped seemed impressed by it as well.

(She likes the feldspar group. I got a lot of good

data from what she said that time.)

(Of course! Look, she's wearing a feldspar; maybe that's her totem.)

So moonstone, labradorite, anorthite, and other feldspars dropped into Karina's open hands until she was all but buried in their silvery shimmer, and Melireenya turned the LAANYE settings from collection mode to analysis mode with a sigh of relief.

(That was a job and a half! These beings can't concentrate at all!)

(Oh, well, it's done now. Let's eat while it's analyzing, then we can put the LAANYE in sleep-teaching mode and in a half turn we should be able to talk to it, I mean her, with mouth-noises.)

(What do you suppose she eats?)

(I hope she likes sprouts.)

Karina wasn't the least bit unhappy to be offered a vegetarian meal. Although her hosts worried back and forth at each other about the poor variety of foodstuffs and the drab flavor of ship-grown fruits and greens, Karina found the meal, at least, to be everything she would have imagined spiritually advanced beings to ingest. She had been a little worried that the unicorn-people would be too spiritually advanced to require any nourishment beyond a little water. The salad they offered her, full of crisp greens, its flavor set off by a tangy dressing of ground seeds that tasted a little like mustard and more like dill, reassured her on those grounds. She wouldn't have minded a tofu brownie or some sprouted-

grains cake for dessert, but the bowl of fruits and
berries was a reasonable alternative. The little
brown berries proved surprisingly sweet and
embarrassingly juicy—the first one she bit into
felt like an explosion of sweetness in her mouth
and startled her into a minor coughing fit. After
that she took the berries with respect, to offset the
tart flavor of the yellow thing that wasn't exactly
an apricot, and found that the combination made a
reasonably satisfying dessert.

After the meal they showed her a tiny cubicle,
high enough to accommodate the unicorn-people
but barely wide enough for Karina, and after some
puzzlement she worked out what the facilities were
for and how she could use them. That solved
another problem she'd been trying not to worry
about and left her feeling quite confident that she
would be able to handle anything else that came
up. And after all the excitement and that really
very filling meal of salad and strange fruits, she
was quite tired and more than willing to lie down
on a couch in the main cabin when they dimmed
the lights in there.

(I'll keep watch this shift,) Khaari volunteered.
(She can sleep on my couch, and you three can use
the LAANYE. I don't really want to hurt my head
learning another barbarian language anyway.)

(Khaari! We must all be able to negotiate with
these people!)

(Why? Somebody's got to stay with the ship,
and I nominate me because I'm the only one who
can navigate you out of here.)

(Self-thinking is un-linyarii.)

(Huh! I'm Liinyar, and I'm doing the thinking, so by definition it's linyarii.)

(This younger generation,) Neeva sighed toward Melireenya. (We would never have talked like that. There's no telling what Thariinye and Khaari will do next.)

(So maybe it's a good idea Khaari doesn't learn their language. In fact, we might be better off if Thariinye didn't either.)

This last comment inspired Khaari to take her turn with the LAANYE after all, sleeping on a reclining chair in the control cabin since the barbarian female was snoozing on her usual couch. As for Thariinye, he was already stretched out on his couch, wearing the headset that connected him with the LAANYE. He hadn't even waited to make sure the barbarian was comfortable . . . but the light snores issuing from Khaari's couch reassured Neeva and Melireenya on that score. With a mutual glance that spoke more eloquently than their thought-images on the subject of this impulsive younger generation, they, too, donned their headsets and settled for a strenuous night of sleep-learning.

By the beginning of the next shift, when Khaari brought up the lights in the main cabin, they could talk to Karina in her own tongue.

Which was very nearly the same as knowing the Basic Interlingua used for trade, diplomacy, and war in all the worlds inhabited by Karina's people.

It was easy enough to explain, now, that they

were relatives of Acorna's who had been searching for her.

(This is not the entire truth,) Neeva fretted. (It is even an untruth, if we allow her to believe—as she surely will—that we came to this portion of the galaxy in search of our lost little one. Should we not tell her of the Khleevi, and that we came to warn her people and seek alliance with them?)

(All things in their proper time,) Melireenya replied. (Remember how the people of that first world were so frightened that they closed themselves within an impenetrable shield? If those harboring 'Khornya (for so Linyaari tongues had rendered her name, turning it into something pronounceable in their language) should do the same, we might NEVER get her back!)

(First we must find our 'Khornya,) Thariinye agreed. (Think, Neeva: she will surely tell us all we must know of these barbarians, so that we can judge whether they are khlevii or linyarii, whether we wish to make alliance with them or to disappear before they can attack our worlds.)

The unspoken interchange went so swiftly that Karina was not even aware of any pause in the conversation; she was still exclaiming in delight over how quickly they had picked up her language.

The Linyaari envoys were equally delighted when Karina confirmed their hope that Acorna was to be found here, on the lunar base to which the shuttle had been bound.

"I had a Lattice note from her, out of this node, just a few days ago," she told them.

"Oh, then you are acquaainit—acquiintee—You

know our little 'Khornya?" Neeva asked eagerly. "How does she? Has she been well treated here?"

Karina looked down. Much as she longed to claim acquaintance with Acorna, was there any point in doing so, when a few hours would prove the claim false? "We have not met in person," she evaded, "only in correspondence. But our auras are attuned." Surely a Lattice note from one person and an acknowledgment from the receiver constituted a correspondence?

"Then she . . ." Neeva fumbled among unfamiliar words. Their shapes in her thoughts were blurry and poorly defined; could the LAANYE be malfunctioning? "Your karma is joined with hers . . . she is expecting you?"

Karina gazed soulfully at the heap of moonstones in her cupped hands. She had been fondling them and playing with them ever since she awoke.

"Will she be conceerin . . . worriid," Thariinye substituted the easier-to-pronounce word, "that you were not on the shuttle?"

"Oh, no," Karina said unguardedly, then tried to retrieve matters. "That is," she said with her tinkling laugh, "we didn't have a definite arrangement. We just left it that if I did not hear from her that this was not a good time, I would be coming to Maganos within the next few days. Synchronicity, you know"—she waved her plump little hands vaguely—"all will manifest for the good of all; we need only maintain the appropriate space in our hearts. But I am quite sure," she said earnestly, "that she is looking forward to finally meeting me on this plane."

"Plane flies through atmosphere," Thariinye said, puzzled. "Atmosphere is not on this moon."

Karina laughed again. "I meant, on the physical plane. We have long been close on the spiritual plane," she said.

(What is she talking about? Do these beings move through different dimensions?)

(They appear to exist in three dimensions and move along a fourth at a fixed rate, just as do we and all other entities,) Khaari told him. (You must have been confused by some idiom of their language. What is the Linyaari for what she said?)

(I don't think you can say it in Linyaari.) "I hear you," Thariinye said aloud to Karina, having picked this up from the LAANYE as an all-purpose phrase meaning, "I don't know exactly what you mean, but let's not argue about it."

Rafik's worries about Acorna grew to monumental proportions when he reached direct-communications range of Maganos Moon Base and got no satisfactory answers to his queries. All he wanted to know was that Acorna was still there and unharmed. All he got from the com techs working the boards at Maganos was static, missed connections, and finally a bland statement that questions about Acorna were to be passed directly to Delszaki Li.

"Fine," Rafik said, "patch me through to Mr. Li's suite."

But Delszaki Li was napping . . . or in a private meeting . . . or investigating some new workings out of reach of the base-to-ship communications system . . .

or simply not to be found at the moment, depending on when Rafik tried to contact him and which technician was asked to forward the message.

"I don't believe it," Rafik said flatly when for the second time he was told that Delszaki Li was visiting the new mine workings on the far side of Maganos. "The man's old and paralyzed and confined to a hover-chair, he's not going to be hopping around Maganos like a performing flea!"

"Mr. Li has a very good hover-chair," said the com tech. "State-of-the-art. And, uh, the light gravity here means that he has more energy, of course. Less, umm, strain on the muscles, you know?"

"Ten thousand bazaar dogs and Shaitans take the hover-chair!" Rafik shouted into the mike. "He doesn't USE those muscles, what difference does gravity make?"

"Transmission unintelligible, please moderate volume," the tech said. "Signal fading . . ." Her voice slowly dissolved into a crackle of static. Fuming, Rafik decided that he would just have to wait until he landed on Maganos. Then he would See For Himself.

Even landing took longer than usual; a vessel of unfamiliar design, whose pilot seemed completely unfamiliar with standard docking facilities and commands, was just before him in the queue and held up docking for everybody else.

"Sorry about that, *Uhuru*," said the breezy voice of the second-shift guidance-control officer. "These idiots just ahead of you in the queue come from some backstars subspace where apparently nobody flies by the regs; according to the pilot they just make it up as they go along. She's having a hell of a time following my instructions—keeps saying, 'I hear you,' and then doing something completely different."

Rafik had a moment's regretful thought for the ancient days of the First Prophet, when in some parts of Earth the Book of the Prophet was interpreted to mean, among other things, that women were not allowed to drive.

When he finally docked, he was in a tearing hurry to reach Delszaki Li's private quarters and much too worried to care about the very odd design of the ship that had held up the queue for so long, or the plump little woman in fluttery lavender draperies who was clambering down an exit stair much too steep for her short legs. He waved at the lunar-base guards and was passed through on sight, without the formalities of identification and checks for contraband that held up strangers arriving at Maganos Base. An old friend of his from the days at MME was now overseeing the Beneficiation and Extraction Department and let him take a slightly illicit shortcut and hitch a ride on a conveyor belt that was supposed to be carrying pulverized material to the oxygen-extraction plant, allowing Rafik to arrive at Delszaki Li's quarters shortly after docking and a good ten minutes before he was expected there.

"Where IS she? Is she all right?" he demanded as he pushed through the iris door, too impatient to wait for it to retract its flexible membranes fully.

Gill and Judit were sitting in the anteroom,

holding hands. Judit looked as if she had been crying; Gill turned red at the question.

"There is no reason to suppose Acorna is in any difficulty," Judit said.

Gill swallowed. "Of course not. Acorna can handle anything that comes up, and Calum . . . well, Calum is very smart, you know, Rafik."

"Calum," Rafik said, "doesn't have the common sense the Prophets would give to a canary, and if we're relying on him to keep Acorna out of trouble, no wonder Uncle Hafiz was worried about her! WHERE IS SHE?"

"Hafiz?" Judit exclaimed. "How did he find out?"

"Find out what?"

"Well . . ." Judit gestured helplessly. "What was he worried about?"

"Don't know, can't find out now." Rafik explained about the garbled message he had received just before a planetary shield closed down all travel to and communication with Laboue.

"And you think there may be some danger to Acorna?"

"Whatever it means," Rafik said, "it can't be anything good. Communication and trade are the basis of House Harakamian's wealth. With Laboue closed off like this, Uncle Hafiz can't check the odds on any of his, umm, interplanetary operations, or keep tabs on the competition, or do any of his other, umm, normal financial and commercial procedures. He wouldn't have done this unless something out there had really scared him." He thought this statement over for a moment. "In fact, I wouldn't have said there was anything that could make Uncle Hafiz nervous enough to forgo a quarter percent profit on the Skarness Relay . . . which he will have lost through not being there to authorize a credit exchange before the news of the Relay's failure came through the regular communications channels."

"Hafiz has advance information on the Skarness Relay?" Gill asked, impressed. "How does he work that?"

Rafik grinned. "You know the Singing Stones of Skarness, in his garden? They're not just a curiosity—they're a communications system. Hafiz broke the code. Those rocks know what's happening on Skarness, no matter where in the galaxy they happen to be."

"How?"

"How does a clam in an aquarium in the desert know when it would be high tide if the desert were underwater?" Rafik shrugged. "They know, that's all. At first the Stones weren't all that useful, because they aren't interested in human affairs—they think we move too fast and die too soon to be studied—but Uncle Hafiz got one of them to make a small side bet on the Relay with him, and now they're all following it. He'd sent to tell me to lay off all our bets just before that last message and the Shield closing down . . . but without his authorization, I couldn't do it."

"Delightful as it is to learn these details of sporting events," Judit said, "I for one should like to find out a little more about what has brought you here in such haste. You don't know what the threat was?"

Rafik shook his head. "Not precisely. But it must have come from space, not from one of his competitors on Laboue, or there'd be no advantage in invoking the Shield. So we don't need to worry about Yukata Batsu or any of that southern continent lot. Uncle Hafiz has effectively divided the universe into two separate boxes," he said somberly. "One box contains Laboue, the other holds the rest of the universe . . . including whatever threat motivated him to take this step. And whatever it is must concern Acorna."

Judit drew a deep breath. "Then . . . perhaps it's for the best that things have turned out as they have. Don't you think, Gill?"

"Could be," Gill agreed. "After all, if even we can't find her, what chance is there that these mysterious enemies will do so?"

"CAN'T FIND HER?" Rafik echoed in shock and outrage. "What—how—Shaitan-begotten spawn of a cretin, you can't have lost the girl on a lunar base this size!"

"Rafik, you really must make an effort not to pick up your uncle's habits of speech," Judit reprimanded him.

At the same time Gill said heavily, "Not on the lunar base. Off it. She and Calum have done a bunk. With a little help from certain other people," he added, giving Judit a dirty look. She flushed but made no attempt to defend herself.

And in chorus, the two of them explained to Rafik how a series of delays in the preparation of the *Acadecki* had so frustrated Calum and Acorna that they not only took off before the ship was

ready but failed to follow the navigation plan
Calum had filed, so that by the time their getaway
was discovered, it was impossible to follow them.

"Impossible?" Rafik repeated, raising his
straight dark brows a fraction of an inch.

Gill gestured helplessly. "You know Calum.
He's not only a brilliant mathematician, but a
devious s.o.b. There are innumerable ways to navigate space from here to the Coma Berenices
quadrant, and trust Calum not to take the most
logical—the one in his filed nav plan—nor yet the
least logical, because we checked that already.
There's absolutely no way to predict what path he
will have taken."

Rafik would have disputed that, and had
already asked for star maps on several scales to be
displayed, but his study of the possible routes to
Coma Berenices was interrupted by the announcement of a visitor for Acorna.

Not being privy to the shortcuts Rafik had used,
nor anywhere near as quick on her feet as he was,
Karina had taken quite a while longer than Rafik
to reach Delszaki Li's headquarters. That she was
there at all was tribute not so much to her increas-
ingly confident statement that Acorna had invited
her as to the Linyaari ability to soothe and calm the
minds of those physically close to them. Neeva and
Melireenya had risked showing themselves to the
guards on duty at the docking station just long
enough to project calming thoughts of "I haven't
seen anything unusual" and "This is a friend of
Acorna's."

Once she entered the interstices of the lunar

base, though, Karina had to make her own way without the help of the Linyaari projections. She had done remarkably well already, ascertaining from "casual" conversations with the people she encountered that either Acorna was to be found with Delszaki Li, or that gentleman would be able to tell her where she was. No one saw any reason to question Karina's statement that she was a friend of Acorna's and an expected guest; if she had not been able to show some valid reason for visiting Maganos, she would not have been allowed past the docking facility, would she? And her statement that she had impulsively come by private transport rather than by the regularly scheduled shuttle both explained why she hadn't been met and gave her an aura of wealth and luxury that helped to smother any doubts. But here, in the anterooms to Delszaki Li's private quarters, she met her match.

The secretary-receptionist who guarded Mr. Li's privacy knew Rafik by sight and had passed him through without question. But Karina he did NOT know—and he was as disinclined to admit somebody who was not on the list of accepted visitors as Karina was to give up so close to her goal. The resulting altercation drew first Judit's attention, then Rafik's, and finally Gill's. They opened the iris door in time to hear Karina "explaining" with some heat that she and Acorna had been in correspondence for some time, that they were closely linked on the spiritual plane, and that it was now their destiny and the will of the stars that they should also be together on the physical plane.

"Stars didn't send me a directive," the secretary said, deadpan.

"Oh, Lor'," Gill groaned, "it was bound to happen sooner or later, but why now, on top of everything else?"

"What was bound to happen?" Rafik asked plaintively. Since reaching Maganos he had continually found himself two steps behind the latest events — only to be expected when he had been absent so long on House Harakamian business, but nonetheless a galling situation to a man used to making his fortune by the timely use of information.

"Nutcases," Gill answered, retreating back into the room behind the secretary's station to make his explanation. "People heard about the healings Acorna did on Kezdet, you know. Can't keep something like that secret. We've put it about that her healing abilities have faded as she matured, but that's not enough to deter the really determined nuts. We've also spread rumors that she's at half a dozen different houses Mr. Li owns in different systems. I think I know how this one got onto her, though — tell you later," he muttered in an undertone as Judit opened the iris again and went through to the secretary's station.

"I am so sorry to disappoint you," Judit said sweetly, "but just now Acorna is . . ."

The pause was fatal to her good intentions.

"Ill. She's not seeing visitors," Rafik said firmly.

At the same moment Gill said, "Not on the base. She's gone to visit old friends."

And, just too late to stop herself, Judit said, ". . . terribly busy."

***

They're all lying! Something's terribly wrong!

Karina's shock and outrage, undiminished by any conscious attempts to focus or channel her psychic abilities, came through to the anxiously waiting Linyaari as clearly as a minor explosion.

(Oh, my head! Tell that female to damp her modulations, will you?) Thariinye complained.

(I can't tell her anything,) Melireenya thought, rather acidly. (She thinks you're in charge, remember?)

(She recognizes natural brilliance when she sees it.)

(Hmph. She probably comes from some culture that has a peculiar caste-ranking system. Maybe they're graded by physical height.)

(In that case, she must be pretty low-caste. I've been looking through the screens at the others of her race who come in and out here. And have you noticed—)

(Not now, you two!) Neeva put in. (Melireenya, you're supposed to be monitoring the female . . . Khariinya. What's happening now? Who are "they," and what are they lying about?)

(I don't know. That was the first I heard from her since she passed those guards at the exit from this docking area. I'm trying to get back in touch now. . . .)

Karina had meant to demand to see Acorna, but some impulse she did not recognize made her ask first, "Who are you people, anyway?" She followed that with her own questions. "Why won't you let me see Acorna—and why are you lying about it?"

"None of your business," Gill said firmly. "Only people on the list of approved guests are admitted to this suite, young lady. You're not on the list—so I strongly suggest you leave now, before we call Security to have you put out."

Karina felt the secretary's mocking eye upon her. She was sure she was turning red with embarrassment, but she stood her ground a moment longer.

"I must see Acorna. Truly . . . you don't understand . . . and I can't tell anyone but her . . . but it is not just for my own sake. There is something she must know. Oh, please!" She was almost in tears. "Please, you don't understand, it's terribly important. If she knew, she'd want to see me, I just know she would."

"Darlin'," Gill said more gently, "I'm sure it's important to you, but there's just no way you can see Acorna. I'll tell you the absolute truth: she's not on this base, and we don't know when she'll be back." He took Karina's hands in his. "Word of honor," he said, looking into her face with those piercing blue eyes that must have persuaded ever so many silly girls to believe whatever he said.

And he radiated truth and sincerity this time, whatever she had felt from him before.

The silver-set moonstone at her throat was cold and dull. And try as she might, Karina could not persuade herself that she "felt" Acorna's presence anywhere near them.

"I . . . I see," she said dully.

Declan Giloglie's blue eyes blazed with a triumphant light that renewed all her suspicions. Karina consciously breathed deeply and thought of Peace and Love. "Well, in that case," she said, "I suppose I may as well go on. I certainly don't want to waste my time looking for somebody who's not even here!" The tinkling laugh was a little flat, and her voice trembled slightly, but that might be put down to disappointment rather than to the sheer fury that possessed her.

(She's absolutely furious now, but I can't tell what about. The silly twit doesn't think, she just stirs the brain-bits around like a nut-and-root stew, you never know what's going to bob up next.)

(Is she in trouble? Where is she?)

(How should I know? She doesn't look, either. You can't transmit images of your surroundings if you never look at them properly. All I can see in her mind right now is blue.)

Karina widened her own eyes and looked straight into Gill's until he released her hands and stepped back. "Well . . . that's that, then," he said. "Sorry for your disappointment."

Karina visualized herself floating in a cool blue cloud that absorbed and masked her utter fury.

(Shit! Now I've lost her completely!)

As the door to Delszaki Li's private suite closed

behind him, the secretary looked at Karina with a touch of pity.

"You're not the only one with a sob story, you know," he advised her, not unkindly. "Take more than that to get in to see Acorna . . . that is, it would if she were here," he added, remembering Gill's story. Not being privy to Acorna's unheralded departure, he took it for granted Gill was lying to protect her privacy. "You've struck out—better go home. They'll call Security if you hang out here, you know."

"I haven't the—" Karina stopped herself before she could disclose her dilemma. The fact was that she didn't have her fare back to Kezdet, much less to her home planet. Everything she owned and as much as she could borrow had been barely sufficient to pay her way this far.

But she did, she reflected, have private transport . . . of a sort. And she did owe it to the Linyaari to go back and tell them . . . well, perhaps not exactly what had happened . . . they wouldn't understand the nuances; she would be false to the underlying spiritual truth if she told them the bald literal truth, wouldn't she?

"You are quite right," she said instead. "I shall return to my personal ship at once."

On the way back, she concentrated on her breathing until she had attained a state of spiritual tranquillity in which she was no longer deceived by the superficial appearance of events and felt quite able to convey the basic truths of the situation to her Linyaari friends.

She'd thought of exactly how to phrase it, too.

***

"She's being kept prisoner!" Karina announced on her return to the ship. She was breathless not only from the climb but from the irritation occasioned by having to push her way through a growing crowd of curious onlookers who were fascinated by the gilt scrollwork and trompe l'oeil scarlet-and-emerald ribbons painted as if they were flowing across the body of the ship.

"Have you seen our 'Khornya'?" Neeva asked, pronouncing the newly learned words slowly and carefully.

"Acorna, not Kornya." Karina sank back onto one of the couches in the main cabin. "No, I told you, they're keeping her prisoner. There's an absolute brute of a man guarding the rooms, he won't let anybody in, and a red-bearded Viking giant who tells the most terrible lies you ever heard. Would you believe it, he actually tried to convince me that Acorna wasn't there at all! And the other two gave quite contradictory stories."

Neeva frowned in concentration as she tried to follow this burst of speech. "But you said she was expecting you . . . had invited you to visit her. Why would she go away?"

"That's just it." Karina sat up. "I don't for a minute believe she has gone away. One of the others said she was sick, and another said she was busy. Obviously they are all lying. I don't know why, but they are determined to prevent Acorna from speaking with anybody outside their little group. Why, for all I know"—she cried, too indignant for caution—"she may never even have seen my first fifty-six messages!"

"Your what?" asked Neeva, now thoroughly confused.

Karina remembered that she was supposed to be a close friend of Acorna's. Well, she was. On a spiritual level. "Never mind, that's not important. The important thing is," she said, enunciating clearly, "there is something very sinister going on, and I intend to find Acorna and rescue her from these people!"

All four of the Linyaari looked at one another for a long time. Karina had the oddest feeling that a very intense argument was going on, though none of them actually said anything. She half closed her eyes and tried to sense their auras. *Breathe slowly*, she reminded herself. *Listen to your breathing, still the mind, expand your awareness.*

It had been a very trying morning. Perhaps she would be able to still her mind and expand her awareness more effectively lying down. . . .

Karina fell peacefully asleep while the Linyaari debated their next step.

(It is brave and generous of this Khariinya to offer her services further, but we must not accept.) Neeva was firm on this. (Bad enough that we have fooled with the minds of those people on the shuttle, making them forget that their flight was interrupted. We must not go on to put this one at risk from her own kind.)

(Besides, she hasn't accomplished much so far.)

(She has found where 'Khornya is being held, and has ascertained that she is a prisoner. That is enough to go on. One of us will have to free her.)

(Oh, dear, oh, dear. I see more fooling with their minds coming up.)

(We are going to have to do that in any case. Have you looked at the screens showing us the docking area recently?)

(Of course not, I've been trying to understand what Khariinya was saying.)

(The other barbarians are behaving oddly.)

(So? It's not as if we knew what was normal behavior for them.)

(I think they are curious about our ship.)

(Why? It's a nice unobtrusive vessel, nothing gaudy.)

(Not by their standards. Look at the other ships docked in this facility.)

Neeva studied the views in the screens and had to concede that Thariinye had a point. Although the Linyaari vessel was not dissimilar in shape to the barbarian ships, the other ships were so . . . well, so dreary! Naked metal and blind ports; nothing to disguise the ungraceful lines of thrusters or to decorate the long plain sweep of the main body; and above all, no color, not even a discreet touch of gilding or a splash of crimson to delight the eye. And by now, quite a number of the short, hornless bipeds were gathered so near to the Linyaari ship that the screens offered only a foreshortened view of them, pointing and talking excitedly among themselves. (Perhaps they are admiring our tasteful decor,) she suggested without conviction.

(I'm afraid it is more than that,) Melireenya agreed reluctantly with Thariinye. (Nobody would choose to make ships look so dull and plain, so it must be that they do not know how to protect painted surfaces against atmospheric abrasion or meteorite damage. This ship must be quite an oddity to them.)

(How could a race be so sophisticated as to travel in space, colonize many systems, even build bases on airless asteroids such as this, and still remain ignorant of the first principles of surface shielding?) Khaari demanded crossly. (It is not logical!)

(Whether it's principle or taste,) Neeva told her, (we are obviously too conspicuous. I am afraid our attempt to make unobtrusive contact has not been successful.)

(We had better not allow them to board . . . or even to pay any more attention to us.)

(I am afraid you are right.) Neeva suppressed a sigh of disquiet. Start bending the ethics of the Linyaari, it seemed, and there was no limit to how far they might get bent. The other three envoys had assured her that the only questionable action they would have to take was to make the crew and the other passengers on the space shuttle a little bit unclear about what had happened mid-flight. But just by being here, they had already exposed the hornless bipeds to a superior technology. Now one of them would have to leave the ship in order to exert a calming presence on the people who were obviously so curious about it. And who knew what that might lead to?

(Don't worry, Neeva. I'll take care of everything,) Thariinye thought blithely.

The base of Neeva's horn ached. Thariinye

would not have been her first choice to take on the task of calming the hornless ones . . . but it was a small task; what difference did it make who did it? Still, her forehead ached as though the horn were warning her of calamities ahead.

And it might have been right, for Thariinye did not stop at showing himself long enough to establish his influence over the bipeds near the ship. Cloaked in his projected cloud of (You haven't seen anything unusual) and (Everything's all right), he went down all the way to the ground level and casually strolled among the bipeds there. The little group gathered near the ship was breaking up now, the members of the group moving away briskly in different directions as if they had suddenly remembered something they were supposed to be doing and couldn't imagine why they were wasting time staring at what was, after all, just another spaceship of the hundreds that docked at Maganos.

Melireenya chuckled at the sight. (Thariinye must have added a bit of "Urgent business" to his projections, to clear them out so fast!)

(I wish he wouldn't. We shouldn't fool with their minds any more than we have to. And— Thariinye! Where do you think you're going?) The young fool was following several of the bipeds toward the guarded exit from the docking facility.

(Quit worrying, Neeva!) Thariinye's images, slightly weakened by distance from the ship, were nonetheless sharp enough to convey a sense of slight irritation. (We agreed that one of us must find 'Khornya, did we not? And since I have already expended the effort to cloud these bipeds' minds into believing that I am one of them, why should I not go on into the base and seek out 'Khornya right now, before her captors have time to hide her elsewhere?)

(He may be right, Neeva. Khariinya's visit may have alerted them.)

(But you do not know where she is! The base is large. . . .)

(Not large enough to hide another Linyaari. I shall simply wander until I sense her presence; then I shall ask her how she is held and what would be the best way to free her. I am not entirely stupid, Neeva.)

And since she could not think of any better plan, Neeva let him go without further protest.

During his first minutes inside the base proper, Thariinye kept letting his calming projections slip as he was distracted by the oddities of this alien construction, then hurriedly projecting extra soothing feelings to relax and distract surprised onlookers. As he cataloged the alien peculiarities, he left behind him a trail of slightly perturbed base workers who had the vague feeling that they'd just forgotten something very important, or that something wonderful had almost happened and if only they'd been looking carefully enough they might have seen it.

The corridors connecting the docking facility to Maganos Central, and that central complex to other parts of the shielded base, were so dark and low that Thariinye felt almost as if he were exploring a mine. After cracking his head on a projecting air vent and catching his horn a really painful blow at a slit-opening door of unfamiliar design, he learned to stoop slightly, walk slowly, and watch the way ahead very carefully for obstructions.

The high dome of Maganos Central, with its seemingly extravagant aerie of scaffolding in a spiderweb design spiraling to the top, was as much a physical relief to Thariinye as a shot of oxygen would have been. But the design itself distracted him for dangerous moments. The spiraling web of scaffolding was hung with green plants that dangled invitingly downward, and in the light gravity of this moon he could easily have jumped high enough to browse at will. What was this place — some sort of cafeteria?

A gasp from a passerby reminded him to maintain his cloaking shields. (You haven't seen anything unusual) he projected, with a hint of (urgent business somewhere else) to hurry her on her way.

The female trotted off and later told her partner in Shipping and Receiving that she'd seen the most amazingly handsome young man just coming into Central, she'd have stopped and tried to chat him up if they hadn't been so behindhand with the monthly report; whereupon her partner gave her a very odd look and said that the monthly report wouldn't be due for another six shifts, and did she think she might be coming down with something?

Retreating to lean against a gently curved wall, Thariinye maintained his shielding and watched the barbarians hurrying back and forth until he concluded, with some reluctance, that the greenery must be merely an atmospheric purifier and not a buffet. At least, nobody else was nibbling on those tempting new leaves.

(Thariinye, you greedy pig! You're supposed to be looking for our 'Khornya, not thinking about brunch!)

(Yeah, yeah, but Neeva, you should just see these plants!) But, reminded of his duty, Thariinye tore his gaze from the succulent new shoots and leaves just above eye level and mentally felt around the central complex for some sense of another Linyaari.

He could sense nothing but the tangled, muddy undertow of a thousand alien minds muttering away, each in its separate little shell, and most too weak and garbled to be intelligible, with here and there a feeling highlighted by surprise or strong emotion: Oh, Jussi, why did you leave me? . . . grubble grubble grubble . . . payday's next shift, then I can get OUT of here . . . grubble grubble grubble . . . Lukia, Lady of Light, help me now!

Startled, Thariinye swiveled to look at the source of that last thought, a grubby kid weaving between the adults so rapidly that Thariinye would have lost him but for the strength of his projections. The words meant nothing to Thariinye, but the image of a radiant Liinyar girl in white-silk robes that accompanied them riveted him.

A sudden thought of "Saints preserve us, what's THAT!!!" accompanied by an image of himself enlarged to ten feet tall and glowing with a strange radiance, reminded Thariinye to maintain his calming projections while he edged through the crowd after the urchin who had so obviously been thinking about a Liinyar girl. He still could not sense any trace of another of his kind in this crowded, smelly base, but that child must have seen 'Khornya at some time, to have formed the image so clearly.

The miner who'd called on the saints stared after Thariinye but could see nothing unusual among the swirling streams of passersby. Ramon Trinidad mopped his forehead and decided not to mention to his mates that he'd had a vision of Acorna. They already teased him enough because he had a small icon of the Virgin of Guadeloupe superglued to the dashboard of his operator cab at the loading station; if he told them he'd been seeing visions, he'd never live it down. All the same, it must mean something that the Lady had appeared to him like that, all in a blinding flash it was, and then vanished. She must be warning him that he'd been marked out for something special.

Ramon Trinidad marched down the corridor to Mining Ops IIID more jauntily than he'd moved since coming to Maganos. At first he'd thought this job, training kids from the gutters of Kezdet to operate lunar mining equipment, was high pay for light work; then he'd considered resigning and telling Personnel that he was a miner, not a kindergarten teacher; then he'd actually begun to like some of the kids. Besides, they didn't laugh at him for invoking the protection of the Virgin and the saints each time he took a group of them out into the long, lightly shielded corridors of the active workings. The kids had their own saints—Lukia of the Lights, Epona, Sita Ram.

The urchin whom Thariinye was following was

also headed for Mining Ops IIID, and praying desperately that he'd get there well ahead of Ramon Trinidad; so the image of Lukia of the Lights kept lighting up in his thought-patterns, guiding Thariinye like a flashing beacon.

Bored by Rafik's intense study of the star maps which were projected all over the walls of Delszaki Li's office, Gill stood up to stretch his legs and wandered over to the one wall not devoted to mapping the outer reaches of the explored and unexplored parts of the galaxy. Rafik had been unable to commandeer this wall because it was filled with vid-screens on which, at any moment, random scenes of the moon base were displayed. Although no one's private quarters were invaded, Delszaki Li took great pleasure in observing all other parts of the base in operation, from the children's school to the outermost mine workings. Before the progress of his disease had robbed him of the ability to control a touch pad with his right hand, the display had been designed for him to call up whatever views he desired. When touching the pad became too difficult for him, the engineers had offered to make the display voice-controlled like his new hover-chair, but he had refused, indicating that it was too tiring for him to issue unnecessary commands and that he would prefer a random display which he did not have to control. Now the images on the more than twenty screens changed constantly, on a randomly activated timer, giving a constantly varying panorama of Maganos Moon Base activities.

Gill stared unseeingly at an image of the glittering dome over Maganos Central, with its overarching glass panels and its garlands of greenery, until it shifted to a view of the bakery attached to the cafeteria, where a cook was setting out trays of fresh pastries in preparation for the shift change, then to an overhead shot of the four major mine workings viewed from a camera atop the central dome. The random changes depressed him, reminding him of the inexorable progress of Delszaki Li's nervous paralysis, and he wondered whether Acorna would return in time to see her benefactor once again. Her image was so clear in his heart that he thought for a moment he was imagining her on one of the screens before him; then his shout surprised Rafik into dropping the laser pointer with which he had been tracing one of the *Acadecki's* possible routes on the larger star map for Pal and Delszaki Li.

"What in the name of the Djinni Djiboutis—" Rafik began before remembering Judit's request that he not swear like the descendant of twenty generations of Arab-Armenian rug merchants.

"What are you playing at, Gill? We're trying to get some work done over here, if you don't mind!"

"Acorna," Gill croaked. "I saw her . . . on one of these screens. She's not gone, Rafik; she's right here on Maganos!"

"She can't be . . ." Pal said, and then, ". . . can she?" Here on Maganos, and concealing herself from him? The thought was almost too painful to bear.

"I saw her, I tell you," Gill insisted. "She was right . . ." He dropped his hand; the screen he pointed at was now showing a row of children chanting the Basic alphabet with hand signs for each letter. "Here," he said, "only it wasn't the school, it was some damn corridor, and the bloody automatic timer had to shift scenes before I could identify it."

"There she is!" Judit cried, pointing at a screen in the far upper right section of the wall.

"That's one of the new workings," Gill said, "somewhere in III."

At the same moment Pal said, "But that's not Acorna."

The picture switched to an image of the docking facility. "Damn that bloody automatic timer, can't we turn it off?" Gill demanded. "And are you out of your mind, Pal? Just how many six-foot people with golden horns do you think we've got around here?"

"More than one, evidently." Pal folded his arms with the gesture of a man who is not to be shaken from his opinion, no matter how impossible and illogical it may seem to the rest of the world. "I would know Acorna among a thousand of her kind. . . ."

Gill snorted. "How do you know? You've never seen a thousand of her kind."

"I would know her," Pal insisted quietly, "and that is not my lady."

Judit had turned away from the screens to look through Delszaki Li's desk. "Judit!" Gill bellowed. "What are you playing at? Get over here and watch the screens. I need some backup in case she appears again! No, first tell somebody to hustle down to III . . . no, I don't know which subsection, there aren't but six open, surely we've got enough security people to cover all of them? Why are you fooling around looking for office supplies, girl? We've got an emergency here!"

"Is searching for manual controller," Delszaki Li put in, his dry and slightly amused whisper cutting through the fog of Gill's emotional bellowing. "My suggestion. You countermand?"

Gill stared. "It still works?"

"Override," Li whispered. "Useful if I wish to see something longer than five seconds . . . but someone else must push pad, now."

Judit scrabbled through a clutter of carved jade tokens, laser pads, used betting slips, fact-flimsies with access codes scrawled on the back, and unlabeled datacubes, and finally held up the control pad with a cry of triumph.

"Try all the workings off III," Gill directed her. "You'll just have to flip through them until we come. . . ."

"Silly," Judit said, "we've got a lot more than six screens to choose from, let's look at them all."

With shaking hands, she tapped out the code for the cameras in IIIA, B, C, D . . .

"THERE SHE IS!" cried Gill and Rafik.

"No, she isn't," Pal insisted.

Mr. Li whispered a command, and his hover-chair carried him across the room to float before the screen showing Mine Working IIID.

"There he is!" the other kids who were in the training session squealed when Hajnal darted into the open area around Ramon's sledger and slid the last twenty feet, triumphant, stopping himself just

inches short of the piles of rough lunar rock that
marked the end of the workings. "Didja get it?
Didja get it?"

"Hajnal, Master Thief of Kezdet, strikes
again!" Hajnal boasted, pulling open his jacket to
reveal an extremely nervous, long-eared, white-
fronted marchare. The marchare squeaked and
leapt out of its hiding place with a powerful thrust
of its long rear legs. The other children scrambled
to catch it.

"Ow! It scratched me!"

"'At's nothing. Look 'ow it got me on the way
here, but I didn't drop it." Hajnal pulled up his
shirt and proudly showed the long bloody
scratches on his chest and stomach. "Now 'urry up,
you lot, and get it into the toolbox in the back of
Ramon's operator cab. I seen Ramon coming this
way. Ain't gonna believe the workings is 'aunted if
'e sees the blasted hanimal, is 'e now?"

"Poor little marchare," crooned a girl who cra-
dled the nervous animal in her arms for a moment,
petting it until its eyes stopped rolling and the long
nervous ears stopped twitching. "Didn't mean to
scratch anybody, did you, poor little frightened
thing? Hajnal, I don't think we oughter put him in
the toolbox, he'll get scared."

"If you don't stop petting him, Eva, he'll go to
sleep on us, and we'll lose our chance."

The little fiends of Kezdet's first graduating class
had been working on Ramon Trinidad for weeks, trying to convince him the combination power unit and
loading station he operated was haunted by the ghost
of a mining engineer who'd been killed in an accident

so grisly nobody who knew the story was ever willing to use that station again. They gauged their success by the number of holy medals and icons Ramon hung on the device, blamed the miners of the next shift for "losing" most of the icons, and competed to see who could drop the most hair-raising hints about what had "really" happened to the mythical dead engineer. But Ramon was beginning to doubt their unsupported stories. It was time for some hard evidence. They were counting on the scrabbling and squeaks of the third-shift pastry cook's pet marchare, concealed in a compartment in the back of the sledger, to provide that evidence. Hajnal, proud of his past as a free thief on Kezdet and no factory slave, had boastfully volunteered to "borrow" the marchare without the cook's knowledge.

"It's mean, putting him in that dark little place," another girl piped up. "Let's not. He's so cute!"

"Cute," Hajnal said darkly. "Lemme tell you, you wouldn' think 'e was so bleedin' cute if you'd had to carry him through Central under your shirt, and 'im gougin' tracks in your belly every time he startled!"

"Sita Ram wouldn't like it," Eva said.

"Huh! Lukia don't mind. She 'elped me get away," Hajnal boasted.

Eva's eyes widened. All the children seemed suddenly to be looking up, over Hajnal's head. Slowly he turned, certain that Ramon had spoiled his plot by reaching the workings before he could conceal the marchare.

But it wasn't Ramon who stood behind him, but a being taller and far brighter than the little miner; a being who seemed clothed in light from Her golden horn to the silvery wisps of hair around Her hooves.

"Epona," "Sita Ram," "Lukia," whispered the children, and then they were all over the bright being.

"I knew you were here, Acorna, I knew you wouldn't just leave us without saying good-bye," squealed Khetala, who had known Acorna as a person rather than a vision of goodness. She threw herself on the tall, silver-haired being in an unrehearsed—and decidedly unwelcome—embrace.

"Get off me!" Thariinye sputtered in his own tongue. In the panic of the moment he could not remember the words the LAANYE had implanted in his cortex a few hours previously.

There was a smaller girl clutching his tunic, now, marring the elegant drape of the fabric, and a boy jumped up and down and swung from his arm as if he were some kind of climbing toy. Why hadn't that plump little woman warned him that the moon base was full of children? Pre-pubes, their psychic abilities still latent, were not susceptible to the mental projections that could be used to calm adults . . . and apparently that particular developmental factor was true across species, or at least it was as true of these beings as it was of his own race. But he had no other projection, nothing else to try! Frantically he projected (You don't see anything unusual) (Nothing is happening) (Need to get back to work).

"But I do see you, Lady Epona, I do! I do!" squealed the smallest girl.

Khetala, the oldest of the group, loosened her embrace and backed off a step, puzzled. Why had she thought this was Acorna? It was obviously only a tall miner . . . she squinted . . . with silver hair . . . and a horn. . . .

"Don't you remember me, Lady Acorna?" she asked, hurt and puzzled.

Hajnal was too high on success and escape even to be touched by the projections. "Whaddaya screechin' about now? I know my Lady Lukia of the Lights!"

Thariinye gritted his teeth and redoubled the force of his projections, but the children were jumping up and down, shrieking with excitement, and far too hyper to receive the calming influence he was trying to put forth, even if they had been old enough to pick up his mental images. Not only that, but they seemed to be insane. They expected him to cuddle them. They thought he was . . .

Under sufficient stress, Thariinye stopped trying to remember the words of the alien language and just used them without thinking.

"Lookh, yuuu liiteli twerpis," he hissed in rage, "I—aam—naat—a—ghiril! See?"

And, just as the security guard requested by Gill arrived at the workings, Thariinye yanked open his blue tunic to display irrefutable evidence that he could not be the "lady" these brats were greeting so ecstatically.

The guard, unlike the children, was affected by Thariinye's projections; so he saw nothing unusual in the sight of a seven-foot horned male with a cascade of silver hair falling down his neck. What that male was doing, however, was both unusual and strictly forbidden on Maganos Moon Base.

"You'd better come along with me, mister," he said.

Seven

Haven, Unified Federation Date 334.05.18

"*T*hat's Hoa," Markel mouthed in Acorna's ear, as they peered down the vent at the first of the innermost security cells, much smaller and more closely guarded than the row where Acorna had been kept.

"Who?"

"Ho—A," Markel separated the syllables. "He's the guy the Palomellese spaced my"—he had to swallow—"my father for—to get control of his work. If he hadn't come aboard the *Haven,* everything would be all right. He's how Rushima's being flooded, burned, blasted, or stormed until they pay Nueva Fallona's gang protection money."

"He?" And Acorna looked down again at the dejected, dark-haired man sitting with his head in his hands. What she could see of his skin had a faintly yellow cast that reminded her of Delszaki Li and made her instinctively wish to trust him. "Then why's he here"—she pointed one hand down—"and not up there with them?"

"Because he trusted our Speakers—my father and Andrezhuria and that Gerezan." The last name was expelled like a curse, and, in the light from the cell below, Acorna could see the tears begin to form in Markel's eyes. He brushed them aside with impatient fingers, taking a deep breath. "He didn't know about what they"—Markel jerked a contemptuous finger upward—"planned. He was scared stiff that the governments of Khang Kieaan, where he used to live, would've figured out that he couldn't just predict weather, he could manipulate it."

"Ooooh." Acorna's mind made leaps of conjecture on how that could be used. "So that's what happened to Rushima?"

Markel nodded.

"But how could Hoa give that sort of power to renegades like them?" Now she, too, pointed upward.

"He didn't. He thought he'd be safe on *Haven* . . . and he would've been, only Nueva and those traitors Gerezan and Sengrat planned a coup and got rid of all the rest of the First Generation. . . ." Markel gulped.

"Like your father." Acorna laid a sympathetic arm about the thin shoulders, thinking proudly of his loyalty and resourcefulness. "Did you escape before they could . . . you know . . ."

He nodded. "They don't know the half of what I know about the *Haven*. I could do anything to this ship . . . sometimes I think I ought to be making more trouble for them, only I don't want to wreck it and kill a lot of innocent people. The other Second-

Generation kids may be pretending to go along, but they shouldn't die for it. I could do anything," he repeated, "if only I knew what to do. . . ."

In that pause, Acorna softly asked, "Like being able to release the clamps on my ship so we can all get away?"

Markel considered, eyeing her, then the lighted vent and the rounded walls of the tube. She didn't think she'd called a bluff: rather she felt, through her arm still about his shoulders, that he was figuring out how to accomplish this.

"I'd be glad if you could alert Shenjemi Federation that one of their colonies is being blackmailed. And my planet that I'm being held hostage."

Markel gave a little snort, muffled by his fingers. "You're not a hostage, you're a prisoner. They got better things to do than collect ransom for hostages. They can hold up whole planets for ransom now."

Acorna gulped, happier than ever that she was no longer trapped in that cell, vulnerable. But Calum was still a prisoner. And, if they had no need to take hostages, Calum was in greater peril than she'd originally thought. They'd have to work fast. She was considering priorities when suddenly she saw that Hoa's face was turned up to the vent. She gave Markel a discreet nudge.

"Oh, oh," he mouthed back at her, and would have led her away, but she stopped him.

"He didn't intend this to happen . . . and he looks ill. I think they've hurt him. Let's free him, too. Maybe he'd know how to stop what they've started. Can we do that? Please?" Markel didn't really have any defense against Acorna in pleading mode—especially with her arm around him and the comforting warmth of her soft feminine body giving him the nurturing love he had needed so desperately for so long.

"He'll have to be quiet," he said.

"I doubt that will be a problem," she replied, and helped Markel unscrew the vent.

Dr. Ngaen Xong Hoa's slender frame made it through the narrow vent with no difficulty, but he was so weak they had to help him far more than Acorna had expected; he did almost none of the work of climbing. When he was finally in the tunnel, she realized why he had been so helpless. Even in the bad light, Acorna could see what had been done to the man's hands and arms. Pretending to bend lower to reset the screws on the vent, Acorna made sure her horn touched—through the fine fabric of her hat—both mangled hands.

Urgently now, Markel directed them away from the empty cell and around a bend in the tubes and over to the other side of the prison block. At the intersection, he firmly placed Dr. Hoa against the curving side and, finger on lips, indicated that he was to stay put. Dr. Hoa nodded, only too happy to comply. Then Markel beckoned Acorna to slither past the scientist. He put his lips to her ears and spoke low but distinctly.

"We got to get your buddy right away now because as soon as they see Dr. Hoa's gone, there'll be nine kinds of alarms and searches and stuff. Might not get another chance. Any way you can help me locate him?"

Acorna closed her eyes. If only her horn had the power of locating people as well as healing them! *Maybe it does,* she thought . . . *I've never known another of my kind. How do I know what I can do?*

She composed her thoughts and tried to visualize Calum's features, but all she could sense was the aura of misery that filled the whole area around the cells . . . and something about . . . maps? She shook her head, trying to clear it. How could she concentrate on finding Calum when she kept getting this feeling that somebody was lecturing her on how to color a map? It felt as if there was a whole geography class going on somewhere under her right hand . . . no, not geography. Strange, half-familiar words floated into her head.

"Conjecture . . . lemma . . . simple closed curve . . ."

Well, how about that!

"I think," she said slowly, "he might be in the cell on the far right."

Calum was so absorbed in the diagrams he was tracing on his cell wall that she had to hiss several times before he finally noticed—and even then he did not look up.

"Just a minute, I'm thinking," he said—and then did a comical double take, looking up so fast that he nearly lost his balance. "Acorna? What the—"

"We're rescuing you," Acorna explained patiently.

"Who's *we*? And do you have anything I can copy this down on? I don't want to lose it, and the trouble with drawing diagrams in the condensation on the wall here is . . ."

"Ten thousand devils fly away with your diagrams and drop them in the dung of the camel pits

of Sheol!" Acorna ripped out a variation on one of
Rafik's favorite curses. "Do you want to wait
around until they come to torture you into releas-
ing the hold on the *Acadecki*? Or do you think you
could drop your mathematical conjectures long
enough to climb up this rope?"

Calum gave a dubious glance at the slender rope
and the narrow space of the air vent through which
Acorna was whispering to him, then looked back
once regretfully at the drawings he had traced on
the wall of his cell.

"Oh, well, I can probably reconstruct it later,"
he muttered.

The vent opening was a tighter squeeze for
Calum than it had been for Dr. Hoa or Acorna, but
when he seemed to be stuck fast Markel inspired
him by mentioning a few of Nueva Fallona's
favorite Palomellese tortures, then commented
that if Calum's shoulders were really wedged
firmly into the vent his feet would doubtless be at a
convenient height for Nueva's attentions.

"She likes playing with matches," he said.

Calum made one last convulsive effort, freed his
broad shoulders, and wriggled upward into the
tunnel, clutching the rope.

"Oh, well," he said, as Acorna exclaimed over
his scrapes, "it's only skin, plenty more where that
came from."

They replaced the vent, went back around the
curve, and collected Dr. Hoa, who was trembling
violently in reaction to his salvation.

"I am not a man of violence," he whispered in
apology. "I am a scientist . . . and I was trying to get

away from people like these. Now we are all trapped. . . ."

Acorna touched his cheek with her horn and the spasms stopped. Toward the end of their passage, they had to tie the rope around his shoulders, and Acorna pulled him behind her, with Markel helping the scientist over the joins and aprons that connected the klicks of interior tubes and conduits. As soon as they reached Markel's nest, the boy picked up his listener, a device that sat comfortably in his ear, and indicated that Acorna should make Dr. Hoa comfortable on the pile of miscellaneous clothing and thermal sheeting behind them.

Acorna was glad to oblige. While she was at it, she also assessed the scientist's other injuries and healed them. He had been badly knocked about before the Palomellese even began their systematic destruction of his fingers and hands; she could not blame him for having given them enough information to use his research, nor for the fear and despair that had all but overwhelmed him in the tunnels. But as she soothed his bodily aches, he seemed calmer and more in control of himself. When she was finished, he caught her by the arm, his eyes once more alive with intelligent curiosity.

"Ki-lin?" he asked in a bare whisper that would not reach Markel, occupied with eavesdropping.

She smiled and put her finger across her lips as their young guide so often had.

He closed his eyes once, indicating he understood, but he also put one frail, healed finger to his lips and then pressed it against hers.

She turned to take a water bottle from the rack above her head and handed it to him. Though he clutched the bottle as possessively as any thirsty man would, Acorna did not have to warn him to take small, slow sips and accustom his body to water again.

Markel was grinning with delight at whatever he was hearing on his earphone. He kept listening, but occasionally would whisper at what was going on.

"They found Hoa missing first, then checked the rest of the cells. They haven't a clue how he and Calum got away, and they got into an argument about it and haven't yet checked to find out that you're gone, too, Acorna. That's as well. Gives us more time to figu . . ." The boy paused, pushed the device more securely into his ear, his eyes blinking angrily. Then he relaxed and smiled again.

"I got to meet someone. And fast," he said, taking out the listener and carefully restoring it to its pouch on the tube wall. "You stay put and stay quiet," he murmured to Acorna and Calum. He glanced over at Dr. Hoa, shrugged his shoulders, and crawled away with the speed of a spider after an intruder in its web.

Acorna saw that Dr. Hoa was asleep, the water bottle securely clutched against his chest with both hands. Briefly she remembered the swollen, distorted knuckles and torn, burned skin she had seen before her healing touch had soothed them. She shivered and tried not to imagine what deliberate cruelty had inflicted those injuries.

"I don't much like this," Calum muttered. "How do you know we can trust the kid?"

Acorna gave him a chilly look. "For starters, he

just saved us both from imprisonment and you, at least, from torture. Then there's the fact that his father was killed resisting the coup that put these people in power—"

"So he says. How do you know he's telling the truth?"

"Well, we're free, aren't we?"

"Are we?" Calum stretched until one elbow banged into either side of the tunnel where they crouched.

"Damn!" Acorna exclaimed. "Why didn't I think of asking Markel to send a message to either Shenjemi or Maganos—or better, both?"

Whatever could Markel have heard that had produced first fury and then humor? Acorna pondered that for a moment. No way to tell now. While waiting, she might as well restore her strength. She took a careful mouthful of water and munched on another carrot as quietly as one can munch a carrot. But they were not vegetables that dissolved even when mixed with her saliva. She swallowed hard, forcing down the half-masticated bits of carrot, so that she could listen once again.

After an interminable wait she heard slight noises coming toward them—but they sounded like the movements of a large man, not like Markel's quick, delicate crawl. She threw a blanket over Dr. Hoa in the faint hope of concealing him from whoever had discovered their hiding place, and looked at Calum with wide, frightened eyes. He squeezed her hand reassuringly—at least, she assumed he meant it to be reassuring.

With her acute hearing, she registered before

Calum did that there were two people approaching them, the smaller one in front.

"It's all right," she whispered to Calum, "Markel's bringing someone."

"That," Calum whispered, "is exactly what I was afraid of."

"Acorna?"

She lifted her head, identifying Markel's whisper. The much larger person behind him looked vaguely familiar, yet the feel of him was completely strange . . . she felt sure she had never been in his presence before, yet his face raised some chord of recognition in her.

He caught sight of her, goggled and gulped and pointed. Markel looked around, then at Acorna, and he, too, goggled.

"Damn," Acorna said out loud. In her hasty attempt to conceal Dr. Hoa, her hat had come off. And her horn was visible.

Calum began chuckling. What was so funny about the situation? A moment ago he'd been sure Markel had betrayed them, now he thought it was funny that her horn was in plain sight?

"It's all right, Acorna," Calum said, "and so is Markel, if he's hanging out with this worthless space drifter."

The man with Markel chuckled in his turn. "Might have known if there was trouble, you'd be mixed up in it somehow, Calum. But what were you thinking of to get young Acorna into it?"

Acorna gasped in surprise, and the man turned to her. "No, you don't know me, but I've heard plenty about you."

"Oh?"

"Gill used to send me holos of you, before we lost touch. Even the Brain, here"—he jerked his head toward Calum—"occasionally mentioned you. When he bothered to write, that is!"

"You can't be . . ."

"Johnny Greene, very much at your service, ma'am."

Acorna took a deep breath of relief. "Of course! Gill has a holo of you in his office, but . . ."

The man in the holo looked much younger, his head thrown back in carefree laughter. This man's features were the same, but now they were drawn in the lines of strain and watchfulness that seemed to mark everybody who had survived Nueva Fallona's coup on the *Haven*.

"You could have told me," she scolded Calum.

"Didn't have time," Calum defended himself. "Look, I didn't know he was going to show up here."

Markel looked about anxiously. "Where'd you stash Dr. Hoa?"

Acorna reached over and gently raised a corner of the cover to show the exhausted doctor sleeping, the tiniest of smiles in the corners of his mouth.

"Is that a relief!" Johnny exclaimed, when he saw the scientist. "I don't know how you did it, Markel. . . ."

"Very carefully," the boy said, sitting with his arms resting casually on his knees, totally relaxed and very, very pleased with himself. "I got them out through the air vents. They fit diagonally through the openings once I took the grates out. Only this one"—he jerked his chin toward Calum—"needed a little encouragement." He frowned as he took a closer look at Calum. "Say, how'd you stop the bleeding? I could've sworn you lost some skin back there!"

"Oh, it was A—" Calum began, then stopped as Acorna gave him a warning shake of the head. It wasn't that she didn't trust Markel, but he was being asked to assimilate a lot at one time. And if something went wrong . . . she refused even to consider that. There would be time enough to explain her unique healing capabilities when they got out of here—and they would! "—a fuss about nothing, as it turned out," Calum substituted for what he'd been going to say. "I sure thought I was going to get scraped raw on the way out, though!"

"Markel," Acorna said urgently, "can you get messages out as well as eavesdrop on their communications? We ought to alert the Shenjemi Federation about what's happening to Rushima—and send to Maganos for help, too."

"Might could," Markel allowed. "Have to tap the main power lines to boost a message, though, and they just might notice the surge. Lemme check on who's on shift now. . . ." He tapped his earphone back in place and listened for a moment. His eyes lit up like those of a much younger child planning some mischief.

"Ooooh, is Nueva furious!" he said. "She's giving all of them what-for and threatening to space the next incompetent who manages to lose a prisoner. 'They'"—Markel thumbed his chest bone—"have got to be found. Oho!" And he sat bolt upright a moment, then relaxed again. But the sparkle was gone from his eyes. "Sengrat's just pointed out that I was never accounted for in the original coup . . . and Ximena reminded him that I used to know ways about the ship in the tubes and stuff." The way he emphasized her name warned Acorna that Ximena was, or had been, someone special to Markel. "They really are on Nueva's side; they're not just going along to save their own skins," he said. "Even Ximena . . . I used to like her. I don't understand people like that."

"Neither do I," Acorna told him.

"You're a couple of charming innocents," Johnny told them, "but I for one would like to know what they plan to do with this information and how Markel thinks he's going to stall them — because I know what that look in your eyes means, kid," he said, ruffling the top of Markel's head.

"Nueva was just going to send someone through that big tube, which would have been a fine game of hide-and-seek in this maze. We could've run the searchers ragged," Markel reported. "Then Sengrat suggested they should use gas. He's still underestimating me." Even as he spoke, he was rooting through yet another hiding place and came out with one hand clasping breathing masks and the other emergency oxygen bottles.

Acorna smiled. "We won't need those."

Johnny shot Acorna a wondering look.

"She is Ki-lin," murmured Dr. Hoa, who had awakened during Markel's excited report. "Her horn purifies water and air and heals. Does it not, most gracious lady Ki-lin?"

"I am not Ki-lin, Dr. Hoa, but the rest of it is accurate," she said.

"See? She has healed my hands and arms from what they did to me." The scientist shoved one sleeve up to show a slightly wrinkled but healthy forearm with a few patches of paler skin replacing the deep burns. "And the rest of me, too," he said with some surprise as he realized he could sit up and move without pain.

"And my knuckles," Markel said, eyes wide as he finally noticed. "My knees don't hurt either, nor my back." He looked at Calum accusingly. "Hey—you did get scraped bad, getting through that vent hole, didn't you? And tried to persuade me I'd been imagining it, when the truth is Acorna healed you?"

"We thought it might be hard for you to accept," Calum said. "Some people don't believe. . . ."

Markel looked reverently at Acorna. "Even with a demonstration? What an asset for our side! They're never going to get their hands on you, lady. Not while I can still breathe."

"I'll see that's a long, long time," Acorna said.

Then Markel pressed the earpiece and held up a hand to stop any further talk. "Yes, that's what they're going to do. Ximena is small enough to make a search once the air has cleared up." His face clouded over. "She doesn't want to . . . I thought maybe she wasn't as bad as the rest of them . . . but she doesn't care about what happens to us, she's just afraid I'll survive the gas somehow and go after her in the tunnels. I couldn't hurt her," he said sadly, "not Ximena, no matter what she's done. I thought she would know that much, at least."

"Well, let's not wait to meet her," Johnny said, changing the subject briskly before Markel's emotions could overpower him. "Markel, can you get us from here to the hangar deck?" He glanced at Calum. "I'm thinking that your ship would make a better command center than this tunnel . . . we could send our messages for sure, and maybe even get clean away if Markel can disable the *Haven*'s grapples."

"No problem! Can't you see, we're already at Red 32 x Blue 16, all we have to do is take a side route through Blue 16–24 and cut across at the intersection of Green 48 . . . well, never mind," Markel slowed down as he sensed the bafflement of his companions.

"I'm just a simple techno-nerd," Johnny said. "I don't happen to keep a 3-D color map of the ship's maintenance tunnels in my memory."

"It's real easy," Markel said. "I'll tell you all about it when we have time."

"That," Johnny said hollowly, "is exactly what I'm afraid of."

"Huh?"

"Never mind!" Johnny gave Markel a friendly push. "Get going, O friendly native guide. Let's hit the road . . . or rather," as Johnny caught Markel's startled look of warning, "let us make noiseless progress away. Do we need anything you have stashed here, Markel?"

"Water?" Markel took down the fabric that had

held the water bottles to the wall and it folded out into a sleeveless tunic, the water supplies on the back of it. "Ration bars. My headset. These . . . no, too heavy . . . but I gotta have these," he mused over a collection of tools, rapidly making his selection. He stuffed the necessary items into another backpack, draping thermal covers over everyone's shoulders, even Dr. Hoa's, and then, lifting up a corner of the tube wall, shoved whatever remained into the opening. It took a few hard pushes to get the opening to resume its normal shape. The area was back to normal. Markel had left no signs of his presence.

"This way, now," he said, pointing before he took Dr. Hoa's hand.

Later Acorna would wonder how they had managed that exodus. The healing properties of her horn were prodigious, as well as its air-purifying abilities; but the constant effort of making the air around them breathable eventually exhausted even her. And there were other problems. They did not have the luxury of sticking to the "safe" routes Markel had mapped out for himself; now they had to follow the passageways that held least risk of detection or offered the shortest path to the hangar. Some of the walls they crept through felt cold, others almost unbearably hot and, over one section— the coil to main drive—Acorna went from one member of their group to another, to heal blistered knees, hands, and other portions of their anatomies they could not keep from touching the hot metal.

"Lousy insulation," Johnny muttered, as Acorna laid her horn up and down his thigh where the material of his pant leg had been seared away.

They rested every time they reached a double tube crossing because there Acorna and Johnny could stand upright and ease their backs.

"You do know where you're taking us, young'un?" Johnny asked.

"I told you, Johnny Greene, I know this ship like no one else, First *or* Second Generation. What's the matter, can't you take the heat?" Markel asked so fiercely that Johnny held up his hands in mock self-defense.

"Lay on, Macduff," the spacer said with a smothered laugh, "and damned be he who first cries Hold, Enough! That is," he added, "if you and Dr. Hoa can manage, Acorna?"

Acorna wanted nothing more than to be through with this claustrophobic journey. She fervently assured Johnny and Markel that there was no need to slow down on her behalf.

Markel had indeed known exactly where he was taking them, a storage room for tools on the hangar deck itself. Through the grill on the narrow window, they could even see the *Acadecki*, clamped tight to the deck but still in front of the other smaller vessels that were part of the *Haven*'s force.

"And that is their first mistake," Markel said with great satisfaction.

As if he hadn't been crawling for days through narrow tubes and inspection conduits, Markel made space on the worktable and started plugging his equipment into some of the power-tool sockets. Everyone else flopped down, exhausted, on the metal floor. Acorna was certain she would retain the honeycomb pattern of the room's floor on the tender parts of her anatomy, but it was worth it to stretch out at last. The cramped journey through the tunnels had tried her sorely; for once she envied Calum his lack of inches.

"Ha! They haven't found anything, and it's going to take them days to inspect the entire network," Markel said. He rubbed his hands together and glanced in the direction of the *Acadecki*. He tried to peer in other directions, but his view was restricted. "Ooops." He pulled back as if someone could have seen his face in the window. "Guards." He peeked out again. "No more than three that I can see. There're usually ten or twelve on hangar duty." Gleefully he washed his hands. "We really have them running up their own . . . sorry." Markel caught himself at Johnny's sharp nudge and shot a quick apology in Acorna's direction. "But that doesn't get us out of here."

"If we could get to the *Acadecki* and power up," Calum asked Markel, "could you patch into the *Haven*'s command centers from there and disable their communications and other systems?"

"Nothing to it," Markel nodded, preening a little.

Calum stood, shakily, and pointed at the window. "Lemme have a look?" Markel moved aside. Calum grunted. "You're sure there're only three here now?" Markel nodded. "What we need is a diversion . . . that is, if you can get us out of this storage room."

"No problemo," Markel said, and, taking an odd-shaped bit of plastic from a thigh pocket, inserted it into the door. They could all hear the light "snick" as the lock was opened. "Only now what? Soon as I open the door, we're in clear sight of at least two of the guards."

"And each of them would like to take credit for the recapture of Dr. Hoa," Johnny said, with a gleam of malice in his eyes. "If you don't mind acting as bait, Doctor?"

"I owe the universe whatever action will repair my disastrous misjudgment," Dr. Hoa said with a slight bow, "even should it require the sacrifice of my life."

"Oh, I don't think it will come to that," Calum said cheerfully, hefting a length of thick steel bar which he had quietly "acquired" during their passage through the tunnels. Acorna looked around the supply room and found a heavy mallet, which she swung about to test its balance.

"That looks good," Johnny said, reaching for the mallet, but Acorna shook her head.

"Find your own weapons," she told him. "I like the heft of this."

Johnny's eyebrows shot up, but he made no further protest.

"I did mention, didn't I, that she's very independent?" Calum asked drily.

"You didn't tell me the half of it," Johnny muttered, rummaging around the cluttered room for something he could use as a weapon. He settled on a length of thin cable that he carefully knotted around a pair of screwdrivers.

"I've got a better idea than using the good doctor as bait," Calum said. "Markel, you said you could hack into hangar security and disable the grapples on the *Acadecki*? If you did it now, that'd distract them for a moment right when we make our break and give us a head start on getting out of here."

"Start opening the door and get ready," Markel said, pressing more key pads. "I got the hangar security on line and . . ."

The sound of the grapples retracting echoed throughout the large hangar. The guards went running toward the ship, and Markel and his followers were out of the storage room before the guards spotted them.

One of the two guards on the catwalk pounded on a device on the wall before he followed his companion down to the hangar floor. The three guards made straight for the *Acadecki*, and the attackers made straight for them.

Acorna let her hammer fly at the nearest guard as he lifted his stunner. Her weapon shattered his hand and sent his stunner skittering across the metal floor, right to Markel's feet. Markel picked it up and downed the top one on the ladder, while Johnny, coming out from behind the bulk of a small shuttlecraft, tackled the third guard before he could raise his weapon. Calum looked around, puzzled that there was no one for him to attack.

"That was too easy," he said.

Markel was taking the stairs to the catwalk two at a time, and running along it, checking the unlocked hatches leading into the interior of the ship.

"We're secure in here now," he called, and saun-

tered to the farthest ladder, sliding down it without
using the actual steps. The boy had had a lot of
practice in such acrobatics. The others followed
him in more conventional fashion but with
scarcely less haste. Even though until Calum pow-
ered up they could not lock the hatches, Acorna
felt more secure once she and all her friends were
inside the *Acadecki*.

"Well done, Markel," Johnny said, throwing an
arm about the boy's shoulders. "But what do we do
now? Once they see us leave, they merely latch the
tractor beam on us and haul us back aboard.
Unless you can disable that . . ."

"Yes, that much I can still do," Markel said,
"but . . ."

"The *Acadecki*'s fast," Calum said, "but, even
with the tractor beam useless, I'd be surprised if
the *Haven* doesn't have laser cannon and missiles."
Markel nodded, looking mournful. "Both—and
there's no way I can get into those controls."

"You mean there's some security on this ship
you haven't worked around?" Johnny pretended
amazement, but Markel looked so hangdog that he
patted the boy on the back and told him it didn't
matter; there was more than one way to skin a cat.

"We may not be able to get clean away," Calum
said cheerfully, "but we can activate the ship long
enough to send out a spurt for help in all possible
directions, then lock down again and . . . well . . ."

They all looked at one another for a long
moment, acknowledging that they might have
come to the end of this particular road. Their
takeover of the *Acadecki* was not likely to go unno-

ticed for long, no matter how cleverly Markel disguised his jamming of the communications between the harbor and the main deck; and they could hardly hold the little ship like a besieged fortress.

"Well, we'll jump through that spacewarp when we come to it," Johnny said with a shrug, accepting the inevitable. "Better get on with it—no telling exactly how much time Markel can buy us with his system manipulations."

Calum started the reactivation sequence while Acorna was busy framing a spurt code message, which she thought should go to Maganos, Kezdet (in case Mr. Li was at home), and Laboue.

"I'm thinking of Rafik's *Uhuru*, too," Calum said. "Won't take more than three seconds a spurt, and it'll quadruple the chances of one message getting through."

"First of all we send one in clear to Shenjemi Federation," Acorna said, and when Calum opened his mouth to protest, she added firmly: "We promised." Calum sighed. "So we did." And looked up the direction code for the Federation. The other destinations he had already long memorized. A low whistle startled them both as Markel, with Johnny Greene assisting Dr. Hoa, came into the main compartment.

"This is some ship," Markel said, awed.

"You can say that again," Johnny added, equally impressed as he helped Dr. Hoa into one of the conformable chairs. "You got a galley on board?" he asked.

Acorna pointed.

"Is there a shield over the hangar entry, Markel?" Calum asked. "Our messages could bounce right back at us if there is."

"I took that off when I disabled the grapples," the boy said absently, far more intent on prowling around the room, running his hands over the soft fabrics and looking into compartments in the furnishings. "There's so much space for everything," he said, standing in the middle of the room, arms outspread and turning slowly around.

Johnny came back with a tray full of steaming cups which he offered first to Dr. Hoa and then to the others. "A pick-you-up," he explained. "This ship isn't just a pretty space, it's well appointed."

"Got your earphone in, Markel? I'm about to spurt, and I want to know if they catch it," Calum said.

"Gotta be outside for that," Markel said, and headed off to the hatch.

"If they do hear us, get back inside in one helluva hurry, lad, because I'll take off and risk their firing at us; we'll just have to hope that everyone's too busy looking for us to see us," Calum warned.

"Gotcha," was Markel's insouciant response.

"On my mark," Calum said, raising his arm, "NOW!" He reactivated the ship and waited tensely through the seconds before the com unit would be ready to function. "Anything on your end, Markel?" After a moment's silence, he toggled down the spurt relay.

"Wait!" Markel cried from outside the ship. "What? You don't—" The boy's cry was too loud to miss, and filled with an unidentifiable emotion.

Calum hit the toggle for the spurt relay and punched in the shutdown sequence for the ship in three quick, deft motions.

"I'm sorry," he said to Acorna. "The Shenjemi message got through, I don't know about the coded spurt to our friends; it was processing the multiple address list when I shut down. With luck, some of the addresses will have been cleared. Where's Markel? What was he yelling about?"

As if on cue, the boy wandered in, a dazed and incredulous look on his face. "I think it's all over."

"What's all over?" Johnny demanded.

"I think . . ." and Markel hesitated, ". . . I think there's been another coup. Nueva and the others were so busy chasing us, they weren't paying attention to the other passengers. Nueva and her gang've been taken prisoner. I think the Starfarers—at least what are left of them—are back in charge again."

"I think we stay right where we are until we know that's what's happened," Johnny said, and gestured for Calum to close the hatch manually. "And let's not reactivate the *Acadecki* just yet. If everything's okay, we have plenty of time to let our friends at home know—and if it isn't, we don't really need to alert anybody who didn't notice that one spurt. We'll just listen in for a bit. You can patch in to the bridge using *Haven*'s systems, can't you, Markel?"

"I think so."

With shaking hands, the boy began to do just that.

Eight

Maganos, Unified Federation Date 334.05.18

*T*hariinye was too stunned to resist the security guard's firm hold on his arm. First the children, then the man seemed to have resisted his projections. Was there some force field in this part of the base that annulled telepathic projections? He sought contact with the Linyaari on board the ship to reassure himself.

(Names of the Four First Mares, what have you gotten yourself into now, Thariinye?)

(Is this what you consider "having an inconspicuous look round"?)

(I told you he was too immature to be trusted with this responsibility.)

Wincing, Thariinye closed his mind to further contact. All right, his mental powers were as acute as ever . . . but what he heard from the three enraged ladies on board the ship was not in the least reassuring! He would just as soon take his chances with the barbarians. After all, they were a puny lot; he could crush this man's skull with one kick from his powerful hooves, if he chose to.

(Thariinye! You'll do no such thing!)
(I am shamed that any blood kin of mine should even contemplate such a khlevii action.)
(Much too immature. I told you so.)

"Oh, do stop nattering at me!" Thariinye snapped aloud, but in Linyaari.

"Don't know what kind of foreign gabble that is, mister," the stolid security guard said, "but iggerance of the law ain't no excuse. If'n you don't speak Basic, you'll get a interpreter."

"You can't take the Lady away!" one of the pestiferous brats around them cried out.

"Kid, this guy ain't no lady," the guard said. "Now git on back to yer mining class. I'm takin' him straight to Mr. Li."

The tallest girl nodded slowly. "I see . . . this is not Acorna." She glared down the protests of the other children. "I know the Lady, and she is like this one, but . . . different. Mr. Li will know what to do."

The guard hurried Thariinye away before the children could start any more fuss.

"What . . . law . . . of yours . . . do I break . . . by existing . . . in this form?" Thariinye had to concentrate to get the words out; it was a harsh, tongue-mangling language, this "Basik."

The guard looked Thariinye straight in the chest . . . about where his eyes would have been if he'd been the same height as this puny biped. So that much of the projection was still working! The man certainly behaved as if he saw nothing unusual in Thariinye's appearance . . . so what was it that had alerted him?

"I ain't interested in your beooootiful form and figure, mister, and neither are them kids back there. But since you DO speak Basic, you oughta know better than to go flashin' in a public place. Specially kids," he added. "Right down on molesting kids, Mr. Li is, and who'd blame him, seein' what them kids already been through? If'n it was up to me, I'd have you deported without a space suit."

The guard's anger lifted his thought-stream momentarily out of the dull "grubble, grubble, grubble" of normal thoughts and gave Thariinye a devastatingly clear image of a tall, handsome, silver-haired biped making sexual overtures to a group of shrieking children, followed by associated images so disgusting he hastily closed his mind against them. He was so shocked that he did not even try to persuade the guard to forget his memories and let him go.

(You idiot, Thariinye! They must have a nudity taboo.)

(Nobody TOLD me!)

(I knew we should have taken longer to study the culture.)

"Lucky for you Mr. Giloglie ordered you brought directly to Delszaki Li's private rooms," the guard said, steering them through a side corridor that opened onto an antechamber lined in crimson silk, with yellow patterns on the hangings. "There's some as would have you lynched for even thinkin' about what you just done."

He nodded at a young man sitting to one side behind a carved wooden console, and an oval opening in front of Thariinye widened like the pupil of a Linyaari eye to admit them.

"Very good, Barnes. You may return to your regular duties now," said a slender, dark-topped biped standing in a tense attitude of expectation just inside the next room, a spacious chamber furnished with soft couches and small tables.

Thariinye ducked to get through the oval opening and redoubled the force of his projections.

(You aren't seeing anything unusual. I'm really very boring. You want me to go away.)

The dark-topped biped swayed and put one hand to its forehead. The gesture tightened the fabric across its chest so that Thariinye was able to see its enlarged mammaries, large enough to indicate it was of the same gender as Khariinya but nothing to compare with hers. Perhaps it was an immature member of the species . . . a nymphet?

"I don't know what's coming over me," she said weakly. "I thought . . . but I did see . . ."

She gazed vaguely in Thariinye's direction with eyes that clearly did not really see him, but only something she would take as "not unusual" in this place. "Excuse me . . . do I know you?"

"Judit, what's the matter with you?" A large, red-topped biped with an amazing display of facial hair burst through an inner door. "Acorna, where the devil have you . . ."

This one slowed, and the same confusion crossed his features. "Wait a minute. I thought . . ."

He backed up through the doorway by which he'd entered, glanced up at something, and looked back at Thariinye. "I don't get it," he said, and rubbed his eyes. "On the vid . . . but you're not . . ."

The hiss of machinery behind him became louder; the red one stepped aside, out of sight, and a very aged biped mounted on a floating box maneuvered through the doorway. Thariinye had an instant impression of fragile, paper-dry, wrinkled skin around a withered frame, bright dark eyes, and a piercing intelligence.

(I deduce some kind of telepathic damper,) the new biped thought.

Thariinye sighed in relief. (Then your people can hear with the heart as well as the ears?)

(It is not a well-understood talent among those of my race, but the possibility has long been discussed. A sage of this man's people once said that when the impossible has been discarded, what remains, however improbable, must be the truth.)

Thariinye tossed his forelock out of his weary eyes. If this was the aged being's first experience of mind-speech, why was he taking it so calmly? And how had he figured it out so fast?

(You young people are so easily excited.)

Thariinye felt the dry amusement in the old being's thoughts.

(Confirmation of a long-discussed hypothesis is

gratifying, not frightening! As for deductions, I could conceive of no other hypothesis which would account for the fact that your image appears as one like Acorna on the vid-screens, yet all who see you in person take you for a man like us.)

(Except those blasted kids!)

(My species often claims that children's sight is purer and more truthful than that of adults. Is this then true?)

(They're too immature for thought-speech. I suppose you could call that pure — I call it damned inconvenient!)

(Ahh. Will be most interesting to learn details of what you call thought-speech. But first things must come first. Let us take tea together, and perhaps you will tell me what you know of our Acorna.)

(OUR 'Khornya,) Thariinye corrected firmly, (and it is for your people to tell us what you have done with her.)

(There are more of you?)

(Introduce us AT ONCE, Thariinye. How could you be so rude? This is clearly not a barbarian but a truly linyarii being.)

(You are so inconsiderate, Thariinye!)

The aged biped's dark eyes widened, and he let out a hiss of comprehension.

"This is wonderful," he whispered aloud. "Judit, you will please make ready tea for . . . how many?"

(There are four of us.) There didn't seem to be much point in concealing their number when this being had so rapidly deduced so much about them.

"I don't see what is so wonderful!" said the female addressed as "Judit"—terrible, tongue-mangling name; how would he ever manage to say it?

"We speak in mind," the old one said in his husky whisper. "I find is much less tiring than manipulating vocal apparatus. You will please learn art of mind-speak as soon as possible, my Judit. Perhaps these new *ki-lin* will be so kind as to teach you." To Thariinye he suggested, (It might reduce confusion if you were to allow my companions to see yourself in your true aspect.)

(How rude, Thariinye! One does not project illusions onto the minds of linyarii beings to whom one has been properly introduced.)

(SHUT UP! Oh, sorry,) Thariinye sent to the old one, (not you, my aunt Melireenya. She is the most terrible nagging—well, you'll see.)

(I look forward to meeting your companions.)

There was a gasp of amazement from the younger bipeds gathered around the old one as Thariinye dropped his cloaking projections and stood before them as himself: a seven-foot-tall Liinyar male in the pride of health and youth, as good a specimen of the race, in his own humble opinion, as they could hope to find.

The momentary silence was broken by a slender, dark-topped biped with a facial structure resembling that of the female, but without the enlarged glands on its chest.

"I told you that was not Acorna," it said smugly.

(WHERE IS SHE? Oh, sorry. I did not mean to shout at you . . . but we are most concerned for the fate of our 'Khornya.)

(Is long story. You will please to take tea first, then when all are calm we will discuss what is to be done.)

Thariinye was chagrined to find that this frail, ancient biped, who claimed to have just now exercised telepathic communication for the first time, was able to shut his mind completely to further queries. The portion of his mind that Thariinye could reach now resembled a wall of polished green stone, so smooth that nothing could adhere to it, so hard that nothing could penetrate it.

Once admitted to the innermost chamber, Thariinye understood how these beings had so easily seen through his calming projections. The vid-screens transmitted the input of mechanical image-sensing devices which, having no thoughts, fears, or emotions, could not be confused by the Linyaari art of projecting illusory feelings.

(Really, Thariinye. You should have realized that beings capable of some limited form of space travel would have other mechanical devices.)

(Huh! I don't recall YOU mentioning the possibility, Aunt Melireenya.)

(The boy is right, Melireenya. We are all culpable of underrating these beings and their intelligence. Already we have discovered that their technology, though crude, is effective and that at least one of them is capable of clear mind-speech. They may well have other surprises in store for us.)

(Let's hope they have something in store that'll surprise the Khleevi. Latest communications from Home say the invasion fleet is definitely targeting this sector.)

(First we get 'Khornya back,) Neeva put in firmly. (THEN we will tell them about the Khleevi. We do not wish to frighten them as we did the first ones we contacted. Thariinye, you are not to discuss the Khleevi until we are with you, do you understand?)

(No fear, Neeva. Now that the old one has closed his mind to me, I am having enough trouble saying ANYTHING in this horrible language of theirs. It hurts my mouth to pronounce the words, and they are so dim they never understand anything until I say it three times.)

Actually, Judit was pleased that her facility with languages extended to being able to decipher Thariinye's accent. He had wakened sooner and spent less total time with the LAANYE than the older Linyaari had, and it showed in his difficulty with Basic Interlingua phonemics. Her name was rendered as "Yuudhithe" and as for his apology for violating their culture's nudity taboo, well, it was a good thing she'd had some idea what he was talking about, or she never would have figured it out.

Once they understood that Thariinye knew no more than they about Acorna's whereabouts, Gill and Rafik were perfectly content to let Judit do the hard work of making conversation with Thariinye and translating his remarks into proper Basic for their benefit, while Mr. Li took one of his quick naps in the hover-chair and conserved his energy for the upcoming meeting. There were fine beads of sweat along Judit's hairline, and she could feel a tension headache gripping the back of her neck before Pal brought the other three Linyaari to Mr. Li's inner room.

(At least you haven't gotten into any more trouble while we were on our way.)

(You can relax now, Thaari. We'll take care of everything.)

"Missiter Li," Thariinye said, "allow me to initraduuse mi khomipaanians." He would have gritted his teeth if it had been possible to do so while working his mouth around the harsh syllables of the alien language. Wasn't it just like Melireenya to come swanning in and take over after he had taken the risks and done all the really hard work? "Neeva of the Renyilaaghe, visedhaanye ferilii. Melireenya of the Balaave, gheraalye ve-khanyii. Khaari of the Giryeeni, gheraalye malivii." At least the Linyaari names flowed easily off his tongue, and he did not put himself to the trouble of translating their titles.

"Inn your speech," Neeva said easily, "I believe I would be knownn as Enyvoy Extraordinyari. My companyaan Melireenya is our Senior Communyications Officer, and Khaari is our Navighation Officer."

Gill nodded stiffly; Rafik bowed; Pal took the envoy's hand and bowed over it, touching his lips to the back of the blunt fingers so like his Acorna's. The pupils of Neeva's eyes narrowed briefly to silver slits, then widened again. The fleeting expression was so like Acorna's that Judit felt tears spring to her eyes.

"We are honored to make your acquaintance," she murmured for Mr. Li, unaware that he was already speaking to the newcomers in their own private manner.

(Is indeed great honor to be the first of our race to greet others of Acorna's kind.)

(Not exactly the first. But that first lot wouldn't even—)

(Thariinye!)

Delszaki Li glanced at Judit, and she moved closer to him, the better to hear his labored whisper. "Can they understand languages other than Basic?" he whispered in his mother's native tongue, which was a first language for more than half the people of Kezdet.

"Delighted to make your acquaintance," Judit said promptly in the same language. Neeva's eyes narrowed to silver slits again.

(Honored Li, I apologize. We thought we had learned your tongue already, but I cannot follow what this person is saying.)

(Not to be concerned. Takes some time to understand obscure idioms of Basic,) Li responded. He quickly called up the image of the Jade Palace to shield his mind once again, lest the Linyaari pick up some hint of his innermost thoughts. "Judit, be polite to our guests," he reprimanded her, "speak Basic, and slowly."

Judit blushed and apologized for her carelessness and gave no sign that she had acted under Mr. Li's orders to begin with.

Delszaki Li was severely embarrassed to confess to the Linyaari that he had lost track of Acorna only shortly before her own people came for her, and he made no effort to conceal his feel-

ings from them. (My house is shamed. I will tell
you that we took all possible care for Acorna from
day of her finding, but how will you believe this
when now she is lost? Descendants of Li will be
mourning this day through centuries to come.)

When this was said aloud, Rafik interpolated,
"Excuse me, Mr. Li, but let us not say yet that Acorna
is lost. We know her intended destination—"

"But not the route," Gill put in.

Rafik's lips twitched. "More than you might
think can be deduced from intelligent study of the
star maps, Declan Giloglie. Given what we know
of the accident to the hydroponics section of the
Acadecki—"

"On't-day ee-bay inay uch-say ay urry-hay oo-
tayell-tay em-thay allay ou-yay ow-knay," Gill
interrupted. Lacking the multilingual background
shared by Li and the Kendoros, he had independently come to his own conclusion about how best
to converse privately in front of beings who could
learn Basic overnight.

"Why not?" Rafik demanded.

Gill glanced at the envoys. "Ee-way on't-day
ow-knay oo-whay ey-thay eally-ray are-ay," he
said. "Ey-thay ight-may ee-bay ee-thay eople-pay
oo-whay arooned-may Corna-Ay."

Rafik put his hand on Gill's arm and drew the
larger man into the antechamber.

"Stop making a bloody fool of yourself with that
pig Latin," he whispered. "We've got no reason to
mistrust them."

"We've got no reason to trust them, either," Gill
returned in a furious whisper. "SOMEBODY set

Acorna adrift to die in space; until we find out who and why, we're not turning her over to the first funny-looking strangers to waltz in and demand her!"

Rafik's lips twitched. "At the moment," he murmured, "we can't turn her over, can we? So while I'm studying the star maps, why don't you sit down with the Linyaari and find out what they have to say about Acorna?"

By that time the tea Mr. Li had requested was ready, and the small social ceremony helped to alleviate the strain all parties were feeling. Knowing Acorna's tastes, he had ordered a blend of herbal tea with alfalfa for the envoys, served in the handleless cups favored by Acorna, while the humans, with their more slender and more flexible digits, drank smoky Kilumbemba Oolong from cups with delicate porcelain handles. Melireenya took pains to tell Judit aloud that she had noticed and did very much appreciate this evidence of attention to their tastes.

"Is no trouble," Mr. Li whispered, so that humans as well as Linyaari could understand them. "We have learned much from our beloved Acorna. Now we hope to learn more from you. Origin of Acorna is still mystery. Gill, you will tell of finding her?"

Gill cleared his throat and briefly recounted their discovery of Acorna, asleep in what they had later deduced was an escape pod, drifting close to an asteroid he and Calum and Rafik had been mining. He downplayed the work the three of them had put into raising the foundling, not to

mention the fact that they had lost their jobs and
almost lost their ship to protect her from becoming the ward of Amalgamated Mining and subject
to whatever experiments their Linguistics and
Psych department could dream up, but his affec-
tion for Acorna came through underlying every
word and moved the Linyaari envoys deeply. He
skipped the tangled tale of her adventures on
Kezdet and ended by explaining that Calum had
come up with an ingenious theory for locating
Acorna's home world and that he and Acorna had
just taken off in search of it—unfortunately without filing a navigation plan.

(One chance in mitanyaakhi!) Neeva silently
exclaimed. (Vaanye could not possibly have foreseen
that the explosion would not only transport Acorna
out of danger but would bring her to another populated sector of the galaxy . . . and into the hands of
these good Linyaari who raised her as one of their
own.)

(Calm down, Neeva. Good they may be, perhaps even linyarii to a degree, but they are not
Linyaari, and I for one am not sure how far we may
trust them.)

(You are too cynical! Can't you feel the truth
and love in this large red one's mind?)

(I agree with Neeva. This one at least is linyarii,
if not technically Linyaari. We should tell them the
truth of our mission.)

(We don't know that all of them are good people. From this man Ghiil's story alone it is clear
that some, at least, of this race think nothing of
experimenting on other sapient beings. Such

behavior strikes me as more khlevii than linyarii.
Let us go slowly here.)

"So," Gill finished, "that's what we know about
Acorna. And what we're all curious to find out is,
exactly how did one of your younglings come to be
floating in our sector, in a pod that couldn't have
kept her alive many more hours, with no signal to
alert anyone to her existence? You folks seem
mighty concerned for her now; strikes me you've
come a long way to retrieve somebody who seems
to've been thrown out with the trash in the first
place." He rested his big, heavy-knuckled hands
on his knees and looked from one of the envoys to
another, his bright blue eyes challenging them to
account for the plight in which they had found
Acorna.

(Neeva?)

(What do you think, Neeva? Shall we tell
them?)

(You are the envoy, Neeva, and 'Khornya is
your sister-child. The decision is yours.)

"Well?" Gill challenged as the silence after his
speech stretched on and on. Most of the humans in
the room waited eagerly for the Linyaari complement to Gill's story; only Rafik, once more
absorbed in his star maps and calculations, was
oblivious to the mounting tension as the Linyaari
looked at one another but did not speak.

(We love Acorna as our own child,) Delszaki
Li told them. (We will not give her over to those
who may have sought to destroy her in the first
place.) He repeated his words aloud so that the
other humans could understand the statement.

Judit nodded firmly, Pal folded his arms, and Gill merely shifted his weight a little forward, like a man in a bar anticipating that fists might soon start swinging.

(The red one does not look so linyarii now, Neeva. He looks quite capable of violence. Do you really want to trust this race on so little evidence?)

(I would not give up my worst enemy to the Khleevi,) Neeva replied violently. (We are ethically obliged to tell them.)

(What if they throw us out and shut down like that first bunch?)

(We will have to take that risk. Anyway, I think they are telling the truth when they say that they do not know where Acorna is now. We have as good a chance of finding her as they do; in fact, if this Khaalum's deductions are correct, she may reach Home before we do!)

Thariinye snorted aloud. (They may be very nice bipeds, but their technology has some major gaps, and most of them can't even mind-speak. I shouldn't be surprised to learn that this Khaalum has gone haring off in absolutely the wrong direction. At least find out where they think he might have gone before you tell them.)

While this silent colloquy went on, Delszaki Li murmured with Pal and Judit in rapid Old Magyar. "They are concealing something from us; I can sense the shields in their minds. Also there is fear and guilt."

"They'll have to tell us more before we give away anything about Acorna. You've said too much already," Pal said, then bit his lip. He had never before ventured to criticize his employer and benefactor.

"Fear you may be right," Mr. Li whispered.

Gill glowered at being shut out of this exchange, even though he understood the necessity for using some language other than Basic Interlingua. Feeling useless among all these polyglots and telepaths, he rose and went over to look at the lines of light Rafik's calculations had produced on the projected star maps.

Thariinye felt much the same. All three of the senior Linyaari were looking at him with deep disapproval, as though taking reasonable precautions against an unknown race were a khlevii act on an ethical par with eating one's young. He could not remove himself from the mental discussion, but he could—and did—leave the tea table to stroll across to the wall of projected star maps, where he leaned over Gill's shoulder and studied the display with growing interest. It was difficult to read, and showed the heavens at entirely the wrong angle, but as he began to understand the alien notation he was able to mentally map these images onto the three-dimensional picture of the stars in space that he carried in his head.

As anybody who has proved even the simplest geometric theorem knows, there is a mental language of geometry that exists independently of any spoken language. First comes a kinesthetic sense of the "meaning" of the theorem—a sort of "Aha! If this moves over there then that has to swing round this point about so far, so it will always be the same length as that-over-there." Afterward

comes the laborious process of translating the intu-
ition into Line AB and Point C and so forth and so on.

Thariinye, looking on as Rafik muttered calculations and traced lines of light on the projection, was
able to follow the logic of Rafik's thinking in these
intuitive terms. And when he touched Rafik's arm,
waggled his eyebrows, and suggested that an arc be
minutely widened to cover a slightly greater subsection of space, Rafik frowned, nodded, and changed
the light-diagram without the necessity of a word
being said. But at the next suggested course correction, Rafik shook his head violently. "You don't
understand," he said. "We know there is a fault in
the hydroponics unit." He had to repeat that very
slowly before Thariinye waggled his eyebrows to
show comprehension. "They must stop before they
leave our explored space. The question is, where
would they be most likely to stop for supplies? If
Calum took this route, he could pick from a salad
bar of ag planets in these two star systems; if he took
this one, there's nothing, he'd have to backtrack.
But I'm betting he would pick neither the quickest
route nor the worst one. Something shaped like a
corkscrew would appeal to the shifty bastard. And
that would bring him out somewhere near here."
Rafik tapped a point representing a distant sun to
bring up a closer view of the system. One panel
darkened, then displayed a glowing white outline
within which was shown a reddish sun with only
three planets orbiting it, two far too close to support
the temperate-region greens Acorna favored.

Thariinye reached out and touched the image of
the third planet. It looked right to him: a little

larger than Home, far enough from the sun to be in the right temperature range, slightly tilted in its elliptical orbit. Two moons, one large enough to cause tides, the other a mere speck, orbited the planet.

The panel beeped, the color of its glowing outline changed to green, and a close-up view of the selected world appeared. Thariinye studied the arrangement of continents and seas approvingly. Yes, this world might well have an ideal climate for farmers. He extended one finger to touch a pattern of light blue triangles and diamonds that looked like a string of beads scattered across the largest continent, and waggled his eyebrows at Rafik rather than hurt his mouth framing a question in this awkward language.

"Ag settlements," Rafik said, "and one spaceport." He indicated the six-armed star set toward the bottom of the chain of blue marks.

(Neeva. They are heading in the right direction.)

(Wonderful!)

(No. Not wonderful. Come and look!)

Thariinye extended his hand with an imperious gesture. Rafik raised his own brows, but after a moment looking in the young Liinyar's eyes, he gave him the laser drawing tool.

"Res-taare fiirist diispla?"

After a moment's pause, Rafik said, "Oh— restore first display? Sure." He snapped his fingers twice. The panel showing a close-up view of Rushima faded back into the general picture.

With swift, sure gestures Thariinye sketched

many parallel lines of light, originating at the far upper right of the screen and approaching the human-settled portion of the galaxy at an oblique angle that would shortly cut right across the bottom of the screen, passing directly through the solar system that hosted Rushima.

(Look, Melireenya, Neeva, Khaari. Our 'Khornya is going here, and so)—Thariinye tapped the parallel bands of light—(are the Khleevi. There is probability eighty-nine percent that the first world they destroy will be the one for which 'Khornya is bound. We have no more time to debate—we must trust these barbar . . .) He jammed the brakes on that thought. (. . . these linyarii beings.) They had better be truly linyarii, for all their sakes!

Neeva's pupils narrowed to threadlike lines of silver as she took in the devastating message of the star map. She could not make the mental translation to their notation and angle of view as rapidly as Thariinye had done.

(Navigation Officer! Do you concur with Thaari's conclusion?)

Khaari rose and joined Thariinye close to the display. After a moment her own pupils narrowed like Melireenya's. (About the Khleevi he is correct, Envoy. As for the route supposedly taken by 'Khornya, I cannot say. It is certainly a possible way to approach our sector . . . but it seems unnecessarily roundabout.)

(This dark one has explained it to me,) Thariinye broke in. ('Khornya left without the permission of these beings. They believe she has taken an unusual route in order to avoid messages ordering her to return.)

All four of the Linyaari turned to stare at the humans sitting round the table.

"Something's wrong," Judit murmured to the others. "Look at their eyes." Acorna's slit-pupiled look of grief or emotional tension was repeated four times over in the long, elegant faces confronting them.

"Delszaki Li." Neeva spoke aloud, carefully, and with only a slight lingering trace of accent in certain syllables. "We . . . haave not been . . . enitirely open with you. We haad anyother purpose inn comiin to your people."

"Is obvious," Li whispered. "Was wondering how long it would take you to admit it. Now we speak freely?"

"Yes, fireeli," Neeva said. "Iss little time." (Calculate expected time of arrival of Khleevi fleet, Navigation Officer! You will aid, Computation Specialist Thariinye! I want an estimate before they ask for one! It is time to take action!)

Nine

Neeva began to tell the story of the Khleevi invasion of the First Home, haltingly in the beginning, then with more assurance as her tongue became accustomed to the awkward syllables of the speech called "Basik."

"Vhiliinyar we called it: 'Home of the People.' What need for another name? And our star was called 'Light of the People.' Other stars, other lands, we named as we first ventured into space: named for their position, for their discoverers, for the color of their light or the quality of their resources. We took what we needed from other systems, and groups of the People dwelt away from Vhiliinyar for a time to explore and use these other lands, but there was only one Home, and now it is no more."

"Vhiliinyar thiinyethilelen, fiinyefalaran Vhiliinyar," murmured the other three Linyaari in their own tongue, a soft ritual plaint of mourning that needed no translation. "We see that your race has seeded itself over many star systems," Neeva continued. "Have you, then, experience of the Khleevi already, that you protect yourselves by this diversity?"

"Population pressure," Gill said. He gave a quick estimate of the rate at which human populations tended to expand, given sufficient food, and Neeva's pupils slitted to silvery lines. "I see! We do not reproduce so quickly," she said with regret. "Many generations will pass before the People recover from the devastation created by the Khleevi. Your race may yet be more fortunate. Even though they destroy one or many worlds, yet will others of you survive and replace those who are lost."

"I think," Pal prompted gently, "you had best tell us exactly what you know of these 'Khleevi.' Where do they come from, what are their customs, and what is the reason for the war between your races? Are they humanoid or completely other? What have they said to you?"

Neeva shook her head. "If I knew these things, I would surely tell you. They . . . they do not communicate. They destroy; and before they destroy, they torture. Of their tongue we have too few samples for the LAANYE to analyze; of their physical structure we know only what is shown on the broadcasts they have sent to cow us into submission. When their first ships appeared in our space, we sent envoys to them, as we have come to you, in peace and friendship. Those envoys never returned, but we know their fate from the images sent back to us. I think I will not show you those vids; there is no need to harrow your hearts with the images engraved on ours. Our envoys, and all of the People who have subsequently fallen into Khleevi hands, have been tortured to death as slowly as Khleevi arts permitted. Fortunately for us," she added drily, "they were initially unaware of how fragile our bodies must be compared to theirs; the first captives died quickly. Since then they have learned more of our physiology."

She explained that at the time of the first Khleevi attacks, the Linyaari had been a space-faring race but not a warlike one; it was all but impossible to make war on or harm beings whose grief and pain you could feel, through telepathic contact, as clearly as your own. Gentleness and empathy had been bred into Linyaari culture until any other way of being was all but unthinkable. And although they had, in their explorations of space, encountered other sapient aliens, none of those races had been so well developed or so powerful as to force the Linyaari to learn the arts of war—or even of elementary self-defense. The only real change caused by their encounters with other races had been the development of the LAANYE, the linguistic analyzer which allowed them to acquire a basic understanding of alien languages from a relatively small speech sample.

"Strange that they would develop such a device when they had no prior experience of language translation," Rafik commented sotto voce.

"Is logical development," Mr. Li contradicted him in a whisper. "No different languages among their own people, hence no false generalizations as to 'true nature of language' such as human linguists produce. Also no development of natural ability to learn other languages, perhaps no brain structures adapted to such task. Is only logical these most intelligent beings would turn to technology for solution."

Rafik shrugged. Having been brought up trilingual, in the Arabic and Armenian of his family house and the Basic of interstellar commerce, he could not even imagine a world in which all intelligent beings spoke but one language and regarded other tongues as codes to be broken by communications software.

"From the Khleevi," Neeva said, "we learned the arts of war . . . but not quickly enough. First we fled them, abandoned Vhiliinyar rather than commit violence against other sapient beings . . . but not all. Too many of the People refused to believe the evidence of the Khleevi 'casts; it was beyond their comprehension that any beings could attack others in this fashion. They learned . . . too late . . . and the Khleevi showed us what happened to them. Even if the Khleevi were to abandon Vhiliinyar now, the People who remain could not return. The land would be alive with the memory of pain and betrayal; the water would be tainted with the blood of innocents."

"Vhiliinyar thiinyethilelen, fiinyefalaran Vhiliinyar," repeated the other Linyaari.

Neeva went to the star map and asked Thariinye to make it display the Coma Berenices quadrant. With Rafik's help, the projection was changed, and using the laser pointer, Neeva traced lines of light showing the Linyaari dispersion to planets in other systems, far enough away, they hoped, to evade Khleevi notice. This flight had bought them enough time to adapt their technology to space war and defense systems, and also time enough to establish certain stringent rules for all their people. "No more Linyaari shall die under Khleevi torture," Neeva told them. "We have all taken a vow to die at our own hands before falling into the claws of the Khleevi. For some years this was not necessary. Having conquered Vhiliinyar, and our neighboring world of Galleni, the Khleevi did not move again for a time. But we did not cease our studies and explorations. We have had two objects; to find a way of traveling much farther and faster than any known spacecraft, so that we might escape the Khleevi for good; and to develop defense systems that might annihilate the Khleevi, both in our own defense and so that other races might not be totally exterminated like the dharmakoi of Galleni."

"Galleni thiinyethilelen, fiinyefalaran dharmakoi," murmured the other Linyaari.

"One of our foremost scientists, Vaanye of the Renyilaaghe, had adapted his researches into the topology of space to weapons research shortly before his death," Neeva told them. "He had discovered a way of temporarily collapsing the dimensional fabric of space at a selected point, which created an inordinately large and destructive explosion at the point of origin. Vaanye had told us only

that there were a few minor side effects to use of the
weapon, such as the fact that it destroyed whoever
employed it as well as the intended target, when he and
his life-mate made the mistake of taking a short cruise
in order to show their first youngling to . . . me."
Neeva's pupils narrowed into vertical silver lines of
distress. "My sister Feriila was Vaanye's . . . wife," she
explained, "and I had been on duty at an outlying
planet in the same system, attempting to establish
diplomatic relations with a race of large quadrupeds
which at first contact had appeared to be sapient. This
was later proved to be an error; they had neither language nor social organization nor any long-term
memory. It was an error which cost Feriila her life,
for Vaanye's cruise coincided with the Khleevi discovery of this star system. Our new planetary
defenses thwarted their first attack—but Vaanye, in
space, had no such defenses. For three ghaanyi we
have believed that Vaanye destroyed Feriila, their
youngling, and the ship rather than allow them to be
captured by the Khleevi. We were astonished to discover that an escape pod from Vaanye's ship had survived the explosion only to be transported to this
remote sector of space . . . and even more surprised to
find that my sister-child had been raised to maturity
among you."

"Ha!" Pal exploded. "So you didn't come for
Acorna."

Neeva inclined her head with a graceful gesture
that indirectly reproved Pal.

"No. Since our present planetary defense systems
have at least temporarily repelled the Khleevi attack,
we have observed that the number of their ships

near the systems we inhabit is greatly diminished.

Some of our people conjecture that their fleet has gone in search of other, easier worlds to conquer. With the smaller number of Khleevi ships patrolling our space, it was possible to send out parties of envoys with some hope of escaping Khleevi detection. We felt it our duty to discover if any other sapient races might exist in the path of the Khleevi fleet, and to warn them if such existed."

"Did you know they were coming this way, then?" Gill asked.

"There were several paths they might logically have taken. We sent groups out in all such directions." Neeva paused, her pupils narrowing again. "Not all ships made a successful escape from the remaining Khleevi . . . but ours did, and we were instructed to continue on our way. Recent transmissions from narhii-Vhiliinyar—you would say, New Home—have emphasized the urgency of our task, as it is now known that a large Khleevi fleet is indeed making a sweep toward this sector of space. We hope to make alliance with you, to share our technology and what we have learned of the Khleevi with whatever resources your race can muster, that they may not fall upon you unwarned as they did us. And now, as well, we hope to find my sister-child and bring her back to the People . . . if she can be saved from the Khleevi into whose path she is heading."

Gill had been moving restlessly in his seat, bursting with questions. How and when had the Linyaari seen Acorna's escape pod and learned of her existence? Who had told them to look for her here on Maganos Moon Base? And why had they been so secretive and indirect in their first approaches on Maganos? But Neeva's last statement thrust all his previous questions into the background.

"Great Gods, woman," he roared, "do you mean to tell us these beasts are headed for Rushima? Why the devil did you draw it out so long? Rafik, send a coded spurt to Rushima immediately! There's no time to waste!"

"Gently, Gill," whispered Mr. Li. "Is important to know all salient facts. Right action can arise only from right understanding."

"I should think the action needed is obvious enough!"

"Declan Giloglie," said Judit firmly, "chill."

Gill subsided into his chair, muttering into his quivering red beard, and Rafik looked at Judit with new respect.

"How did you do that?" he murmured in her ear.

"Practice," Judit replied, equally quietly. "My first employer on Kezdet had a hunting dog which it was my responsibility to train. Behavioral training principles turn out to be applicable across species."

"When we have a moment," Rafik responded, "I want to see if you can get him to heel."

Judit's lips twitched. "No, but given the right motivation he will sit up and beg."

Rafik intercepted a meaningful glance from Mr. Li and, abandoning this badinage, he slipped out of the room to consult with Li's secretary about the fastest route by which to send a coded spurt-message to

Rushima for immediate transmission to the *Acadecki*. The message would have to have a header that would persuade Calum and Acorna not to reject it unheard, yet it must not contain anything that would start a general panic on Rushima. Hmm . . . Wasn't Rushima an outlying colony of the Shenjemi Federation? Best apprise the Federation, too, of the situation . . . or as much as could be encapsulated in the very condensed but fast-traveling spurt. Let the Shenjemi decide whether to defend or evacuate Rushima; Rafik's first responsibility was to get Acorna and Calum out of there at once. Then perhaps the Linyaari envoys could set up a communication link with the Shenjemi to discuss their next step.

The messages sent, Rafik returned to the deliberations in Mr. Li's innermost office. All the interior walls except the one devoted to vid-screens now glowed with star maps; arcs of light radiated from one system to another, and geometric shapes denoting star fleets moved with agonizingly deliberate velocity to converge on the Rushimese system as various parties put forward their suggestions for mobilizing a defense against the Khleevi attack. Gill pointed out that Kezdet's own Guardians of the Peace had a large space fleet at their command, testimony to Kezdet's acquisitive ways and tendency to demand "taxes" or "reparations" from neighbors on the slightest excuse.

At his command, the star-map projector displayed a fleet of golden rhomboids moving from Kezdet toward Rushima, but taking a far more direct route than that presumably chosen by Calum. "They could be there within five days."

"You can't be serious!" Judit flared up at him. "Shake hands with Kezdet, count your fingers," she quoted a proverb popular in this and neighboring star systems. Pal nodded his agreement. Having escaped the infamous system of child bondage on which Kezdet's old industrial empire had been built, a system protected by the Guardians of the Peace, neither of the Kendoros was inclined to trust a Kezdet Guardian in the slightest.

"Oh, they're not all that bad," Rafik said. "Smirnoff and Minkus, for instance—"

"Smirnoff's a psychopath!" Gill interjected. "And out for your blood, in case you've forgotten."

"True," Rafik nodded, "but he did save my life by disarming the bomb Tapha meant to kill me with. Whatever else you may say against Des Smirnoff, he's no coward."

Gill snorted. "Maybe not, but he's still an idiot. Remember who let Tapha get past security with that bomb in the first place? No, thank you. We don't need clowns like Smirnoff and Minkus in this operation. They're liable to get your whole hand blown off instead of just taking a couple of fingers!"

"This insignificant old person has dealt with Kezdet for many years and still has all fingers intact, though unfortunately not functioning," Mr. Li pointed out. "But Kezdet fleet is designed for small-time piracy and aggression on weaker neighbors, Gill, not for defense against armada. Send Guardians to Rushima is to sign their death sentence."

"Well, now," said Pal and Judit simultaneously, their brows clearing, "if you put it that way . . ."

"Besides," Li added, "Kezdet is not known for altruism. Will hardly strip their system of defenses in order to protect agricultural colony belonging to Shenjemi Federation."

"Rafik, has Shenjemi responded to the spurt yet?"

Rafik glanced at the small portable com unit which he had set to display all incoming messages from Shenjemi—or Rushima.

"More or less."

A voluminous spurt from Shenjemi was still being expanded and decoded; the words scrolled across Rafik's screen as he watched.

"First, they request proof that this so-called attack on Rushima is not a hoax, and they want to know what connection this message has with the spurt they recently received from Rushima claiming the planet was under attack by space pirates."

"The Khleevi—already?" Judit paled.

"I don't think so," Rafik replied. "The Rushimese seem to think they're being attacked by some group called the Starfarers. . . . Now, where have I heard that name before? Oh, yes . . . Uncle Hafiz mentioned them once; they used to be the Free Nation of Esperantza. Amalgamated diddled them out of the planet they'd just settled and stripped it for mineral assets, but they refused to take the resettlement offer—claimed they'd been cheated and would settle for nothing less than having Esperantza restored and returned to them. They turned their space station into a mobile colony and have been wandering around for yonks, staging protests and doing odd jobs in space to finance themselves." He frowned. "But they were always very ethical . . . obnoxiously ethical. I can't see them turning to piracy, no matter how hard up they were. This must be some other group with the same name."

"Besides," Gill said, "Rushima's not exactly the ideal target for pirates, is it? What sort of loot could they take off an ag planet? Loads of grain? Some nicely rotting silage?"

"To get back to the Shenjemi Federation," Rafik said, "they have sent a spurt direct to Rushima requesting confirmation and have as yet received no reply; third, Rushima's ROI—return on investment," he translated for the Linyaari, "is too low to justify the expense of a full-scale defense. They are considering sending a small fleet to evacuate the planet and relocate the colonists, should there be any basis for our 'hysterical' message." He shrugged slightly and touched the display of red stars for Shenjemi ships to stop the forward movement of the simulation. "Let's hope they make up their minds in time. How much time do we have?"

(Khaari?)

(I'm working on it!)

(Between one and two enye-ghanyii,) Thariinye announced.

Khaari sighed and rolled her eyes. (I hate to admit it, Neeva, but the brat's probably right. I'm trying to get you a closer estimate.)

(Brat! I like that! You're only one age group ahead of me, Khaari!)

(Children, quit squabbling! I can't hear myself think!)

After a few minutes' consultation with Judit and Gill, Neeva said, "If the Khleevi observe Rushima and choose to take it, they will probably beginn operations in . . . I think eight to"—she counted on her digits for a minute, murmuring—"I do wish somebody would add arithmetic capabilities to the LAANYE; I cannot add in base tenn." She muttered to herself in Linyaari for a moment, then lifted her head. "Yes. Two-tenn to six-tenn of your days."

"Twenty to sixty?" Gill asked hopefully. "Or twelve to sixteen?"

The number words were within the LAANYE's capacity, if the arithmetic was not.

"Twelf to six-teen," Neeva said firmly.

Gill whistled. "You didn't give yourselves much lead time, did you?"

"Be reasonable, Gill," Judit said. "They risked their lives to get away from narhii-Vhiliinyar at all. Are you going to criticize them because they reached us just ahead of the Khleevi?"

"It's a whole lot better than getting here just after the invasion," Pal pointed out.

"Let's just hope the Shenjemi Federation get their collective finger out in time." Gill said. "And in the meantime, let's have Acorna out of there. Rafik, what word from Rushima? They must have received our spurt by now."

Rafik shook his head. "It didn't get through."

"WHAT???" Gill lunged half out of his chair. "What did you do wrong?"

"Chill," Rafik said firmly. He was disappointed to see that the word was not effective when it wasn't delivered in Judit's calm voice. "Look,

Gill, nothing is getting through to Rushima right now. The Shenjemi couldn't raise a reply either. And the *Acadecki* isn't receiving OR transmitting."

"If these Khleevi have already got there—"

"Imm-possible," Thariinye said in an atrocious accent, but with great authority.

"More likely it's space weather," Rafik pointed out. "A bad disturbance in the ionosphere could bring satellite communications down for several hours, even days."

Judit touched Delszaki Li's desk-console screen with one finger, murmured a few words, then tapped the screen again. "Unlikely. The Galactica-pedia says Rushima is noted for its temperate and even climate. Atmospheric and ionospheric storms are virtually unknown."

"In any case," Mr. Li put in, "dare not wait days, or even hours. Someone must go to warn Rushima, and to bring Acorna and Calum back. Here, we continue to resend spurt message, make plans for defense, encourage Shenjemi to evacuate Rushima."

"And what happens if the Khleevi bypass Rushima?" Rafik asked.

"They find richer pickings closer in," Gill said grimly. "Depending on their tastes ... Neeva, what do these Khleevi want?"

Neeva shook her head. "You know the fate of our envoys. We have never established communi-cation; whatever they want, it is not that. I know only what they do. They destroy."

"Do they colonize the planets they take? Are they looking for living space?"

Neeva thought that over. "They . . . yes, they now inhabit Vhiliinyar; but our scouts report that we would not know our home again. They . . . they . . ." She choked, could not find words in Basic to describe the devastation, but Delszaki Li's eyes widened as he took in the images of desolation that filled her mind and the thoughts of the other Linyaari.

"Valleys and green hills become plains," he said, straining his voice to communicate what he perceived to the others. "Orchards and cities are leveled. All native life is destroyed, down to the insects in the air and the bacteria in the earth. A river becomes a foul marsh breeding clutches of small Khleevi in the thousands. Dry land is an ocean of grass in which the mature Khleevi fly. And the bones of the Linyaari are piled in monuments."

"The Mongols meant to do the same to Western Europe, once," Rafik said. "It would have been in the"—he paused and flicked fingers swiftly over the string of amber beads knotted in his belt—"in the thirteenth century, Old Reckoning. Chroniclers of the time say they advanced like locusts, devouring and destroying all before them, and attacking so swiftly that the mounted knights of the West had no time to assemble a defense. Impregnable walled cities went down before them, whole lands were depopulated, and they boasted that they would make of the entire world nothing but a vast steppe over which they might ride wherever they would. Fortunately," he said, "this was before our people had space travel, so it did not occur to them to extend the devastation to other planets."

Neeva drew in her breath in shock at this revelation.

(Did you hear that? Their own histories recount such behavior!)

(Have we made a mistake in seeking alliance with them? Perhaps they are more khlevii than linyarii after all.)

(What choice did we have?)

(I think we are safe enough. They, too, have no choice. How could they ally with the Khleevi, who destroy anyone who lingers long enough to communicate with them? They must help us to turn back the Khleevi, else their own worlds will suffer as did our Home.)

Gill thought the Linyaari simply had nothing much to say. "Very interesting, Rafik," he said. "But the Mongols did not succeed. I've seen Earth; it's not a featureless steppe, and Europe has cities and monuments dating from long before the time you mention. So what turned them back?"

Pal and Judit turned to Rafik, hopeful.

Rafik shook his head slightly. "Their leader at home died," he said, "and they thought it was more important to go home and vote than to continue the conquest; they could always destroy Europe some other time. Fortunately, they never got back to it."

"Oh," Gill said, disappointed. "I don't suppose we can count on that happening again. You'll just have to think up some ruse, Rafik."

"Me?"

"You and Delszaki Li are the brains of this outfit,"

Gill told him blandly. "Me, I'm just a simple, horny-handed son of the lunar regolith. You two work out how humanity is going to exterminate this swarm of killer bees, and I'll just pop off to Rushima and fetch our Acorna home again. Mr. Li, what's the fastest ship Maganos has available right now?"

"Wait just a minute," Rafik protested. "You'll go for Acorna? Excuse me, but I believe I have some interest in this matter as well."

"And I," said Pal.

"You're not going anywhere without me," Judit said.

"You two can't go," Gill protested, "Mr. Li needs you. And Rafik has to stay here and think."

"I could think just as well on board a ship as anywhere else," Rafik said, "and anyway, I'm not nearly twisty enough to solve this problem. What we need is somebody who can persuade all the major planetary federations to disburse large sums of cash and most of their defense systems, up front, to guard against an alien threat that they've never heard of and that is being described only by some other aliens."

He paused, appalled at the magnitude of the task, so described.

"What we need, in fact," he said finally, "is Uncle Hafiz." He pounded one fist into his palm in frustration. "And he is walled up behind the Shield, where no one can communicate with him . . . or the rest of Laboue . . . at all."

(Walled up behind the 'Shield'? Khaari, I have a bad feeling about this. Do you suppose that first planet we approached . . .)

(Oh, no!)

(Oh, yes.)

Aloud, Neeva said, "Where is it, this Laboue?"

"Not on the maps," Rafik said. "My uncle and the others who make it their headquarters prefer their privacy. And I am sworn to House Harakamian now; on the lives of my unborn sons, I may not tell you its location."

Neeva nodded. "Tell us nothinn, thenn," she acquiesced, "but I am not forbiddenn to tell you that before we approached you onn Maganyos . . . Maganos," she corrected herself, "we had made contact by vid with residents of another planet on the fringes of your settled area, the first one we identified. Since at that time we did not have the LAANYE programmed to teach us your language, we attempted to communicate by vid; we showed them some of the scenes broadcast from Khleevi torture ships, to make them aware of the danger. We received a brief vidcast from the planet . . . there was a biped . . . human . . . dark as you, Rafik, who showed us pictures of Acorna and a drawing of her escape pod. That was how we learned of her existence. But before we could question this human further, the entire planet was shut down under an impenetrable shield that blocked all communication, even visual transmission. Our only clue was a message sent from the location we had been communicating with, indecipherable but for the one word 'Acorna.' That message went to a ship which then departed hastily in this direction; we followed the ship to Maganos in the hope that its owner might lead us to Acorna."

She inclined her head gracefully toward Rafik.

(Khaari, point out the location of that first planet on these maps.)

Khaari took a light-wand and illuminated a star some distance from Maganos and lying well away from the more populous parts of this sector.

"I very much fear," Neeva went on, "that it is we who were responsible for your . . . your mother-sib's retreat behind the shield."

Rafik looked at the illuminated area, lips set in a grim line.

"Without breaking my oath to House Hara-kamian," he said, "I think I can say that you are very probably correct. And you know," he went on in a slightly more hopeful tone, "perhaps it's not Uncle Hafiz's brains we need so much just now . . . perhaps what we need is the Shield. If such a device could be installed on every inhabited planet, beginning with those in the direct line of the Khleevi fleet . . ."

"But the secret of the Shield," Pal pointed out, "is presently behind the Shield, together with your uncle's invaluably twisty mind. So perhaps our first priority ought to be finding some way to crack the Shield. Surely Hafiz has told you something about how it functions?"

"Nothing," Rafik admitted. "I am not sure he even understands it himself. The genius of our House is in finance, not technology. But we always hire the best technicians."

"Then the engineer who designed and installed the Shield . . ." Pal began.

"Martin Dehoney," Rafik said. There was a moment of silence.

"Well," Gill said slowly, "he was the best, no question about it!"

He was also dead; the design of Maganos Moon Base had been Dehoney's last creation.

"Provola Quero worked with Dehoney," Judit said. "Perhaps she might have some ideas. Why don't you two get together and discuss the matter with Mr. Li while we . . ."

"Oh, no," Rafik said. "I'm going, too."

"And we," said Neeva. "Acorna is my sister-child; it is my responsibility to see to her safety. Besides, our ship is faster than any your people could design."

Rafik's teeth flashed white under the thin dark line of his mustache. "We'll just see about that!"

"As for planetary defense," Mr. Li put in, "House of Li has excellent liquidity, as does House Harakamian. Why not hire mercenaries from Kilumbemba Empire?"

Gill whistled through his teeth. "The Red Bracelets? If anybody can take out the Khleevi, they should be able to." Delszaki Li's personal bodyguard was rumored to have served with the Red Bracelets at one time, and he had never met any human being tougher or more frightening than Nadhari Kando.

"Say," Rafik put in, evidently thinking along the same lines, "Is it true that Nadhari used to—"

"She prefers not to discuss her past."

"Oh. Well . . . but, Delszaki, it would cost a fortune."

"House Harakamian and House Li command

two fortunes," Li said calmly. "Also, Kilumbemba mercenaries will work on commission. Percentage of profits in captured alien ships, alien technology could be powerful lure."

"And," Gill said slowly, "they're probably bored right now. The Kilumbemba Empire hasn't expanded in several years. The Red Bracelets are expensive to maintain and dangerous when bored, but Kilumbemba daren't release them from their contract for fear of a revolt in one of the new, um, 'acquisitions.' It just might work. Rafik, you and Delszaki are the best negotiators; before we go anywhere, why don't you see if we can subcontract from Kilumbemba for the best part of their mercenary space fleet?"

"And pledge Uncle Hafiz's credit to support them, I suppose," Rafik said with resignation. "Not that I don't think it's money well spent," he hastened to explain, "but Uncle Hafiz is going to kill me when he comes out from behind the Shield."

"He wouldn't grudge the credits to save Acorna," Gill pointed out.

"No—but what do you bet he'd find a way to make somebody else pay them?" Rafik grinned and sat down at a com unit. "After this little maneuver, I had better make tracks for Rushima . . . and I'm not sure it would be wise to come back! I don't want Yukata Batsu wearing my ears on his trophy belt!"

"Shhh," Gill said in a rumbling attempt at an undertone, "I think that kind of talk upsets our guests." He felt it would definitely be unwise to tell

the Linyaari about Yukata Batsu, Hafiz's chief
competitor on Laboue, and his unpleasant habit of
keeping trophies from his defeated enemies . . .
including the ears of Hafiz's own son, Tapha. Hafiz
himself had been more upset about Tapha's stupid-
ity in letting himself be captured than about the
mutilation, but somehow Gill felt the Linyaari
were not used to taking such matters in their stride.
They are still not sure we're civilized enough to deal with,
he thought. *Maybe we'd better not let them listen in on
the negotiations with the Kilumbemba mercenaries, either.*
And on the excuse that Rafik and Delszaki Li
needed absolute privacy for this ticklish task, he
offered to escort the Linyaari on a brief tour of
Maganos Moon Base while the necessary wheeling
and dealing took place.

"That is—if you can be sure nobody will notice
your . . . um . . . unusual appearance?" One thing
they did not need to deal with was the effect on
Maganos of seeing four "Acornas" suddenly
appearing in their midst.

"We attracted no attention on our way here,"
Melireenya pointed out. "As long as Thariinye
does not lose his temper again, we should have no
trouble."

"Just keep us away from those blasted kids,"
Thariinye said.

Since the raison d'être of Maganos was the education and training of the bondchildren liberated
from Kezdet, Gill found this directive rather difficult to follow, but with Judit's help he managed to
keep the Linyaari occupied for some time in child-
free areas of the base. Indeed, Provola Quero alone

would have been able to lecture them indefinitely
on the design of the base living quarters, mining
facilities, and engineering shop; but even the
Linyaari thirst for knowledge was eventually sati-
ated by the seemingly endless string of facts and
sketches at Provola's disposal, and at last Gill
could think of nothing but to bring them back to
Delszaki Li's rooms before they became too tired
to maintain their shielding projections.

He was relieved to deduce that the negotiations
had gone well; Delszaki Li was napping in his
hover-chair, and Rafik was sprawled on cushions
with a look of satisfaction on his thin, dark face
and a glass of something that would probably have
been forbidden by the First Prophet in his right
hand.

"All done?" Gill asked cautiously.

"All fixed." Rafik tipped the glass to his mouth
and took a sip of the amber-colored liquid. "He"—
he jerked his head toward the sleeping Delszaki—
"is a genius at this. I think he might even be able to
teach Uncle Hafiz a thing or two," he said with
surprising generosity. "Would you believe he's got
Kilumbemba underwriting half the costs of the
expedition, because they feel it's to their benefit to
keep the mercenaries busy and in training rather
than having them at loose ends where they might
stir up trouble? Although I'm not sure they realize
it yet," he added thoughtfully. "The way Delszaki
put it was that we would save Kilumbemba a lot of
money by paying half the retaining salaries of the
mercenaries for the duration of this expedition.
Which means that effectively they are still paying

half the costs . . . and then House Li is covering seventy percent of the remainder. I only had to sign over the profits on a couple of planetary systems in Uncle Hafiz's name, he might not even kill me when he finds out what he's paying for, but I don't plan to stick around and check it out. Very generous of Delszaki."

Mr. Li's eyelids flickered. Gill suspected the old man was not really asleep, and he wondered just how "generous" Delszaki Li's offer had really been. He would have a controlling interest in the expedition now, and if he was right about the profits to be made from exploiting Khleevi technology, the lion's share of those profits would go to House Li rather than House Harakamian. Insensibly Gill began to feel more confident about the whole project. The Linyaari were so convinced that no one could withstand a Khleevi attack, they'd infected him with their pessimism—but Delszaki Li was no man's fool, and if he was already maneuvering to control profits, he must be counting the war as good as won.

"The only problem is," Rafik went on, "I did have to throw in a little extra inducement to Admiral Ikwaskwan."

"Admiral?" Gill said sharply. He had heard the notorious leader of the Kilumbemba mercenary forces called many things, but never anything so flattering as that.

Rafik waved a languid hand. "It's not exactly a formal military structure. If the man wants to be an Admiral, or a Brigadier, or High Potentate, let him take the title. Thing is, he wanted a share in Rosewater's Revelation."

"You sold your uncle's best racehorse to Ikwaskwan?"

"Only a part share, and it is in a good cause. You think he'll mind?"

"I think you'd better head for Rushima and not come back, like you were saying at first," Gill told him. "What have you been drinking to make you think Hafiz is going to be happy about teaming up with a—a—" It wasn't so much that words failed him, as that Judit's presence inhibited him from using any of the words he felt to be appropriate. "With Ikwaskwan," he finished weakly as a familiar smoky scent, wafting through the air, distracted his attention. He took another deep sniff and recognized it. "MY BEST SCOTCH, THAT'S WHAT YOU'VE BEEN INTO!"

"I earned it, weasel-wording and sweet-talking Ikwaskwan and half the Kilumbembese Cabinet while you were playing tour guide," Rafik said without bothering to move out of the way of Gill's furiously working hands. "Judit, call off your husband before he damages these precious vocal cords. Oh, and by the way, we had a spurt-message from the *Acadecki*."

"You did?" Gill's hands dropped to his sides. "Oh, all right, I won't kill you until you tell me what was in it."

Rafik grinned up at him. "That's not very good motivation."

"Very well, then, I'll let you live. This time."

"It was a little confusing," Rafik confessed. "Basically it said, 'Disregard previous message, everything all right here, stopping for R&R on Rushima.'

I doubt that means they've defeated the entire Khleevi fleet single-handedly; it probably just means they've outwitted those space pirates Rushima was complaining to the Shenjemi Federation about. That should be well within Calum's and Acorna's abilities," Rafik said with sublime confidence.

"Did you tell her to get out of there?"

"Couldn't. The *Acadecki*'s not answering; they must all be on Rushima, and Rushima isn't transmitting. I expect the space pirates knocked out their satellite communications. I did send a long spurt telling Acorna about her people showing up here, and that we'd be with her in five days. If anybody picks up on the *Acadecki*, they should get that much."

"You didn't tell her about the Khleevi?"

"That sort of message is not something you want to leave lying about a ship's com system until somebody is inspired to pick up," Rafik pointed out. "What if the Rushimese hear it? There could be panic, rioting—and Acorna's somewhere on the surface, we don't know where. I thought it better to wait until we can patch through some sort of direct contact."

Gill had to admit the logic of this, but knowing for sure that Acorna was on Rushima—and unwarned about the deadly danger approaching—made him more impatient than ever to take off. The hours they would have to wait for the Kilumbemba forces to mobilize dragged like lead.

Ten

"So, what do we do now?" Calum asked. "Wait till the dust settles and there's someone we can talk to about leaving?"

"I think we better be sure they know it's us who are leaving and not some of the enemies escaping," Acorna said. "I'm going to check on my 'ponics."

Calum watched her go. He hoped there was enough there for her to eat. He also hoped that she was going to change out of those rags and into some outfit suitable to the real Acorna.

"Anyone else for a bite to eat while we talk this over?"

He looked first at Dr. Hoa, who hadn't moved since sinking into a seat. The man's color was better and his expression more alert. "Are you feeling well enough for a meal?"

"There's nothing wrong with me a good cup of tea won't set right in next to no time," the scientist said with a little smile. "That is, if you should happen to have tea."

"In fact, I do," Calum said, making his way to the galley. "Tea for all?"

"What's 'tea'?" Markel asked.

"You can find out after you've cleaned up a bit," Johnny Greene said.

"Why should I do that when I might just have to do a flit again?"

Johnny closed off his nostrils and raised his eyebrows. "In this fresher air, ol' buddy, you stink. So do I, I'm sure, but not quite as badly."

Calum, whose back was to Markel, grinned. He hadn't wanted to mention the fact.

"If you happened to have any clean clothes, Calum," Johnny went on, "I could sure stand a change myself. Any old ship suit'll do."

"Second cabinet in the first cabin on the right. And there's a sanitary unit directly opposite the bunk."

Dr. Hoa was on his second cup of tea and looking far more alert when Acorna came back, wearing more normal attire. Then both Johnny and a far cleaner Markel showed up, although the boy looked a trifle surly.

Markel took the cup of tea and some finger foods that Calum had defrosted, and went to the place where he had deposited his equipment. He put in the earphone, and in a few seconds was smiling with great satisfaction, but then he glowered again.

"If I hadn't been stuck with you, I'd've been in it, too," he said.

"If you hadn't been able to save Acorna, Calum, and Dr. Hoa first, young 'un," Johnny Greene said in firm contradiction, "there wouldn't have been a coup at all. I gather someone had the sense to gas the searchers in the tubes?"

For a moment, Markel stared in astonishment at his friend. Then his expression was both smug that he had actually been a crucial element in the rebellion and surprised. "How'd you know how they got them?"

Johnny shrugged. "That's what I would have done. Nueva, Dom, Sengrat, and the others would have been so intent on wanting to get at least Dr. Hoa back into their hands, they'd've depleted their guard points." He waved to indicate the guards they had overcome. "We'd've been up the crick without a paddle if the full complement of guards had been here in the hangar." Then he grinned at Markel. "Whaddaya bet that Kerratz, Andreziana, and Zanegar led the revolution?"

Markel's eyes went wide. "How'd you know?"

He ruffled Markel's hair. "You were doing all you could in your fashion, Markie, lad, and your father was one of those spaced. It's only logical that the ones who hurt worst would try hardest to get back at the murderers of their parents. Now, find out if they need to know where Dr. Hoa is hiding. I'd ask for Kerratz. Always thought he was the smartest of 'Zhuria and Ezkerra's brood."

"No, Andreziana's the one we want," Markel said in his blunt fashion as he found the mouthpiece in his backpack and attached the speaker J-bar. "I need to speak to Andreziana. This is Markel."

Johnny Greene and Calum both gestured for Markel to patch in the *Acadecki*'s system so they could hear, too. Markel shook his head emphatically, but Johnny caught him by one ear and gave him such a malevolent glare that Markel capitulated just in time for them all to hear the contralto voice of Andreziana.

"Where the hell have you been, Markel?"

"Clearing the decks so you could act, of course," the boy replied, laughing. "Caught 'em all napping, didja?"

"No, we caught them hunting in the tubes for you. So we closed 'em off and gave them a dose of their own," the girl replied.

"S-spaced?" Markel looked slightly green.

"We didn't have a lot of choice," Andreziana said. "They refused to surrender. I wasn't going to lose more of our own people going after them in the tunnels, not to mention risking that they'd win a tunnel fight."

"No," Markel said. "No, you—you couldn't do that. It's just . . ."

"I'll say this for those Palomellese," Andreziana interrupted like someone eager to change the subject, "most of them were right with us. Seems that Nueva Fallona and her group weren't that popular with their own people after all."

"So, what did you promise the Palomellese to get their cooperation?" Markel asked, accepting the change of subject.

"They'll take a landfall on Rushima and help undo the damage done for the chance to stay on."

"Won't we have to go through the Shenjemi Federation for permission for that? At the very least, they'll want to sue the *Haven* for the havoc caused," Markel said, dubious.

With an arm around Markel's shoulders, Johnny

positioned himself to speak through the J-bar. "John Greene here, 'Ziana, and congratulations on handling the retaking. That'll all be on log, and I think we can reason with the Shenjemi. We've sent a message about the condition of Rushima, by the way. . . ."

"You did WHAT?"

Her protest even shook Dr. Hoa, making him spill a bit of the tea he had been so happily imbibing. He held up a finger.

"We've been down on the surface," Calum said, speaking directly into the com unit of the *Acadecki*, "and promised the survivors that we would get a message to their sponsors. This is Calum Baird, pilot. By the way, do you have wounded?"

"Sure we do." The girl's voice softened. "Did you think we could manage a bloodless revolution? Why? We've some medics. . . ."

"But you do not have a *ki-lin*," said Acorna, elbowing her way beside Calum.

"What the shards is a *ki-lin*?"

At that point, Dr. Hoa angled his way between Acorna and Calum. "Very good, very unusual, useful, miraculous person. Saved me. Saved Markel, saved Calum. Save you pain and healing time."

"Who's that?"

"Dr. Hoa—and this is the *ki-lin*."

Acorna took a deep breath. "For what now appear to be very sensible precautions," Acorna said, her voice rippling with amusement, "I disguised myself as a procuress when my ship was captured by Nueva and her gang. I am, however, Acorna Delszaki-Harakamian."

If Johnny and Markel were jumping up and
down in dismay at Dr. Hoa's revelation, Calum was
tearing at his hair over Acorna's admission.

"Harakamian?" There was a certain awed tone in
'Ziana's voice. "Of House Harakamian?"

"Delszaki?" added a baritone. "Not THE Delszaki Li?"

"Yes, to both questions. How may I help you
now?"

There was a babble in the background, then a
new person was speaking.

"Look, I'm medical, but we've got some really
badly off wounded on the infirmary deck and some
people who'll die if we can't clear that gas out of
their lungs," the man said.

"I'm on my way," Acorna said, and gave a decisive
nod at Calum, who was staring hopelessly at her.

"C'mon, we'll all go. Lock down your ship, Cal,
will you?" Johnny Greene added. "Just in case
there are some survivors creeping down to the
hangar."

With some regret, Calum did as Johnny suggested.
He had been thinking of trying to raise regular contact
with Delszaki Li's headquarters on Kezdet . . . just to
allay any fears Mercy might have for his safety if the
original spurt had gotten through . . . but Johnny was
right. It was too soon to cry safe and far too soon to
omit any possible precaution.

Before they reached the end of the hangar deck,
there was banging on the hatches that had been
locked against Nueva's group.

"We're coming, we're coming," Johnny Greene
roared, deftly assisting Dr. Hoa up the steep risers.

"I am better, much better," Dr. Hoa kept protesting. "And what has been done can often be undone. With my process," he added with a little smile, "we can set much right in little time."

"That'll go down well with the Rushimese and the Shenjemi," Johnny said with a wry grin.

As soon as Dr. Hoa reached the bridge, 'Ziana, the late Andrezhuria's daughter, greeted him with considerably more warmth than she accorded those accompanying him. One eyebrow went up at the sight of Acorna, but she politely did not comment on Acorna's unusual appearance. Her face composed, 'Ziana was sitting in the bridge command chair, which dwarfed her slight figure. Her bandaged hands dangled from the armrests, but not far from the festoon of weapons hanging to her lap from the belt she wore. Not much taller than Calum, slender, with fair hair braided tightly in many small strands and tied together at the base of her neck, she looked her age, not the principal in a major coup. She certainly didn't look as if she could have been capable of the deeds she and the other teenagers lounging around the bridge had recently planned and executed.

"Dr. Hoa, is there anything you can do to help Rushima?" she asked. Her slightly accented Basic was delivered in the tone of a much older, self-possessed woman.

"I do believe I can, Andreziana," he said, as courteous as ever as, with a querying lift of his brows, he nodded toward one of the empty chairs on the port side of the bridge.

"Go to it, Doctor," she said, gesturing with one

graceful, if bandaged hand. Blood had leaked down her forearm and clotted.

Acorna sucked in her breath and looked at Johnny, who gave his head the slightest of negative movements.

"Who're the strangers, Markel?" 'Ziana went on, steepling her bandaged hands in front of her. It was a gesture, Acorna instinctively felt, that had been one of her mother's.

"Acorna." Markel might have been introducing a reigning planetary leader for the pride in his voice. One of the teenage boys lounging around the bridge snickered. Markel bristled, relaxing when Acorna touched his shoulder. "You only show how little you know," Markel said.

"She's the one can heal?" the lad said snidely. "What does she use? That horn on her head?" His hair had been cut into bristle which was dyed in uncomplementary colors. 'Ziana's gesture silenced him, and he seemed to cave in over his diaphragm at her displeasure. He wore a sloppy bandage on one shoulder: the sear mark of the stun bolt was partly visible.

So swiftly that no one could have stopped her, Acorna was beside him, her derided horn performing its miracle.

"Hey, whaddya go and do that for?" The boy raised his unharmed arm to push her away, but she had already retreated.

"Hey." His tone was completely different. He peeked first at the now healed flesh, then pulled off the rest of the bandage and saw clean, pink skin. "Hey, how'd you do that?"

"However she does it, I'll have some of the same, if you wouldn't mind, Acorna?" 'Ziana said, holding out her bandaged hands. "Can't really use the fingerpads with all this on me."

Although Acorna was as delicate as possible in peeling back the wadded fabric, little flickers in 'Ziana's eyes showed how painful the process was. Her hands were so badly burned they were weeping blood and scrum. Acorna lowered the horn to each palm, then the girl's torn wrists. Flesh seemed to flower instantly across the wounds.

"Let me tell you, that is a relief," 'Ziana said, briefly sounding her chronological age. "There're injured down below who need a lot more help than I do . . . did. Thank you. And, you, Brazie, I didn't hear your thank-you."

Brazie of the multicolored hair stammered out his gratitude, still fingering the now smooth ex-wound.

"You're both welcome. Anyone else?" Acorna asked, looking around at those who occupied the bridge.

"Aw, it ain't much," one of those beside Brazie said, but his companions pushed him toward Acorna. Another pulled up the rags left of the back of his shirt and revealed encrusted welts. Acorna had never seen anyone whipped and beaten, but, when she maneuvered the boy into the light to assess his injury, she knew that that was what had been done to him. Calum uttered a low whistle.

'Ziana now turned to Johnny Greene and Markel. "I need to talk to you two," she said, once again in that firm, uncontradictable voice. "You were within an ace of getting spaced, Johnny. Did you know? How'd you know to hide? And where did you hide?"

Johnny settled himself in the chair just below her level, and Markel took a seat next to him. "Well, I figured I was running out of Nueva's good graces. She was never sure where I stood with the First-Gen group, since they sort of picked me up because they were short a docking expert. Esposito and I had had a couple of run-ins. . . ."

'Ziana chuckled. "So you had. Dom never liked you either."

"True, though I had no intention of cutting him out with Nueva. She wasn't my type. But that's all history, 'Ziana. Let's talk about now. You've control of the *Haven*, but are there enough competent people left after two sets of wholesale slaughter to staff and crew a ship of this complexity?"

"My mother didn't raise me stupid, Johnny. Any more than Illart did Markie-boy here." 'Ziana was slightly contemptuous.

"Then you do have someone who can dampen the electromagnetic resonances in the navigation controls," Calum said, pointing to some orange flashing lights on one drive control board.

'Ziana swore and swung down off the command chair to take a closer look.

"If I could make a recommendation," Calum said at his most tactful, "I think the problem is more drift than immediate danger, and I can do some calculations to see how much thrust you'll need to apply, but this is one panel that should be manned at all times. And the life-support system seems to have been damaged from the look of the signals it's giving." He pointed to a board several positions down.

"You a pilot or something?"

"I've belted around the system for most of my life and never lost a ship," Calum said. "All modern ships use about the same basic controls . . . just some are bigger'n others, like this one."

"He's an expert and very experienced pilot," Acorna said. "Approved and recommended by both Delszaki and House Harakamian."

"Who's them?" Brazie asked, frowning in suspicion.

"Only two of the biggest interstellar firms," another lad said, and came up to Calum, extending one hand in greeting. "I'm Kerratz. My father was . . ." and Calum surmised that the father had been one of those spaced, ". . . teaching me his specialty. I've had a little time on the board, so I could take it over—if you'd do the calculations. I wouldn't want to do them, and be wrong."

A girl, heavy-boned and wearing flashily dyed blue-and-orange hair, pointed to the life-support board. "'Ponics system suffered a lot of damage when we were trying to weld the access panels shut so they'd all die in the tubes." Those deaths didn't seem to bother her as much as the harm to the plants. "Want I should get a gang together and see what damage is done?"

Calum turned politely toward 'Ziana.

"Go to it, Neggara," 'Ziana said, waving her off. "You help her, Brazie, Dajar, Foli. You've had a long enough rest now. And Rezar," she added, pivoting on one heel to address a tall, well-built boy cultivating a fine mustache on his handsome face, "you take the com board. This bridge needs to be properly controlled."

Then she turned to Johnny with a "how'm I doing?" glance that was challenging.

"What's happening on the decks below?" he asked. "There may be some good 'uns among the Palomellese who can spell your folk."

'Ziana didn't much like that suggestion from the expression on her face.

"Well, you'll be standing long watches, then," Johnny said with an indolent shrug.

"You go find some loyal enough to help," 'Ziana said. "I'm not leaving the bridge."

"I agree. You shouldn't," Johnny said, "but, if Acorna's finished here and Calum can hang about with the technical advice, I'll leave our *ki-lin* at the infirmary on my way down the levels."

'Ziana nodded agreement, but, as Acorna walked away toward the door, her eyes spoke volumes of gratitude to the spacer that 'Ziana's pride would never allow her to utter.

"You've done well, 'Ziana," Johnny said, then chuckled. "Nueva's mistake was in not spacing the whole kit and kaboodle: First AND Second Generation."

"You're damned right there," 'Ziana said as she resettled herself in her command chair, "but she considered us 'kids'!" She snorted as she steepled her fingers.

"A mistake for several reasons," Johnny said suavely. "How about communications below? Are they in working order?"

"Most of 'em," said Rezar, surveying his board. "Some holes, but call here to the bridge anywhere you can. I'll patch you through." He began running a diagnostic on the system.

"You okay where you are, Dr. Hoa?" Johnny asked before joining Acorna by the lift shaft.

"Oh, go on, go on, I've so much to set right I won't miss you at all," Dr. Hoa said, absently waving a hand over his head in the direction of the speaker, but focusing all his attention on the graphics in front of him. He was tsk-tsking over something as Johnny and Acorna left the bridge.

"Surely those children cannot run a ship this size?" Acorna said.

"Oh, I dunno about that, Acorna," Johnny said with a grin. "Seems to me I heard that Cal, Gill, and Rafik had you managing a lot of basic controls before you were three years old."

"My species evidently matures more quickly than yours," she said.

"And those kids who put down Nueva's coup were apprenticed, as a matter of course, to specialists once they turned fourteen."

"They can't be much older now," Acorna protested.

"On the contrary," Johnny said in a very droll tone, "they are much, much older . . . now." With a hand under her elbow, he signaled her to jump to the level they were nearing on the shaft. "If they're beginning to find out how complicated it is to do it all themselves, it'll make my job easier."

"Finding someone a little more senior with enough experience to direct them?"

"Precisely." He pointed to starboard. "Infirmary's that way."

Since she could hear the moans and sobbing, his direction was unnecessary.

"I'll come back this way and see how you're doing. Even medics were not safe from Nueva's wholesale spacing orgy."

"Calum?" Rezar asked. "Could you come look at this? I don't know this kind of code."

Calum had been overseeing several panels for the appointed novice crew as well as giving Dr. Hoa a hand with the math. ["Never my strong suit, Mr. Baird." "Well, it is mine, and you've merely inverted the matrix that defines nonlinear diffraction-process interaction too soon—or tried to; the matrix can't be inverted, so you have to transform it to this form first. See? Now you get the right answer."]

"That's beamed at Rushima, which no longer has any com units. Broadcast on a wide beam so we're catching the edges of it. Use the finer tuner and put it up on screen. No, this toggle."

The message immediately began blaring from the bridge speakers until Rezar figured out how to modulate its volume.

"This is Blidkoff of Shenjemi Federation calling." Even the tone sounded bored with the words. "Rushima, reply. Urgent. You must respond if you expect any aid."

"He sounds real interested," Rezar said sarcastically.

Calum glanced up at 'Ziana. "I'd say Rushima needs help from whatever source it can get it."

•

'Ziana regarded him steadily. "But this ship caused the damage."

"Ah"—Calum held up one finger—"yes, my initial message to them said Rushima was under attack by the Starfarers."

"The real Starfarers"—'Ziana indicated herself—"are once again in control of *Haven*. Our . . ." she had to swallow before she could continue, ". . . mothers and fathers believed that peaceful protest would allow us to use some uninhabited world as a new home, since Esperantza was destroyed."

"You have been traveling a long time," Calum said kindly.

"The Shenjemi could demand reparations from us. . . ." she said.

"Not you . . . and you've logs to prove it," he said, pointing to a ceiling device that was the visual log of all proceedings on the bridge. "I can answer as myself. Shall I? And we can sort the *Haven*'s part out later. We have to give some answer. The Rushimese are in a bad way down there."

"We've been in a bad way up here, too, Baird."

"Ah, but I can restore much of the normal climatic pattern in just a few days," Dr. Hoa said, "after first inducing some more . . . extraordinary . . . weather to quickly counteract the worst effects of what has been done."

"Can you?" 'Ziana looked around at the frail man, who nodded vigorously.

"This is Blidkoff, Second Undersecretary of RUI Affairs, calling Rushima. Can you respond, Rushima? Are you under attack?"

Calum moved to the com unit. "Blidkoff, this is Calum Baird of the *Acadecki*, a private vessel. I sent the message you received. The planet has been under attack, and the first thing to go were the satellite communications."

"Baird? Calum Baird? No such name exists on the planetary roster." Blidkoff was plainly skeptical.

"Because I'm not Rushimese," Calum said. "I'll repeat. I am Pilot Calum Baird of the *Acadecki*, a private vessel. We had a 'ponics problem and thought Rushima could help us with it. Instead, we had to help them by informing you of the attack. The whole planet's in a bad way. They're going to need a lot of help to get sorted out down there."

"View please," Blidkoff answered, his skepticism coming through loud and clear.

'Ziana was wagging her arms in protest, but a grinning Rezar made a frame around Calum's face, indicating that he'd broadcast just the face. Calum looked over his shoulder for 'Ziana's permission, and, after a moment with her eyes closed, she nodded.

"Oh, sorry, didn't realize the view was off on my end," Calum said. He beamed at the screen for Blidkoff's benefit.

"And what exactly did you perceive was a problem with Rushima? Apart from their failure to communicate through normal channels?"

Pompous brainless regolithic idiot, Calum thought to himself, keeping his smile intact. "Storms, floods, and drought."

"They must be inventing disaster to get off paying their taxes. That planet was selected for its incredibly boring and stable climate."

"It's a large planet, Blidkoff," Calum said, no longer willing to be the victim of the man's incredulity. "And as your first spurt informed you, these disasters were artificially created by their attackers . . . who have now been disposed of, but the settlers are in dire need of basic supplies to help them start over. You do what you want. I promised Joshua Flouse I'd send you a Mayday. I have. Good day to—"

"Now, let's not get in a huff, Pilot Baird. Joshua Flouse . . . eff—eel—o—"

"U ess ee," Calum finished.

"Well, he's a reliable community leader."

"I suspect he is. Decent chap, gave us seed and enough vegetation to keep us going, even though they'll be in need themselves. So why don't you go on and keep him going?"

"I fear that's beyond my area of command," Blidkoff began. "Rushima's return on investment is insufficient to justify the expense of further Federation assistance."

"That's your problem, Blidkoff, and I'm sorry for the Rushimese, but at least I've kept my promise." And Calum himself cut the connection.

A buzz interrupted the silence on the bridge.

"He wants to talk to you again," Rezar said, looking hopefully up at Calum.

Calum looked around at 'Ziana, who seemed in an equal quandary.

"You kids got rid of the nasties, but now what?" He could see 'Ziana swallow.

"Now we have to carry the can for those

Palomellese bastards' mistakes," Rezar said.

"That's what being adult is," Calum said gently, feeling sorry for so much shit dumping on these teenagers who, only a few weeks ago, probably had been nice normal kids, fussing because no one would take them seriously.

"We should have a meeting about this," Kerratz said.

"Mother said that, too, that adults . . ." and, Ziana paused a moment before she rushed, ". . . are not afraid to accept responsibility. I took that one to heart when we gassed the tubes and spaced the murderers of our parents. I guess it applies here. We'll stay, and we'll make good as much as we can . . . with Dr. Hoa's help."

"And then I am taking myself and my weather program out of reach of anyone else," Dr. Hoa said.

"I think I may be able to help you there, Dr. Hoa," Calum said. "How much longer do you need?"

"Oh, I'm just starting, Mr. Baird. What was done to Rushima cannot be undone as quickly, but we're making progress. Yes, indeed, we are making progress. Now, would you check my equations again? I shouldn't like a simple error on my part to undo what I've been able to accomplish so far."

"But this is your program, isn't it?" Calum said as he went to the doctor's position.

"Oh, it is, but I always had a mathematician assisting me. Meteorology is science, my boy, but mathematics is a black art."

"Did you want me to help with the damage

reports, 'Ziana?" Johnny, returned from escort duty to Acorna, said so suavely that none of the people on the bridge could take offense. It was obvious none of them had thought of that.

With great dignity, 'Ziana nodded in his direction. "Please, would you, Johnny? You've had a lot more experience in that area than we have."

"You're learning," he said with his engaging grin.

Johnny concentrated on checking out the essential functions for the *Haven*. and apart form some damage by weapons fire—fortunately only stunners had been used rather than missile hand-guns—the hull had taken no integral damange. The conduits wuld need further flushing and venting to remove the traaces of the gases used . . . and any remaining bodies had to be found and removed. Not the most agreeable of duties, but it needed to be done.When Johnny looked around to see whom Markel could suggenst for the task, the lad was gone.

Markel, in fact, had gone back to the quarters he had shared with his father to see if any of his things were still there. The rooms had been trashed. He took one look and pressed the lock. He'd find himself somewhere else to stay. He'd also find himself some clean clothes. He'd had enough of these.

The main clothing storage was locked, of course, but his little strip of plastic did its trick, and he was in. The place still had a faint trace of the gases that had been used to trap Nueva and her gang, proba-bly the stuff was still trickling from any vents that hadn't been closed. Something would clearly have to be done about it soon. So he made a quick selection of clothing and new ship shoes—Acorna had healed all the cuts and bruises he'd acquired in his adventures, but ship shoes would add to his new dignity. He also picked up a tool belt and a notepad, since his was still on the *Acadecki,* with the few personal items he had managed to save when he decided he'd better not be found by Nueva or any of her conspirators.

He did wonder that there were so few people in the corridors and halls. Maybe 'Ziana should make a shipwide announcement that Second Gen had complete control of the *Haven.*

Then he shafted over to 'ponics, which was looking very sad indeed, though Neggara and her group were already planting some vats.

"I need some stuff for Acorna. She'll be using up a lot of energy healing, you know," he said.

Neggara craned her neck around at him. Then she grinned. "Since it's you, and for her, you're welcome to anything that's edible. Though that ain't much."

"You've got the big leaves still." Markel pointed to the basic pumpkin, rhubarb, and legume leaves that would indeed be essential to air refreshing. He said nothing at all about Acorna's ability to clean air. But he was pretty sure that was what this ship was operating on right now.

Neggara was shaking her head. "Don't understand it. According to the manuals, they aren't enough to do what they have to be doing in terms of restoring clean air to the entire ship."

"We got lucky, I guess," Markel said, and picked

what he thought would be a useful bouquet of greens and some early legume pods for Acorna.

What Neggara didn't know wouldn't hurt her — or Acorna — but, as he left the 'ponics section, he did worry that the Lady would not have enough strength both to heal the wounded AND purify the ship's air. However, he had managed not to smirk with his covert knowledge of who was really responsible for the fact that they weren't all gasping for breath on the *Haven*.

Acorna was just bending over an unconscious Palomellese with serious stun bruising all down his left side when Markel arrived at the sick bay. As Markel approached, he heard her sigh, and knew he'd been right to rustle up some food for her. She seemed to be working her way into the infirmary, for there were already many empty bunks at the front of the room. Medics were buzzing in small groups, watching her surreptitiously.

Markel waited just out of Acorna's range until she had finished the current patient.

"Gotcha something to help you," Markel said, holding out his bouquet to her just as one of the senior medics started to protest his interference.

Acorna held up one hand, then smiled with weary gratitude for his thoughtfulness. She couldn't know it, nor did Markel realize the significance of his altruism, but seeing that Acorna was fed was probably one of the first unselfish things he had ever done. Even in rescuing her, he had been acting out of self interest.

"And I think you'd better lie down when you've eaten . . . you look absolutely transparent," Markel

said, giving a level and accusing glance at the medic.
"I don't see anyone bleeding to death," he added,
having made a quick assessment of those still abed.
"I'll never hear the end of it from Calum and 'Ziana
if you pass out on us, you know."

The way Acorna wobbled as she rose was sufficient evidence to the medical staff that this
intruder's assessment of her condition was undeni-
ably accurate. The head medic almost leapt forward
to assist her, but Markel was closer and took her
arm as if by right.

"You haven't used up all the private compartments, have you?" Markel asked.

"This way." The medic ushered her into one of
the cubicles. "We're very grateful, lady, and didn't
realize that you . . ." Markel firmly closed the panel
on the apologies.

"There's not much selection in 'ponics, right
now," he said, placing his gleanings on her lap.

"Doesn't matter," she said, stuffing chard into her
face and chewing with weary efficiency. "Anything
green'll do fine. There are so many more—"

"Who can probably recover just fine in the usual
way," Markel cut in firmly. "We need you more to
keep the air fresh in this ship with the 'ponics in the
condition it's in."

Acorna gave a weary sigh, munching on the
legumes and the stalks, too.

"You can't do everything yourself, you know," he
said. "Isn't there anything else you can eat that we'd
have on board? Somehow just those . . ." His fingers dismissed the limp chard leaves as insignificant.

"Any vegetable ration bars? I cannot live on them

for any long stretch of time, but they will keep me from starving through the immediate future."

"Thousands," Markel said, immensely relieved. "That's what we've had to feed the Palomellese with. I'll be back in a flash."

As soon as he exited the compartment, the head medic caught him.

"Is she all right? We didn't . . ."

"Well, it takes a lot of energy to do what she does, you know," Markel said, trying to make out Acorna was worse off than she was to be sure they wouldn't interrupt her until she'd had some rest. "You don't happen to have any vegetable ration bars up here, do you?"

They did and loaded Markel down with as many as he could carry. He took them in to her. She had finished all the fresh greens—if that was what you could call the limp leaves—and gratefully shed the packaging film protecting the first bar. She ate nine before suddenly she seemed to collapse inward and sprawl across the bunk.

"Acorna?" Markel reached for her delicate arm, even if he hadn't a clue where he'd find a pulse on it.

She clasped his arm, weakly, but turned her head and smiled at him.

"I'll be fine. You stand guard, will you, Markel? I'll just need a bit of sleep while I digest that fine meal."

Markel could not agree with her notion of a "fine meal" as he spread the light thermal over her and tiptoed out of the compartment.

"She's sleeping," he told the head medic, then snagged a four-legged stool, which he put against the door. He sat, crossed his arms over his chest, and assumed his role as guardian.

He was also asleep, head drooping over one shoulder but supported by the door he guarded, when Calum and Johnny came down to find Acorna.

"You know," Johnny said thoughtfully, hands on his belt and elbows cocked to the side, as he looked down at his protégé, "Markel might turn out to be a fine man after all. Though"—he waggled a finger at Calum—"never tell him I said so."

"Last thing on my mind," Calum said, making a cross over his heart.

So they waited until Acorna emerged from the room, and just managed to catch her guard before he fell into the compartment. His reflexes had him on his feet and in a defensive position against the wall before he was awake enough to see who was there.

"Well, you look a lot better," he said to Acorna in the tone of a worried parent, straightening his tunic and brushing back his hair. "Sleep did you good, didn't it?"

If Calum had to turn away and Johnny had to cough to disguise his chuckle, Acorna affectionately smoothed Markel's hair.

"Yes, it did." She looked past Johnny to see the head medic eagerly approach her. "There's an urgency—"

"Well, it will have to wait," Johnny said firmly, taking Acorna by the arm. "The bridge has need of Acorna right now!"

In point of fact, it was the 'ponics system which

needed Acorna, and she did what she could to clean the air.

"How much of that gas was used?" she asked, sneezing.

"The kids wanted to be sure," Johnny said at his driest.

"We could rig blowers," Calum said, remembering how they had managed to clear air in the early days of Maganos Moon Base. "What sort of equipment is available, Markel?"

"Well, we can find out easy enough," Markel said, and turned toward the nearest shaft. "But it'll have to be from the bridge computer."

"I'll go back to the infirmary then," Acorna said, starting in that direction, but it was Calum this time who grabbed her.

"No. You are going back to sleep," he said firmly. "Your horn is practically transparent, and the rest of you doesn't look much better."

"There are still people in need—"

"Nothing our own medics can't handle," said Andreziana, who had been calling up reports from the infirmary while they talked. She backed Calum up. "You have done too much, Acorna . . . and we have other problems to solve now that you cannot help with."

"What?"

"First, we must repair the damage to the *Haven.* Then, Dr. Hoa has promised to work on his weather program, to see if there is some way he can control it so as to correct the damage done by our ship and his science to Rushima . . . if they will accept the offer." Andreziana's emotional and physical exhaustion made her look, briefly, much older than her chrono-logical age. "Whether by use of Dr. Hoa's technical expertise, or by the work of our own hands, we must make what reparations we can to the settlers of Rushima. That is our problem, not yours."

"The Shenjemi Federation . . ."

"Have realized that the situation is critical, yes," Johnny Greene said, "and help is on its way. But 'Ziana is right. The First-Gen Starfarers were men and women of honor who would have done every-thing possible to repair the damage caused by use of their ship. I'm proud to see these kids following in the tradition."

With this assurance, Acorna felt justified in taking a few extra hours for rest. Hours turned into several days, as she fell into a deep healing sleep from which she awakened at intervals only long enough to con-sume immense quantities of the most mineral-rich greens the *Haven* could provide. "I wish I could get her dirtside," Calum fretted. "Rushima's a mess, but she needs to run, and breathe air that hasn't been recycled, and eat something that didn't grow in a vat."

"I think that can be arranged," Markel told him. Calum had been watching over Acorna too obses-sively to pay much attention to the repair work on the *Haven* or the ongoing discussions with the Rushimese. "Hoa's ready to work his weather magic now, but we're going to need to temporarily resettle the Rushimese from the worst flooded area while he arranges a few minor cataclysms to fix things up."

"Good idea," Calum approved absently. "Now, Acorna—"

"Is going to have to be with our resettlement party," Markel said. "Otherwise, they won't go anywhere with us. Acorna's the only one they trust. In fact, we were hoping that you and she would be willing to use the *Acadecki* to ferry settlers—because they have a pronounced, if justifiable, aversion to any of our landing craft."

"Sounds good to me," Calum said. "Soon as she's really awake, we'll get started."

Acorna was clearly healing herself in these periods of deep sleep, restoring the energies depleted by her efforts on behalf of the Starfarers and their wounded ship, and he had no intention of interrupting that process. He returned to watching over her obsessively, feeling more relieved than anything else that their friends on Maganos did not know to transmit queries to the *Haven*. After sending a "Disregard previous message, everything's all right," from the *Acadecki* immediately after they were sure the countercoup had succeeded, he'd shut down the *Acadecki* and joined in the work of rebuilding the *Haven*. He did not particularly want to communicate with Maganos again until he could assure them Acorna was perfectly well. Call him a coward, but there were some things he'd rather not tell Gill and Rafik, much less Delszaki Li and Uncle Hafiz. This—an Acorna too worn-out to stay awake—was definitely one of those things.

Eleven

Laboue, Unified Federation Date 334.05.22

*H*afiz had never been so long out of communication with his various colleagues
and interstellar financiers. No amount
of pacing up and down his underground refuge
would ease his churning mind.

"There is really NO point at all in such ferretlike
isolation. There hasn't been a single explosion registered on the equipment. There haven't been any
landings anywhere. Am I a slave, to live in prison,
or a woman, to dwell in purdah?"

His pacing had brought him back once again to
that portion of the garden where the Skarness
Stones were located. Although his establishment
was completely underground, and shielded by formidable appliances, he could actually stand just
beneath the position of the Stones.

He clapped his hands to summon a human ser-
vant. "Bring me a thin rod, of metal, not silver nor
gold, but base metal, of two arm-spans' length. No,
misbegotten whelp of a djinni's basest lusts, how
should I know where such a thing is to be found?

Inquire of the steward, and do not trouble me with such matters." Once the rod had been located, he demanded a ladder. "Now position it . . . no, never mind. Guard the door to this corridor, and let no one enter until I give permission. I shall be . . . at my devotions." No need for any to observe the procedure which he had invented for communicating with the Stones from this underground refuge; and if they wondered what sort of devotions required this equipment, why, let them wonder!

The manual labor of placing a stepladder was beneath his dignity, but by great good fortune he hit the D Stone with his first try. Then, placing his forehead and both hands on the rod, he tapped out his urgent query.

"Has Laboue been invaded?"

There was no immediate answer. He hadn't expected a prompt reply—but he expected some reaction. Besides, it was undignified for a man of his eminence and prestige to remain in this semisubservient posture, even if he had taken care not to be observed. Also, the metal rod was beginning to wear a groove into his forehead. He daren't relax either his grip or the contact with the rod because he had to catch the rhythm of whatever message the Skarness Stones had for him.

"Clear sky."

Hafiz thanked them and stood upright, dropping the rod with a clang as he alternately rubbed the ridges on his hands and forehead. Then he wondered just what that cryptic message did mean. "Clear skies" because the weather was fair; "clear skies" because these monsters had landed; or "clear skies" because whatever had been headed toward Laboue had gone around the planet?

He convinced himself the last interpretation was the most likely, since no detection equipment known to mankind could have pierced the shell currently protecting the inmates — and there was no truer definition of those who resided on, or under, Laboue right now. So it had to be safe. The Stones would not have lied to him. They didn't know how.

Hafiz did get in touch with Qulabriel as protocol required.

"I'm going above, Qulabriel. I must be in touch with my people, to reassure them. I will report on the condition of the surface once I have ascertained if any damage has been done. But I must surface."

"If you must, you must," Qulabriel replied in a grudging tone. "However, do not respond if there is any change in the surface at all. And a thorough scan, please."

"Has not the Second Prophet admonished us, 'Do what thou shalt do, but do all in order and as fitting My children'?" Hafiz replied genially, while vowing that some day Qulabriel would pay for the tone of voice he had just used to the Head of House Harakamian.

The process of unshielding and rising took time. Hafiz had the ladder placed in one of the upper rooms, at the tallest window near the ceiling so that he could countermand the action if he found reason to do so.

He saw no danger, as his dwelling made a stately ascent into the fresh, clear air of Laboue. All around, of course, where other gardens should be, and other dwellings hidden within them, there was blank and featureless space. For the Shielding provided Laboue with a sterile desert surface in some places or rampant, impenetrable jungle vistas which clearly said to any observer that this planet wasn't worth further inspection.

Clambering down the ladder while his extensive household was still climbing up out of its basement retreat, Hafiz made his way to his office and reactivated his contact with the receivers implanted in one of Laboue's little moons.

Messages came flooding in to his receiver. Those from Rafik went from queries to near-hysterical demands for reply. Some of the later ones from his associates also ranged from moderate concern to the hysteria that characterized Rafik's.

"It's nice to know that I've been missed," Hafiz said, until he realized that he had also missed out on a fine coup and a large profit. He got more and more upset as he began to tote up just how much money the isolation had cost him in terms of deals unanswered and missed opportunities. When he got his hands around the necks of those . . . those . . . what had they called themselves? . . . Linyaari, he would show them not to deceive the Head of House Harakamian with such dramatic hoaxes.

Yelling for his servants to ready his spacecraft and telling his chief steward to report to Qulabriel, Hafiz almost ran to the hangar in his anxiety to be airborne and back in the midst of the world from which he had temporarily excluded himself. He must show himself in person at the trading centers of his personal empire, and at once. Who knew how long it would take him to repair the damage done? Who knew what negotiating it would take to prove that the Head of House Harakamian was not a coward, diving underground at the first sign of danger? What had made him panic so badly at those obviously manufactured scenes shown by the Linyaari?

He was already demanding a nav plan for Twi Osiam when he calmed down enough to wonder, again, whether the scenes broadcast to Laboue might not have been real and not a hoax. After all, the people who had broadcast their warning were Acorna's folk. He'd never known her to lie . . . but of course, his beloved nephew had raised the girl so she would value truth. A pity, that . . . with better training, she might have been most useful to him in the business dealings of House Harakamian. But she was so incurably candid that he suspected her species could not be other than straightforward. And why would they have shown their own species being tortured if there were not some substance to their outrageous claim that this part of the galaxy was in danger? That those . . . those . . . barbaric savages were on the loose in the immediate vicinity?

He sent a lucid message to Rafik on the *Uhuru*, mentioning that he was again in circulation and asking what Rafik had been able to save of their current deals without his authorization, which, in some cases, Rafik still must present to seal a contract.

He got back the signal, which meant the *Uhuru* was recording the message. Now where was Rafik?

If not on board his ship, he had better be doing business for House Harakamian. He received back the somewhat reassuring report that the *Uhuru* was currently docked at Maganos.

What but a threat to Acorna could have taken Rafik from his assigned business deals to Maganos? And should she not be apprised of the arrival of others like her? Worry and concern and a kindly desire to give Acorna this news in person inspired Hafiz to do something he had not considered in all his adult life: he put aside his business plans for a purely personal trip to Maganos Moon Base.

"At least the time of travel need not be a total loss," Hafiz told himself. Some at least of his complex business dealings could be rescued by long-distance communication, and he spent the time of the journey doing just that. He was requesting landing permission from Maganos Moon Base when a final message in the long line he had been receiving was from Rafik.

"Uncle, having no way of communicating with you, I have asked Delszaki Li to make arrangements on Acorna's behalf. I trust they will meet with your approval. I will report as soon as we reach Rushima."

"Rushima? Grushima?" Hafiz was totally outraged. He'd never heard of the place and tapped in a request for information, trying to control his temper. After all, he had authorized Rafik to operate on his own, finely tuned instincts. . . . "An agri planet?" he bellowed when the information came up. "Sponsored by the Shenjemi?"

Hafiz's dealings with the Shenjemi Federation

had not been all that remunerative, and Hafiz made his value judgments on profits made. He'd had few enough from the Federation.

"Why has Rafik gone off to Rushima anyway? It almost sounds as if he is following Acorna. What possessed the girl to take off just when her people appear in our space? Provola had better know exactly what's happening, or I may have to wait until Rafik's firstborn son shows what promise he might have," Hafiz said to the ship in general and no one, certainly not his crew, in particular.

When his ship docked at Maganos Moon Base Hafiz went straight to Delszaki Li's private offices, only to find them deserted. Not even the secretary who usually guarded the inner sanctum was at his post. As a consequence, Hafiz had no way of finding out that Mr. Li had briefly collapsed after the strain of the past few days and had been ordered to bed in Maganos's small hospital facility. The secretary who should have been receiving visitors and directing inquiries was instead hovering outside the closed doors of the hospital unit, waiting to hear of the recovery of an old man he had come to love like . . . well, not a father . . . more like a great-grandfather.

To be fair, Li had no reason to expect any need for his services; since the triumph of the Child Liberation League had obviated the need for secrecy, Mr. Li had more and more left the day-to-day management of his financial and business affairs in the hands of trusted subordinates. Furthermore, when he visited Maganos he considered himself "on holiday" and expected—and received—no visitors except those in his immediate circle of beloved friends—the three miners, the Kendoro siblings, and, of course, Acorna—all of whom were gone now. Not expecting Hafiz to lower the shield, let alone journey to Maganos, none of them had thought to leave him any explanations for their sudden departure. And the secretary, who, like most of the rest of Maganos, was not privy to the tale brought by the Linyaari envoys, had little to offer when Hafiz finally located him.

"Acorna and Calum left first, in the *Acadecki*—" Hafiz began.

"You know about that?" The secretary was stunned.

"I should," Hafiz said, "she's my ship. Continue, please."

"Well. Everybody was worried about that. The ship wasn't fitted up properly, you see. . . ." The secretary started off in some detail about the remodeling and improved defense plans for the *Acadecki*, which he did know something about, until Hafiz interrupted and very politely suggested that the man go on with his story about what had happened to cause a mass desertion of Maganos and Delszaki Li's collapse.

"Well, um, they arrested this . . . person," the secretary went on doubtfully, and wondered why his own tongue seemed to be fighting him. Of course it had been a person, a young man, he'd seen him, what else would you call him? But something else was diverting his attention from the story. . . .

"It's hard to talk with my collar twisted so tightly," the secretary said, "if you could . . ."

"A thousand apologies." Hafiz released his grip on the man's tunic, but not the steely-eyed glare that somehow brought to mind much worse things than simple assault . . . archaic words like bastinado and strappado floated through the secretary's jangling brain. Once released, he told Hafiz everything he could; unfortunately, that wasn't enough to allow any reconstruction of what had been going on in Li's private rooms. Other . . . "people" . . . had come. . . . For some reason, he had a hard time describing them or even remembering their appearance; all he knew for sure was that they were good people who meant no harm, and there was nothing unusual about them.

"And how," Hafiz inquired silkily, "do you 'know' all that?"

The secretary shook his head. "I just know. . . ."

Judit, Gill, and Pal had all gathered with Mr. Li to speak with them, and so had Rafik when he arrived. They kept the door closed, and the secretary couldn't hear anything except when somebody went in or out. Once he heard the new visitors speaking in a language that he couldn't identify.

"I didn't get it," the man said. "They had their own ship; they looked rich; doesn't everybody speak Galactic by now? I can't imagine where they could have come from."

"Who cares?" Hafiz snapped. "Go on."

There wasn't much left to tell. The strangers had left in their splendid ship; Judit, Gill, Pal, and Rafik had all left in the *Uhuru*; Delszaki Li had been so fatigued that despite frequent short naps while the talking went on, he had collapsed immediately after their departure and had been resting in the high-security medical unit ever since.

"They won't let anyone in to see him," the secretary said. "They just keep saying he's resting comfortably and doing as well as can be expected and all the usual blather." He looked at Hafiz with some hope. "The doctor might let you in."

But the Harakamian will met its match in a youngish, tired doctor whose first medical experience had been as a volunteer to patch up bruised and broken children on the day of the Liberation, and who revered Delszaki Li as a near saint.

"He's been heavily medicated and will remain so until I am satisfied that his physical condition has stabilized," the doctor snapped, "and until then, nobody disturbs him!"

"If you've got him doped to the eyeballs," Hafiz tactlessly translated the medicalese, "I don't suppose it would do me much good to look at his sleeping body."

Consumed with curiosity, he decided to pass the time until Li awoke or a message came from the *Uhuru* by finding out what had been done since his last visit to complete the mining facilities. A sudden thought struck him as he turned to make his way to the engineering offices. "Ah—Provola didn't take off for the back end of beyond also, did she?"

Reassured that Provola Quero was in her office as usual, Hafiz made his way there after leaving instructions that any news was to be forwarded at once to Provola's office, the suite which was kept for him in Maganos's living quarters, and any other place he might conceivably be found.

∗∗∗

The door to Provola's office was open, and from some distance Hafiz could hear a tearful voice pleading with Provola Quero and that woman's calm, cool, responses, obviously unmoved by the petition. As he entered, his eyes were taken by the unexpected sight of a generous womanly figure in lavender, nicely set off by white trim, and enhanced by a number of glittering crystals of various colors which quivered enticingly from the fine silver chains which draped the woman's voluptuous body. She would have made two of wiry little Provola Quero, with her ascetically cropped head and single tight braid—and in Hafiz's estimation, a true woman like this was worth ten of an engineer-female like Provola.

"My dear Mr. Harakamian," Provola said with more warmth than Hafiz had ever heard in the woman's voice before. She was not his type, and not even feminine in her appearance, but she was an excellent manager. She turned to the female. "I must ask you to leave now."

"But where can I leave TO?" was the tearful reply, plump white hands with beringed fingers wide open in appeal. "I only had enough credit to get here to help darling Acorna. . . ."

"And why, my dear . . ." Hafiz paused to allow for an introduction.

"Karina . . ." both women said at once.

Hafiz could not resist seizing the delightfully plump white hand now extended in supplication to him. And he kissed and stroked it while with his other hand he gestured to Provola that he would handle this.

As he guided Karina out of Provola's inner office, he could hear her sigh of relief.

"My dear Karina, why did you think that Acorna needed help?" Hafiz said, gesturing around at the well-appointed waiting room and the busy corridor outside.

"But she does," Karina insisted, and then his name dropped into the proper slot in her retentive memory, "dear Mr. Harakamian."

"Let us discuss this matter in the privacy of my quarters," Hafiz said at his most persuasive and in his silkiest tone. He hadn't seen a woman of these delicious proportions in so long. Nowadays the emphasis was on trim, slim, svelte, bony feminine figures, and he'd about given up the hope of finding one that would be so enticing to him. It was an added attraction that she seemed to know something about Acorna's present situation.

Karina's eyes widened. "You have rooms here . . . on Maganos?"

"I have many personal and business connections with the House of Li," Hafiz explained, leading her toward Living Quarters A. "A suite of rooms is kept constantly maintained and at my disposal . . . or is supposed to be." He finished with a scowl as he placed his palm on the reader beside the door to his suite and the door slowly irised open to reveal rooms that had clearly quite recently suffered from the recent invasion of a careless bachelor. Datacubes and vids littered the floor, never having been put back in their individual cases; a natty suit in lime green and fuchsia lay crumpled at the entrance to the shower cube; and a half-empty glass making rings on the polished Tanqque purpleheart wood of the nearest table testified by its smell that the recent occupant of these rooms had taken to heart the Second Prophet's relaxation of the restrictions on spirituous liquors.

"My heir," Hafiz growled. "Soon to be my ex-heir if he does not mend his ways!" He activated the wall console and requested a thorough cleaning for the suite, then suggested to Karina that they should repair to one of the small dining rooms off the main cafeteria instead. "And when Rafik comes back," he said, "if he comes back, I shall enroll him in the Personal Hygiene and Cleanliness classes taught to the children of Maganos, for clearly he is in sore need of basic instruction!" The thought of tall, dignified Rafik cramped into a child's desk and lectured on the need to clean his teeth properly tickled Hafiz's fancy and dispelled most of his anger.

Karina dispelled the rest of it by asking how he could possibly be annoyed with such a fine, brave, handsome man as Rafik, and vowing that she had recognized him instantly from his resemblance to Rafik. If she had in fact done so, it would have been a remarkable feat of imagination, since Hafiz was six inches shorter and thirty pounds heavier than Rafik, and his creased face, now consciously amiable, bore a strong resemblance to that of a crocodile hoping that some day another fat, brown child would tumble down the bank. However, to Karina, hungry and stranded for days on a strange planet without credit, Hafiz looked truly beautiful as he led her to a small dining room where he requested a tray of cream pastries and his special blend of kava.

"Now, dear Karina, do tell me how it happens that a friend of Acorna's should have been left in this sad plight," Hafiz invited her, "and what you would like me to do to the villains who abandoned you so."

"Oh," Karina said, "they are not villains, they are Enlightened Beings, and I am almost sure they did not mean to leave me in desperate straits, only they were in a hurry, and, of course, I had not told them I had no credits left. How could I? You do see, don't you?"

"Of course," Hafiz agreed urbanely, although totally confused.

"They have beautiful auras, you know," Karina rambled on, "as of course you'd expect of Acorna's race—"

"The Linyaari are here?" Hafiz interrupted her. Although he had put aside both his current business dealings and the tempting thought of making an exclusive trade agreement with the first sapient aliens to contact human civilization in order to look after Acorna, now that he was actually at Maganos and nobody seemed to be panicking on Acorna's behalf, he could not help thinking how lucrative such an arrangement might be . . . and that he, as one of Acorna's two guardians, should by rights have first pickings. He had not reckoned on her other guardian somehow magicking the Linyaari to his residence first.

"Well, not anymore. They went after—"

"Ten thousand Shaitans! I should have known that crafty old dog of an unbeliever would get ahead of me!" Hafiz drummed his fingers on the tabletop, temporarily oblivious to Karina. "But perhaps Rafik has protected my interests. Yes, that must be what he meant by 'arrangements.'" The downward creases on his face lifted slightly. "In that case, I may well forgive the boy after all. Karina, my dear lady, I must speak with Delszaki Li's secretary again at once; can you ever forgive me?"

Karina's eyes darkened with a sorrow that was not entirely due to the fact that she had not quite finished the last of the pastries. "But we've only just met!"

"And I look forward to many delightful hours improving our acquaintance," Hafiz assured her. "And although my business is pressing, I refuse to leave unless you promise me that you will take proper care of yourself and eventually retire to my suite to rest. You must eat to keep up your strength and to maintain your exquisite beauty." He called for a portable console and left orders for Karina to be able to request anything she desired at the charge of House Harakamian.

That should be safe enough, he thought cynically; there was nothing to buy on Maganos Moon Base except food and the simplest of basic necessities. Later he would give himself the pleasure of ordering new garments from Kezdet for this generously endowed beauty, a project that would absolutely require him to acquaint himself with her exact dimensions, and later . . . who knew what might not follow? Best not to alarm her; he would not want such a treasure of voluptuous womanhood to take flight while he was occupied in business talks.

His first order of business was to extract from

the secretary the terms of any trade agreements that
had already been filed. With any luck there had not
been time to put anything on disk. Opportunity
abounded when a man was prepared to take advantage of it. Then, if Li was still not available, he could
while away the hours of waiting by courting his
lovely Karina. It seemed his trip to Maganos would
be profitable in more ways than he could have ever
predicted.

Twelve

*I*t was nearly six days before Acorna started staying awake for more than a few minutes at a time, but then she returned to normal within a few hours of her last awakening.

"You mean those poor people have been waiting all this time only for me?" she exclaimed, horrified. "Calum, why did you not go on without me?"

"I," Calum said, "do not possess a sweet voice, a pretty face, or a magical horn. The mere fact that I was around and helped to repair their com system doesn't seem to be enough to make me Trustworthy. It's you or nobody."

"Then you should have wakened me sooner!"

Markel and Calum looked at each other and tried not to laugh.

"We should've taken vids," Markel said. "Acorna, you *have* been awake, off and on—vertical, anyway. Just long enough to use the facilities and devastate our chard and spinach beds. Then you'd stagger off without saying a word and go back to sleep."

Acorna shook her head. "I cannot believe it."

"Next time we *will* take vids!"

"There won't be a next time," Calum said. "I'm not letting Acorna wear herself out to that extent ever again."

The Rushimese required that the *Acadecki* land first with only Acorna and Calum on board; they did not trust vids of Acorna speaking to them from the *Haven*.

"I just hope that you'll be able to convince them that the kids really want to make reparations for the devastation caused during Nueva's coup," Calum said wearily as they landed. "If they won't let us use the *Haven*'s shuttlecraft as well as the *Acadecki* to ferry settlers from the flooded area to high ground, we'll be here for weeks before Dr. Hoa can start work on drying out this settlement."

"I will try to persuade them," Acorna said, "but it may take time. . . ."

Calum chuckled weakly. "And to think we thought we were saving time by skipping out of Maganos before the repairs were complete! If we'd waited until the 'ponics were fixed, we wouldn't have been caught up in this mess, we might have been well on our way to searching the Coma Berenices quadrant by now. . . . Well, my mother always told me, 'Haste makes waste,' but I was always in too much of a hurry to listen to her."

"It is not a waste if we are able to help people desperately in need," Acorna said, but her lovely eyes clouded over at this reminder of how much time the stopover at Rushima had cost them. "Someday we will find my people . . . and you know, Calum, if we had waited for Pal and Mr. Li to agree that the *Acadecki* was ready, we would still be on Maganos!"

Calum had to agree with that. Still, he hoped that the Rushimese got over their suspicions of the *Haven* quickly. The longer he was away from Mercy, the more he missed her . . . and since he had promised himself to see Acorna safely with her own people before he was free to be with Mercy, it was a kind of torture to be delayed and delayed here, where they had barely begun their quest.

"The settlers are arriving," Acorna said. "Let me see what I can do to get them organized, and you can try to raise Maganos." She gave him an understanding smile. "Mercy, I mean, all our friends, will want to know what we are doing."

Calum found that he did not particularly like being "understood." One of the many things he liked about Mercy was that even if she could guess what he was thinking, she never told him so!

Oh, well, soon enough they would be on their way out to the Coma Berenices quadrant, and he could apply himself to nice straightforward problems of astrogation instead of the most chaotic, unpredictable problems of all . . . people.

Still, this might well be his last chance to communicate with Mercy in private; it was thoughtful of Acorna to give him the opportunity. For the first time in days, Calum activated the *Acadecki*'s com unit.

Before Calum could enter his request, though, the com unit gave forth the nerve-wracking squeal that signaled an incoming spurt-message. He sighed and waited the interminable seconds while the spurt codes chattered across the screen, then watched a blurry image gradually become clearer and clearer as the *Acadecki*'s computer expanded the compressed message. As the face on the screen became recognizable, Calum sat upright and tensed.

What was Rafik doing in this sector, close enough to send compressed visuals? Had their first message from the *Haven* gotten through after all, sending Rafik on a wild-goose chase to rescue them? He'd never live that down. . . .

Rafik's first intelligible words, once the entire spurt was expanded, proved this was not the case; the call for help had not in fact been received, but the "all clear" message had. And Rafik was coming on a completely different errand. Calum listened with growing surprise, replayed the message not once but twice to make sure he had understood it correctly, then set the com receivers on "automatic." He had to find Acorna at once!

They had set the *Acadecki* down in the muddy lake where they'd first landed, thinking that a logical place to start the restoration of Rushima would be with Joshua Flouse and the settlers who already knew Calum and Acorna. Once these waterlogged hectares had been dried out and restored to productivity, the Rushimese would be more likely to trust the good intentions of the Second-Generation kids who now controlled the *Haven*. But Dr. Hoa had warned that the process of draining and drying the area through weather modification was likely to be brutal; even with Calum's mathematical help, they could neither predict nor control effects with the accuracy desirable when working over populated communities.

Calum was rather disconcerted when he came out to find the landing area deserted, while Acorna stood fetlock-deep in the clarified water, absentmindedly picking up and tasting small floating strands of filamentous algae. "Hey, where'd everybody go?"

"They are building rafts," Acorna informed him, "to ferry their possessions across the pond. There was some discussion of asking us to set down in a drier spot, but they could not agree on one; every little hill that is not actually underwater is too full of livestock and refugees."

"Oh. Well, their choice, I guess," Calum said, "as long as they don't take too long about it. . . ." With Rafik's amazing news to impart, he couldn't really get too interested in the settlers' logistical problems. "Anyway, I've got something to tell you. Acorna, we don't need to go on in the *Acadecki*. There'll be no need to test my program to find your home."

The jubilant note in Calum's voice startled Acorna.

"What are you talking about?" She had never seen Calum like this before. His eyes blazed, and his fair hair stuck up in an untidy quiff along the top of his head.

"I've heard from the *Uhuru*. Rafik is coming here."

"Rafik?" She felt slow and stupid, unable to think clearly. Something very important was about to happen, or had happened; she couldn't tell which. It wasn't about Rafik, though; so she

focused on the details to slow down the important
thing, which she was not ready to hear. "But he was
not on Maganos or Laboue. How did he know we
were here?"

"He was on Maganos when our message got
through. And you'll never guess why!"

Acorna thought she did not want to guess.

"Does he know everything is all right now?" she
asked.

Calum had sent another message as soon as they
knew the situation on board the *Haven*, but perhaps
Rafik had taken off for Rushima before that spurt
came through. Why else would he be coming?

"I guess so." Calum scrubbed one hand over his
head; the short yellow hair flattened like hay under
a great wind, then sprang up again, quivering with
excitement. "I mean, he must; I gather only the second message got through. The first one must have
been killed when I shut down so fast. But there's
other news. Acorna, he's not coming alone. Like I
just said, we don't need to go on with the search for
your home."

It had been the first thing he'd said, and she had
known at once what it must mean. She had been
holding the meaning away from her, bracing herself
against it, trying to keep him from saying it with all
her questions about Rafik. But it could be delayed
no longer.

"They have found us," she said, slowly, and
regretted it the next instant. Half the bright exulta-
tion drained from Calum's face.

"Yes—I wanted to tell you. How did you know?"

"I guessed. Why else would he stop here?"

Acorna felt as if she were feeling her way with bare hooves across a shaking quagmire, treacherous ground that might dissolve under her at any moment. "So . . . they are coming for me?"

Calum confirmed her guess.

"With Rafik?"

"They have their own ship, of course. They think it is faster; Rafik is not so sure, but he wanted to be sure you had the news before they reached Rushima. He thought it might be too great a shock if you saw them without warning."

"That was . . . considerate of him." Shock? What was that? This numbness through which she moved, half-disembodied, half-sinking under feelings she did not recognize—was *that* shock? She felt as if she had been poisoned; her limbs tingled, and her eyes could not take in the light that had been there a moment ago. If she had really been poisoned, though, she would be able to heal herself. And this moving darkness was not something she could heal with a touch of her horn.

"Acorna?" Calum sounded far away. "Acorna! Are you all right? I thought you'd be happy!"

"Of course I'm happy," she said with an effort. She forced a smile to her lips. "My people. My dream come true. How could I be anything else but happy, dear Calum?"

"Well, that's what I thought," he said, still sounding doubtful, "but for a moment you looked almost ill. Are you coming down with something, do you think? But you shouldn't . . . you don't get sick."

"No more I do," she agreed, with another smile. "I think I was a little dizzy for a moment. It was quite a shock, you know." She thought of the disappointment that Calum must have been loyally concealing. Such a good friend . . . he and Gill and Rafik had always been so good to her, the only family she had ever known. He had wanted to discover her home himself, not have the location handed to him. The least she could do now was play up to him.

"And, Calum, now we will not have to wait months to find out whether your deductions were correct. My . . . people will surely be able to tell us the exact location from which they came. Won't it be interesting to find out whether it matches the destination we chose on the basis of your program?" He could still have the satisfaction of being proved accurate . . . if he had been correct.

Calum grinned. "You're right! We don't need a construction proof; we'll have an existence one! And another thing—"

"Calum, you know I don't speak mathematics," Acorna said in warning.

"Not about my program. About your people! Rafik says they are telepathic, isn't that wonderful? And they have a very high code of ethics; it took them quite a time to decide whether we were worthy to know them." Calum blithely condensed what Rafik had already abbreviated, the Linyaari discussion over whether humans were linyarii or khlevii. "Oh, by the way, they call themselves Linyaari, although I expect it just means something like 'People' in their language. Their technology is way beyond ours in some respects—apparently they've got some kind of automatic language-learning system. The ones who are coming already speak Basic, so you'll be able to talk to them right away, isn't that great? And best of all, Acorna, one of them is your aunt!" Calum beamed as if he were giving her a wonderful present.

"Talk to them?" Acorna said faintly.

"Yes, right away. Although now I think of it, you probably won't need to use Basic. If they're telepathic, you must be, too. You'll just be able to merge minds with them."

"That's . . . wonderful."

Calum looked suddenly uncertain. "Your own people, a family of your own . . . Acorna, don't quite forget us, will you? Gill and Rafik and me?"

Acorna stood up, pleased to find that her legs would, after all, support her. Standing, she was now taller than this one of her three foster parents.

"Calum, I will never forget you. You three are my family, and nothing can change that," she said firmly. "But I . . . I need to think. Do you mind if I go out for a run now? I can think better in the fresh air."

"All right, but be careful, won't you? All that heavy weather's done some funny things to the terrain. You don't want to go spraining an ankle or getting your mane snagged in a wire fence," Calum warned, exactly like any overanxious parent who can't quite grasp that his or her child is grown-up.

The fetlock-deep water slowed Acorna and forced her to lift her feet high as she set off at a steady pace for the distant horizon. She had to stay constantly aware of minor changes in the underlying ground which she could not see through the mud her running stirred up. She was grateful for the difficulties of running; they were a welcome distraction from her thoughts.

All too soon, however, she reached the edge of the lake bed and was running upward over a gentle slope covered with soggy wet grass that squelched underfoot but required no particular attention from a runner. The oversweet smell of rotting vegetation came up to her nostrils with each breath; the land was waterlogged, water-poisoned. But under the cover of soggy, rotten dead grass there might be living roots and the promise of new life in a gentler season. Was there a similar promise for her, of life in an environment that was truly hers? Or was she a misfit, neither of the Linyaari nor of the race that had fostered her? As Acorna's pace evened out she found unwelcome thoughts and fears once again plaguing her. Her people . . . did that mean Calum and Rafik and Gill were no longer hers? Calum had asked her not to forget them, but was the truth not more likely to be that they would soon forget her?

What had she ever been to them but a burden and a complication? They'd lost mining time to raise her from infancy, lost their jobs to protect her from Amalgamated's unethical scientists, and then had been thoroughly entangled in her crusade to rid Kezdet of child labor . . . a cause they might sympathize with, but would surely never have undertaken but for her. Even now their lives were being distorted around hers. Did Gill really want to be a foster parent to the children relocated on Maganos, or did he secretly long for the freedom of asteroid mining? Did Rafik resent being called away from House Harakamian business? Was he only coming to Rushima because his sense of duty required him to be present when Acorna met her own people? And as for Calum—would he ever have undertaken the long and risky voyage they'd planned if he had not felt it his own duty to restore Acorna to her home? Certainly he had not seemed all that disappointed to learn the voyage and search were no longer necessary.

As she breasted the hill and began loping down into the long valley before her, Acorna decided that the three ex-miners would probably be only too happy to hand her over to "her people" and know their responsibility to her was ended.

And what of her? She was supposed to be ecstatically happy at being reunited with her own race. Wasn't that what this whole voyage had been about? Now Acorna faced the fact that she had never really imagined an end to the voyage. The planet Calum had targeted as her probable home lay so far away that the prospect of reaching it had never been quite real to her. Now, without the expected months of waiting and preparation, suddenly she was supposed to rejoice at being thrown into the arms of these strangers. They might look like her, but what else would there be to link them? "Linyaari," she whispered to the wind, trying out the unfamiliar word. "Linyarrri? Liiinyar?"

The word evoked no recognition in her, any more than the syllables of her native language that Gill and Rafik insisted she had pronounced when they first met her. "Avvi," she'd said aloud then. "Lalli." They were nonsense syllables to her now, nothing more.

***

Calum was occupied with figuring the rate of thrust required to take off the mass soon to be inserted into the spaceship when Acorna got back to the *Acadecki*, tired and sweaty from her long run. She used most of their fresh water in frantic showering, afraid the approaching Linyaari would be disgusted by the sight of a hot, sweaty, barbarian relative, then purified the water and let it trickle back into the tank. Wrapped in a dark green towel, nervous over the coming meeting and what it might mean to her, she considered the meager wardrobe choices available to her. She hadn't been thinking of clothes when they made their getaway from Maganos. The only important thing then had been to begin the search and escape from well-meaning attempts to delay. Now, as she surveyed the available choices with mounting dismay, perhaps sublimating her fear over what the next few hours might hold, clothing assumed an importance it had never before had for her.

All she had brought were plain ship's coveralls and an assortment of gaudy disguises such as the one she had donned while pretending to be a Didi. All the disguises were frothy and elaborate, to match the large, lavishly decorated hats she used to cover her horn; they were not to Acorna's taste at all. She would not meet her newfound relatives in something she considered vulgar and garish—but would they be insulted if she wore only her everyday ship's coveralls? What would such highly civilized beings wear? Did they dress for dinner, like the characters in historical vids? Maybe they were clothed in shimmering force fields of light and would think anything she donned quaint and provincial. . . .

Calum was aroused from his brown study by a tall, slender, agitated female wearing nothing but yards of green towel, a silver mane, and a sprinkling of water droplets. "Calum, this is impossible!" she declared. "I don't even know when they will be here or what they wear! What if they don't like me? What if they think I look barbarian and provincial? What if . . . and I can't even talk to them," she exclaimed, flinging up her arms. "I don't remember—" The towel slipped, and she made a hasty grab for the top edge just in time to avert disaster. "I don't remember any words of their language. My language. They're telepathic. I'm not, so what if I'm some kind of a mental defective by their standards? You said they had trouble deciding whether human beings were worthy of an alliance with their race, and look what they had to study—Gill, Judit, Rafik, Mr. Li . . . if they aren't good enough for the Linyaari, how will I ever measure up?" Her eyes were silver lines in dark pools of distress, and she was beginning to make the whinnying sound that was as close as she ever came to sobbing aloud.

"Hold on a minute, girl," Calum said, "you're not being rational here."

"Oh, yes, I am!" Acorna contradicted him. "I am being quite rational; I have thought this whole thing out very carefully, and Calum, this—is—not—going—to—work! I cannot meet them, don't you see?" She whirled away from him, silver hair flying through the air, and he thought that not all the moisture on her face had come from her recent shower. He wished to God Judit were here, she'd know how to calm Acorna down. Or Gill. Or even Rafik! Why did it have to be him who was stuck with the task? A man didn't specialize in mathematics because he had a rare talent for human relationships. All Calum had was reason and logic, and he made one more attempt to apply it.

"Acorna, how do you know you're not telepathic? If it only works between members of your race, and you've never been around any others—"

"I just know," she interrupted him. She had thrown a second towel over her head and shoulders and was rubbing vigorously as if to dry off her hair; her voice was muffled by layers of fuzzy fabric. "I'd have felt something before now if I were a telepath. I shouldn't be surprised if they exposed me at birth. You know the ancient Greeks used to do that with defective offspring, or even superfluous girls—I am certainly superfluous to them, don't you think? What would they want with some barbarian who can't even speak their language? Only, being such a high-tech race, naturally they wouldn't just leave me on a mountaintop. A space capsule must be a much better means of disposal, don't you see? After all, the mountain thing wasn't totally reliable—look at Oedipus."

"Who's he?" Calum was completely out of his depth now.

"Really, Calum," Acorna said in tones of freezing superiority from the depths of her covering towels, "don't you read anything? He was exposed because of a prophecy that he would murder his father, only a shepherd took him in and raised him, and then one day he met his real father at a crossroads and they got in a fight and of course Oedipus didn't know who he was, so he killed him, and then . . . well, after then he behaved most improperly, all through not knowing anything about his origins, and I think eventually he blinded himself. So you see why I can't meet them."

"I see you're talking a lot of nonsense," Calum said. "I never met this Oedipus chap, and what's more I don't want to, because he sounds quite loopy to me. You're not loopy, and you're not going to kill anybody, and the Linyaari want you. They've come one hell of a long way for you, so I most seriously doubt that they sent you off in an escape pod to begin with. It'll have been some kind of accident, that's all, and no doubt they'll explain it all when they get to Rushima."

Acorna had dropped the towel that covered her head and was nodding silently. Under the illusion that he had calmed her fears, Calum made the mistake of adding, "Now why don't you just get dressed; pick out some pretty thing; you want to look nice when your people get here."

"You don't understaaaand," Acorna wailed, and was off again, hiccuping and whinnying. Calum patted her shoulder and prayed to the Gods of Balanced Equations that Gill, Judit, Rafik, somebody who understood females would reach them before the Linyaari showed up and wanted to know why he'd been upsetting their foundling. But to his great relief, she calmed herself quickly enough and was once again—at least on the surface—the quiet, sweet-tempered girl he had raised. It was the arrival of Joshua Flouse with the first rafts that restored her to normal. On hearing the splashing approach of the settlers, Acorna quickly dashed cold water over her face and slipped into her coveralls. "I am sorry," she said. "I have been foolish, and we have work to do. Calum, do you not need to go to the *Haven* and collect that working party?"

"Might as well take the first load of settlers to high ground, then go on to the *Haven* from there," Calum decided. "But they'll have to leave their goods here for now, except for what each one can carry; when I get the kids dirtside, they can do the heavy lifting."

That decision, announced by Calum, caused a furor, which only Acorna could calm. As she waded through the lake, speaking quietly to each group of settlers with their raftload of treasured personal possessions, the cries of outrage died down and the Rushimese farmers grudgingly poled their rafts back to the soggy "shore." Once there, Joshua Flouse displayed the talent for leadership that had made him spokesman for this settlement, quickly separating each pile of personal goods into those that were too fragile to be left and those that might reasonably survive Hoa's weather modifications if carefully stored in an outbuilding.

Even with this division, and with Calum's requirement that each refugee carry his own possessions, he and Acorna wound up doing far more than their share of physical labor. Children and old people and invalids had to be helped into the *Acadecki*, and the helpers could not carry anything else. Calum personally stowed a tea set brought at great expense from the Shenjemi home, piece by fragile piece, and then cursed himself for wasting time with such trinkets when he saw Acorna wading through muddy water with twin infants clinging to her neck and caressing her horn. By the time the *Acadecki* was filled with refugees, Calum and Acorna and the able-bodied men and women of the settlement, who'd chosen to see their weakest members to safety first, were all exhausted and dripping with mud and sweat. But the labor seemed to have been good for Acorna; or perhaps it was the twitters and coos of the babies who were entranced by her horn and silvery mane that had restored the shine to her eyes.

The settlers' hard-won calm almost disintegrated, though, when Calum told Acorna to board the *Acadecki*, that they could take no more passengers on this trip.

"How do we know you'll be back?" cried a burly man who'd all but exhausted himself helping weaker settlers board the ship.

"You're not going with my babies, and me not with them!" a young mother exclaimed fiercely.

The imminent danger of a riot was averted when Acorna stepped out of the ship before Calum could stop her.

"I will stay with you," she said in her clear, sweet voice, and the uneasy group subsided at once.

"Well, if she stays . . ."

"You're a dammed fool, Kass," somebody said to the burly man who'd begun the protest. "Oughta know there's no funny business when the likes of her is involved."

"'Ow'd I s'posed to know that?" the unlucky Kass protested. "Never seen nothin' like her before, did I?"

"Just gotta look at her . . . besides, she cleared the water for us, didn't she?"

Acorna gently urged the people away from the base of the ship and waved at Calum. "Go on," she urged him. "Everything will be all right."

Not without misgivings, Calum lifted off once the settlers on the ground were well clear of the area. What would Rafik and Gill say to him if they knew he'd left Acorna alone, even briefly, in such circumstances? But there seemed little choice . . . and with any luck, they never would know.

Acorna was not the least bit concerned for herself as Calum lifted off; she didn't have time for that. There were too many wet, muddy, disgruntled people to be helped into some semblance of organization, too many piles of hastily abandoned household goods which the owners had left with anxiety and a great many last-minute messages: "Mind and keep all my things together and don't let that Auntie Nagah be poking around in them. . . . Be sure they stow those datacubes of mine somewhere safe and dry, that's the only library on all Rushima. . . . Now be sure and keep that table upside down, see, one of the legs falls off if you pick it up the other way, but 'er's a good table and solid."

Solid "'er" certainly was; Acorna had to enlist the help of Flouse and Kass to get it carried as far as the soggy bank. "Leave it there," Flouse said. "I'll ask one of the dryland settlements to send a motodray— all ours are fair ruined with this wet, see?" He wiped his sweating forehead. "Blest if I know how old Labrish ever got it that far, and him half-crippled with the rheumatics."

Acorna rubbed the small of her back in rueful agreement. Although strong, she was already tired from carrying most of the children to the ship. But they seemed calmer in her arms than in anybody else's, even their parents'.

One of the parents was sitting at the water's edge, uncaring of the mud that smeared the cuffs of her coveralls, crying quietly. The woman's tears ran in an unending stream down her face to join the silty water of the acres-wide shallow "lake."

Acorna recognized the young mother who'd protested against her children being taken off without her.

"They will be all right," she said quietly, sitting down beside the grief-stricken woman without regard for her own clothes. "I promise you that. And very soon Calum will come back for more people, and you will be with them again, in a nice dry place where you can get them clean and they can sleep dry and warm; won't that be better?"

"They'll be frightened without me!"

"But you'll be with them very soon," Acorna repeated, "and in the meantime . . . they do have your own elders from this settlement to watch them, and Calum himself is very good with children."

The young woman sniffled. "Doesn't look like a man who'd have much patience with their little ways."

"Looks are deceiving," Acorna said with a smile.

"Calum raised me from infancy, and he is much more patient than he seems."

"You? Garn!" The woman looked up and down Acorna's tall body. "He ain't hardly old enough!"

"Looks," Acorna repeated, "are deceiving." She did not add that it was her appearance, not Calum's, which was deceptive; the settlers had accepted her strange looks with surprising equanimity. She did not wish to remind them of her alien nature by explaining that she came of a race which could apparently grow to physical maturity in just four years.

By personally promising to see that the young woman was taken on the very next shipload, and talking in a low, soothing voice, Acorna got her somewhat calmed down; and that calm seemed magically to spread through the crowd. This was shattered as the roar of a ship's engines filled the air and all but drowned out the voices of those on the ground.

"Oh, good," Acorna said cheerfully, "see, here's the *Acadecki* back already. . . ." But it didn't sound like her own dear ship; in fact, it didn't sound quite right for any ship she had ever heard. It came down much too quickly, and the roar stopped too abruptly, and she had barely glimpsed a flash of gold and scarlet before it landed with a hiss of escaping heat that turned the shallow lake bed to a wall of steam clouds.

As the clouds cleared, Acorna saw a craft not dissimilar in shape to the U-class starships of Delszaki Li's fleet, but ornamented with gaudy scrollwork of scarlet-and-gilt ribbon shapes that curved about the hull. She blinked and rubbed her eyes. How did they do that? No decorative paint could survive repeated searing journeys through a planet's atmosphere . . . no paint known to humanity, she thought with a flash of panic, and suddenly the ship seemed utterly and completely alien.

Around her there were sudden cries of fear, and the young mother beside her leapt to her feet with the evident intention of running away. Acorna jumped up, too, if only to keep the girl with her; if these people ran in panic, this frail young woman and many others might slip and be trampled . . . who were these new arrivals? They could only be the Linyaari . . . her people.

My people—alien, alien, alien—no, my own people. Her heart thudded irregularly, and the young mother pulled away from her with the strength of sudden, desperate panic. Acorna realized suddenly that she herself was contributing to the fear of the crowd. Perhaps if she could calm down and set an example . . .

"There is nothing to be afraid of," she said, trying to keep her voice from shaking. She raised it slightly. "You don't know who is in that ship, but I know. These are more of my kind. You aren't afraid of me, are you? Well, then! They've come to help, not to hurt you."

As her commonsense words percolated through the crowd, the momentary danger of a panic-stricken flight passed. The settlers were still nervous, Acorna could feel that in the tense movements of their bodies and the way they stood poised on both feet as if ready to fight or flee; but they were listening to reason again.

If indeed it was reason . . . she could not be sure that this alien ship held her own people, could she? And yet, beyond all reason, Acorna was sure of it, even before a hatchway too far up the side of the ship opened and let down a ladder whose treads were too steeply set for human legs, even before the eerie sensation of looking in a distant mirror came over her at the sight of tall, slender, silver-haired people slowly descending the ladder with their hands open in a sign of peace and the golden horns on their heads glittering in the Rushimese sunshine.

Thirteen

(*T*here she is . . . my 'Khornya . . . our 'Khornya!)

(We must tell her . . . them . . . now. It would be wrong to keep them in ignorance, Neeva, and there are surely enough of us here to prevent any panic.)

(Let me greet my 'Khornya first. Can we not have this one moment in peace without being reminded of . . .)

Acorna had a confused image of something alien and terrifying, something like a metallic ant heap writhing with hatred and destruction.

(As you will. But she must be told soon.)

They were within speaking distance now, lifting their long, elegant legs clear of the muddy water with each delicate step. Behind them, Acorna recognized Nadhari Kando, Delszaki Li's personal bodyguard. She had no energy left to try and figure out what Nadhari was doing here; all her attention was on the beings so like and yet unlike herself, who were so rudely discussing her to her face.

Acorna couldn't figure out how she had heard them so clearly even when they were still quite some distance away, but it didn't really matter now.

"What is it you need to tell me?" she asked.

The tall woman in the lead blinked and said something in a rush of liquid, nasalized sounds that meant nothing to Acorna. She shook her head, feeling dull and stupid, and suddenly all too aware of the sweat that soaked her coveralls and the mud that ornamented them in soggy brown blotches.

(I thought you said she was old enough to speak when Vaanye and Feriila took her on that trip, Neeva! What's the matter with her? Is she retarded, do you think?)

(Probably neglected. They wouldn't know how to care for one of us.)

Well! In all her childish fantasies about finally meeting her own people, she'd never imagined anything like this! Acorna blew out an indignant "Whuff!" through her nostrils and lifted her head proudly, forgetting the mud on her coveralls and all her doubts about being acceptable to these Linyaari.

"There is nothing the matter with me," she said slowly and clearly, "except that I am afflicted with inconsiderate relatives. I used to imagine all sorts of things about the people of my race, but one thing I never thought of was that they would be rude. I am not retarded, and Calum and Gill and Rafik took better care of me than you can conceive, and I am proud to have been raised by them!"

Beside her, the young mother she'd befriended stirred uneasily.

"Whatcha talkin' about?" she demanded. "They ain't said nothing yet, 'cept that foreign gibble-gabble, and I don't think you understood that any more than I did!"

Acorna frowned, puzzled. It was true—she had not understood the only thing that had been spoken; and yet they had said those other things . . . hadn't they?

(Oh, my dear 'Khornya! Have you never heard mind-speech before?)

(Of course she hasn't, Neeva. Remember, barbarians raised her.)

(Don't pay any attention to Thariinye, my dear. He is incurably rude . . . hardly linyarii!)

The untranslatable word carried, in mind-speech, all its connotations of "real-people-like-us," "civilized," "sapient," and "ethical."

Acorna started to speak, then deliberately closed her lips and thought at the others.

(Perhaps . . . I am not . . . linyarii . . . either. It is true . . . I was raised by these people . . . you call "barbarians". . . AND I LOVE THEM!) she finished in a desperate unmodulated rush.

A woman standing behind the leader winced. (Do try and teach her not to SHOUT, Neeva.)

Then Neeva's arms were about Acorna, and she touched horn to horn, and with that contact came a flood of emotion not translatable into any words: joy, and mourning for the parents Acorna could not remember, and absolute, unconditional welcome.

(You are both linyarii and Liinyar, and you are ours,) Neeva thought with absolute conviction. (I am Neeva of the Renyi-laaghe, visedhaanye ferilii of this expedition, and you are 'Khornya of the Renyilaaghe, my sister-child. Your parents were Feriila and Vaanye of the Renyilaaghe; you have Feriila's eyes.) And Neeva's clan memories surged into Acorna: a blue-green grassy world of rolling hills and bright streams. A tall man with eyes the deep silver of the shadowed grass, who smiled and tossed a laughing baby up in his arms; a sweet-faced woman whose silver eyes were the mirror of Acorna's own; feast days of flowers and singing, little furry animals that chattered in the trees . . . .)

"My dream!" exclaimed Acorna aloud.

Neeva drew back slightly, but still keeping both hands on Acorna's shoulders. "Your . . . dream?" she asked in slightly nasal Basic.

It had been a treasured dream that sometimes came to Acorna in the drowsy moments between sleeping and waking, sometimes not for months at a time, sometimes two or three times in a single week. It was among her earliest memories, and it had been in her mind even before that, for Gill and Rafik had told her that as soon as she learned a few words of Basic she had occasionally wakened speaking of strangely colored skies and demanding angrily to know the name of an animal they had never heard of.

Haltingly, Acorna told Neeva of the fragments she retained from a dream that had always left her feeling safe and loved. "There was a garden where the grass was soft and almost blue, and someone held me up to see the singing-fuzzies in the trees. . . ."

"No dream," said Neeva, and the silver pupils of

her eyes narrowed to vertical lines. "That was a garden in the clan-house of the Renyilaaghe. Your father Vaanye used to take you to see the thiliiri in the trees there; he said you sang like a thiilir instead of crying like an ordinary youngling. And Feriila and I would chat while Vaanye played with you . . . don't you remember?"

Acorna shook her head, feeling her own pupils contract like Neeva's.

"No matter, no matter." Neeva rested her horn against Acorna's for a brief moment of infinitely reassuring contact. "You are ours, our memories are your memories, you will share them all as we do." Underneath the spoken words Acorna could hear a cry of grief and pity. (How could you survive so, all alone?)

(I was NOT alone,) she thought, and her own memories of Gill and Rafik and Calum flooded into Neeva's mind.

(I see,) said Neeva in a much-altered tone. (We had not expected there could be a bonding. . . .)

"Not a bonding, not like that," Acorna said, since Neeva's sense of bonding meant a physical, sensual tie. (They nurtured me, taking turns. . . .) She touched horns again with her aunt and let loose a myriad of scenes from being bathed as a small child in a small sink to her sampling all the plants in the 'ponics, to understanding "no," and then learning how to read and write, and how to do more important things like find rhenium where they didn't know it would be, and understanding equations and how to place bets to win. And, most of all, protecting her from those who thought her deformed. . . .

(Deformed?) And the others echoed the word, shocked. Especially the tallest, who stood slightly apart from the other two women. From that one, Acorna sensed masculinity and pride and something else. If that was what a grown Liinyar male looked like . . . well . . . Acorna forced her thoughts away from that area.

(Yes, deformed. They nearly took it off.)

(They nearly what?) All four Linyaari cringed, and the male actually put a quick hand up to his horn, as if protecting it from the very thought of such an action.

(So you see, I owe much to Gill, Rafik, and Calum. They never, ever left me alone.)

(Yes, my dear child, we will express our gratitude for their care of you in a substantial manner.) Neeva drew Acorna a little farther away from the clutch of settlers who were distinctly interested in what was going on.

"I ain't heard 'im say much at all," the young woman complained. "Just touchin' them horns together like stags back on Shenjemi. And they ain't neither of them stags."

Neeva beckoned to Khaari to join them in a three-point touching so that Khaari's personality could reduce the shock of what they had to impart to Acorna.

So it was that Acorna learned about the Khleevi and why her parents had needed to send her from their ship to prevent her capture. Both Linyaari cushioned her against the horrible scenes of torture that the Khleevi perpetrated on helpless Linyaari. Acorna pitied the poor victims and understood why her parents had wanted to spare her from it and give her that one slim chance to live.

(We are also here to warn this quadrant of the galaxy that the Khleevi are on their way here,) Khaari said, nuzzling Acorna with her horn to reduce the shock that did, indeed, shudder its way through Acorna.

She broke their hold, looking about in shock at the poor bedraggled settlers.

(Be easy, Acorna) Khaari said sharply. (You are broadcasting fear, and they will sense it. Melireenya, help us dampen this. Thaari, you, too. As I said, help is on its way. This Rafik has called upon an army. . . .)

"Is that why Nadhari's here?" Acorna managed to peek over at the short woman who was standing in a parade-rest position, not seeming to look at anything, but, if Acorna knew the woman, and she did, seeing everything. Only what could Nadhari do, trained and intrepid as she was, against people who frightened the tall, elegant Linyaari?

(Several come. These people will be safe. But you must be in the safest place,) Neeva said, sliding one hand around Acorna's slim shoulders. (For we must not lose you again. Come, into our ship.)

"No. I promised that I would stay here until the *Acadecki* comes to take another load away from here. And these are not the only ones that must be protected," Acorna said, backing away from her own people. "I can go nowhere until the entire planet is evacuated if the Khleevi things are coming this way."

"We can take zum in our ship," Neeva said,

glancing over and doing a mental count of the heads she could see. "But not all."

"All, or I don't leave this planet."

(It is obvious she is linyarii,) Thariinye said in a bored tone. (Only females will support a lost cause.)

(Be still with such foolish talk, Thaari. We must get her to safety. And I do not think we will have much time.)

(The armies are coming. We know that.)

(But when? And soon enough?)

"I don't go without these people and as many others as we can find," Acorna said, and suddenly Nadhari Kando was beside her.

"That's telling them, Lady Lukia," said the bodyguard in her gravelly voice.

Meanwhile, Rafik had reached the *Haven*, fully expecting to see Acorna awaiting him. The first ship he spotted in the huge hangar bay of the Starfarer ship was the *Acadecki*. He did not see the Linyaari ship. But his instrumentation had shown that the Linyaari ship had been far enough ahead of even his superfast *Uhuru* to have landed, collected Acorna, and been back before he could arrive. Calum was there, and Rafik charged angrily toward the one familiar face, only to stop and stand stock-still when he realized that the man next to Calum was familiar, too.

"Johnny Greene, what in the name of misbegotten imps, djinni, and Shaitans are you doing here?" But he thumped Johnny on the back with more enthusiasm, Calum thought, than he had ever displayed on being reunited with his old mining partners. "Is Acorna on the bridge? Where's that fancy ship of the Linyaari? I know they made it to Rushima ahead of me."

"We expect them at any moment, Rafik," Calum said absently. He was absorbed in counting the other old friends who were even now disembarking from the *Uhuru*. Judit, Pal, Gill . . .

"Mercy?" he inquired hopefully.

"She felt it was her duty to stay with Mr. Li. He wasn't looking so good—oh, nothing to worry about," Rafik said. "We've been in touch with Maganos; he was in bed for a few days but he's okay now, and anyway Uncle Hafiz is with him. Apparently he decided to raise the shield and"—he gestured helplessly—"it's rather a lot to explain. Now where's Acorna?"

"On Rushima."

"You left her alone? On Rushima?" Rafik's coffee brown face faded to a dingy gray.

Calum gave Rafik a dirty look. "I'm sure you would have arranged everything much better if you'd been the one to get kidnapped by Palomellese space pirates. Forgive me, all I managed to do was rescue us"—actually Markel should have gotten the credit for that, but Calum was past being reasonable—"help recapture the *Haven*, and work out the mathematics needed for Dr. Hoa to reverse the weather devastation on Rushima. She's needed there now to help with relocating the settlers to high ground, and so am I. I just stopped to get a working party of kids off this ship."

He had the slight satisfaction of seeing Rafik's eyes widen.

"Like you said," Calum added in an offhand tone, "it's rather a lot to explain. Now, if you don't mind, I need to get on with the relocation. We have to have all these people on high ground or off the planet before Dr. Hoa can start. . . ."

"Forget the high ground," Rafik said in a strangled voice. "A different planet is exactly what we need for them. Maybe a whole different system."

It was Calum's turn to goggle. Quickly Rafik filled him in on the threatened invasion which had brought both the *Uhuru* and the Linyaari to Rushima.

The com unit on Johnny Greene's belt squawked suddenly.

"Armed force approaching. . . ."

"That'll be the Red Bracelets," Rafik said, and added, "I hope . . ."

On their way to the bridge he sketched the situation for Calum and Johnny, who relayed the information to the *Haven*'s young crew so that no further explanations were needed when they reached that area. Full-screen displays gave a view of nine approaching ships: a dreadnought, flanked by two battle cruisers and six destroyers, all of whom were capable of carrying light fighters within as the fleet now angled down to the same plane as the *Haven*'s position.

Rafik gave a sigh of relief. "Yes, they're our people . . . so to speak. We've bought them for this engagement—that is, Delszaki and Uncle Hafiz together have."

Calum's eyes widened. "The entire Red Bracelet fleet? How are you—we—going to pay for that?"

"That's all of your friend's fleet?" the kid in charge of the displays snapped over his shoulder. "Then who're these guys?"

The scene altered, and, although the screen's magnification had not been changed, it was obvious that another triangle of nine ships—of a design Rafik had never seen before—was also closing fast on this same position.

"The Khleevi?" Calum asked.

"Must be," Rafik said. "I got a—well, a picture in my head from Neeva, she's Acorna's mother's sister. . . ."

"Her aunt . . ."

"I think they've got a different kinship structure. She calls herself mother-sib to Acorna, and the feeling I get is that it's more like a second mother than an aunt."

"What the hell difference does that make with the design of the Khleevi ships?"

"None, but that's them," Rafik said, pointing. "And they're still far away, because close-up, Melireenya says the smallest of them is twice the size of the *Haven*."

Calum swore with great verve and imagination, impressing Markel.

"And Acorna's on Rushima with those things coming after her? Why didn't it occur to any of you great thinkers to mention this little invasion when you were sending that joyous let's-reunite-the-family spurt-message?"

Calum's scathing glance swept over Rafik and his companions. Gill turned red, Pal stared straight ahead, and Judit dropped her eyes.

"Rafik thought we shouldn't risk starting a panic among the Rushimese," Gill mumbled.

"It was your idea, actually," Rafik said.

"Whatever! Anyway, we all know now; and what are we going to do to protect those people from what's coming at them?"

"First step," said Calum, "is to get Acorna and the Linyaari up here, find out what exactly they know about these Khleevi. These mind-pictures you're talking about can't be any substitute for a good discussion of strategy and tactics. And as soon as the Red Bracelets are within range, we need to get their head honcho in on the talks. You stay here and work on opening communications with the Kilumbembese, Johnny; I've got to collect Acorna."

"I'm coming with you," said Pal in a tone that brooked no argument.

When the *Acadecki* returned to settle in the extensive but shallow mud puddle that the *Haven* had created from a hectare of low-lying fields, Pal was first out of the hatch. He stopped in mid-stride, shocked by the appearance of the gaudy scarlet-and-gold ship that sat a short distance away, and even more shocked by the sight of the Linyaari envoys scattered through the crowd of Rushimese settlers. Actually it wasn't that so much that bothered him; it was the fact that Acorna was neither with the four envoys nor alone. The tall, overbearing young male who'd been arrested by a security guard on Maganos was by her side, bending over her with an attentive expression that made Pal want to deck him. Behind them stood Nadhari Kando, apparently relaxed . . . until one noticed that she was lightly balanced on the balls of her feet, hands free, eyes constantly scanning the space around Acorna for possible threats.

"Look at that oversize . . . stallion," Pal muttered to Calum in tones of disgust, as the other man joined him. "Making time with my girl while we've got an emergency on our hands!"

"I don't think she's your girl now, Pal," Calum said sadly. "I don't think she's any of ours, now."

"Yeah, but—"

"Save it for later," Calum advised him. "For now, help me figure out how we're going to get Acorna and the others up to the *Haven* without being mobbed by the Rushimese."

Pal hadn't served as Delszaki Li's personal assistant for years without learning how to keep a poker face and, more important, how to spin a convincing lie on the spur of the moment. As he moved through the crowd, grinning and repeating his tale about a purely temporary glitch in the resettlement and the need to get help from these aliens in preparing adequate facilities for all the waiting settlers, Calum could almost believe it himself. Certainly none of the Rushimese questioned Pal's story, though Calum thought he saw a quizzical look on the face of Joshua Flouse—a man who, as settlement leader, had undoubtedly had his own experience with making up plausible tales.

Even Pal, though, could not keep the whole group of settlers calm without the help of the Linyaari. That became evident as he began, like a good sheep dog, cutting out the aliens and neatly herding them out of the crowd and back to the

Acadecki. He had to get them one at a time, and as each one left, ripples of unease stirred through the crowd, only settling when the remaining Linyaari spaced themselves out more evenly in the mass of humans.

Acorna was reluctant to come with Pal, but he explained that they needed information from the Linyaari, and that she, as the only person who could communicate with them telepathically and who was also familiar with Basic Interlingua, might be needed to make sure that they understood the Linyaari information about the Khleevi correctly. She and Thariinye were the last but one of the Linyaari to come aboard, followed by Nadhari Kando, who was taking quite seriously her orders to guard Acorna at all times; only Neeva remained with the Rushimese.

"She's not coming," Pal reported.

"Oh, yes, she is!" Calum started down the steps, prepared to bring the Linyaari Envoy Extraordinary to safety by force if necessary, but Acorna caught his arm. "Calum, one of us must remain here," she said in an urgent undertone. "If I am truly needed to interpret—"

"You are," Pal said in a firm tone that brooked no argument.

"Then one of the envoys must stay." Her pupils narrowed. "I wish it were not Neeva . . . but we Linyaari cannot all leave."

"I don't see why!" How quickly she had identified herself with them: "we Linyaari" indeed!

"Yuu would not," drawled Thariinye. "We haff skills yuu know nothinn of . . . anny one of us cann

keep these beings calm in ways yuu do not unner-
stan. Eeven little 'Khornya could do it!" He put his
arm around Acorna's shoulders and patted her arm
patronizingly.

"It is true, Calum," Acorna said. "They . . . we . . .
can put forth an aura of peace and calm that will
keep the settlers from panicking. But if we all go,
and the *Acadecki* as well, they will surely think we
are abandoning them."

Calum thought grimly that this might well be
true, unless the Linyaari and the humans on board
the *Haven* could come up with some way to protect
an entire continent full of far-flung, scattered settlements from imminent invasion. Right now, he'd kill
for the secret to Uncle Hafiz's planetary shield. But
with the only man capable of installing it and making it work buried six feet under on some distant
planet, the Rushimese—and anybody else on the
surface of Rushima—were dangerously, potentially
fatally, exposed.

But he did not wish to say this to Acorna, nor to
confess that his own immediate objective was to get
her to the relative safety of the *Haven*. Rushima was
virtually without defenses, and the *Acadecki* didn't
have top-flight weaponry and defenses owing to his
and Acorna's eagerness in leaving before the retrofit of the weapon systems was complete.

He began to forgive Rafik for his reticence about
the Khleevi invasion. It was not the sort of news
one wished to broadcast to an already unhappy
crowd.

Nor did he care much, himself, for the idea of
abandoning the Rushimese to their fate. He would

bring Acorna and the Linyaari back to the *Haven*, but after that he would be free to use the *Acadecki* up to the last minute in ferrying the Rushimese . . . where? The *Haven* could hardly provide space, let alone life support, for all the farmers in this and other settlements. Perhaps there were caves where the people could hide.

He would worry about it later, Calum decided, as he broke all records and several safety regs in his eagerness to blast away from Rushima and get Acorna to safety . . . and, as a minor objective, to get her out from between Pal and Thariinye, who had strapped in on opposite sides of her with the evident intention of glaring at one another and exchanging barely veiled insults all the way back.

Fortunately, it took only a matter of minutes to reach the *Haven* and dock, and once on board, Calum discovered that a solution to the problem of the Rushimese settlers had already been found . . . if the Red Bracelets would go along with it. Already a harsh Kilumbembese voice crackled from the spurt decoder.

"Admiral Ikwaskwan to *Haven*, regarding your request: Denied. My men came to fight the enemy, not to baby-sit civilians. It is not in our contract to perform transport services for these . . . farmers!"

Rafik spoke into the recorder. "With respect, Admiral, we believe you will find that Section 19, Subsection iii, Paragraph (b) of your contract requires you to operate under my direct command in all matters not specifically military. I do hope we can resolve this matter amicably; penalties for forfeiture are explicit and . . . ah . . . rather steep. I fear my uncle is not at all of a forgiving nature in such matters." He hit the code and transmit buttons and sat back with a sigh as the response was compressed for spurt to the lead ship of the Red Bracelets.

Seconds later, another transmission was received, this time accompanied by vid. Ikwaskwan's harsh, high-boned face stared out from a gray background slashed by a single curving red line. "We shall reach Rushima orbiting range within the hour, at which time we will discuss this in person," he snapped. The screen went blank with no parting formalities from Ikwaskwan.

"Dear, dear," Gill said, "seems the wee mannie is just a tad annoyed with us, Rafik. You had better take me along for this personal discussion he wants."

"And me," said Nadhari Kando in her low, gravelly voice.

"You're going nowhere," Rafik said briefly, "and neither am I. Really, Gill, one would think you had learned nothing of the art of negotiating from all those years of watching me in action! Uncle Hafiz would not have chosen an heir so stupid as to conduct difficult bargaining sessions on the opponent's home turf." He thought that over briefly. "Well, Tapha probably would've," he conceded, "but Uncle didn't exactly choose Tapha." Hafiz had expressed no particular grief when his dim-witted, conceited son had died in an attempt to assassinate Rafik before he could be disinherited in Rafik's favor, and none of his friends believed this was because of his iron control of his feelings. . . . He had, in fact, been heard to comment that Tapha's untimely death saved him a fortune in legal fees.

"Nothing difficult about it," Gill said. "It's in the contract, isn't it? He has to do whatever you say, apart from direct battlefront decisions."

Rafik regarded his erstwhile partner with amusement. "And just who," he inquired lightly, "is going to enforce said contract at this distance when they're heavily armed and outnumber us by a factor of thousands? As for later . . . Ikwaskwan is, I'm sure, quite as well aware as I am that time, distance, dead witnesses, and lies can blur the definition of just what was or was not a direct battlefront decision. No, we will have to find other methods of persuading him."

"To do what?" Calum, a latecomer to this discussion, demanded.

Rafik briefly explained to him that on the nearest star system to Rushima, but well out of the current sweep of the Khleevi fleet, they had identified a planet with acceptable gravity, atmosphere, and water where the Rushimese could take refuge until the battle was over . . . if the Kilumbembese mercenary fleet could be pressed into service to transport them there.

"Will we have time?"

"That," said Rafik, "depends to some extent on exactly how long it takes to persuade Ikwaskwan to accept our views."

Although he was present for the subsequent discussion, opened as soon as the Red Bracelet flagship *Ta'anisi* was within hailing range, Calum was never quite clear on just how Rafik managed to persuade "Admiral" Ikwaskwan to come aboard the *Haven* rather than the other way round. All he could say was that there had been an exchange of compliments in which Rafik so carefully veiled whatever threats or bribes he was offering that it would take the twisty mind of a Harakamian . . . or a Kilumbembese mercenary . . . to figure out what was going on. All he knew was that Rafik sighed when the exchange was over and commented that this could be expensive, and he hoped Uncle Hafiz and Delszaki Li were prepared to pay for cost overruns beyond the scope of the original contract.

"You're bribing him to move the Rushimese?"

"I am hinting that cooperation will not go unrewarded," Rafik corrected Calum's surmise. He sighed again. "We'll doubtless have to commit ourselves to explicit promises and named sums before he agrees; I just hope I can keep his demands down within reason."

Nadhari Kando broke her customary silence. "I may be able to help persuade him."

"Any help you can give would be most appreciated," Rafik said with a courtly bow. He started to ask whether it was true, then, that Nadhari had once served with the Red Bracelets; but something in her cold, expressionless stare put him off. He had heard that Li's bodyguard did not discuss her past; it would be impolite to bring it up now. Risky, too. Decidedly risky.

Acorna turned and looked up at Thariinye. "Cannot we help, too? If it is a matter of persuading . . . you were so good at calming the Rushimese!"

"Calum tells me you did pretty well at that yourself!" Pal exclaimed.

Thariinye smiled and patted Acorna's shoulder. "Little 'Khornya will learn, but she is unpracticed. Best to leave this to those with the experience to be tactful and diplomatic."

(Well, that leaves you out, Thariinye! I'd sooner have 'Khornya handle it; at least she knows how to be nice to people!)

(Will you just get off my case, Khaari?)

Acorna's pupils narrowed to slits, and she looked back and forth between the Linyaari while the others wondered just what was going on.

(Please, Khaari, don't be angry on my account. What Thariinye says is true, you know; I have not practiced your . . . our . . . arts and I would likely be only a hindrance to you.)

(Never a hindrance, dear child, but we do not wish you to exhaust yourself. Thariinye, Khaari, save your energies for this visitor; do not waste yourselves in quarreling.) Melireenya's firm intervention quashed the momentary altercation and brought the four Linyaari together in at least superficial unity—for Acorna unconsciously moved to stand with her kinsfolk as they drew closer together.

When "Admiral" Ikwaskwan boarded the *Haven*, Calum understood why he had not been afraid to negotiate on Rafik's turf. He was accompanied by a squad of mercenaries in dark gray uniforms, each man visibly armed and alert. Calum noticed that some of them wore one red bangle on the left wrist, others two or even three, while Ikwaskwan himself was bare-armed. Some kind of rank symbol? Nadhari would know; he wished he had asked her before the Red Bracelets came aboard. Perhaps Rafik already knew.

Nor was the bodyguard Ikwaskwan's only protection; his first words—he dispensed with the time-wasting formalities of greetings and introductions—made it clear that his flagship had weapons trained on the *Haven* and that at least one member of his bodyguard carried a fully armed tungsten bomb.

Rafik smoothly agreed that it was desirable to take all possible precautions when visiting, mentioned with a deprecating smile that the *Haven* was itself not without weaponry both offensive and defensive, and said that he personally would deeply deplore any dissension which should cause injury to their honored ally.

(Meli, are you sure these "humans" are on our side?)

(No . . . but at least they are not Khleevi.)

(That is beginning to seem less and less of a recommendation. Like us in form, perhaps, but hardly in ethics.)

(That may not be entirely a bad thing. If they meet their friends with weapons in both hands, what do you suppose they do to their enemies?)

(Thariinye, you have abominable taste. Besides, if they are so suspicious, they will likely destroy one another before the Khleevi even arrive.)

The Linyaari continued their internal debate. Acorna listened, wanting to cry out in defense of her friends, but also concerned that her newfound kinfolk would think her, too, a warlike barbarian. If only Neeva were there! Acorna longed for her aunt's wisdom and acceptance.

Once the opening dance of establishing ascendance was over, with neither side a clear winner, Ikwaskwan demanded to know exactly what additional compensation would be granted his troops for the service of ferrying dirt farmers from one planet to another.

Rafik cleared his throat and prepared to equivocate to the best of his not inconsiderable ability; but before he could speak, Nadhari Kando sauntered out from her semiconcealed position behind the group of tall Linyaari.

"Hi, there, Ikki," she said, her usual gravelly drawl muted to an almost husky tone, "it's been a long time."

Not long enough! was written on Ikwaskwan's bony face at sight of Nadhari, but he had too much self-control to voice the feelings. "Nadhari Kando. I had heard you were dead."

"The rumors were gravely exaggerated," replied Nadhari without cracking a smile. "But since we appear to be on the same side again, Ikki, I hope you are a little better at carrying through your plans now than you were then."

"I could hardly be worse," Ikwaskwan muttered, as if to himself. "How did you . . . never mind. So you're doing security-guard work now, Nadhi?" His scornful tone made it clear he thought she had come down in the world.

"I am under contract to the House of Li," Nadhari said without blinking, "as are you and your troops, Ikki. Tell me, did M'on Na'ntaw ever hear what became of that credit exchange from Theloi?"

Ikwaskwan licked suddenly dry lips. Nadhari

waited patiently, thumbs hooked into her belt, one knee slightly bent toward the man she called "Ikki."

"Or did the data get lost when his second-in-command was assassinated?" Nadhari prodded. "Remember? Everybody thought it was counter-revolutionaries, but no one could explain how they'd gotten hold of the plans for our camp. Very clever of them to go straight to Skomitin's tent and back out again without getting caught, wasn't it?"

"So delightful to talk over old times," Ikwaskwan said with a tight-lipped smile that did not reach his eyes. "We must have another little chat some time, Nadhi dear, but just now I am needed at my own bridge. Rafik Nadezda has indicated that there is some urgency about this little population transfer, and you know my feelings on honoring the wishes of the client."

"I certainly do," Nadhari agreed. Her own smile was echoed in her wickedly glinting dark eyes. "So does E'kosi Tahka'yaw . . . oh, no, I should say, he did know, did he not?"

"Later, later," Ikwaskwan mumbled. "Must return to the *Ta'anisi* now. Nadezda, have the goodness to transmit orders and location of the targeted system, also a map of the settlements to be evacuated here on Rushima."

Rafik nodded, stern and unsmiling. "All necessary data shall be at your disposal . . . Admiral."

Not until the closing of the outer ports indicated that Ikwaskwan and his bodyguard were physically off the *Haven* and on their way by shuttle back to the flagship did he allow himself a long sigh of relief.

"Nadhari—" he began, but the quiet woman had vanished.

"Who were those people she was talking about?" Gill asked.

Calum shook his head. "Never heard of 'em. Meant something to Ikwaskwan, though. Ikki?"

"I don't," Rafik said gravely, "believe I want to ask. We owe her, though . . . and I'd better get busy transmitting those orders!"

(See, Khaari? These humans aren't so bad after all. They settled everything quite amicably.)

(It must be that a pretense of force is part of their greeting ritual,) Thariinye suggested. (You know, like a singing-fuzzy erecting his tail spines when he's courting.)

(Isn't it nice that the Admiral met an old friend on board this ship?)

(But who'd have guessed it? Nadhari is such a sweet, gentle girl, how do you suppose she got to be friends with a professional fighter?)

Acorna listened to this exchange and once again decided not to say anything, either out loud or mentally. Her kinfolk seemed to have totally missed the point of that tense, threatening conversation; but why disturb them, if they were happy with their own interpretation?

Fourteen

*I*f some of the Red Bracelets were offended at being assigned to evacuate settlers rather than to strictly military tasks, two of the newest officers were complacent at the prospect. Ed Minkus and Des Smirnoff joined in the grumbles of their unit but then Smirnoff, in a surprising volte-face, volunteered himself and Minkus to pilot one of the shuttles that was to be sent to outlying areas. Although most of the small settlements on Rushima consisted of clusters of homes and storage sheds along the single primitive road that snaked through the eastern part of the main continent, there were always those individualists who desired privacy, unspoiled territory, or simply the chance to acquire a larger grant of land in compensation for developing areas far from existing transport. Some of these settlers might not be able to get to the collection points currently being specified by continent-wide emergency broadcasts on the hastily replaced com-sat equipment. Others might not even hear the 'casts since their equipment might be down or damaged. Some individualists were prone to turning off their com systems for weeks at a time. Ikwaskwan reluctantly agreed to send a few low-flying shuttles to seek out stragglers, although he was adamant that all his people should be back at their stations well before the ETA of the Khleevi force.

"You crazy, Des?" Ed Minkus grumbled as they prepared to board the shuttle assigned them. "Never volunteer for anything, that's what you told me was the first principle of surviving in this outfit."

Des Smirnoff laid one finger to the side of his bulbous nose and winked, while saying in a loud voice that echoed through the hangar, "Why, Ed, didn't we swear an oath of loyalty to the Red Bracelets? And doesn't a loyal comrade enthusiastically support whatever his superiors order? Duty and honor, Ed!"

Captain Ce'skwa, their Unit Leader, heard the speech and gave Des a long, disbelieving look. "Suck-up," murmured one of the Red Bracelets working on the next shuttle.

Des gave the man a wide, brilliant smile and a thumbs-up sign before clambering into the pilot's seat of his own shuttle.

Ed started to ask what all that nonsense had been about, but Des silenced him with a sign. The chatter of takeoff instructions filled the cabin; Des went through his checklist and said nothing that was not strictly business until their craft was well on its way to a landing on Rushima. Then he slapped the com unit off, turned to Ed, and grinned.

"You always were thick between the ears, Minkus."

"Not thick enough to put myself out for work I don't have to do," Minkus grumbled. "Ikwaskwan's not fool enough to send all of us on transport duty. Some lucky sods will get to stay behind, manning the battle stations and polishing command chairs with their rears, and we could've been among them."

Des snorted. "Not bloody likely, with us so new there as to've accumulated no seniority and no friends with strings to pull! We were for this duty, my friend."

"So you thought volunteering would make you look good?"

Des winked again. "I thought, Ed me boy, him as volunteers first gets the pick of the assignments. Now which would you rather be doing for the next six hours—commanding a troop of slogs to ferry the dirt farmers back and forth, with some two-bracelet type watching your every move, or taking your pick of what the evacuees left behind in their hurry?"

"But we're supposed to . . . oh," Ed said as understanding belatedly dawned. "You aren't going to look for settlers at all, are you? You're going to look for places they've already left!" He guffawed. "Neat trick, Des. Okay, we'll take it easy and say too bad, couldn't find no stragglers, Captain Ce'skwa, ma'am!"

"We will not take it easy," Des contradicted him. "We've got just six hours Standard and who knows what goodies to collect and stash in that time."

At the rendezvous landing they were met by a sweating dirt farmer who offered them their choice of datacubes or a hand-drawn map showing where he thought most of the outlying settlements were. Des was about to spurn the paper map when Ed discovered that the datacubes were in a format incompatible with the shuttle's computer. "Okay, okay, we'll take the map," he said, grabbing it before some of his colleagues could make the same discovery.

Captain Ce'skwa glanced at the map and quickly assigned each of the four shuttles on outlier duty to a different quadrant. Des grinned in satisfaction as he saw the generous sprinkle of X's marking probable settler huts all over his quadrant.

"Eager for work, Smirnoff?" Ce'skwa said drily. "You surprise me."

"Hope to continue doing so, ma'am!"

As she turned to the next pair of pilots, he continued under his breath to list the ways he'd like to surprise the uppity, interfering bitch, then snarled at Ed. "Well, what are you waiting for? Get going! We've only five and three-quarter hours Standard left to collect . . . all these poor, unfortunate souls," he finished with a sanctimonious smirk.

The first two places they flew over looked not only deserted but too poor to be worth looting: ramshackle huts whose roof timbers had been lifted off by some freak wind, the interiors soaked by torrential rains. "Nobody's lived here for some time," Des grunted, "if you could call that living . . . and if there was any good stuff, it's long gone or buried in mud. Whoever built here was an idiot anyway; obviously the area is subject to flooding—he shouldn't have settled on low ground."

The third place looked more promising. A long, low stone building tucked into the shelter of a cleft in a rocky hillside, it had been high enough to escape the floods, and the cliff must have sheltered it from the worst of the storms that had devastated the forest at the top of the hill. Des's eyes sparkled, and he guided the shuttle to a landing place on a barren outcrop of rock above the building. "Now this looks more like it!"

The scramble down to the building was rougher than it had looked from the air; the thin layer of topsoil over the rocks had been washed away by pounding rains, leaving a barren, slippery surface with precious little to hold on to and not even any good footholds. Ed wished that Des had landed in one of the waterlogged fields below the house instead, but he knew that saying anything would only ignite Smirnoff's temper and would not spare him the slippery descent. He took his time, though, testing what miserable footholds he could find and tugging firmly on roots before trusting his weight to them. Des slid recklessly down, bouncing and bruising his anatomy on various outcropping ledges of rock, got to his feet at the base of the cleft, and lumbered toward the house, blaster in hand, before Ed had even finished praying to all the gods he could bring to mind that he wouldn't break his neck on the last fifteen feet of the descent.

He was dangling by one hand, eyes closed, feeling for the ledge that had bruised Des on his descent and praying that the burly man hadn't bro-

ken the rock off entirely, when a bellow of delight
from within the house startled him into letting go
and dropping the last few feet.

"Minkus! Get your worthless butt in here and
help me shift this stuff!"

"Shit," Ed said, not exactly in reply, "I think I
broke something."

"You better not have, ol' buddy," was the
response. "If I have to choose between carrying you
back to the shuttle or carrying this load of furs, well,
the furs have some market value. . . ."

With this encouragement, Ed limped as far as
the outer door of the house—more of an elongated
cabin, really—and decided that his right ankle
was not really broken after all. Sprained, maybe.
A bad sprain. He ought to be lying down with his
foot up and an ice pack on the sprain, not hob-
bling around pretending to rescue settlers. Whose
idea had it been to join the Red Bracelets anyway?
Probably Smirnoff's, but he couldn't remember
for sure. They had both engaged in some heavy
drinking after being thrown out of the Kezdet
Guardians for embezzlement, peculation, and
abuse of suspects to a degree that revolted even
the other Guardians.

It had been after one of those drinking parties
and the subsequent blackout that Ed had wakened
to find himself dressed in a gray uniform and being
addressed as "Scumsucker," by the broad he had
quickly learned to call "Captain Ce'skwa, ma'am!"
What followed had been the most strenuous and
miserable weeks of his life; Captain Ce'skwa had a
talent for convincing them that they would really

rather attempt whatever bone-crunching, muscle-tearing "exercise" she assigned than explain their failure to her.

And that had been the officers' training; his and Smirnoff's experience in the Kezdet Guardians had at least bought them a single red bracelet apiece on entry. He didn't even want to think about what the rank and file of the mercenaries went through as basic training.

Now he turned a jaundiced eye toward the stack of half-cured furs Smirnoff was fondling and inquired where exactly Smirnoff planned to stash those things that they wouldn't be noticed by Captain Ce'skwa. "They stink, too," he pointed out. "Whoever had this place wasn't through tanning them when he lit out. Even if you could hide them, she'd be bound to notice the smell. I'm sorry, Des. We need to look for smaller stuff."

Des scowled. "Do you know how much furs of this quality would fetch in the Zaspala Imperium? And I've got a perfect fence . . . uh, buyer; my cousin Vlad has a furrier's and tailor's emporium, caters to the Zaspala aristos. Shit!"

And he signaled his acceptance of Ed's strictures by whirling the bundle of furs around at arm's length, then tossing it at the open cabin door. Ed dodged. The bundle landed with a thud, the bindings split, and furs spilled out into the thick black mud left by the rains that seemed to have assaulted this whole area.

Des dropped his blaster and went through the cabin with the recklessness of rage, spilling out food stores in case they contained jewels or antique money, smashing crude pottery cups and dishes that all too obviously had no resale value even on Rushima, let alone anywhere civilized. While he smashed and destroyed he cursed monotonously, taking out his disappointment over the furs on the inanimate objects in his path.

"Why couldn't the jerk have been a prospector instead of a fur trapper?" he demanded of the ceiling.

"He is," cackled a dry, crackling voice behind them. "One-One Otimie, explorer, trapper, prospector, and misanthrope extraordinary, at your service, gentlemen! Don't do anything reckless, now; I ain't real familiar with this here de-vice, wouldn't want to set it off accidental like."

Both men turned slowly to see a dried-up little stick of a man in the doorway, holding Des's blaster with two dismayingly shaky hands.

"Broadcast said as the enemy was comin', and we was to clear out," One-One said with a cackle, "but I don't reckon on leavin' my place to no in-vaders, nosirree! You fellas was turrible careless and noisy. Give me plenty of time to hide out up yander." He jerked his head toward the cliff they'd descended with such pains.

Des glanced at Ed and moved his head slightly to the left. Ed knew what he was thinking: if they got far enough apart, the old geezer wouldn't be able to keep the blaster trained on them both, and while he shot at one the other would be able to tackle him. But what, Ed thought, if he was the one who got blasted? Damn it! He'd known the Red Bracelets was no outfit for him.

✽✽✽

"No TACTICS?" Rafik raised both arms in total incredulity and flopped back into his chair. "You've been captured, tortured, pursued for generations. You've had your home world disintegrated, and you have still developed NO TACTICS to fight these Khleevi?"

Gill, Calum, and Ikwaskwan looked equally confounded by Melireenya's remonstrative expression.

"Linyaari do not kill."

"That's fine and dandy if someone isn't trying to kill you," Johnny Greene said.

"You mean all you've been doing since those . . . those devils started extinguishing your race was run and tell everyone the wolves are coming?" Rafik asked, still staring with disbelief at the calm Linyaari.

"No, we have . . . designed defensive weaponry," Thariinye said, not at all liking Rafik's reaction. "We have designed ships—"

"Which can outrun them," Rafik finished for him, as Thariinye drew himself up to his not inconsiderable height with indignation. "Fine, fine. Do you know what sort of firepower they have? What sort of weaponry they can bring to bear on us?" Rafik had risen, come out from behind the table, and was advancing on the tall Linyaari in as belligerent a pose as anyone had ever seen him use on another sentient being. "Because we sure as hell are NOT running away. Nor are you in that fancy fast ship of yours. The chips are down, the game is up, and it's here or never." Rafik finger-combed his hair back into order because he had been emphasizing his words so vehemently, his longish hair half covered his face.

"We, too, are armed and ready," Khaari said firmly. "They"—she pointed to the phalanx of Khleevi ships—"have missiles of great strength, capable of destroying all but your largest ships . . ." Khaari found herself unable to get out the syllables of the mercenary leader's name. ". . . Add-mee-ral," she got out. "They attack and attack until the ship is so . . . made holes in . . . that it can no longer return fire."

"That's not tactics," Rafik muttered, "that's suicide. At least"—he glanced thankfully at Ikwaskwan—"we've the proper attitude and experience to hand right now." He went to the screen. "Have your ships power enough to flank them, Ikwaskwan?"

"Of course we do, and considerably more firepower than they are likely to have if all their kills have been as easy as these horned types say. I mean, no contest. Go for the drive, the bridge, a few shots midships, and you've disabled it."

"Now that the settlers are safe," Melireenya said, "would it not be wiser to depart this system before the Khleevi arrive? Thus no one will be harmed."

"This time," Rafik said. "Your own experience has shown that running away won't work forever. And we barbarian bipeds have a strange reluctance to hand over real estate we've worked hard to claim."

Acorna felt enclosed in an isolation cell from all that was said around and about her. Somehow, in those few moments she'd allowed herself to envision her "own kind," she thought they'd be . . . well, wiser. More aloof, more self-contained: not that Melireenya wasn't, but Thariinye stood there with this supercilious expression on his face, which didn't become him at all, and he obviously loathed Rafik for making all Linyaari seem craven. But, if you weren't raised to kill, or hate, or scrabble for a living as her Kezdetian children had, why would you need to know tactics?

(One uses tactics in maintaining peace and accord, 'Khornya,) said the soft voice of Melireenya. (But, at first all we could do was run, or be certain none of us were captured alive. The vid we showed you is from our earliest contact with the Khleevi. And it was your father who invented the most devastating weapon we have. We dare not use it against the Khleevi because it destroys the destroyer as well. So we do not mention it until there is no other recourse. Do not fault us that we have been tardy in learning the skills of aggression and the weapons of defense. Had we not come to warn you, you would not have known the threat approaching you now.)

Though Melireenya stood on the opposite side of the conference room, Acorna was abruptly "in" the room again and not isolated from her kind or her defenders.

"So, let's get this tub"—Rafik paused to bow a smiling apology to Andreziana—"behind the moon, where it is not immediately apparent to the enemy converging not so slowly but very surely upon us. You don't want to have a few of Admiral's

Ikwaskwan's gunnery officers stay aboard the *Haven*, do you?"

"I'm gunnery officer," Johnny Greene said, appointing himself into that position on the spot.

The flush of indignation faded from 'Ziana's cheeks. "We've all had battery practice, Admiral. We'll pick off anything that eludes your attack."

"Well, now, will ya, li'l lady?" Ikwaskwan's eyes glittered.

"Leave it, Ikki," Nadhari murmured, and the light in the Kilumbembese mercenary's eyes dimmed to their normal shrewd gleam.

And, suddenly everyone was leaving to whatever posts they had been assigned, and Acorna was alone.

('Khornya,) — Thariinye leaned into the room again, smiling an invitation at her — (you're with us.)

Calum pushed past Thariinye and got her by the arm. "You'll be on the *Acadecki*. Rafik thinks we can move nonessentials about and make room for more ammunition. Even if we didn't fit in the extra banks Pal wanted, if we have enough ammunition, we'll achieve the same effect. More or less. If we get the chance."

Acorna accompanied Calum, but she bestowed an apologetic smile on Thariinye and a soft (good luck) as she passed by him. He was still watching her when she and Calum took the grav shaft down to the hangar level.

What Rafik thought of as nonessential was not so regarded by either Calum or Acorna, but in the end they acceded to his demands, and racks of additional missiles were stacked wherever there was room for them, up to and including Acorna's cabin, the space where her escape pod had been strapped, against the walls of the main lounge, Calum's bunk, and the spare cabins. The bunks happened to be exactly the same length as the missiles, and eight were strapped on top of the mattresses.

This was done with great effort and much sweating and swearing, finished just in time to hear the Klaxon that warned of an important message about to be given.

"Captain Andreziana here. Ikwaskwan reports that Rushima can be considered cleared of settlers. There is one shuttle still missing, but it is expected to report shortly.

"We will now proceed to our assigned position. All escort ships please prepare to disembark. And good luck, *Acadecki*, *Balakiire*."

"Good luck to you, *Haven*," Rafik said, reaching across the control panel to open the comlink. He settled himself in the pilot's chair, and, turning his head, said, "Prepare to leave the hangar."

"Hey, I pilot the *Acadecki*," Calum said, pushing at Rafik to leave the chair.

"I'm the tactician, remember," Rafik said as his slim brown fingers flew across the control panel. "You're the mathematician. And whichever you are, strap in."

Calum was still mumbling under his breath when he complied. Acorna muffled a giggle, and Gill turned his head away. To herself she thought how much like Thariinye and Khaari Calum and Rafik sounded.

(Not a bit like that undersized egotistical by-

blow of a twilit and a barsipan,) said Thariinye's
voice in her head.

(Do be quiet,) Melireenya said at her firmest.

Despite the speed at which Rafik prepared the
Acadecki for takeoff, the Linyaari ship had already
slipped out of its hangar position and was speeding
to take its position in the battle line.

Fifteen

Acadecki, Unified Federation Date 334.05.26

*T*he Kilumbembese mercenaries got back in the nick of time from ferrying as many of the Rushimese to safety as possible. As the combined space force of the Kilumbembese, the gaudy Linyaari courier ship, the three armed pinnaces of the *Haven*, the *Uhuru* under Nadhari's command, and the *Acadecki*—with Rafik in the pilot's seat—ranged themselves in their assigned battle positions, a certain steely calm descended in the main cabin of the *Acadecki*. The pinnaces were a last-minute addition, but they upped the odds against the Khleevi squadron.

Ikwaskwan had decided on a frontal approach. If things went as planned, as soon as the ships came into firing range, the coalition defending Rushima should divide their forces into two, confining the Khleevi within their pincers. This meant that each of the larger ships could bring its port or starboard missiles into action, swing around, and come back to deliver a second blow to the attacking ships. If any of the Khleevi ships should break off for a direct attack on the helpless planet, the smaller ships should attempt to slow their progress and/or their landing.

"Naval maneuvers need not be complicated, especially when we have never fought with you before," Ikwaskwan said. Rafik would have preferred a more sophisticated or subtle attack, but he had none to offer. These weren't asteroids he was attempting to make surrender their valuables, but sapient—although that was not a certainty—aggressors who had managed to terrorize the more sophisticated Linyaari. At least more sophisticated in some areas of technology.

The Khleevi liked to fight, so a fight they would get. Only this time the buggers wouldn't win so easily. The heir to House Harakamian was no lifesaving altruist: he was the descendant of red-blooded warriors who had for millennia taken by force what they desired, and held on to it. Since bargains were impossible with the Khleevi and force the only thing they understood, he would fight them as they had never seen fighting before.

Nevertheless, when the first, seemingly endless missiles spurted out of the Khleevi vanguard, Rafik prayed to those warrior ancestors with a fervor he had never before used. It was Gill who triggered the *Acadecki*'s missile ranks. He heard Acorna applauding, then Calum raging at Markel . . . who shouldn't be on board this ship . . . and then Gill tapped him on the shoulder.

"We're reloaded. Your turn."

This time, Rafik snarled as he sent more missiles after the first lot and recoiled at the bursts of flame and spewed fragments as the *Acadecki*'s missiles contacted and exploded the oncoming Khleevi warheads.

"Sheer off, we're going right into the mess," Gill cried, and Rafik hit the thrusters in a two-second blast that took the ship safely away, and their proximity sensors indicated they had missed being blown up by the skin of their collective teeth. Suddenly it was Gill in the pilot seat, though how he had relocated Rafik in the second chair, the heir did not know. But Gill's lips exposed his bared teeth in a snarl, and the intense expression on the big man's face suggested that his ancient Viking ancestors were a lot more accessible than Rafik's warriors.

"Oh, just look," Acorna cried, pointing at one of the auxiliary screens, aimed at where they had just been. "The lead Khleevi ships are breaking up."

"NO!" Calum's negative shout had more than a tinge of fear in it. "They're breaking OFF."

As Gill turned back to where the mercenaries were pounding the V formation of the Khleevi, it seemed that the three lead ships were disassembling themselves into smaller separate units. Far too many smaller units.

They watched, horrified, as the little pinnaces, like minnows against sharks, followed, their forward lasers punching at the shark tails . . . in three cases making direct hits. But only three instances . . . and luck had to have been on their side because there were far too many of the smaller Khleevi ships heading directly toward Rushima.

One of Ikwaskwan's dreadnoughts engulfed a Khleevi ship in such a holocaust that there were only a few units left to peel off the mother ship, like dry seeds falling out of a pod. But they made no attempt to correct their downward direction.

"Dead!"

The battle cruisers took out three more Khleevi mother ships, and sent their fighters after the few that escaped the devastating firepower of the cruisers. The destroyers worked at the lowest level of the V of Khleevi, but the instant the mother ships were attacked, the smaller units detached.

"There're thousands of them," Acorna cried. "Oh, how will we ever destroy them all?"

"We'll give it a mighty big try, Acorna acushla," Gill said. "What's the state of our weapon supply, Cal?"

"We'd do better to try launching singly, bringing down a small ship with each missile, than any more broadsides," Cal said.

"I think . . ." Acorna added her opinion, ". . . that we ought to go for the mother ships. I know they're now a much smaller target, but if we kill all of them, the Khleevi will be forced to land on Rushima, and they'll be sitting targets."

"Good thinking, Acorna," Gill said, giving her a grin over his shoulder as he maneuvered the *Acadecki* to bracket one of the now-spindly-looking mother ships in his launch sights.

They were so oddly shaped they didn't even appear to be dangerous, though the ovoid upper structure was clearly armed, to judge by the laser beams and lance missiles it was throwing at any target in range. From the upper ovoid a long stem depended, the stem on which the smaller units had been attached, making the Khleevi ships seem so much bigger than they actually were.

The dreadnought immolated one of the rear Khleevi in a ball of fire and slowly began to swing round to target a second. One of the battle cruisers took a bad hit and swerved out of range, while its fighter ships returned to defend it.

"That's two of the nine gone," crowed Rafik, waving his fists about.

"No, three," Gill corrected him, pointing to one that was no longer firing.

"Yes, but how many dozens of the smaller ones have gotten completely away?" Acorna asked.

"Let's harry a few to their deaths," Gill said, and altered course once more, bearing down on a covey of them.

"We're down to laser fire," Cal said.

"Misbegotten son of a syphilitic camel driver," Rafik said, and swore on. "If you'd listened to Pal in the first place, we'd've been able to go for one of the mother ships instead of having to go after the small fry."

"Let's fight them," Gill said, "not each other. Ah, got one."

Which he did, but the small ships seem to explode into even smaller divisions.

"How long can they keep separating?" Gill complained in exasperation.

Fighters from the battle cruisers and the pinnaces, which had survived against incredible odds, began shooting the new lots like so many swallows in a seasonal pilgrimage. However, the swallows had barbs in their tails, and one after another the three pinnaces following their primary targets were hit.

"Sowing space mines?" Gill asked rhetorically. Some pods had escaped each of the pinnaces. "We better get as many survivors as we can."

The brilliantly colored Linyaari ship and the *Uhuru* had had much the same idea and collected the pods, which attached themselves to their rescuers' hulls with tractor beams. But that meant the loss of any high-speed maneuvering capabilities for the rescuers.

"Let's get this lot back to the *Haven*," Gill said, pointing to the bulk of the Starfarer ship just visible at the edge of Rushima's primary moon. The small one that rushed around in orbit beyond the bigger one wouldn't have hidden a Khleevi parasite.

By the time the *Acadecki*, the *Uhuru*, and the Linyaari had brought the pods safely back to the *Haven*, Captain Andreziana had received orders from Ikwaskwan to come out of hiding and get the last three ovoid mother ships. The other six had been accounted for and were destroyed.

"All Khleevi are now on the planet, or about to land. We can move in now with kinetic energy weapons and smash them," Ikwaskwan said, his voice vibrant with triumph. "Pick on our clients, will you, you parasitical, piratical, putrefied parcels of puking pus-filled perverts. You won't be back in this part of space again, I can tell you! We'll pick you off like nits from a nanny."

Rafik listened to Ikwaskwan's harangue with the air of one master of the art of invective listening to another.

"But there are now so many of them down there," Acorna said.

"Thousands." Ikwaskwan grinned. "It could be expensive . . . lucky our clients are rich."

The *Haven*, with them on the hangar deck, moved out from behind the moon and, one by one, turned her big lasers on the ovoid stems that were attempting to find refuge behind the moon from the dreadnoughts and battle cruisers chasing them.

Amid the cheers as the last mother ship blew up, Markel said with great satisfaction and in anticipation of what was to come next—

"Well, it's up to Dr. Hoa now, isn't it?"

He became the center of everyone's attention.

"Well, isn't it?" he asked in a slightly speculative tone.

"Look," Ed Minkus said patiently for perhaps the twentieth time, "we aren't the invaders you were warned about. There are aliens—real aliens—heading for Rushima. And they're nasty bastards. They'll torture and kill every last one of you and turn this planet into a wasteland. We were sent to get you off-planet before the fighting starts. We're the good guys, damn it!"

"Sure," One-One said. "Sure you are. That's why you was wreckin' my cabin. You all seen the damage they done, didn't you, fellers?"

There was a general murmur of agreement, broken only by one dissenting voice that said he personally had seen One-One do worse than that to the bar at Crip's Crossing more than once.

One-One frowned the dissenter down. "Caught

'em in the act, din't I? And you ain't never seen me toss me own good stock of furs in the mud, have you, Quashie?"

Over the hours while Des and Ed had been held prisoner, there had been a steady trickle of other settlers who'd remained behind, coming in twos and threes in response to a message put out by One-One on some incredibly primitive homemade broadcasting device that seemed to operate on quartz crystals, wire coils, and curses. The gist of his message seemed to be that the bastards who'd messed over Rushima's weather had finally made the mistake of coming down to mess them all over in person; he'd caught two that they could use for hostages or execute depending on how things went, and everybody within range should come to his cabin as soon as they could get there, and bring their weapons.

The motley crowd that now filled the cabin inspired Ed with no very sanguine hopes as to his and Des's future. There were too many of them, and the cabin's tiny windows let in too little light, for him to see them all clearly, but he was just as glad of that. The faint light from the windows showed lean, weary-looking men and a few women, dressed in limp rags or stiff, awkwardly tanned leather. Their skin and clothes were crusted with engrained grime, their eyes glittered with the dangerous light of people who'd been pushed too far and isolated too long, and, collectively, they stank of old sweat and stale liquor. And the weapons they had collected inspired him with no more confidence. There were a few fairly up-to-date laser pulsers and blasters, but more common were edged weapons that looked to have been improvised out of farming equipment and whatever could be found for handles—sharp blades, things with rows of pointed hooks, a kitchen cleaver. There were even a few ancient projectile weapons that looked as if they belonged in a museum.

"Individualists" was in Ed's private opinion an overly polite name for the Rushimese who'd chosen to settle the backcountry and stay there in the threat of an invasion by overwhelming forces. Several more appropriate terms came to his mind, including, "nuts," "wackos," and "psychotic bastards." But he was careful, considering his company, to keep those opinions strictly private. One of the first arrivals had been carrying a long rope with which he bound Des and Ed together, seated back-to-back on the floor. He'd cut off the unused length of rope and coiled it again. Whenever the settlers discussed what to do with their prisoners, this man's lean, grimy fingers began stroking the coil of rope, and Ed watched it with horrified fascination.

From One-One's broadcast and subsequent conversations, Ed and Des had learned how the land and huts they'd overflown had come to be in such poor condition and why the settlers were so hostile to strangers now. They'd likely have been received with suspicion even if they hadn't been caught wrecking the cabin in search of valuables to loot. Ed had to admit that little fact did rob their story of some credibility . . . but damn it, he was actually telling the truth, and it was in these people's interest to listen to him; they'd all be in deep kimchee if they didn't untie him and Des and let them take them off-planet.

Ed kept trying to convince them of that, though with less and less hope of doing it as the hours wore on. The changing quality of the dim light warned him that much precious time had already passed . . . how much he didn't know; One-One had relieved him and Des of their chronometers and other equipment as soon as someone showed up to hold the blaster on them while he patted them down for weapons.

Des was unable to join in the argument for their lives, having exploded in such bursts of fury and blasphemy when first tied up that One-One had told the man with the rope to gag him. All Des could do now was rock back and forth and breathe stertorously through his nose to express his fury and indignation. Ed decided to make one more try at convincing with the colonists.

"Look," he said reasonably, "I can understand why you wouldn't trust us on our unsupported word; you have suffered terribly from strangers. But if you'd just let me use our ship's com system, I could bring other people who'd tell you the same thing."

One-One cackled. "Right, sonny, you could bring some more of your thieving buddies down on us, couldn't you! Don't waste your breath; I sent somebody to shut down the com units hours ago. And there's three guys guardin' the ship, so don't get no ideas about that bein' your ticket home, neither! Reckon we c'n use it to ambush yer buddies when they do show up."

"Hours . . . What time is it?" Ed demanded. "For God's sake, just tell me how long we've been here already?"

One-One squinted at Des's shiny chronometer, which hung awkwardly off his skinny wrist.

"Cain't read these little bitty numbers so good as I used to, sonny. What you reckon it says, Quashie?"

Quashie scowled. "Funny numbers," he said finally. "Don't look like no clock I ever seen. Change too fast, too. What's that one mean, the one keeps getting bigger? Look, it was ten a while ago, now it's up to twenty-five . . . twenty-six. . . ."

Sweat beaded on Ed's forehead and rolled down his face in an agonizingly tortuous, ticklish path. He tasted the salt on his dry lips.

"Is that number in a little blue square at the bottom right hand of the chronometer face?"

"Was blue," Quashie said. "Now it's red."

Ed sagged against the ropes that held him more or less upright and closed his eyes.

"I'm tired of hearing all your arguing," One-One told him. "You shut your trap now, or we'll shut it for you like we done the other 'un."

"It's okay," Ed said tiredly. "There's no hurry now. We're all dead, we just don't know it yet."

The chronometer had been set to display the time left before Admiral Ikwaskwan's deadline for clearing the planet. The changeover from blue to red meant the time had elapsed and the chronometer was now measuring the time since the deadline had passed.

Ed didn't know what Ikwaskwan expected to happen now, but he was fairly sure that the Admiral wouldn't change or delay his plans for the sake of two new recruits and one shuttle—and it must have been something fairly disastrous he had in mind; otherwise, their employers wouldn't have been so insistent about the necessity to evacuate all Rushimese from the planet before the deadline.

As if to corroborate his statement, a distant blast rumbled through the sky. Several of the Rushimese startled nervously; two of them blocked the tiny window, trying to peer out of it.

"More of their dirty tricks," one of them said. "Thunderstorm, I reckon. That could of been a lightning strike on Crip's Crossing. Any more rain, and that cliff's gonna come down on this-here cabin, One-One."

"Held up all right so far, din't it?" One-One retorted, but his eyes slid uneasily upward.

"Naah, that ain't lightning," the man called Quashie argued. "More like the dam upcreek of Crip's busting. I heerd the big one down to the reservoir go. Sounded just like that there."

Three more booms and a series of sharp cracks canceled the argument. The last noise was so close to the cabin that Ed shut his eyes and tried to contract his body, as if that would protect him from aerial attack.

"Hellfire," somebody at the window shouted, "they done got the shuttle!"

"Get my Pyaka outa there!" screamed a gray-faced woman.

"Winjy," said Quashie, putting an arm around her shoulders, "ain't nothing left to get nobody out of. I'm dreadful sorry, but we be mournin' Pyaka and them other two fellas. They gone, Winjy."

Now we are really dead, Ed thought, and if he

thought he'd known despair before, he knew the difference now. There'd been no reasonable hope that these maniacs would untie him and Des and give them a chance to reach the shuttle . . . but as long as it existed, the hope of escape had been there, the chance in a million that they would somehow be able to get out of this crazy place and back to the narrow berth on a Red Bracelet ship which now, in retrospect, seemed a haven of comfort and safety.

So deep was his despair, he paid no attention to the low-voiced conversation going on between One-One, Quashie, and one or two other settlers who seemed to be leaders of the group. Their words were almost drowned out anyway by the woman Winjy's hopeless sobbing and by the blasts and roars of distant battle . . . not all of them all that distant, either!

Ed leaned against the cabin wall, eyes closed in despair, and ignored his surroundings until something hard poked him in the ribs, and One-One gruffly demanded to know what he thought.

"About what?" He didn't even bother to open his eyes.

"About settin' you loose, peanut-head, what you think we been talkin' about here?" A second, harder dig inspired Ed to look at the old guy. "Reckon if these here invaders wanted to blow up your shuttle, them and you might not be on the same side after all. And they's ship looks different from yours, too. Different from anything I ever seen before, truth."

"Christ on a crutch!" somebody yelled. "They *is* aliens! Some kinder giant bugs!"

Des grunted and thumped from side to side,

shaking Ed with each excited movement. "Mmmp? Mmmb nnn mmmph!" he grunted emphatically.

"'Course, you're still damned looters, and we'll probably still hang you after we done fought off these here fellas, but if'n you'll give your parole while the fight lasts, well . . . reckon we c'n use ever able-bodied person we got here."

Ed couldn't swear loyalty fast enough.

"Your buddy, too?" One-One regarded Des critically.

"Mmmm-mmmp," Des told him.

"Good enough . . . you ain't got nowhere to run to, anyways. Might wanta keep that in mind." One-One sliced through Des's gag with a casual swipe of his sharp tanning knife, then cut the ropes binding both men with two more slashes.

"Hey," the man with the rope protested, "that's me good rope you wastin'!"

"Ain't got time to fool with knots," One-One said. "Cover the back winder, willya?"

He handed a blaster to Des and pointed out that he still had the other blaster, and that there'd be someone watching their backs, in case they had any cute ideas.

Des shook off the ropes and gag like feathers and charged for the back end of the cabin as if he'd been doing sitting-up exercises instead of sitting tied up in a corner for hours. Ed moved more slowly, feeling the pins and needles of returning circulation in his extremities and the cramping sensation of muscles protesting their long confinement.

"Pick it up, Ed me boy!" Des shouted. Somebody handed him a wicked-looking iron pole with a row of sharp points roughly welded to its far end.

"A lot of good that does," Ed protested. "Where's our other blaster?"

One-One grinned and shook his head. "Ain't got enough distance weapons to waste two on one winder, me boy. Your buddy'll try an' hold 'em off. Any of 'em gets in close, you use this best way you can, got it?"

When Ed reached Des, his partner was wearing a maniacal grin intensified by the foam that had flecked his lips while he was gagged and the blood where One-One's pointed knife had cut his cheek as well as the gag. His chin was blue with an incipient beard and, all in all, he looked as desperate and uncivilized as the worst of the settlers in the cabin.

"Luck of the Smirnoffs, Ed old buddy!" he greeted Ed.

"Luck?" Automatically, Ed took position beside Des, his iron pole at an angle where he could jab it out the window at anything approaching. "Our ship's been destroyed, we're trapped on this planet between crazy settlers and invading space bugs, Ikwaskwan's gonna pound the bugs and doesn't care what he does to us in the process, and you say we're lucky?"

"If the bugs hadn't moved in," Des said cheerfully, "these maniacs would've likely hung us. And as for the ship, there's a simple solution now, isn't there? We'll just have to take theirs!"

"Simple." Ed almost choked.

"No alternative, buddy. Oh-oh, here comes a bug. Let's see if their armor holds up to a . . ." Des squeezed off a shot. A cloud of steam went up from the advancing alien's hard brown carapace, and one of its many legs disappeared, but the other limbs kept inexorably moving. Some of the legs fired green energy bolts at the cabin.

Des ducked, looked at the weapon in his hand, and swore. "Damn fools gave me your blaster!"

"What's wrong with that?"

"Got mine fitted with a PowrChargr last station," Des said, naming one of the many enhancements that was considered illegal and immoral in the civilized world. This particular one was supposed to allow an ordinary hand blaster to spread its stun range over half a klick, or alternatively to narrow and concentrate its power in one needle-sharp pulse that would vaporize the object it hit.

"Shit!" Des squeezed off half a dozen more shots as the alien advanced, coolly picking off the jointed legs along one side of its flat body until they were all gone. The alien toppled to one side and lay wriggling its other legs helplessly.

"Give me the pole." Des squeezed his bulk through the open window with a few rips, scratches, and curses, dropped with a thump onto the muddy ground, and charged without stopping to catch his breath. The hooked pole went into a bulbous, gleaming structure on the alien's head and sank deep within, splashing Des with the black fluid that spurted from the sphere. Ed clenched his teeth against the wave of nausea rising from his guts.

A moment later Des was back at the window, saying, "Come on, get 'em all out this way. We can't stay in the house, it's an obvious target."

"What's the point of leaving it?"

"Easy," Des said. His teeth gleamed white among the blood, foam, and black droplets that decorated his face. "We'll lure the bugs into the house, then fire off a couple of blaster shots and bring that cliff down on 'em . . . it's not all that stable now, didn't you notice that when we were coming down the track?"

Ed certainly had. And though he had little or no faith in Smirnoff's plan, he couldn't think of anything better—so he begged, bullied, or persuaded the remaining settlers to crawl through the back window and follow Des along the narrow track he had temporarily cleared.

For one dark moment he wondered exactly how Des planned to "lure" the Khleevi into the cabin and who was going to play "bait," but One-One Otimie solved that question once he understood the plan. From an overlooked cupboard above the food stores he produced battered musicubes and a solar-powered player.

"Kirilatova," he said, jamming a cube into the player with ruthless disrespect for the delicate workings of the machinery. "*Figaro.* Remastered from the originals." He cackled at the look of surprise on Ed's face. "Thought we was all uncultured backcountry folks, din't you, sonny? Hee-hee-hee. I like opera just fine; it's people I wanted to get away from."

As they scrambled through the back window, the last two humans to clear the cabin, the seductive strains of Susannah's aria, *"Deh vieni, non tadar,"* floated through the air. Ed only hoped the song would be as enticing to the Khleevi as it had been meant to sound in the opera.

He was almost disgusted at how well Des's crude plan worked. The cockroachlike Khleevi approached the cabin, cautiously at first, then more openly as no one fired on them. They made sharp crackling noises among themselves as they drew closer, firing occasional bolts into the cabin; Ed could almost have sworn the two in the lead were laughing and rubbing their forelegs together in anticipation of a jolly time. He remembered the vids Ikwaskwan had copied from the Linyaari and used as training films, and felt sick all over at the memory of what the Khleevi considered light entertainment. He had a terrible moment as he worried that everybody was out of the cabin. He couldn't have left a dog to the mercies of those—those things. . . .

Every muscle of his body screamed to run, run now before they noticed their quarry had escaped, but Des coolly waited through agonizing seconds until all but one of the advancing aliens was out of sight inside the cabin. Then he and One-One fired blasters at the designated weak spots, dissolving a long line of muddy earth and stone into a bubbling liquid that let the front face of the cliff slide downward with a long, final sigh. Slabs of stone tilted slowly forward and smashed the cabin roof flat; one of them fell half across the one Khleev who remained outside, turning his body into a mangled mess that leaked black fluid and curls of steam. The stone slabs were followed by a slow but inexorable tide of wet dirt and the molten lava created by the blasters, which buried the cabin and its occupants under a newly created hill.

"Come on," Des hissed before the wave of mud

and lava had settled, "gotta take their ship before they catch on to what just happened!"

"Before who catch on?" gasped Ed, at his side. "We just killed—oh." More cockroaches were pouring out of the squat, alien-looking ship that stood in the clearing.

"You are so damn dumb, Minkus. Would you leave a ship totally unguarded while everybody chased the natives?" Des gave him a look of disgust. "Yeah, you probably would. Give me that pole, you don't know what to do with it." And he plunged in among the Khleevi with a battle yell of pure, savage joy, stabbing the pole down with unerring aim into the enemies' soft spots.

Someone thrust a cleaver into Ed's hand, and the wave of yelling settlers carried him on until he found himself in the thick of the fight, chopping off legs with his cleaver, dodging the energy bolts, frantically waving his free arm to defend himself from the gouts of black acid the aliens spat . . . and then, before he knew it, they were through and on the farside of the aliens, and Des was shouting at them to follow him into the ship itself. Ed stepped over blobs of black guck, already crusting over, and kicked a dying Khleev off the ladder with one booted foot.

There were no more Khleev inside . . . no more living, that is . . . though the stench of their dying and the acid whiff of their black . . . blood? . . . whatever . . . infested the entire ship. The settlers crowding after Ed forced him forward and into the tiny section covered with unreadable instrumentation that Des already occupied. He was squatting on the low, narrow bench that the Khleevi must have used instead of chairs.

After a moment's uncomfortable experimentation, Ed decided that Smirnoff had found the only possible adaptation of the human anatomy to these furnishings. Wide metal columns behind them, their outer walls curved in a concave form that must have been designed to fit a Khleev carapace, promised support and protection during takeoff, and the straps that dangled from the columns could, with some ingenuity, be arranged to hold a human body. Ed hoped the settlers had made their own accommodations to the Khleev interior; Des was already punching buttons with mad abandon in search of the one that would fire up the ship's engines.

"You think you can fly one of these things?" he asked doubtfully.

"Can't be all that different from ours," Des said. "Same problems, same type solutions. They gotta get free of gravity, navigate, correct position, and tilt . . . Yeeehaw!" he screamed in triumph as one of the buttons he'd punched resulted in a wild blast of flame that lifted the ship from its landing place with a sickening double punch and sway. "Ikwaskwan, here we come! See if you can find a portable com system among all that crud the settlers dragged on, Ed. It might be polite to announce we're on our way!"

Sixteen

With the Khleevi mother ships disabled and their pods pinned down on Rushima by the orbiting ships of the Red Bracelets, there was time to discuss Markel's suggestion of using weather-modification technology to destroy the Khleevi rather than the expensive, and destructive, kinetic energy weapons favored by Ikwaskwan.

"I had intended this system for peace, not war," said Ngaen Xong Hoa sadly. "But it seems that technology of this sort must be used always for destruction—if not by the warring parties of my homeland, then by whoever controls it." He gave Markel a long, steady look. "I trusted your father's honor. He died rather than permit Nueva Fallona and her cronies to make war on Rushima with my weather-modification system. Now you ask me to do the same thing."

"Not on Rushima, on the Khleevi—" began Gill.

"Wait!" Markel swallowed hard after interrupting Gill, but his face showed a maturity and resolution that had not been there short weeks earlier. "Yes, Dr. Hoa. We wish to use your scientific knowledge to kill . . . those who would otherwise . . . exterminate us. So we would be using it in self-defense, which is not the same thing as using it for making war on the helpless. . . . You know what the Linyaari have told us about these invaders. If they had come in peace, we would have greeted them in peace . . . but they come to destroy us. And, yes, I will use any means at my disposal to defend my people and myself. I believe Illart would have done the same thing."

"We do not know they have come to make war," Hoa said.

"Actions speak louder than words," Rafik pointed out.

"Ah. But words have not spoken yet." Hoa clasped his hands together in front of him. "Before I give consent to this further misuse of my research, I must insist that we make every effort to communicate with our alien visitors."

"Markel? Is this necessary?" Andreziana glanced at Markel and raised one eyebrow.

"Yes," Markel said in the most decisive tone. He paused and gave an indolent shrug more like his usual mannerisms. "Anyway, I could probably deploy the weather-intervention technology without Dr. Hoa's consent. Just as Nueva Fallona did! By analyzing the programs Nueva's people implemented we could deduce those things that were left out of the research notes." He paused, and all his aggression seemed to dissipate suddenly. He swallowed again. "But . . . I believe . . . Illart would also have said we must first attempt peaceful negotiation."

"Ridiculous!" Andreziana was on her feet. "Markel, as captain of the *Haven*, I could order you to implement the technology now."

"But you will not," said Pal Kendoro sharply.

Pal was so quiet that all were startled at this interruption and watched as he came forward to grip Andreziana's arms at the elbows, forcing her to look up at him. "'Ziana, don't you know better than to give orders that Markel will feel honor-bound to disobey? You and the other kids did a grand job of recapturing the *Haven*. You're a bunch of infant experts at everything from astro-gation to life-support systems, but you've still got a few things to learn about people . . . and the art of command."

"I know what we need to do in order to deal with the Khleevi," Andreziana snapped, freeing herself from Pal's grip with a quick, vicious twist of her body. "Unlike some around here, I'm not afraid to take responsibility for it—any more than I was afraid to space the murderers who killed my mother and father!"

"And you're still feeling bad about that, aren't you?" Pal said in a low, gentle voice. "They were murderers, and you had no other option, but you see their faces in your nightmares . . . and so to prove you made the right choice then, you have to keep choosing the toughest path, whether or not it's necessary."

Tears sparkled in Andreziana's eyes, and she stared up at him wordlessly.

"You don't have to do that now, 'Ziana," Pal said. "This responsibility belongs to all of us; you don't have to carry it alone. Whatever we do, we'll all discuss it, and we'll all share in the decision. You and the other kids did a fine job when you were left on your own, but the point is, that you're no longer alone anymore. We're in this battle, fighting right beside you."

Andreziana's lips trembled, and Pal put his arm about her, shielding her face from the view of the others for a long, tense moment. When Andreziana finally turned away from him, she looked composed, more at peace than she had since the Palomellese coup on the *Haven*.

"I'm sorry, Markel," she said. "Understand," she warned him, "I'm still captain of the *Haven* . . . but this can't be just the captain's decision. This decision belongs to all of humanity . . . all who are here to speak, at least . . . and to the Linyaari, too," she said. "Shouldn't they be here? And the Red Bracelets—"

"Let's not overdo it," Johnny murmured. "I think we know how the Red Bracelets would vote. Besides, they're needed where they are . . . in low geosynchronous orbit, making sure the Khleevi don't go anywhere."

"And we cannot afford to keep them there indefinitely," Gill pointed out.

After more discussion, it was agreed that the *Haven* and the *Acadecki* would attempt for a period of two Standard hours to establish some communication with the Khleevi on Rushima, using the universal codes that had long been agreed on for first contact with any sapient alien race, should one ever be found. Therefore, mathematical formulae and physical constants were broadcast in steady sequence, using different base systems and with regular pauses to invite reply.

"No response," Calum said wearily after more than an hour had gone by. "Perhaps we should try something else."

"We could shoot at them," Gill muttered. "That sure got a response!"

"No, not—*waitaminute*, wait a minute!" Calum punched at the control panel to bring up an enlarged view on one screen. "Something's leaving the planet—and heading straight for us. Coms, tell Ikwaskwan not to shoot it down!"

"Trojan horse," Gill suggested, while Acorna efficiently raised Ikwaskwan's flagship and requested the lone vessel be allowed to exit Rushima unhindered.

"He's not heading straight for anywhere," Calum exclaimed. "Look at that—yawing all over the place . . . don't these people know how to stabilize their ships?"

"They did just fine in the battle," Gill pointed out. "Maybe this one is damaged." His fingers twitched, indicating his complete willingness to do more damage.

"Acorna, are you open on all frequencies?"

"Of course, Calum," Acorna said. "Intruder is not transmitting."

"If they don't correct their course and identify themselves somehow in the next sixty seconds," Calum said tensely, "rescind the hold-fire request and give Ikwaskwan permission to destroy them. They're now, more or less, on a collision course with US. I'm sorry about Dr. Hoa's sensibilities, but not sorry enough to die while waiting for the other fellows to parley. The Linyaari said they don't parley, and it looks like . . ."

Fortunately for two newly hired mercenaries and a group of weary Rushimese settlers, at that moment Ed Minkus found a portable com system.

"Don't fire! Don't fire!" he squawked first, and then, regaining a little control, "All Red Bracelet ships and allies: this is Ed Minkus for the ship . . . uh . . . what is it called, Des?"

A rumbling growl seemed to be telling the speaker not to waste time on nonessentials. "Call it Jurden, it smells like one!"

"Right! Uh . . . this is the ship Jurden, a prize of war captured from the Khleevi, requesting permission to rejoin . . . and, uh, could somebody tow us in with a tractor beam? We're having a little trouble figuring out the controls on this thing."

"Jurden, this is the *Haven*," came a crisp young voice on the frequency Ed had found. "We have a fix on you now. Can you verify this is not a Khleevi trap?"

"Dammit, we just got away from the Khleevi . . . wait a minute!" There were scuffling sounds and Ed's voice muffled by distance, protesting; then a crackly old voice came on.

"Girlie, this here's One-One Otimie, free settler of Rushima, and you bring us on board right fast, you hear me? Got things to tell you about them big ol' bugs like you wouldn't believe! And I ain't goin' back there, no how, no way, so if you think us is bugs, you just go right ahead and blow us out of the sky, you hear? Rather that than goin' back, right, folks?"

"Jurden, prepare to be towed," Andreziana's voice responded.

The exchange was shut off as *Haven*'s tractor beam attached itself to the Khleevi ship. Gill and Calum leaned back, laughing weakly, while the others exchanged puzzled glances.

"What's so funny?" Acorna finally asked.

"Smirnoff. The bastard can't be all bad," Gill said. "He must have some Celtic ancestors somewhere."

"I fail to see that as a guarantee of respectability—look at you two giggling idiots!" Rafik said, crisply critical.

"Jurden," Calum calmed himself long enough to explain, "is an old Scots word for a chamber pot. So I guess we know Smirnoff's opinion of the Khleevi!"

And once Smirnoff and Minkus and One-One had described how the Khleevi came in firing and attacked immediately, even Hoa regretfully agreed that the Linyaari account of their enemies seemed to be completely accurate.

"Talk is better," Hoa said ruefully, "but some warlords do not talk, only kill. Markel, you will assist, please?"

The weather-intervention process fascinated Calum, who was watching every detail of Hoa's work. There was plenty of time for all interested observers to assemble because Hoa insisted that the Red Bracelet ships must clear out of their low orbit.

"Ionospheric intervention of this magnitude can affect orbiting ships' communications and electrical systems," Hoa explained. "*Haven* must maintain a certain distance in order to fire laser beams, but all others should retreat as far as possible."

While the Kilumbembese ships were moving to a safe distance, Hoa studied real-time displays of Rushima's atmosphere and terrain and hummed softly to himself.

"Mmm, mmm, good unstable cloud masses here, yes, much instability in the troposphere, electrical potential building up . . . a little nudge here. . . . We begin with lightning," he said, "using ship's amplifiers to simulate action of hybrid Oscillator/ Regenerative Amplifier which I used in scientific studies. Spaceships, being tall and metal, should attract lightning before any other objects on ground. Communications and electrical systems will be destroyed."

"Get on with it, can't you?" Calum murmured under his breath. "Pulling back the Red Bracelets may have been necessary for their safety, but it's got to look to the Khleevi like we're retreating. They'll see if they can escape. They know they're trapped on the surface."

Hoa's fingers played over the console pad before him, and he snapped requests to Markel for confirmation of the numbers he produced.

"Hurry!" Andreziana said from her own seat. "I'm seeing hot spots, probably ships igniting their engines. . . ."

"Now," Hoa said, and the screen in front of Andreziana went wild with a display of crackling lights.

"What was that?" she gasped.

"Series of short pulses cause electron migration, propagation, collisions, avalanche ionization," Hoa said. "Conduction path will be formed wherever possible. Lasers would provide more focused strikes, but in absence of information about location of ships, general ionization is best bet."

Three Khleevi ships had launched off-planet during the lightning storm, but two of them behaved so erratically as to make Des Smirnoff's approach in the Jurden appear a marvel of accurate navigation. After a series of staggering loops, one failed to escape Rushima's gravity and fell back toward the planet; the other one transmuted into a searing burst of light that left only fragments. The third ship darted through a space just recently vacated by the Red Bracelet fleet and escaped Rushima, but not to attack, only to flee. One of Ikwaskwan's warships swung out of line and followed.

"How did you make that second one explode?" Calum demanded, awed.

Dr. Hoa shrugged slightly. "Impossible to predict what goes first when electrical systems are destroyed. Steering, power . . . in this one, I think fuel controls. It is not at all an accurate action," he said with disapproval. "Is not science; science deals with predictable results. Now you will see! Markel, bring up titanium-sapphire lasers, please."

"Aren't we too far away for laser warfare?" Calum asked. "The beam will spread until it's so weak . . ."

"Sufficiently intense light pulses are trapped in three dimensions," Hoa replied without looking up. "Self-compensating nonlinear effects. End result, dispersion, diffraction, and scattering are balanced by self-stabilizing processes. I cannot prove how it happens," he said, "only demonstrate results of focused high-intensity laser strikes on appropriate cloud material. Laser forms a tunnel of ions, which attracts lightning. . . . My intent," he said sadly, "was to use such tunnels to draw lightning away from structures, which needed protection. Instead . . ." He twiddled with controls and adjusted the focus of the laser with infinite precision. "Instead," he repeated, as lightning arced through Rushima's atmosphere, "I now direct it at structures. . . ."

"Which need destroying," Calum reminded him gently.

Ikwaskwan's com technician reported that the Khleevi ship had escaped; having so little mass, it had been able to reach lightspeed long before the heavier battleship, and they had been unable to catch it within the limits Ikwaskwan had set for his fleet's range.

"Quite right, too," Calum agreed. "They'd do themselves and us no good by following one Khleevi ship until their fuel was exhausted. Still, I'd like to know where they come from. . . ."

"Several ships have been captured," Markel reminded him, "and we have the virtually intact pod that Smirnoff and Minkus escaped in. We can study their computers and charts. . . ."

"And maybe Dr. Zip can help analyze the metals," Calum said, remembering how that eccentric astrophysicist had applied the latest upsilon-V imaging techniques to provide Calum with a basis for working out where Acorna's home world probably lay. That world was long since laid waste by the Khleevi, and the Linyaari envoys could provide them with the location of the new home, narhii-Vhiliinyar; but there still might be a use for his computational and astroplotting program, to help locate the home base of the Khleevi. That possibility cheered him immeasurably, and while Dr. Hoa pounded Rushima with storms and floods to destroy any remaining Khleevi, he began jotting notes for an amended version of the program.

When Dr. Hoa patently began to tire Calum and Markel both vied to take over from him. Calum was chosen but, when Dr. Hoa saw Markel's sullen expression, he put his hand under the boy's chin and forced him to meet his gaze.

"There will be time for you, too. Watch and be ready to take your turn. You are well able when all is said and done."

Johnny Greene leaped forward to help the exhausted man who, at first, waved off the need for assistance until he stumbled at the steps leading up to the main level of the bridge.

"Come." Andreziana was beside the doctor, firmly taking his hand. "You may rest in the captain's ready room," she said, indicating the door that gave onto the bridge.

"Your ready room, my dear, your ready room," Dr. Hoa said, smiling as he patted her arm but quite willing to let her escort him. That accomplished, Andreziana returned to her command chair with just the slightest of smirks at having been more effective than Johnny Greene. And Pal moved just that much closer to her chair, subtly informing the older man that his efforts were redundant.

Johnny turned away, with a broad grin that

Acorna and Rafik noticed: Acorna with considerably more sympathy and relief than Rafik.

That would certainly solve a problem for her. The way Pal had all but challenged Thariinye disturbed her even if she did see it as only the usual posturing of males for a desired female. The incident had also taken away from Acorna's eyes the scales of infatuation over her first encounter with a male of her own species.

However, she too was tired and wanted to retire as discreetly as she could to the *Acadecki*, now once again on the *Haven*'s hangar deck.

So, too, was the Linyaari ship, and, as she passed it, Neeva called out to her.

"Join us, my sister-child," and then added as Acorna switched her direction, (You cannot know how rewarding it is to see the Khleevi overwhelmed as they have overwhelmed us for centuries. To know that we, we four, have been witness to their rout.)

(I don't feel much like cheering, I'm afraid) Acorna said truthfully.

Neeva pressed her horn against Acorna's. The scene of Acorna's dream reappeared. (This is what they destroyed for you. But it is good to see that you are more linyarii than khlevii in the matter of dealing death. This is indeed a novel way of defeating one's enemy.)

(IF you can get them to land on a planet) Acorna said.

Neeva nuzzled Acorna. (You are heartsick, my sister-child, and it is because we are not what you thought we should be. Is that not correct?)

Acorna gasped. She hadn't realized just how

deeply Neeva could delve. (I mean no offense, truly. It's just that you . . .)

(Are what our world and genetics have made us, just as these humans are the product of their worlds and genes.) It was Melireenya whose deep voice chimed into their conversation. She appeared in the open hatch of the brilliantly decorated ship. (You wish to know HOW do we manage to keep the paint so bright? Ah, that is one of our secrets. Come. Come. Let us relieve your anxieties and confusions, dear 'Khornya.)

Acorna was mind-weary enough to wish surcease and entered the Linyaari vessel. Thariinye was not in evidence.

(You must have just passed him on the way to the *Haven's* bridge,) Neeva said. (He wishes to know more about this most unusual and spectacular method of dealing with the Khleevi.)

(Huh,) Khaari said with a nasal snort of disagreement, (he enjoys seeing the ships blown up and was counting them. "That is for the Selinaaryi." "The next kill will be for the Juveniiryi.")

(Who?) asked Acorna, confused, though she did realize that these were family names.

(Ancestors and friends who were lost to the Khleevi over the centuries,) Khaari answered.

(Will there be ships enough to satisfy that lust in Thariinye?) Neeva asked ruefully.

She led Acorna to a pile of cushions and settled her in their comfort. Then she began to knead the muscles of Acorna's neck, and work her fingers up and down the length of the mane, into the vertebrae themselves. More often than not, Acorna winced at the pain as Neeva touched places which Acorna hadn't even known were sore.

(When we bring you home) and there was a subtle triumph in Neeva's use of the word, (we shall introduce you to the ways whereby we dissipate tension and fatigue. This ship was not large enough to contain the unit, which is why we do not appear at our best to you. We, too, have suffered from the stress of reaching your quadrant of space soon enough to give you warning.)

(We are not always as contentious as we have been these past few weeks,) Melireenya said sorrowfully. Then her silvery eyes brightened. (What glad tidings we bring, along with one we thought lost and gone to us.)

(Do I have many relations?) Acorna asked, though she already knew that she had been the only youngling born to her parents.

Neeva's silvery neigh filled the room. (Hundreds! But we shall not require you to meet them all at once.)

(I will want you to meet a few) — Khaari smiled, her eyes sparkling — (a chosen few of mine.)

Melireenya gave Khaari an affectionate shove. (I am the elder. I shall have the first chance.)

(Chance for what?) The inferences were beyond Acorna, though she sensed them in the subtle nuances of the interchange.

(Why, to introduce you to a suitable mate, of course) Neeva said, as if that should have been obvious. (You are well old enough to need a mate. In fact, I marvel that you have been able to contain yourself.)

(She has had no one to stimulate that part of her nature yet) Melireenya said. (Or have you experienced . . . well, unusual sensations at all?) She turned to the other two females. (It can happen, you know, for someone isolated as she has been.)

(I . . . well) — Acorna bowed her head in confusion — (there have been moments . . .)

(Not for much longer, sister-child,) Neeva assured her, and continued to massage her neck.

(It will have to be for a while longer,) Acorna said regretfully.

(WHY?) all three Linyaari demanded, shocked.

"Well, there are things I must attend to at Maganos. . . ."

(Nothing that Rafik fellow cannot handle) remarked Melireenya firmly. (We are YOUR people. You must first come with us. Then, if there are any problems that you must indeed deal with yourself, we can return with you.)

Khaari's neigh was closer to a snicker. (And with your life partner.)

(WILL one find me suitable? I've lived so long. . . .) Acorna stopped because even Melireenya was convulsed in Linyaarish laughter.

(Wait and see, 'Khornya. Wait and see.) Then the other two made excuses of tasks to be done and Neeva altered the rhythm of her gentle kneading, and, before Acorna could help herself, she was dozing off.

It was dawn on the *Haven* before anyone came looking for her. Calum had finally deferred to Markel and gone back to the *Acadecki*, falling asleep the moment he lay down. He never thought that

Acorna would be anywhere but in her own quarters. So, when Gill and Rafik came looking for her, and him, to announce the arrival of Uncle Hafiz, with his voluptuous and veil-swathed Karina, they were startled and dismayed to find her missing.

"She is here, close by," Karina said through her veil. It wasn't a very thick gauze, Calum noticed: much more transparent than the silks he'd once been dressed in for Uncle Hafiz's benefit. It allowed someone to get a glimpse of a rather attractive face, if much too plump for Cal's taste.

Now Karina gracefully placed her much beringed hand on her forehead.

"Very close." She slowly turned and looked at the Linyaari vessel. "There in fact. And oh, they're all there. And fast asleep."

"Uncle," Rafik said in an undertone, "since when have you followed the outmoded and barbarous custom of veiling your women?" Only a few years earlier Hafiz had been shocked and dismayed to find Rafik apparently converted to the Neo-Hadithians and reverting to the strictures practiced by those who denied the Second and Third Prophets, keeping women veiled and refusing spirituous liquors. He had professed great relief to discover that Rafik's apparent conversion to a fundamentalist sect had been only a clever business trick—even if he had been its victim.

"Since I acquired this pearl without price, my lovely Karina," Hafiz replied in the same discreet undertone.

"Acquired? Uncle, the last time I looked, slavery was forbidden by the laws of all known states and federations. Even on Laboue, I do not think you can legally own a concubine!"

Hafiz put on a disapproving expression. "Nephew, I might take offense did I not love you so dearly. Karina is my beloved and dearly cherished wife in the sight of the Three Prophets. We have sworn our vows upon the Three Books."

Rafik's mouth dropped open. "You've married that . . . that pseudopsychic charlatan?"

"Dear boy," his uncle said in a warning tone that held more than a hint of steel, "you are speaking of your new aunt. It is a shame to all discerning men that such a flower of beauty should have been forced to work for a living instead of reclining upon silken cushions and being fed on marzipan and cream cakes. Her previous lifestyle," he said grandiloquently, "is unimportant to me; the cherished gazelle of Hafiz Harakamian need never lift a finger again."

Rafik reflected that if his uncle really intended to feed his new acquisition upon marzipan and cream cakes, she might well be incapable of lifting a finger in a few years. Even now, "gazelle" was hardly the word that came to mind when describing her.

"Is she not voluptuously beautiful beyond your wildest dreams?" his uncle sighed rapturously. "Even my Yasmin could hardly have compared with Karina."

Mention of Hafiz's first wife, the long-dead Yasmin, reminded Rafik that his uncle had already shown a definite predilection for women whose most prominent attributes lay somewhere south of their brains. Yasmin had been a dancer in a zero-G topless bar when Hafiz abducted her.

"Karina, my little lily," Hafiz said to his new wife, "pray do not exhaust yourself in using your powers to contact the Linyaari. They will awaken soon enough of their own accord, and I would not see your lovely face lined with fatigue. Sit here and rest yourself, and I will see to it that some light refreshment is brought to restore your psychic energies."

Karina smiled up into his face with a look of such radiant love and trust that Rafik's last objections to the marriage melted like snow on Laboue, and he was devoutly thankful that the words "gold digger" had not passed his lips. No one looking at the pair could doubt that they were truly infatuated with one another. Still, when he remembered his uncle's cynical strictures on the subject of women and marriage, he could not but be amused to see Hafiz, of all people, swept away on a tide of sugary-sweet romance.

"What are you laughing about?" Calum inquired out of the side of his mouth after Rafik had greeted Karina with all the respect due to his uncle's wife and retired to the farside of the *Haven*'s main cabin to release his amusement.

"Hafiz," Rafik said. "To see him billing and cooing with that . . . I mean, with my beloved aunt . . . and if you had ever heard the Old Earth poets he used to quote on women and marriage! He used to compare marrying to buying a horse." And he recited four lines of Hafiz's favorite poet's from memory:

> *If it be pleasant to look at, stalled in the packed serai,*
> *Does not the young man try it and pace ere he buy?*

If She be pleasant to look on, what does the young man say?
'Lo! She is pleasant to look on. Give her to me today!'

"And if she produces a son to cut you out of your inheritance?"

"Is it not written in the Book of the Third Prophet, 'Count not the light from a distant star among your assets, for that star may have been long dead by the time its light reaches thine eyes'? I have not been such a fool as to count on stepping into the shoes of a healthy man with many years to live, Calum. While trading for Uncle Hafiz I have built up quite a respectable line of credit on my own account . . . which, come to think of it, he may need to borrow against." Rafik raised his voice. "Tell me, Uncle, how stands the credit of House Harakamian after these disasters?"

Hafiz interrupted a low-voiced colloquy of his own with Admiral Ikwaskwan and Johnny Greene. "What disasters, my beloved nephew?"

"Well . . . the interruption to your trade . . . and, ah, paying the . . ." Rafik stammered. He had been so flabbergasted by the introduction of Karina as his uncle's wife that he had not even noticed Admiral Ikwaskwan's arrival, and now he had to hastily suppress the comments that had risen to his lips about rapacious mercenaries.

Hafiz gave the broad, closed-lip smile that many competitors had learned to dread. It usually meant he had just swallowed their pet canary.

"I confess there were some minor difficulties initially," he said pleasantly. "In fact, Delszaki Li and I were forced to combine our businesses in order to command enough liquid credits for the initial great expenses. But with the advantage of House Li's trading contacts and capital added to my own superior communications system, I am happy to say that House Harakamian-Li now commands an even greater share of the galactic market than before ... and from what Mr. Greene here tells me of the technology to be discovered in the captured Khleevi ships, we expect to recoup our initial losses quite quickly. There is also," he said thoughtfully, "the small matter of trade agreements with the Linyaari. Now that Delszaki and I are no longer in competition, that should also be resolved quite profitably."

"House Harakamian-Li?" Calum repeated, stunned.

"What's the matter with that?" Gill demanded. "Sounds like a good idea to me."

Calum groaned. "Gill, you have no business sense whatever. With those two ... rapacious old pirates ... working together ... and about to reap obscene profits off their contacts with the first two space-faring alien races we've ever encountered ... well, let's just say they make the Khleevi look like a minor threat to civilization!"

Admiral Ikwaskwan cleared his throat. "As to the matter of profits," he reminded them, "a half share in the Khleevi captures belongs to the Red Bracelets."

"One-third," Hafiz said quickly.

Ikwaskwan hooked his thumbs in his belt and rocked back and forth slightly on the balls of his feet. "The agreement was that all parties to the contract should share equally in the spoils of war. Since Harakamian and Li are now one House, clearly they constitute only one contracting party and should share half and half with the other party—me."

"One-third," Nadhari Kando said from behind Hafiz and Greene. "You were content with that originally. Play fair, Ikki!"

Ikwaskwan's bony face looked even sharper and more angular at sight of Nadhari. "But . . ."

"E'kosi Tahka'yaw," Nadhari said, sounding relaxed, as if she were saying a private mantra to the ceiling. "M'on Na'ntaw. And, of course, Skomitin. You haven't forgotten Skomitin, have you, Ikki?"

"Skomitin's dead," Ikwaskwan said quickly.

Nadhari gave him a sweet smile. "But I'm not . . . am I, Ikki?" Her light rocking movement mirrored Ikwaskwan's own, but she seemed considerably more relaxed; one hand was on the back of her head, the other in a pocket of her dark, close-fitting coveralls. Calum remembered that Nadhari was said to keep poison darts in those tight black braids that coiled around her head.

Ikwaskwan moistened his lips. "You seem in the best of health . . . as I am. I trust we all expect to stay that way! One-third, then," he said more loudly, turning back to Hafiz, "as was agreed in the original contract. God forbid I should seek to defraud my honored clients! The Red Bracelets' reputation for probity and fair dealing is known throughout the galaxy."

"He didn't say what it was known as," Calum muttered in Rafik's ear.

"Can't use the appropriate language in front of the ladies," Rafik responded, equally sotto voce.

What exactly constituted a fair one-third share of
the captured ships required quite a lot more hag-
gling, as neither Ikwaskwan nor Hafiz wished to
allow the other party to conduct a detailed survey of
exactly what had been captured before the spoils
were divided. By the time they had agreed on how
to share out the loot, another complication had
arisen. Des Smirnoff and Ed Minkus, rested and
recovered from their ordeal on Rushima, put in
their own claim for credit to the salvaged pod
known as the Jurden.

Ikwaskwan listened to their claim without
speaking, while his dark eyes slowly looked over
the two very junior Red Bracelets from head to
foot and back again. "What recruiting officer took
these in?" he demanded eventually. "If I had
known any of my officers thought us so desperate
for warm bodies . . ."

"Hey," Des interrupted, "you're looking at experienced men. Trained with Kezdet Guardians of the
Peace, y'know." He puffed his chest out and threw
his shoulders back, looking as tough and military as
he could manage.

"*Tchah! Höwötiáwak, thsiöwötiya thé!*" Ikwaskwan
dismissed the claim with a phrase in his own language that made Nadhari laugh aloud. "Bumbling
incompetents who allowed themselves to be captured by the dirt farmers—I have heard all I need of
these. It's not the looting I object to, you understand," he explained to Hafiz, "it's the incompetence.
My Red Bracelets would be the laughingstock of the
galaxy were it known that I had taken in such gutter-
sweepings as these. I dare not even dismiss them."

He sighed. "I cannot afford to let them loose with the claim that they were once, however briefly, officers of my force. There is only one solution." A hand twitching toward the blaster on his hip made it quite clear what he thought that solution was.

"Quite so," Hafiz agreed. "Clearly they must be properly trained up to the standard of your forces. You do have something corresponding to the regular army's basic training, do you not?"

Ikwaskwan's lips twitched as he took in the proposition. "On Kilumbemba . . . we have, indeed. It is, of course, mostly geared to the young and exceedingly fit; admission tests for the lower ranks are stringent. But I think these two should be able to survive it," he said in a casual tone that revealed his disinterest in the outcome. "Smirnoff! Minkus! Give me your bracelets; you are reduced to the ranks and ordered to Kilumbemba for training."

Ed stripped off the single red bangle that was his badge of rank without a word, but Des was foolish enough to push his luck. "And the credit for our capture?"

"Ahhh," Ikwaskwan breathed. His head moved like that of a serpent about to strike. "As it was told to me, the Jurden was helplessly out of control when *Haven* took her under tow. By the laws of space salvage, she is *Haven*'s prize, no? Now, you two—to the shuttle, march! You will consider yourselves under arrest until you can be delivered to the brig aboard one of the battle cruisers." He lifted his wrist com and delivered a series of short, sharp instructions in his native tongue which presumably

alerted the shuttle crew to the imminent arrival of
two disgraced ex-officers.

Once Smirnoff and Minkus had shambled off,
Ikwaskwan turned to Nadhari. "Nadhi. It has been,
as you say, a long time. I believe some of our new
armaments may be of interest to you."

"I have a duty here," Nadhari said. She sounded
almost regretful.

"Go, go," Hafiz said with a beneficent smile on
his face. "Acorna is in the care of her people now.
You have earned some time off." Especially considering that she had just increased the profits of
House Harakamian-Li by one-sixth.

Nadhari looked thoughtfully at Ikwaskwan.
"You do understand that should I fail to return
within . . . let us say two hours Standard . . . your
shuttle would not be permitted to depart?"

"And you," Ikwaskwan returned, "understand
that the security precautions put in place by my predecessor for safeguarding the person of the Admiral
have been not only retained but improved? My staff
officers would die to avenge any harm to me."

Nadhari shrugged. "With the primitive tactics
you employ, Ikki, they will likely die soon enough
anyway." But she put one hand on his arm and
sauntered off toward the docking bay where the
shuttle rested.

"Well," breathed Calum, staring at the two
retreating short, slight figures with their air of coiled
menace, "seems like romance is bustin' out all over!"

Rafik glanced at the corner where Pal was holding Andreziana's hands and talking earnestly. "It
does indeed."

"Come up and see my battle lasers some time," Gill said, in a voice trembling with suppressed laughter. "I don't know, I've never tried that line. . . ."

"And you never will," said Judit firmly, tucking her arm through his. "Didn't you have a proposition to put to Johnny, Gill?"

Johnny Greene was tempted by Gill's suggestion that he return to Maganos to help with the development of the mining base's third stage, but shook his head regretfully. "I can't leave these kids to run the *Haven* all by themselves."

"Looks to me as if they won't be completely on their own." Rafik jerked his head toward Pal and Andreziana.

"Still . . . it's bad enough they've lost their parents and their home. . . ." Johnny said, incautiously loud.

Markel, never far from Johnny's elbow, overheard this. "What do you mean, we've lost our home? *Haven*'s in perfectly good shape . . . at least she will be, once we make the repairs which we should be well able to pay for, now that Dr. Hoa has agreed to stay on with us. We should be able to earn more than enough to maintain the ship by selling his weather-modification services to ag planets . . . honestly," he added, "not as a protection racket!"

Johnny raised his eyebrows. "You can keep the *Haven*, yes. But Esperantza . . ."

"Was dear to our fathers," Markel said, "and we weren't about to hurt their feelings by telling them it was a dream we didn't share. Hey, 'Ziana," he yelled, breaking into her tête-à-tête with Pal, "you want to live dirtside?"

"No way!" Andreziana shook her head so vigorously that golden ringlets bounced around her face like scraps of a broken halo. "Give up being captain of the *Haven* just to get worn-out fighting atmospheric weather and planetside gravity? You gotta be kidding!"

"You can take a poll if you like, Johnny," Markel offered, "but I think you'll find the rest of us feel the same way."

"And between Dr. Hoa and Pal," Rafik pointed out, "they will hardly be without adult guidance. Trust the kids, Johnny. They know what they want, and they can be fairly ruthless about getting it."

He withdrew to a reasonably private corner with Gill, Judit, and Calum. "Looks like everything is getting settled," he said glumly.

"Yeah," Gill said with equal lack of enthusiasm.

"There's really no excuse . . ." Calum began.

". . . to keep Acorna here with us," Judit finished, tears sparkling in her eyes. "She needs her own people."

"Do not grieve," Karina advised them, a lofty smile on her round face. "She will not leave you . . . not for long. I can sense her presence with us now."

"Of course you can!" Gill snorted rudely, "you know damn well she's on the *Balaküre*, sleeping."

"Not anymore," Karina said smugly, and on her last word, the Linyaari delegation came in, Acorna glowing with light and happiness.

"I must say farewell to Mr. Li before we leave for narhii-Vhiliinyar," she was telling Melireenya, quite firmly. "Even if the return to Maganos does delay you . . . us."

"Then you have decided to leave us," Gill said heavily. "Well, it's the right thing for you, Acorna acushla, and we all wish you . . ." His voice trembled with suppressed sobs, and he could not go on to save his life.

"I must go back with Neeva and Khaari, yes," Acorna said, "to be educated in the Linyaari ways, and to find . . ." She blushed. "Well, to complete my education."

(Yes, you're going to have all sorts of educational experiences,) Khaari teased, and Acorna's blush deepened.

"But after that . . ."

"Yes?"

Gill, Rafik, and Calum all waited with bated breath.

"We must maintain diplomatic contact with your race," Neeva said, "and as our only expert in human ways, Acorna will be too valuable an envoy to be wasted in any other position. Melireenya will be staying with you for the time being, to be joined by her life-mate; but as soon as our 'Khornya has found her own life-mate, I expect that she will be permanently assigned to this sector as special attaché to the Linyaari embassy."

Karina was the only one who could speak after this announcement. "Told you so!" she grinned.

Meanwhile, far away from the human-settled sector of space, a damaged ship fled homeward with its traumatized crew. Their speech could not be transcribed in the letters of any human language, consisting as it did of a series of rapid clicks whose changing rhythms carried their meaning; but the meaning itself would have been perfectly clear to any of the iniquitous, warlike race from whom they fled.

"We must warn our masters to have nothing more to do with this race," Senior Click-Off Long-legs announced to clicks of agreement. "They are barbaric and vicious beyond belief: when attacked, they actually fight back!"

As for whether the human race would remain equally content to have nothing to do with the Khleevi . . . this they did not consider.

Glossary of Terms

Acadecki — the ship Calum and Acorna journey in to find Acorna's people.

Acorna — a unicorn-like humanoid alien discovered as an infant by three miners — Calum, Gill, and Rafik. She has the power to heal and purify with her horn. Her uniqueness has already shaken up the galaxy, especially the planet Kezdet. She's now fully grown and searching for her people.

Aiora — Markel's mother, now dead.

Amalgamated Mining — a vicious intergalactic mining corporation, famous for bad business dealings and for using bribes, extortion, and muscle to accomplish its corporate goals or cut its costs.

Andreziana — Second-Generation Starfarer, daughter of Andrezhuria and Ezkerra.

Andrezhuria — First-Generation Starfarer, and Third Speaker to the Council.

Balaküre — the ship in which the envoys from Acorna's people reached human-populated space.

Balaave — Linyaari clan name.

barsipan — jellyfish-like animal on the Linyaari home planet.

Blidkoff—Second Undersecretary of RUI Affairs, Shenjemi Federation.

Brazie—Second-Generation Starfarer.

Calum Baird—one of three miners who discovered Acorna and raised her.

Ce'skwa—a captain and Unit Leader in the Red Bracelets.

Child Liberation League—an organization dedicated to ending child exploitation on Kezdet.

Coma Berenices—the quadrant of space most likely to hold Acorna's ancestors.

Dajar—Second-Generation Starfarer.

Declan "Gill" Giloglie—one of three miners who discovered Acorna and raised her.

Delszaki Li—the richest man on Kezdet, opposed to child exploitation, made many political enemies. Paralyzed, he floats in an antigravity chair. He's clever, devious, and he both hijacked and rescued Acorna and gave her a cause—saving the children of Kezdet.

Des Smirnoff—an unsavory sort, a former Kezdet Guardian kicked out for failure to share the proceeds of his embezzlement with appropriate superiors, now an officer with the Kilumbembese Red Bracelets.

dharmakoi—small, burrowing, sapient marsupials known to the Linyaari, now extinct as a result of Khleevi war.

Didi—Kezdet slang for the madam of a brothel, or for one who procures children for such a madam.

Didi Badini—a madam on Kezdet who tried to kill Acorna.

Dom—a Palomellese criminal posing as a refugee aboard the *Haven*; a key member of Nueva Fallona's gang.

Ed Minkus—a companion of Des Smirnoff's who has followed him from the Kezdet Guardians of the Peace to their present employment with the Red Bracelets.

E'kosi Tahka'yaw—former ally of Admiral Ikwaskwan's, betrayed by him in some manner which the Admiral would prefer not to discuss.

enye-ghanyii—Linyaari time unit, small portion of a *ghaanye*.

Epona—a protective goddess identified with horses and, by some children of Kezdet, with Acorna.

Esperantza—a planet taken away from the colonists by quasi-legal manipulations on the part of Amalgamated Mining.

Esposito—a Palomellese criminal posing as a refugee aboard the *Haven*; a key member of Nueva Fallona's gang.

Eva—Kezdet orphan training on Maganos.

Ezkerra—First-Generation Starfarer, married to Andrezhuria.

Feriila—Acorna's mother.

Foli—Second-Generation Starfarer.

Gerezan—First-Generation Starfarer, Second Speaker to the Council.

ghaanye (pl. ghaanyi)—a Linyaari year.

gheraalye malivii—Navigation Officer.

gheraalye ve-khanyii—Senior Communications Officer.

Giryeeni—Linyaari clan name.

Hafiz Harakamian—Rafik's uncle, head of the interstellar financial empire of House Harakamian, a passionate collector of rarities from throughout the galaxy and a devotee of the old-fashioned sport of horse racing. Although basically crooked enough to hide behind a spiral staircase, he is fond of Rafik and Acorna.

Hajnal—a child rescued from thieving on Kezdet, now in training on Maganos.

Haven—a multigeneration space-colonization vehicle occupied by the Starfarers, who had been pushed off the planet Esperantza by Amalgamated Mining.

Ikwaskwan—self-styled Admiral of the Kilumbembese Red Bracelets.

Illart—First-Generation Starfarer, First Speaker to the Council, and Markel's father.

Johnny Greene—an old friend of Calum, Rafik, and Gill; joined the Starfarers when he was fired after Amalgamated Mining's takeover of MME.

Joshua Flouse—mayor of a flooded-out community on Rushima.

Judit Kendoro—assistant to psychiatrist Alton Forelle at Amalgamated Mining, saved Acorna from certain death. Later fell in love with Gill and joined with him to help care for the children employed in Delszaki Li's Maganos mining operation.

Karina—a wanna-be psychic with a small shred of actual talent.

Kass—Rushimese settler.

kava—a coffeelike hot drink produced from roasted ground beans.

Kerratz—Second-Generation Starfarer, son of Andrezhuria and Ezkerra.

Kezdet—a backwoods planet with a labor system based on child exploitation. Currently in economic turmoil because that system has been broken by Delszaki Li and Acorna.

Khang Kieaan—a planet torn between three warring factions.

Khaari—senior Linyaari navigator on the *Balaküre*.

Kilumbemba Empire—an entire society which raises and exports mercenaries for hire—the Red Bracelets.

Kirilatova—an opera singer.

Khleevi—name given by Acorna's people to the space-faring enemies who have attacked them without mercy.

ki-lin—oriental name for unicorn; Ki-lin is also a name sometimes given to Acorna.

Kisla Manjari—anorexic and snobbish young woman, raised as daughter of Baron Manjari; shattered when, through Acorna's efforts to help the children of Kezdet, her father is ruined and the truth of her lowly birth is revealed.

Laboue—the planet where Hafiz Harakamian makes his headquarters.

Labrish—Rushimese settler.

Linyaari—Acorna's people.

Lukia of the Lights—a protective saint, identified by some children of Kezdet with Acorna.

madigadi—a berrylike fruit whose juice is a popular beverage.

Maganos—one of the three moons of Kezdet, base for Delszaki Li's mining operation and child-rehabilitation project.

Mali Bazaar—a luxurious bazaar on Laboue,

famous for the intricate mosaic designs which
decorate its roof.

Markel—First-Generation Starfarer, son of First
Speaker Illart.

Martin Dehoney—famous astro-architect who
designed Maganos Moon Base; the coveted
Dehoney Prize was named after him.

Melireenya—Linyaari Senior Communications
Specialist on the *Balaküre*.

Mercy Kendoro—younger sister of Pal and Judit
Kendoro, saved from a life of bonded labor by
Judit's efforts, she worked as a spy for the
Child Liberation League in offices of Kezdet
Guardians of the Peace until the child-labor
system was destroyed.

Misra Affrendi—Hafiz's elderly trusted retainer.

mitanyaakhi—generic Linyaari term meaning a very
large number.

MME—Gill, Calum, and Rafik's original mining company. Swallowed by the ruthless, conscienceless,
and bureaucratic Amalgamated Mining.

M'on Na'ntaw—high-ranking Red Bracelet officer,
cheated by General Ikwaskwan in a way that
threw the blame on someone else.

Moulay Suheil—fanatical leader of the Neo-
Hadithians.

[Auntie] Nagah—Rushimese settler.

narhii-Vhiliinyar—second home of the Linyaari.

Nadhari Kando—Delszaki Li's personal bodyguard,
rumored to have been an officer in the Red
Bracelets earlier in her career.

Neeva—Acorna's aunt and Linyaari envoy on the *Balaküre*.

Neggara—Second-Generation Starfarer.

Neo-Hadithian—an ultraconservative, fanatical religious sect.

Ngaen Xong Hoa—a Kieaanese scientist who has invented a weather-control system. He seeks asylum on the *Haven* because he fears the warring governments on his planet will misuse his research.

Nueva Fallona—Palomellese criminal who poses as a refugee to the Starfarers until she can carry out a coup leaving her and her gang in control of the *Haven*.

One-One Otimie—a Rushimese trapper and prospector.

Pal Kendoro—Delszaki Li's assistant on the planet Kezdet. Brother to Mercy and Judit. Acorna's dear friend, and possible love interest—though they haven't tried to do anything about it. Given that they come from different species, it could be problematic.

Palomella—home planet of Nueva Fallona.

Provola Quero—woman in charge of the Saganos operation.

Pyaka—a Rushimese settler.

Quashie—a Rushimese settler.

Qulabriel—Hafiz's assistant.

Rafik Nadezda—one of three miners who discovered Acorna and raised her.

Ramon Trinidad—one of the miners hired to direct

a training program on Maganos for the freed children.

Red Bracelets—Kilumbembese mercenaries; arguably the toughest and nastiest fighting force in known space.

Renyilaaghe—Linyaari clan name.

Rezar—Second-Generation Starfarer.

Rosewater's Revelation—Uncle Hafiz's best racehorse.

Rushima—agricultural world colonized by the Shenjemi Federation.

Saganos—second of Kezdet's moons.

Sengrat—a pushy, bossy, whiny, bullying know-it-all with a political agenda on the ship *Haven*.

Shenjemi Federation—long-distance government of Rushima.

Sita Ram—a protective goddess, identified with Acorna by the mining children on Kezdet.

Skarness—planetary source of the famous (and rare) Singing Stones.

Skomitin—somebody in Admiral Ikwaskwan's past of whom he does not care to be reminded.

Starfarers—name adopted by the Esperantzan settlers who were displaced by Amalgamated's manipulations. They refused unsatisfactory resettlement offers and turned their main ship, the *Haven*, into a mobile colony from which they carried on a campaign of nonviolent political protest against Amalgamated.

Ta'anisi—the Red Bracelets' flagship.

Tanqque III—rain-forest planet; export of its coveted purpleheart trees is illegal.

Tapha—Hafiz's ineffectual son, who made several attempts on Rafik's life before he himself was killed during yet another murder attempt.

Thariinye—a handsome and conceited young male Linyaari on the envoy ship.

Theloi—one of many planets where the miners had to leave hastily to avoid their many enemies.

thülir (pl. *thilirii*)—small arboreal mammals of the Linyaari home world.

Tianos—Kezdet's third moon.

Twi Osiam—planetary site of a major financial and trade center.

twiilit—small, pestiferous insect on Linyaari home planet.

Uhuru—current name of the ship owned jointly by Gill, Calum, and Rafik.

Vaanye—Acorna's father.

Vhiliinyar—home planet of the Linyaari, now occupied by Khleevi.

visedhaanye ferilii—Linyaari term corresponding roughly to "Envoy Extraordinary."

Vlad—cousin of Des Smirnoff's, a fence, probably descended from Vlad the Impaler.

Winjy—a Rushimese settler.

Ximena Sengrat—Sengrat's beautiful young daughter.

yonks—a subjective and general measurement, a great deal of passing time. Roughly equivalent to "it took forever."

Yukata Batsu—Uncle Hafiz's chief competitor on Laboue.

Zanegar—Second-Generation Starfarer.

Zaspala Imperium—backward planetary confederation, original home of Des Smirnoff.

Dr. Zip—an eccentric astrophysicist.

Notes on the Linyaari Language

1. A doubled vowel indicates stress: *aa*vi, ab*aa*nye, khlev*ii*.

2. Stress is used as an indicator of syntactic function: in nouns stress is on the penultimate syllable, in adjectives on the last syllable, in verbs on the first.

3. Intervocalic n is always palatalized.

4. Noun plurals are formed by adding a final vowel, usually -i: one **Liinyar**, two **Linyaari**. Note that this causes a change in the stressed syllable (from **LI-nyar** to **Li-NYA-ri**) and hence a change in the pattern of doubled vowels.

For nouns whose singular form ends in a vowel, the plural is formed by dropping the original vowel and adding -i: **ghaanye**, **ghaanyi**. Here the number of syllables remains the same, therefore no stress/spelling change is required.

5. Adjectives can be formed from nouns by adding a final -ii (again, dropping the original final vowel if one exists): **maalive**, **malivii**; **Liinyar**, **Linyarii**. Again, the change in stress means that the doubled vowels in the penultimate syllable of the noun disappear.

6. For nouns denoting a class or species, such as **Liinyar**, the plural form of the noun can be used as an adjective when the meaning is "of the class," as in "the Linyaari language" (the language of the Linyaari rather than the usual adjectival meaning of "having the qualities of this class")—thus, of the characters in *Acorna*, only Acorna herself could be described as "a **Linyaari** girl" (a girl of the People), but Judit, although human, would certainly be described as "a **linyarii** girl" ("a just-as-civilized-as-a-real-member-of-the-People" girl).

7. Verbs can be formed from nouns by adding a prefix constructed by [first consonant of noun] + **ii** + **nye: faalar**—grief; **fiinyefalar**—to grieve.

8. The participle is formed from the verb by adding a suffix **-an** or **-en: thiinyethilel**—to destroy, **thiinyethilelen**—destroyed. No stress change is involved because the participle is perceived as a verb form, and therefore stress remains on the first syllable:

enye-ghanyii—time unit, small portion of a year **(ghaanye)**

fiinyefalaran—mourning, mourned

ghaanye—a Linyaari year, equivalent to about one and one-third earth years

gheraalye malivii—Navigation Officer

gheraalye ve-khanyii—Senior Communications Specialist

Khleev—originally, a small vicious carrion-feeding animal with a poisonous bite; now used by the Linyaari to denote the invaders who destroyed their home world.

khlevii—barbarous, uncivilized, vicious without reason

Liinyar—member of the People

linyarii—civilized; like a Liinyar

mitanyaakhi—large number (slang—like our "zillions")

narhii—new

thiilir, thiliiri—small arboreal mammals of the Linyaari home world

thiilel—destruction

visedhaanye ferilii—Envoy Extraordinary

9. Like all languages, Linyaari has a number of irregular constructions, each of which must be explained on a case-by-case basis.

Don't Miss Any of the
ACORNA ADVENTURES

"Good spacefaring fun."
Publishers Weekly

ACORNA
by Anne McCaffrey and Margaret Ball
0-06-105789-4/$7.50 US/$9.99 Can

ACORNA'S QUEST
by Anne McCaffrey and Margaret Ball
0-06-105790-8/$6.50 US/$8.99 Can

ACORNA'S PEOPLE
by Anne McCaffrey and Elizabeth Ann Scarborough
0-06-105983-8/$6.99 US/$9.99 Can

ACORNA'S WORLD
by Anne McCaffrey and Elizabeth Ann Scarborough
0-06-105984-6/$6.99 US/$9.99 Can

And in Hardcover

ACORNA'S SEARCH
by Anne McCaffrey and Elizabeth Ann Scarborough
0-380-97898-9/$25.00 US/$37.95 Can